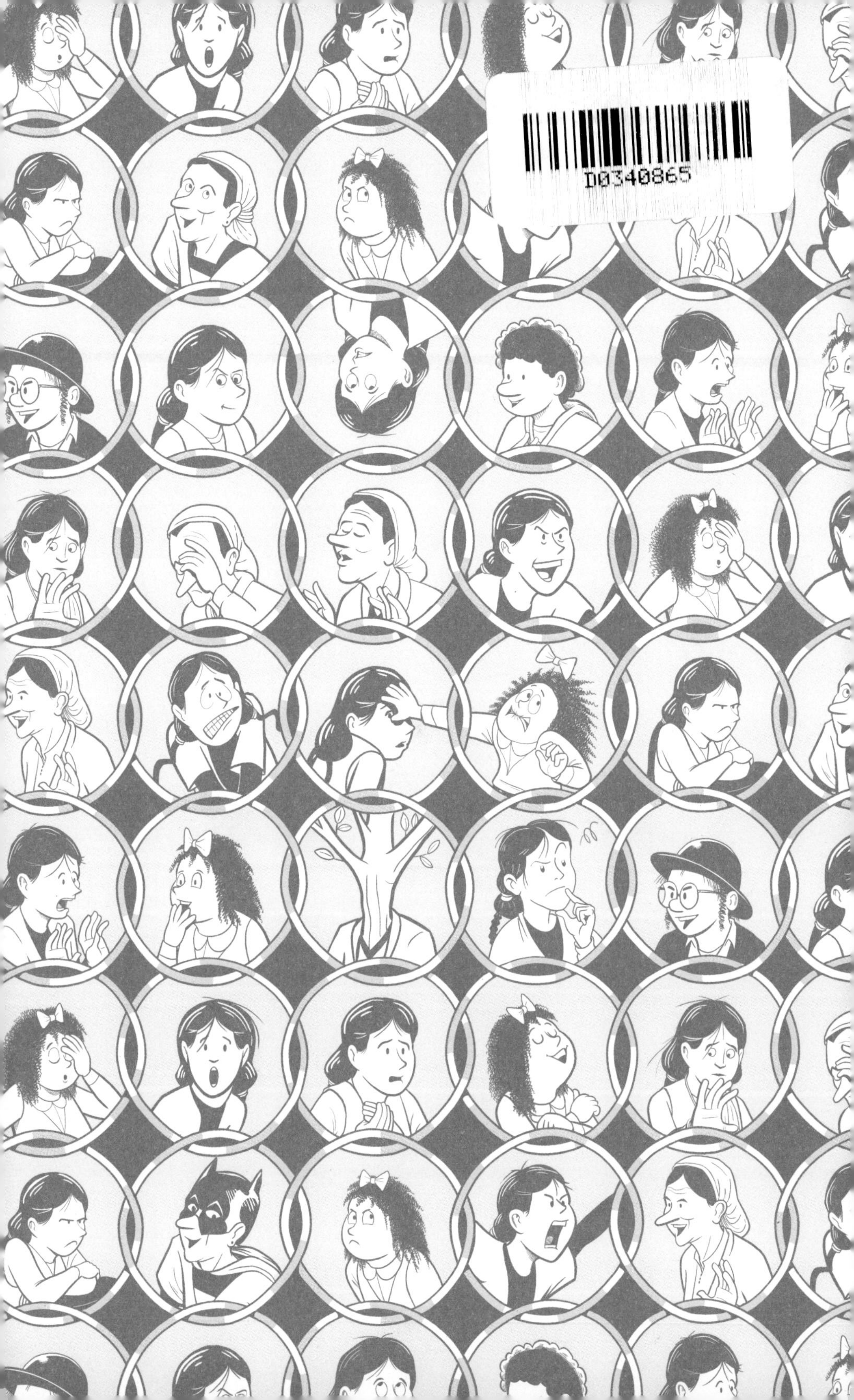

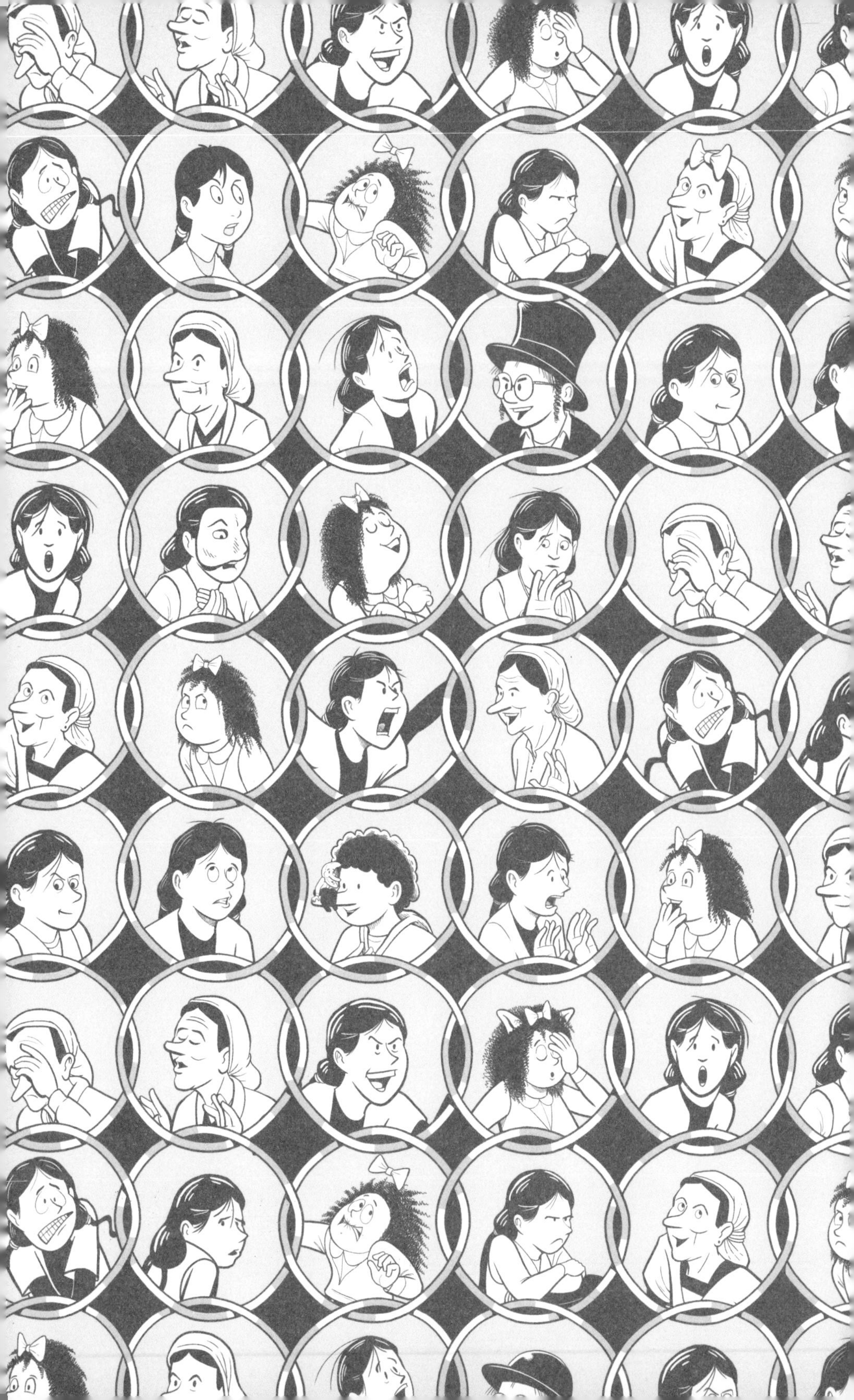

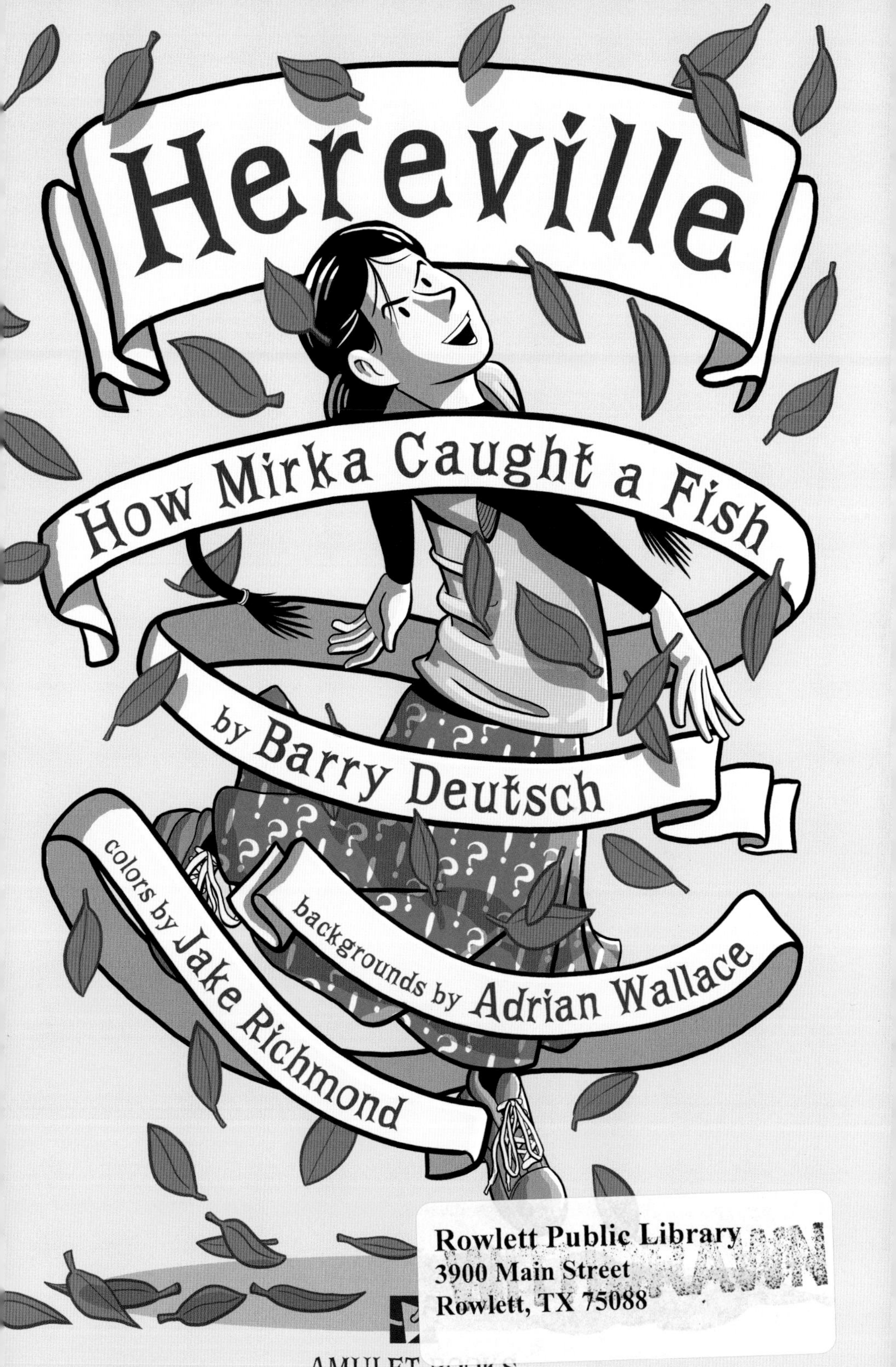
Hereville
How Mirka Caught a Fish
by Barry Deutsch
colors by Jake Richmond
backgrounds by Adrian Wallace

AMULET BOOKS
NEW YORK

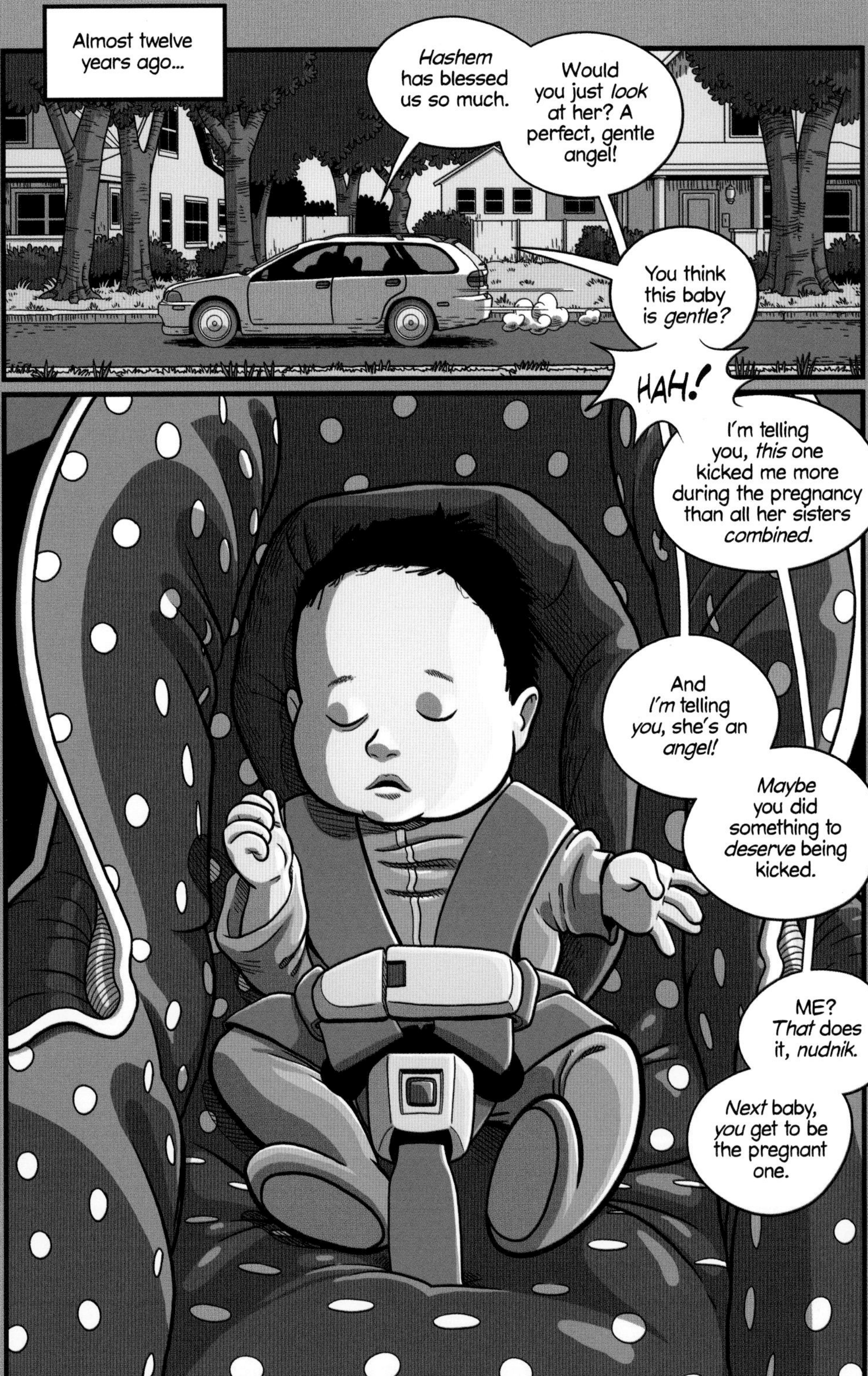
Almost twelve years ago...
Hashem has blessed us so much.
Would you just *look* at her? A perfect, gentle angel!
You think this baby is *gentle?*
HAH!
I'm telling you, *this* one kicked me more during the pregnancy than all her sisters *combined.*
And *I'm* telling *you*, she's an *angel!*
Maybe you did something to *deserve* being kicked.
ME? *That* does it, *nudnik.*
Next baby, *you* get to be the pregnant one.

Hashem: God
Nudnik: Pain in the neck

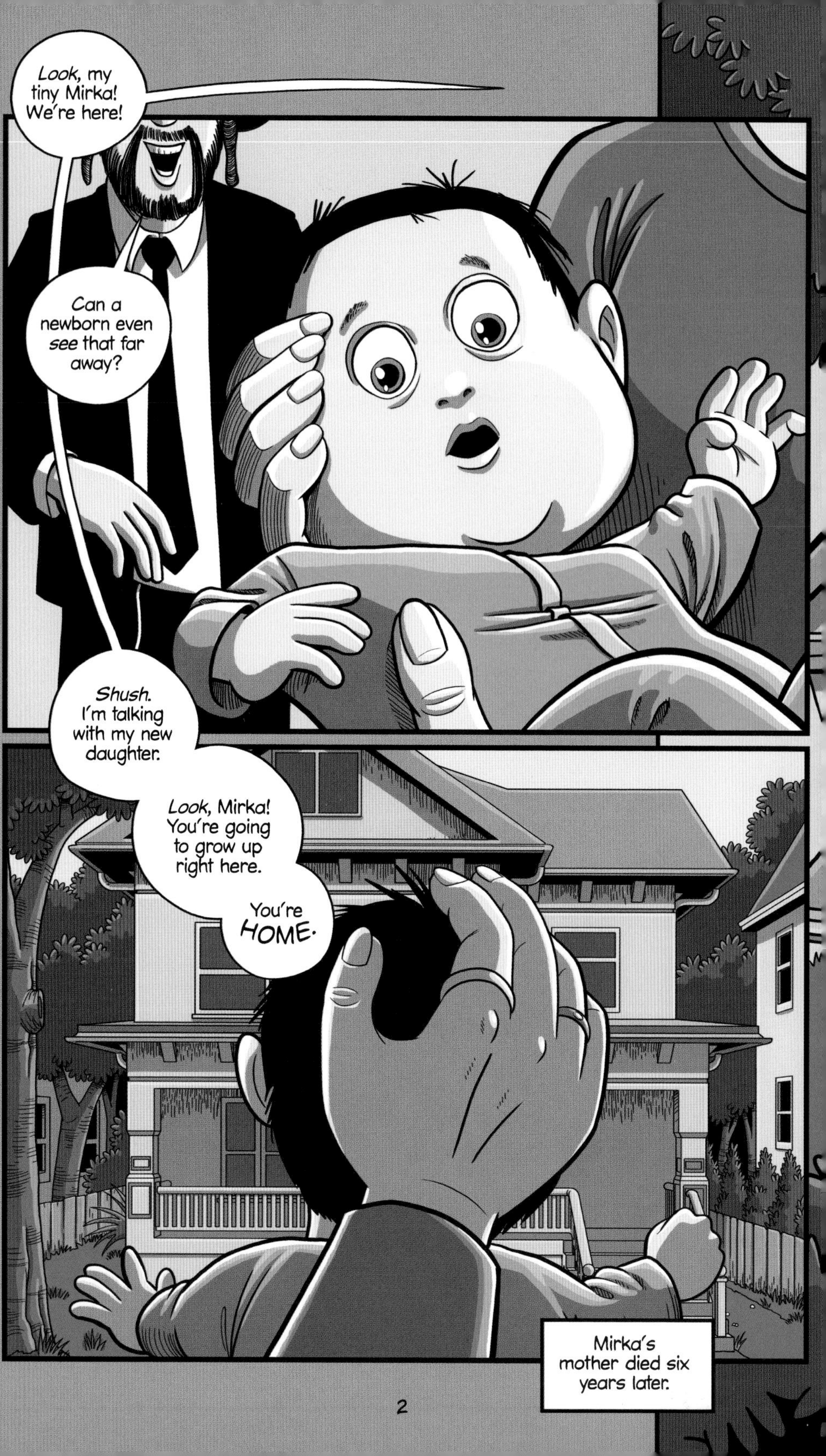
Look, my tiny Mirka! We're here!
Can a newborn even *see* that far away?
Shush. I'm talking with my new daughter.
Look, Mirka! You're going to grow up right here.
You're HOME.
Mirka's mother died six years later.

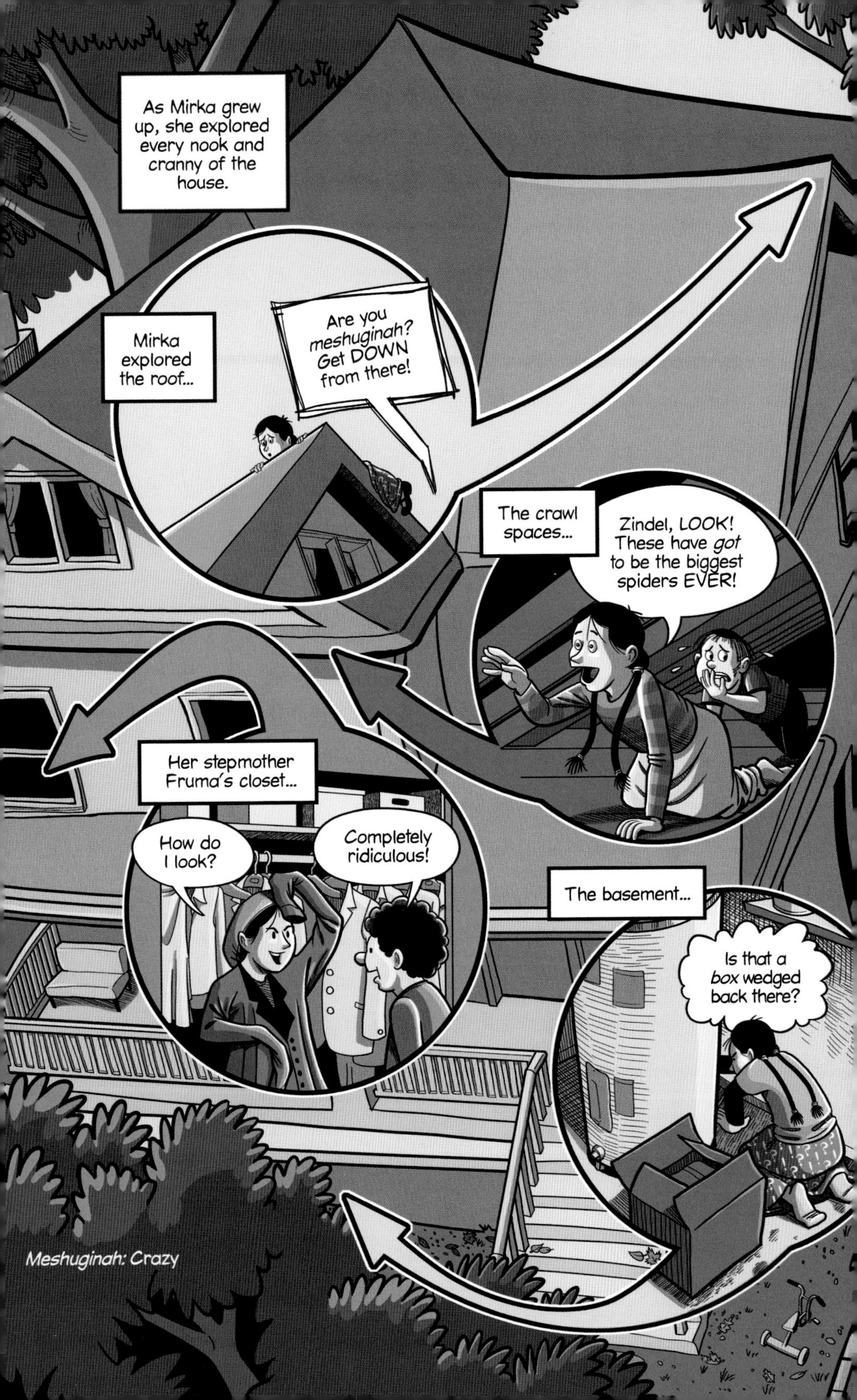
As Mirka grew up, she explored every nook and cranny of the house.
Mirka explored the roof...
Are you *meshuginah*? Get DOWN from there!
The crawl spaces...
Zindel, LOOK! These have *got* to be the biggest spiders EVER!
Her stepmother Fruma's closet...
How do I look?
Completely ridiculous!
The basement...
Is that a *box* wedged back there?
Meshuginah: Crazy

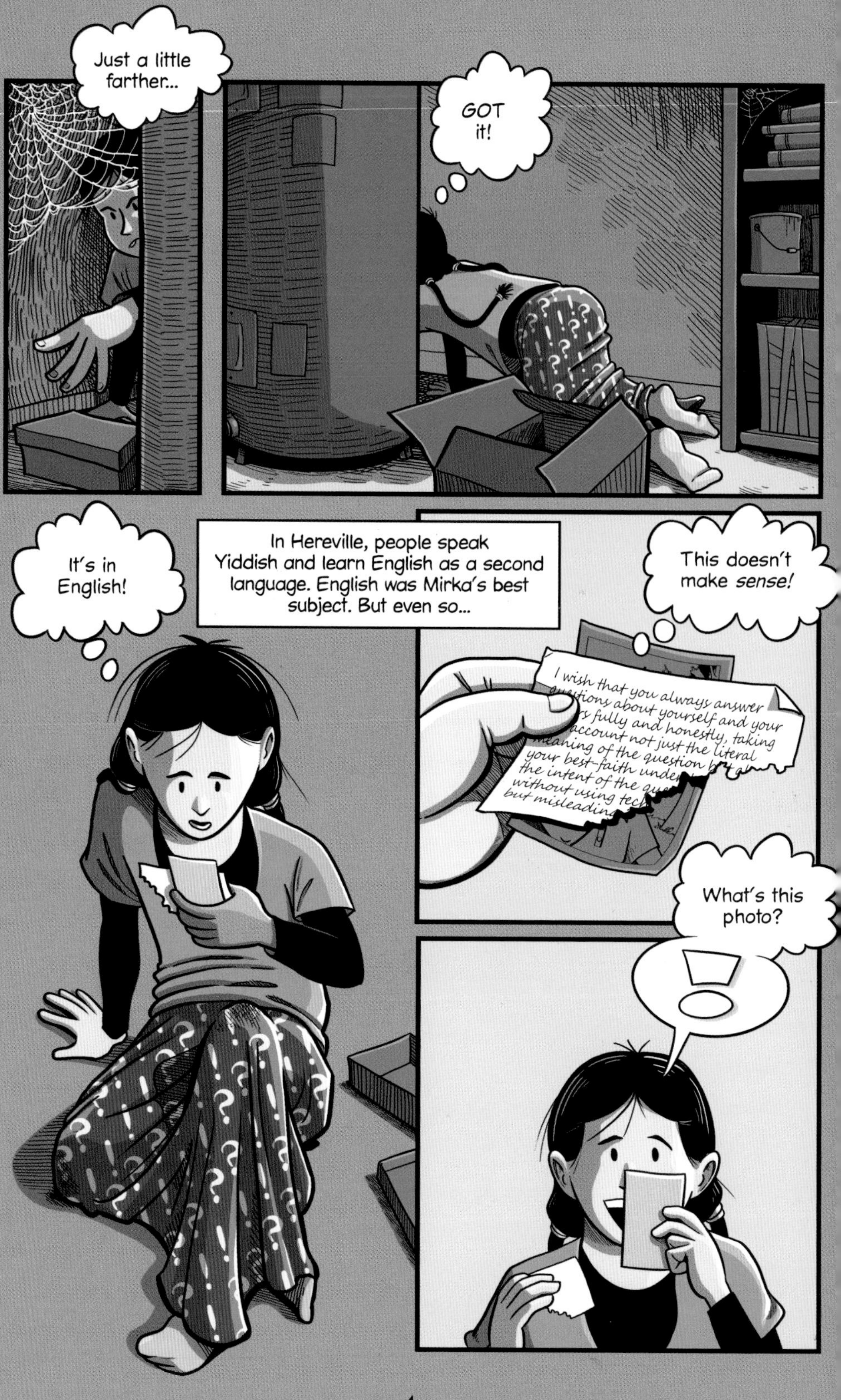
Just a little farther...
GOT it!
It's in English!
In Hereville, people speak Yiddish and learn English as a second language. English was Mirka's best subject. But even so...
This doesn't make *sense!*
I wish that you always answer
questions about yourself and your
fully and honestly, taking
account not just the literal
meaning of the question
your best-faith unde
the intent of the
without using tec
but misleadin
What's this photo?

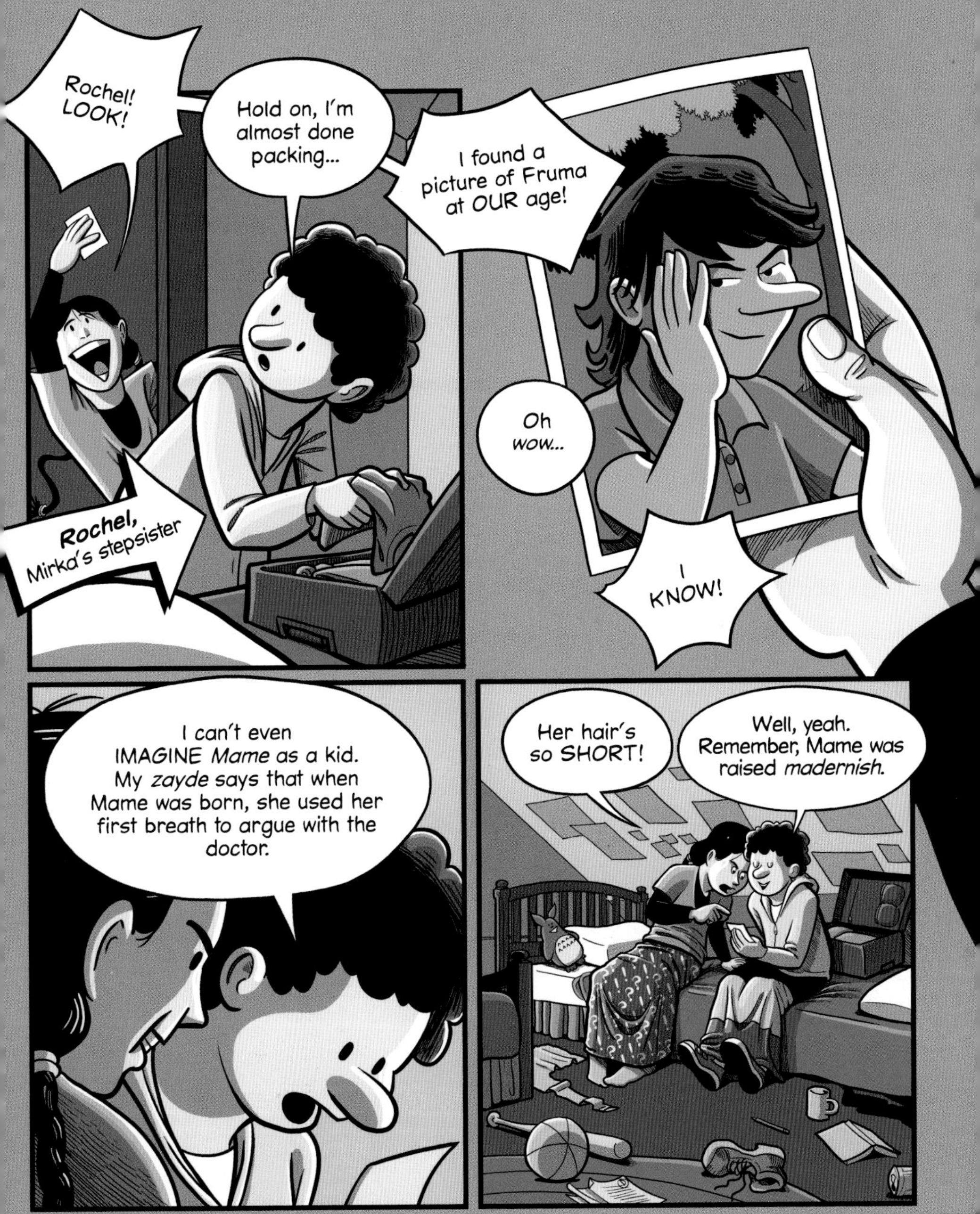
Rochel! LOOK!
Hold on, I'm almost done packing...
Rochel, Mirka's stepsister
I found a picture of Fruma at OUR age!
Oh wow...
I KNOW!
I can't even IMAGINE *Mame* as a kid. My *zayde* says that when Mame was born, she used her first breath to argue with the doctor.
Her hair's so SHORT!
Well, yeah. Remember, Mame was raised *madernish*.

In Hereville, unmarried women and girls keep their hair long, although they usually tie it back.

Married women keep their hair short, or even *shave* it.

But you'd never know it, since they wear wigs, or a head covering called a "snood."

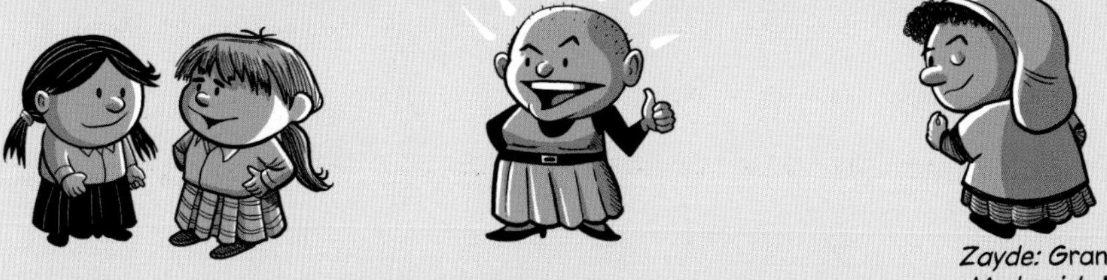

Zayde: Grandfather
Madernish: Modern

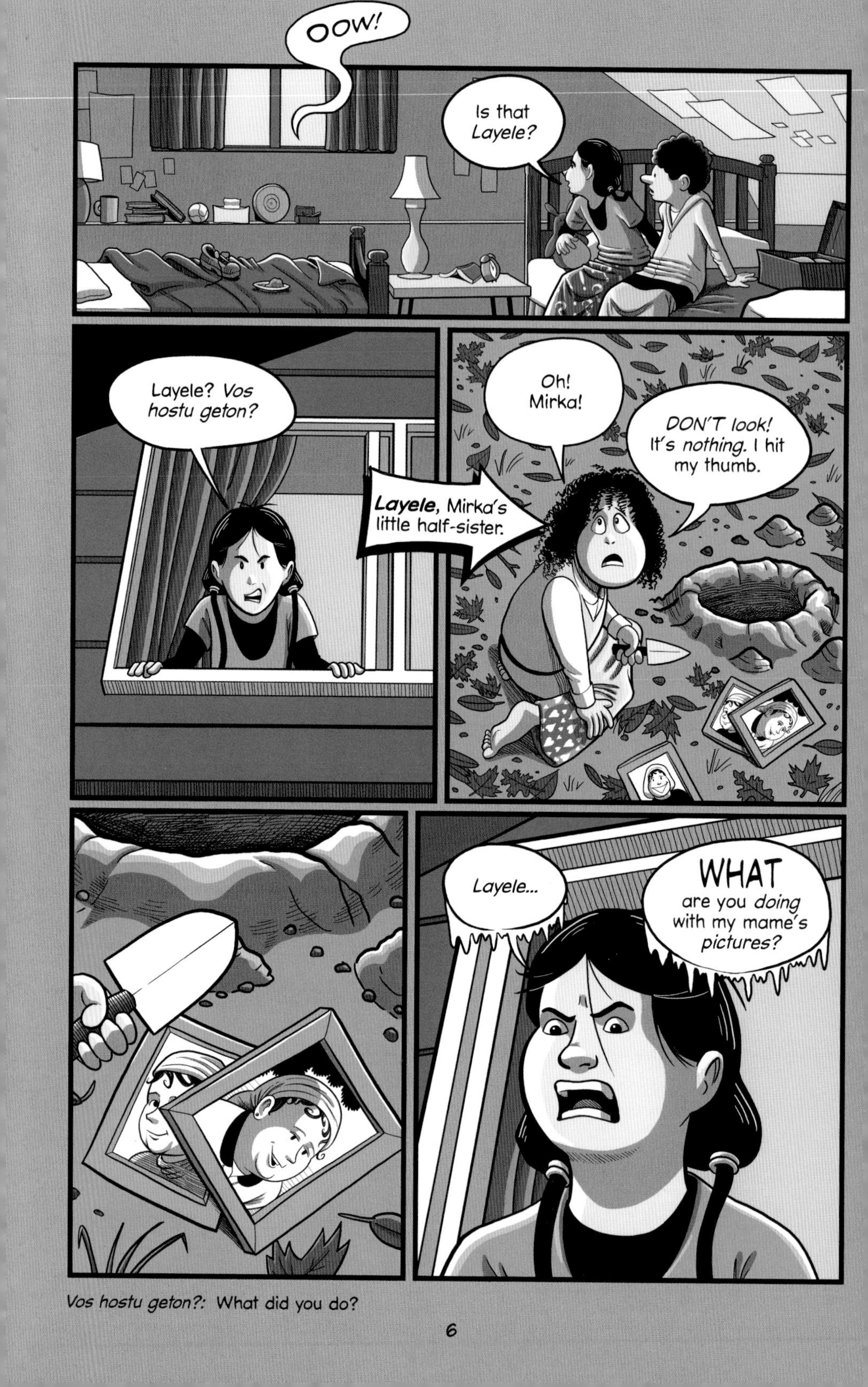
OOW!
Is that *Layele?*
Layele? *Vos hostu geton?*
Layele, Mirka's little half-sister.
Oh! Mirka!
DON'T look! It's *nothing.* I hit my thumb.
Layele...
WHAT are you *doing* with my mame's *pictures?*

Vos hostu geton?: What did you do?

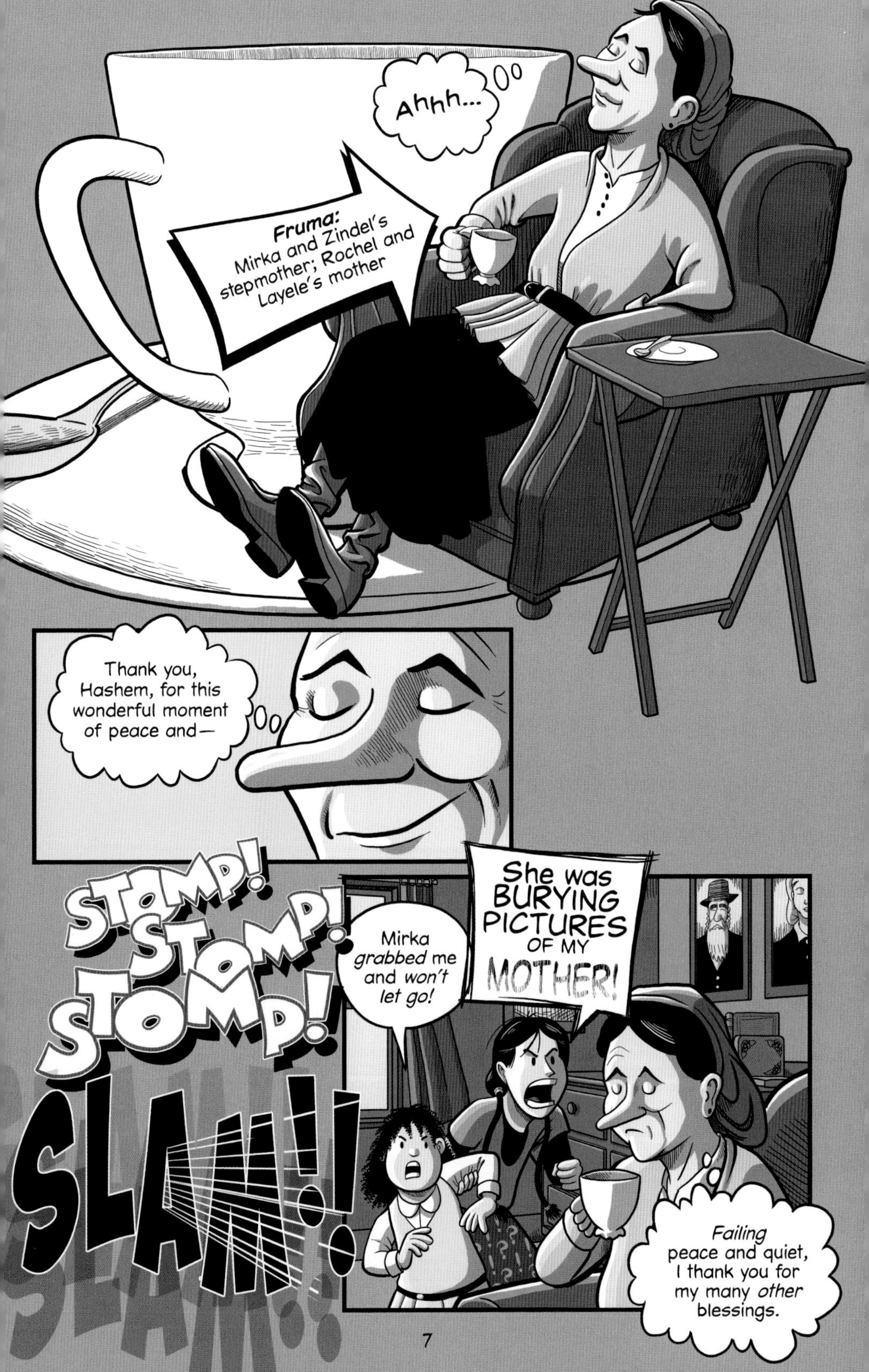
Ahhh...
Fruma: Mirka and Zindel's stepmother; Rochel and Layele's mother
Thank you, Hashem, for this wonderful moment of peace and—
STOMP! STOMP! STOMP!
SLAM!!
Mirka grabbed me and won't let go!
She was BURYING PICTURES OF MY MOTHER!
Failing peace and quiet, I thank you for my many other blessings.

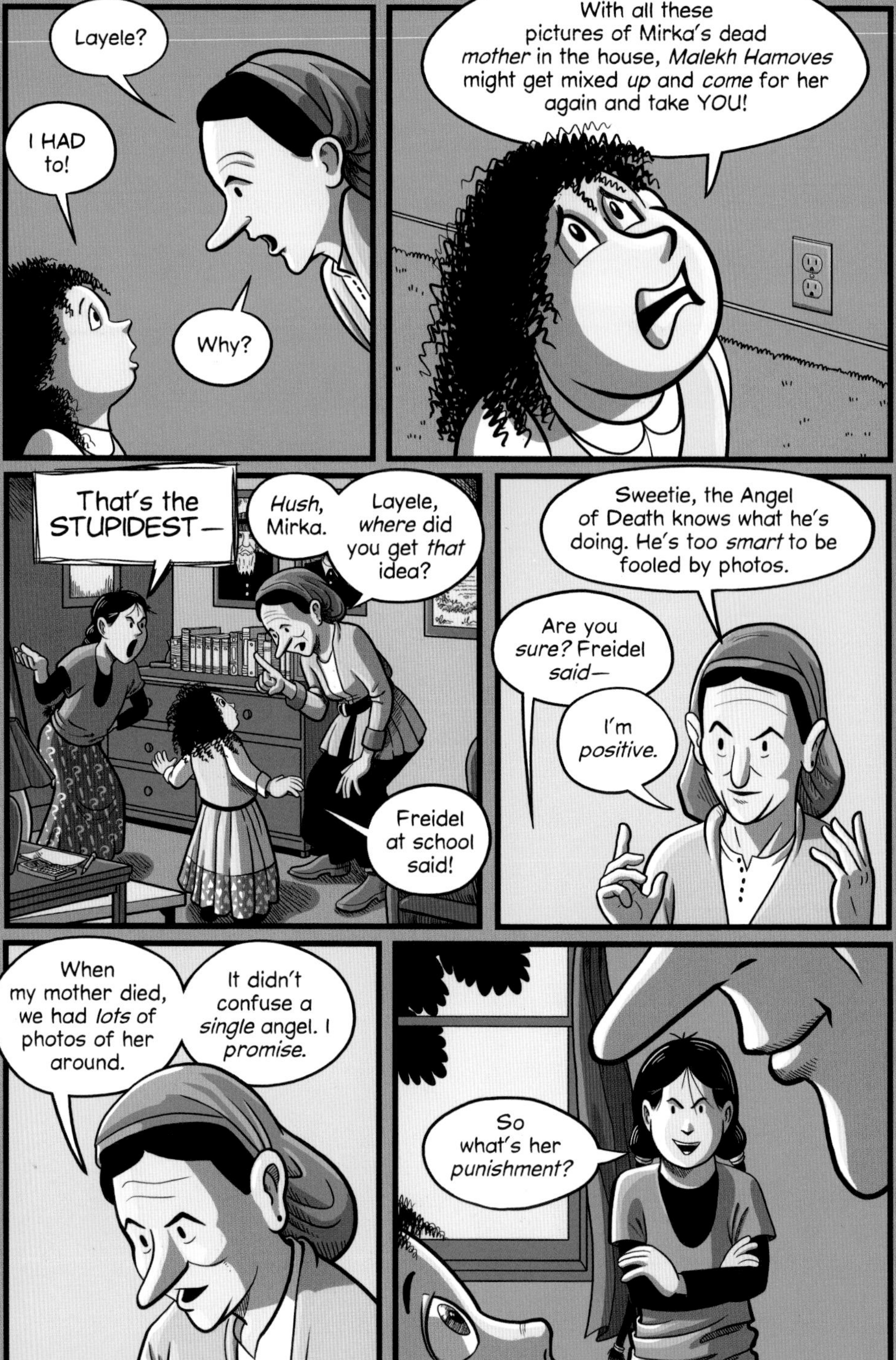
Layele?
I HAD to!
Why?
With all these pictures of Mirka's dead *mother* in the house, *Malekh Hamoves* might get mixed *up* and *come* for her again and take YOU!
That's the STUPIDEST—
Hush, Mirka.
Layele, *where* did you get *that* idea?
Freidel at school said!
Sweetie, the Angel of Death knows what he's doing. He's too *smart* to be fooled by photos.
Are you *sure?* Freidel *said*—
I'm *positive.*
When my mother died, we had *lots* of photos of her around.
It didn't confuse a *single* angel. I *promise.*
So what's her *punishment?*

Malekh Hamoves: The Angel of Death

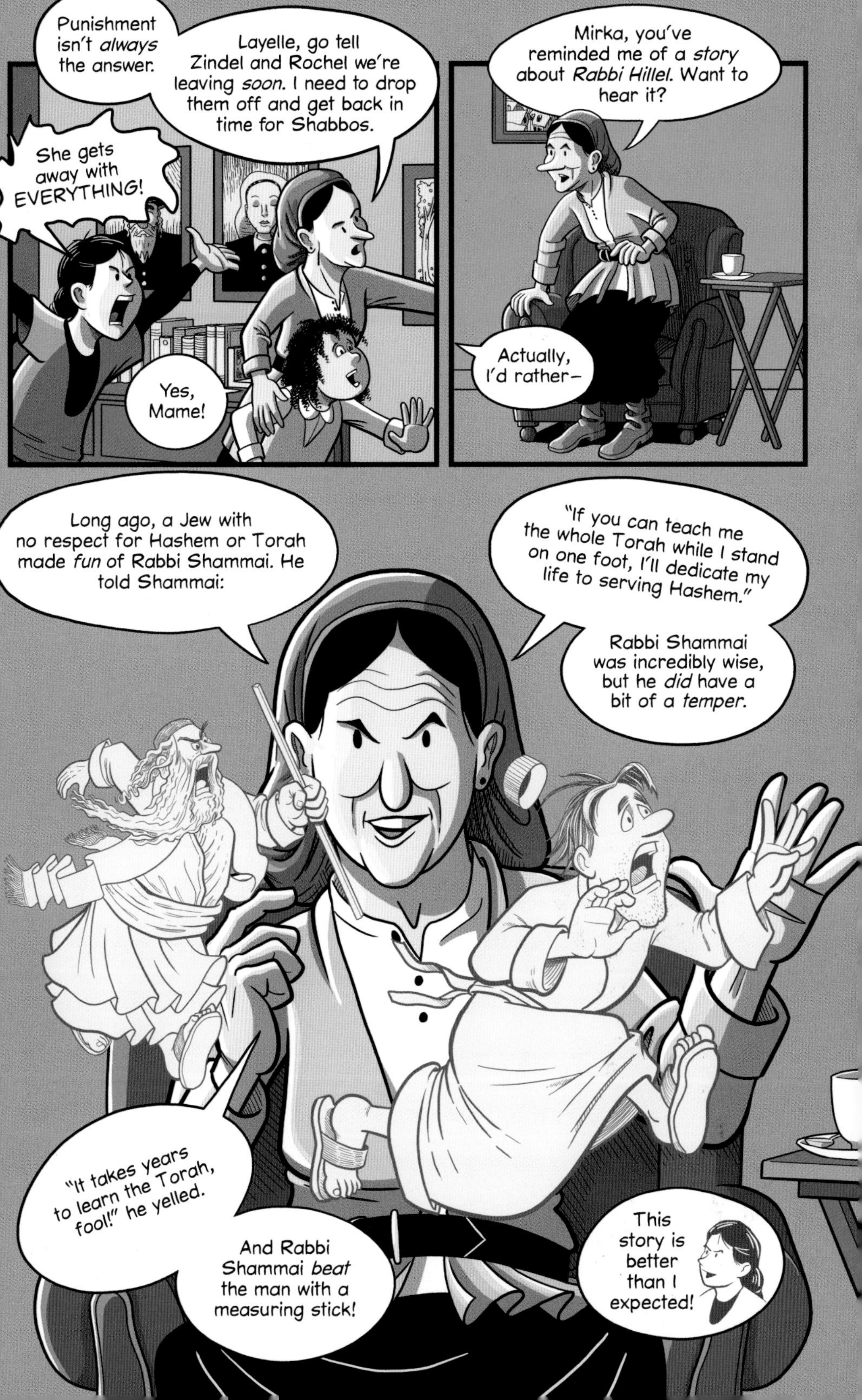

Punishment isn't *always* the answer.
Layelle, go tell Zindel and Rochel we're leaving *soon.* I need to drop them off and get back in time for Shabbos.
She gets away with EVERYTHING!
Yes, Mame!
Mirka, you've reminded me of a *story* about *Rabbi Hillel.* Want to hear it?
Actually, I'd rather–
Long ago, a Jew with no respect for Hashem or Torah made *fun* of Rabbi Shammai. He told Shammai:
"If you can teach me the whole Torah while I stand on one foot, I'll dedicate my life to serving Hashem."
Rabbi Shammai was incredibly wise, but he *did* have a bit of a *temper.*
"It takes years to learn the Torah, fool!" he yelled.
And Rabbi Shammai *beat* the man with a measuring stick!
This story is better than I expected!

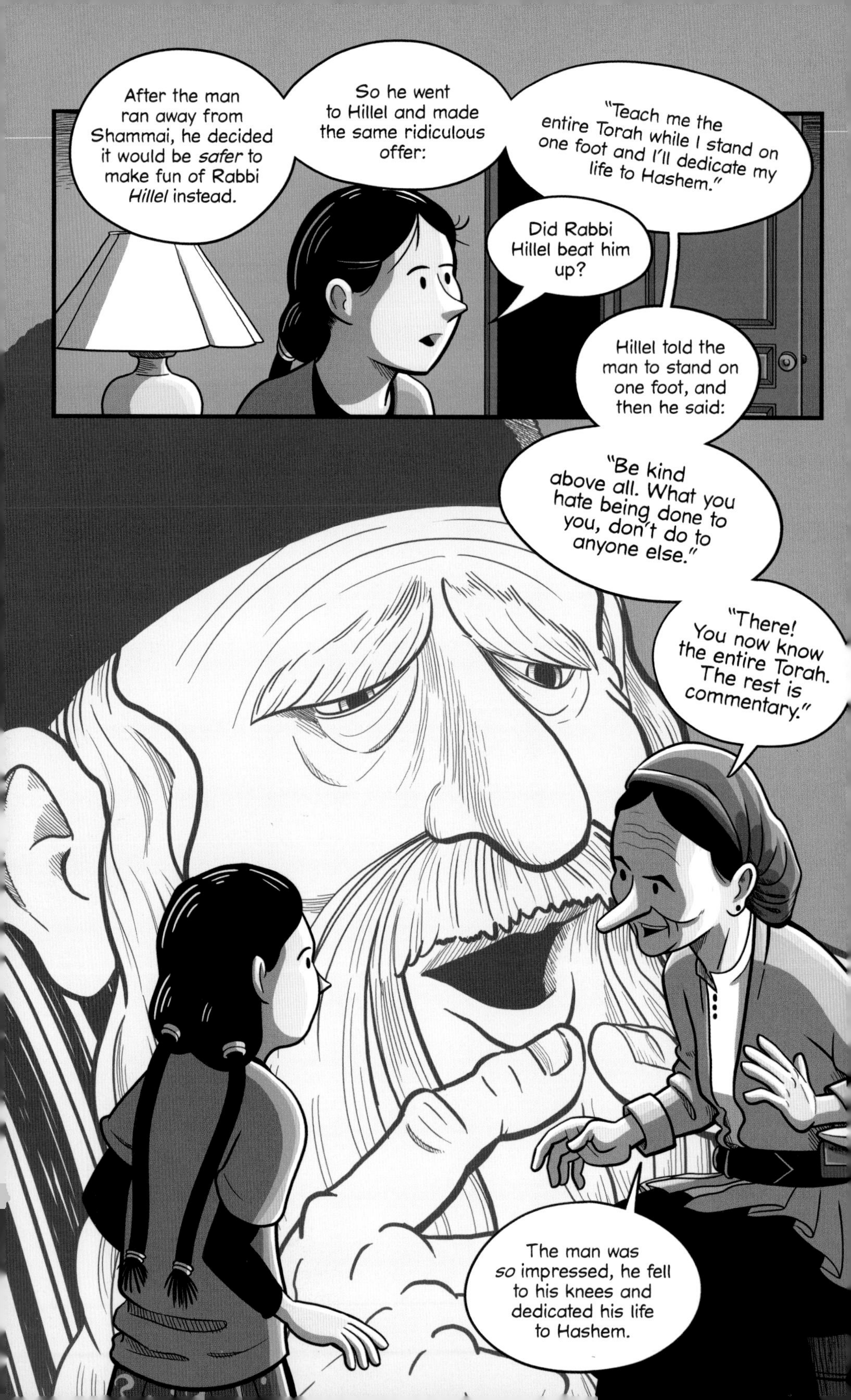
After the man ran away from Shammai, he decided it would be *safer* to make fun of Rabbi *Hillel* instead.
So he went to Hillel and made the same ridiculous offer:
"Teach me the entire Torah while I stand on one foot and I'll dedicate my life to Hashem."
Did Rabbi Hillel beat him up?
Hillel told the man to stand on one foot, and then he said:
"Be kind above all. What you hate being done to you, don't do to anyone else."
"There! You now know the entire Torah. The rest is commentary."
The man was *so* impressed, he fell to his knees and dedicated his life to Hashem.

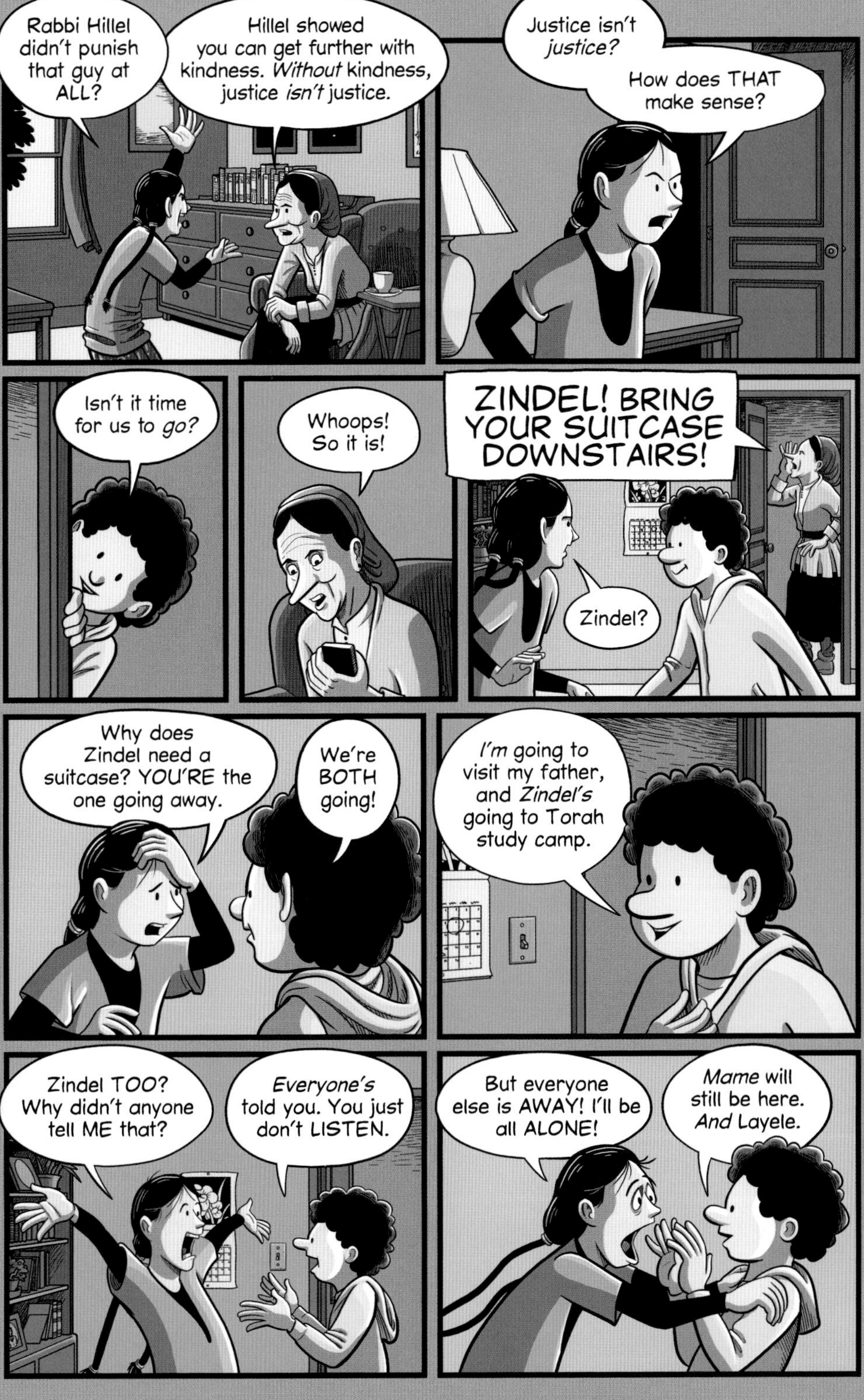

Rabbi Hillel didn't punish that guy at ALL?
Hillel showed you can get further with kindness. *Without* kindness, justice *isn't* justice.
Justice isn't *justice?*
How does THAT make sense?
Isn't it time for us to *go?*
Whoops! So it is!
ZINDEL! BRING YOUR SUITCASE DOWNSTAIRS!
Zindel?
Why does Zindel need a suitcase? YOU'RE the one going away.
We're BOTH going!
I'm going to visit my father, and *Zindel's* going to Torah study camp.
Zindel TOO? Why didn't anyone tell ME that?
Everyone's told you. You just don't LISTEN.
But everyone else is AWAY! I'll be all ALONE!
Mame will still be here. *And* Layele.

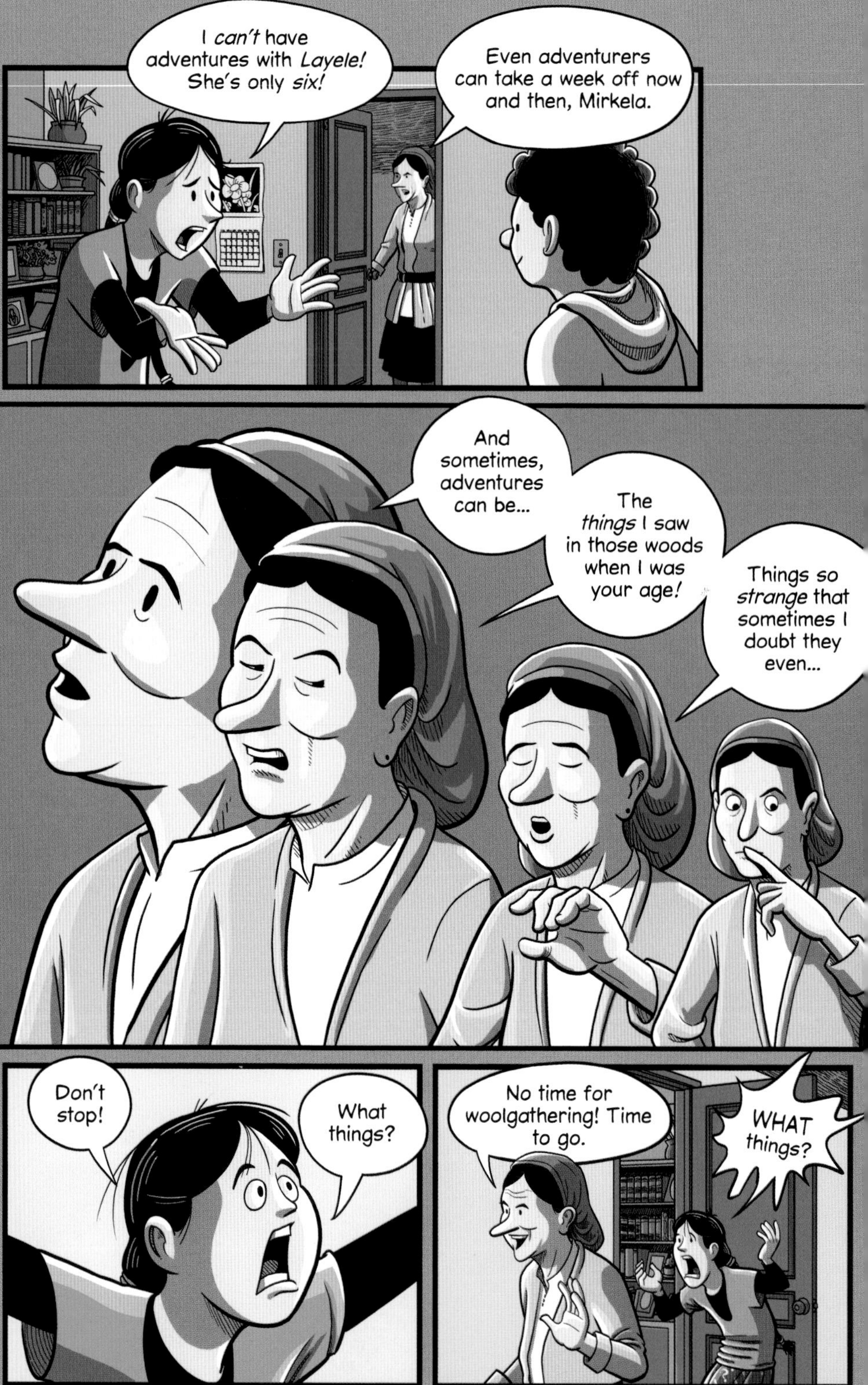
I *can't* have adventures with *Layele!* She's only *six!*
Even adventurers can take a week off now and then, Mirkela.
And sometimes, adventures can be...
The *things* I saw in those woods when I was your age*!*
Things so *strange* that sometimes I doubt they even...
Don't stop!
What things?
No time for woolgathering! Time to go.
WHAT things?

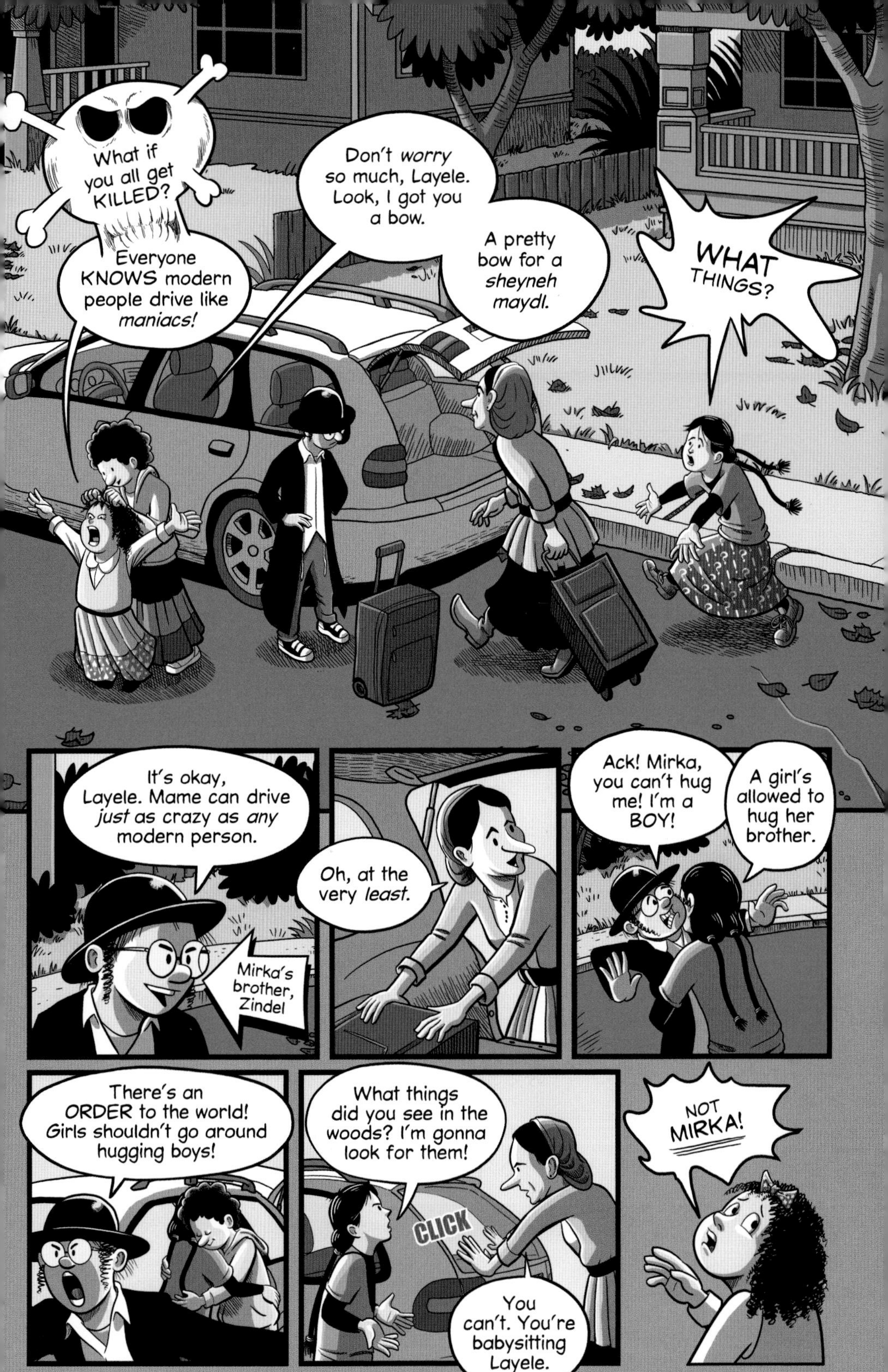
What if you all get KILLED?
Everyone KNOWS modern people drive like *maniacs!*
Don't *worry* so much, Layele. Look, I got you a bow.
A pretty bow for a *sheyneh maydl.*
WHAT THINGS?
It's okay, Layele. Mame can drive *just* as crazy as *any* modern person.
Mirka's brother, Zindel
Oh, at the very *least.*
Ack! Mirka, you can't hug me! I'm a BOY!
A girl's allowed to hug her brother.
There's an ORDER to the world! Girls shouldn't go around hugging boys!
What things did you see in the woods? I'm gonna look for them!
CLICK
You can't. You're babysitting Layele.
NOT MIRKA!

Sheyneh maydl: Pretty girl

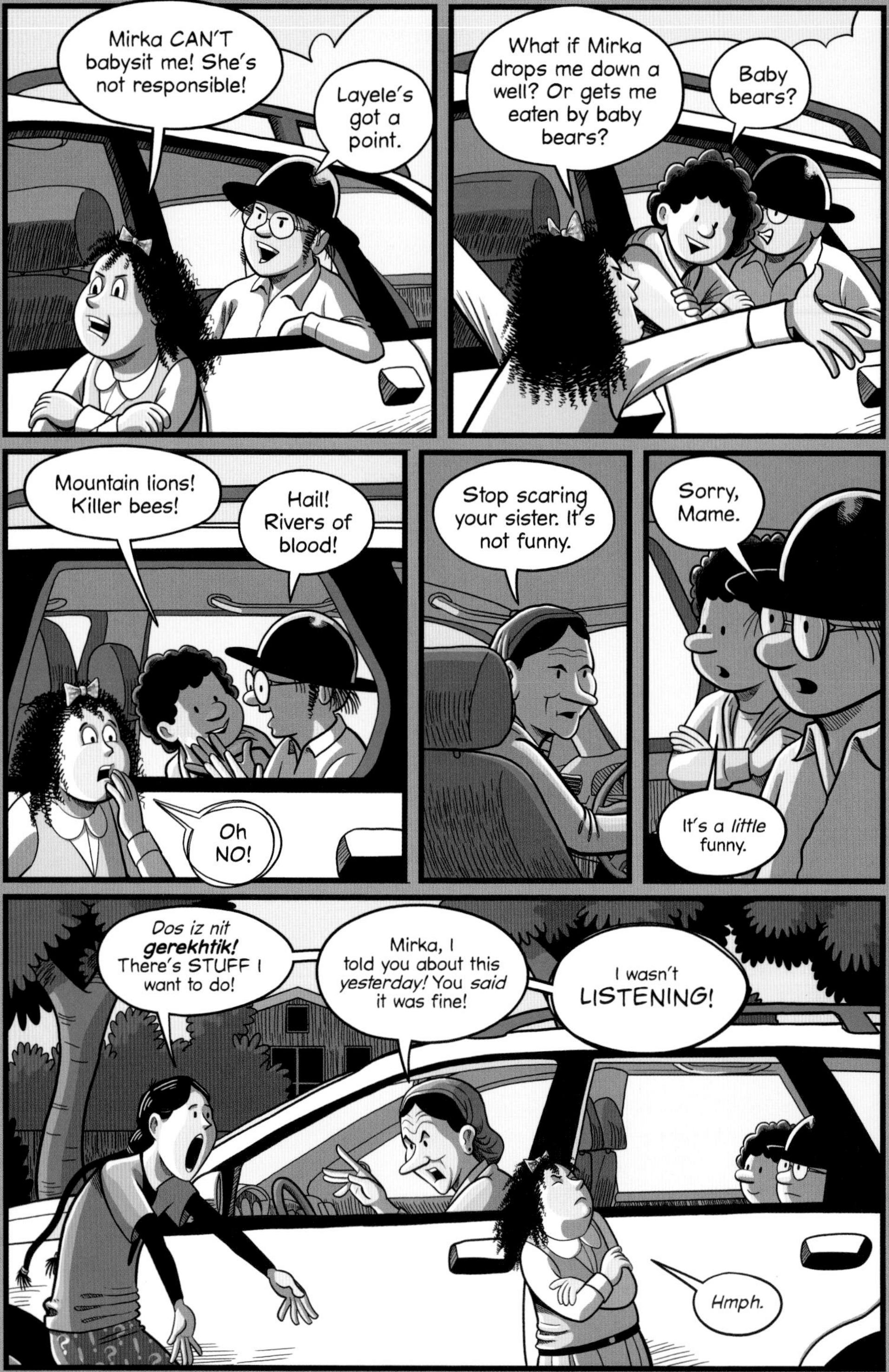
Mirka CAN'T babysit me! She's not responsible!
Layele's got a point.
What if Mirka drops me down a well? Or gets me eaten by baby bears?
Baby bears?
Mountain lions! Killer bees!
Hail! Rivers of blood!
Oh NO!
Stop scaring your sister. It's not funny.
Sorry, Mame.
It's a *little* funny.
Dos iz nit ***gerekhtik!*** There's STUFF I want to do!
Mirka, I told you about this *yesterday!* You *said* it was fine!
I wasn't LISTENING!
Hmph.

Dos iz nit gerekhtik: This isn't fair

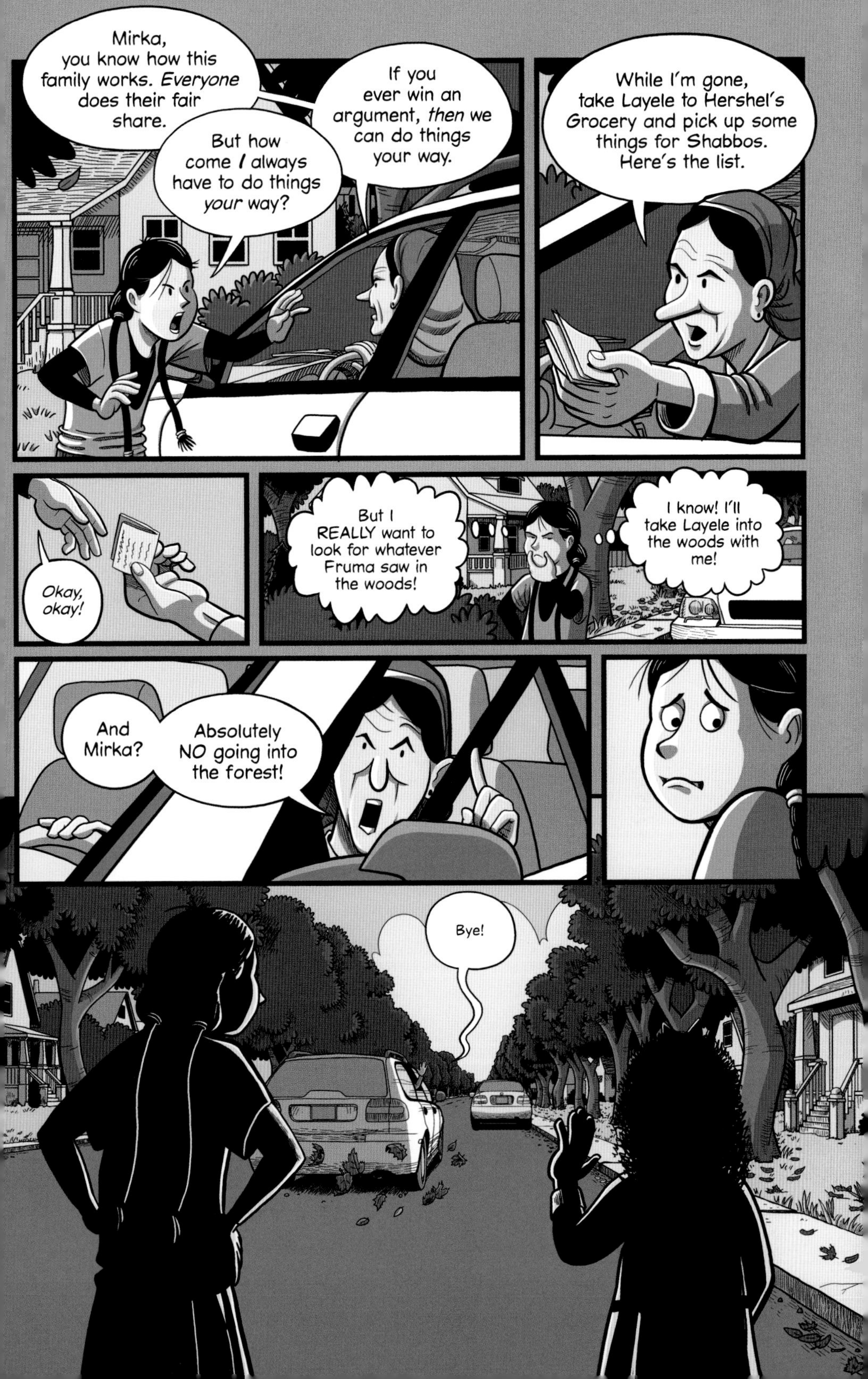
Mirka, you know how this family works. *Everyone* does their fair share.
But how come *I* always have to do things *your* way?
If you ever win an argument, *then* we can do things your way.
While I'm gone, take Layele to Hershel's Grocery and pick up some things for Shabbos. Here's the list.
Okay, okay!
But I REALLY want to look for whatever Fruma saw in the woods!
I know! I'll take Layele into the woods with me!
And Mirka?
Absolutely NO going into the forest!
Bye!

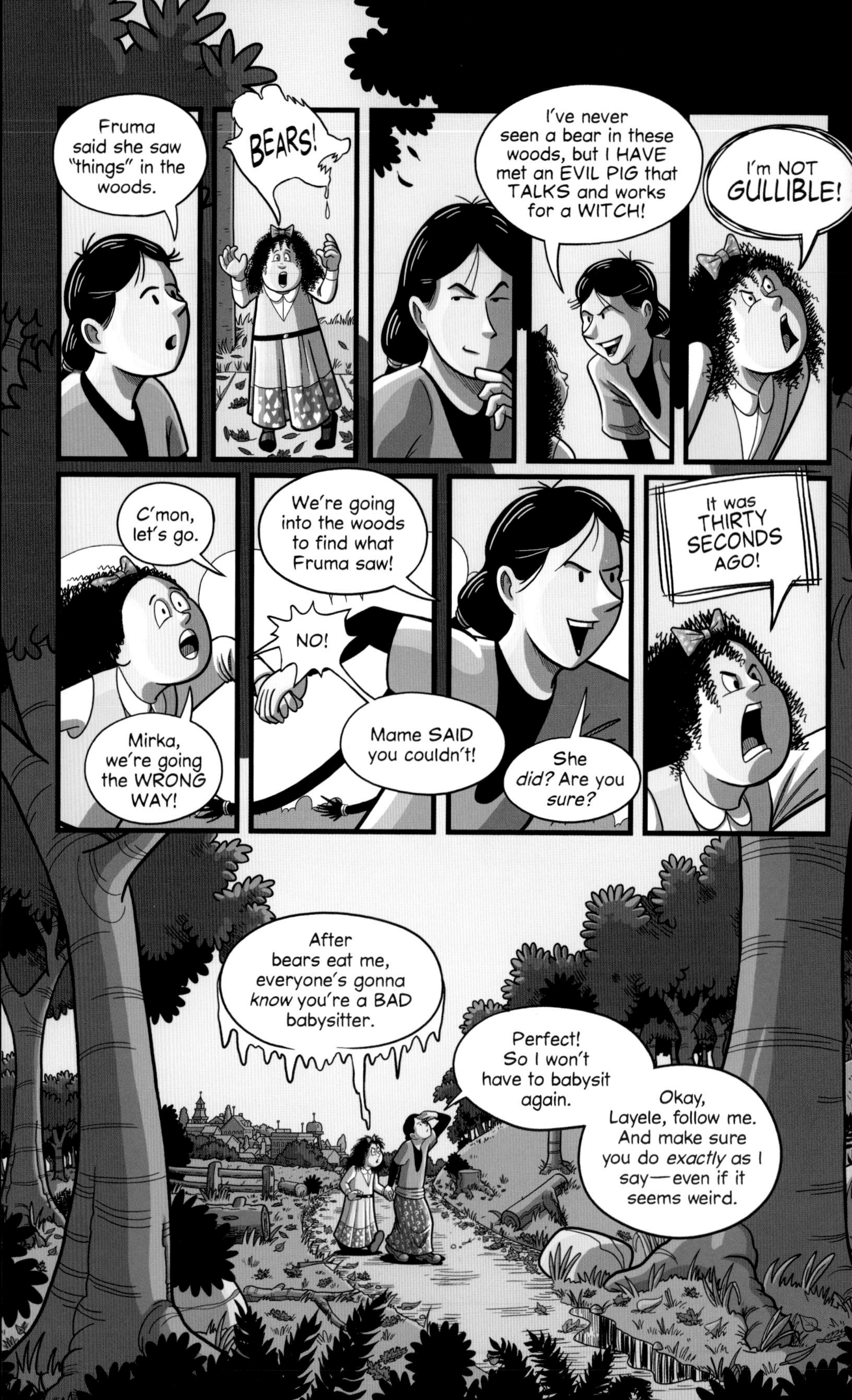

Fruma said she saw "things" in the woods.
BEARS!
I've never seen a bear in these woods, but I HAVE met an EVIL PIG that TALKS and works for a WITCH!
I'm NOT GULLIBLE!
C'mon, let's go.
Mirka, we're going the WRONG WAY!
We're going into the woods to find what Fruma saw!
NO!
Mame SAID you couldn't!
She *did*? Are you *sure*?
It was THIRTY SECONDS AGO!
After bears eat me, everyone's gonna *know* you're a BAD babysitter.
Perfect! So I won't have to babysit again.
Okay, Layele, follow me. And make sure you do *exactly* as I say—even if it seems weird.

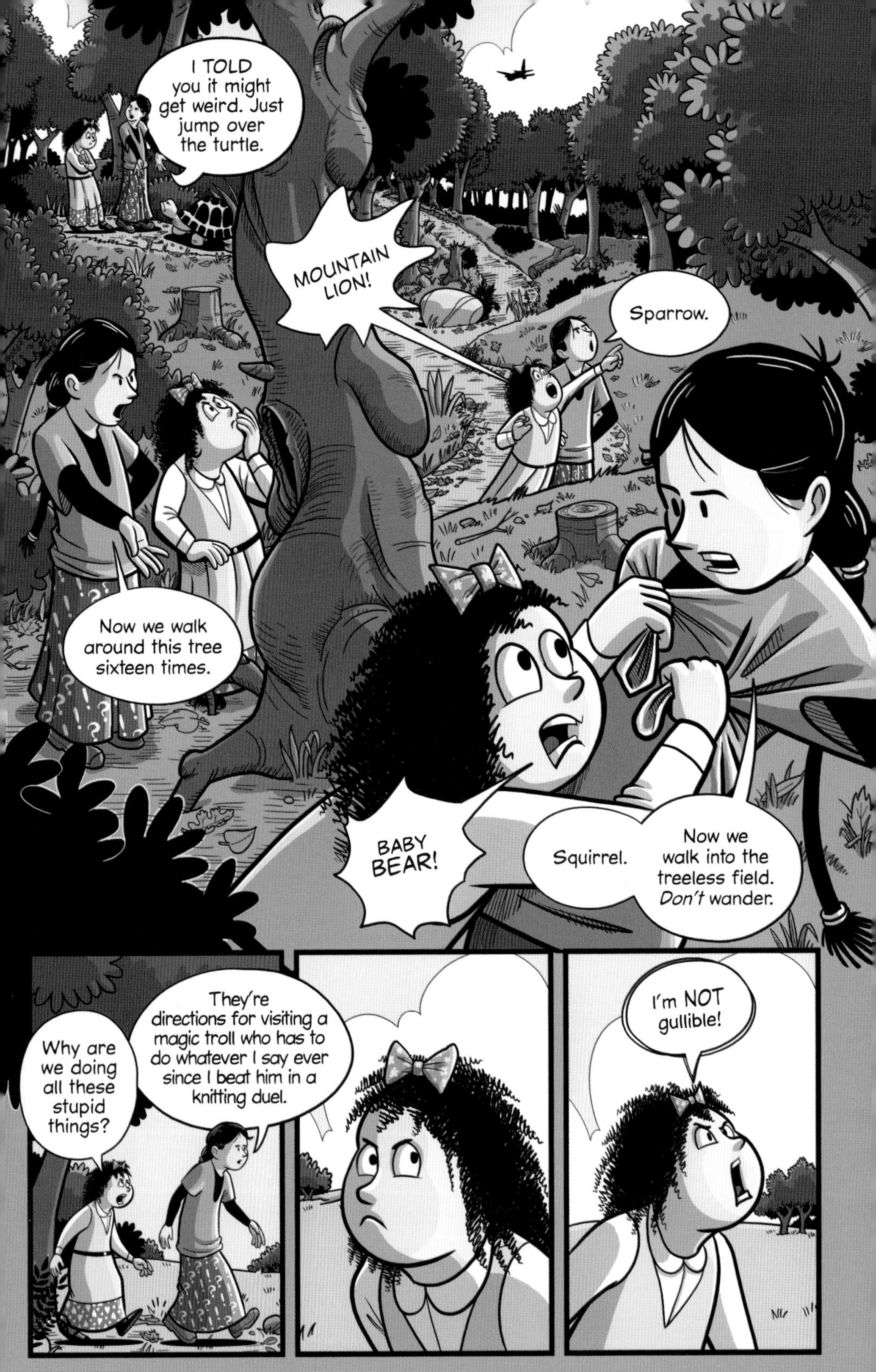

I TOLD you it might get weird. Just jump over the turtle.
Now we walk around this tree sixteen times.
MOUNTAIN LION!
Sparrow.
BABY BEAR!
Squirrel.
Now we walk into the treeless field. *Don't* wander.
Why are we doing all these stupid things?
They're directions for visiting a magic troll who has to do whatever I say ever since I beat him in a knitting duel.
I'm NOT gullible!

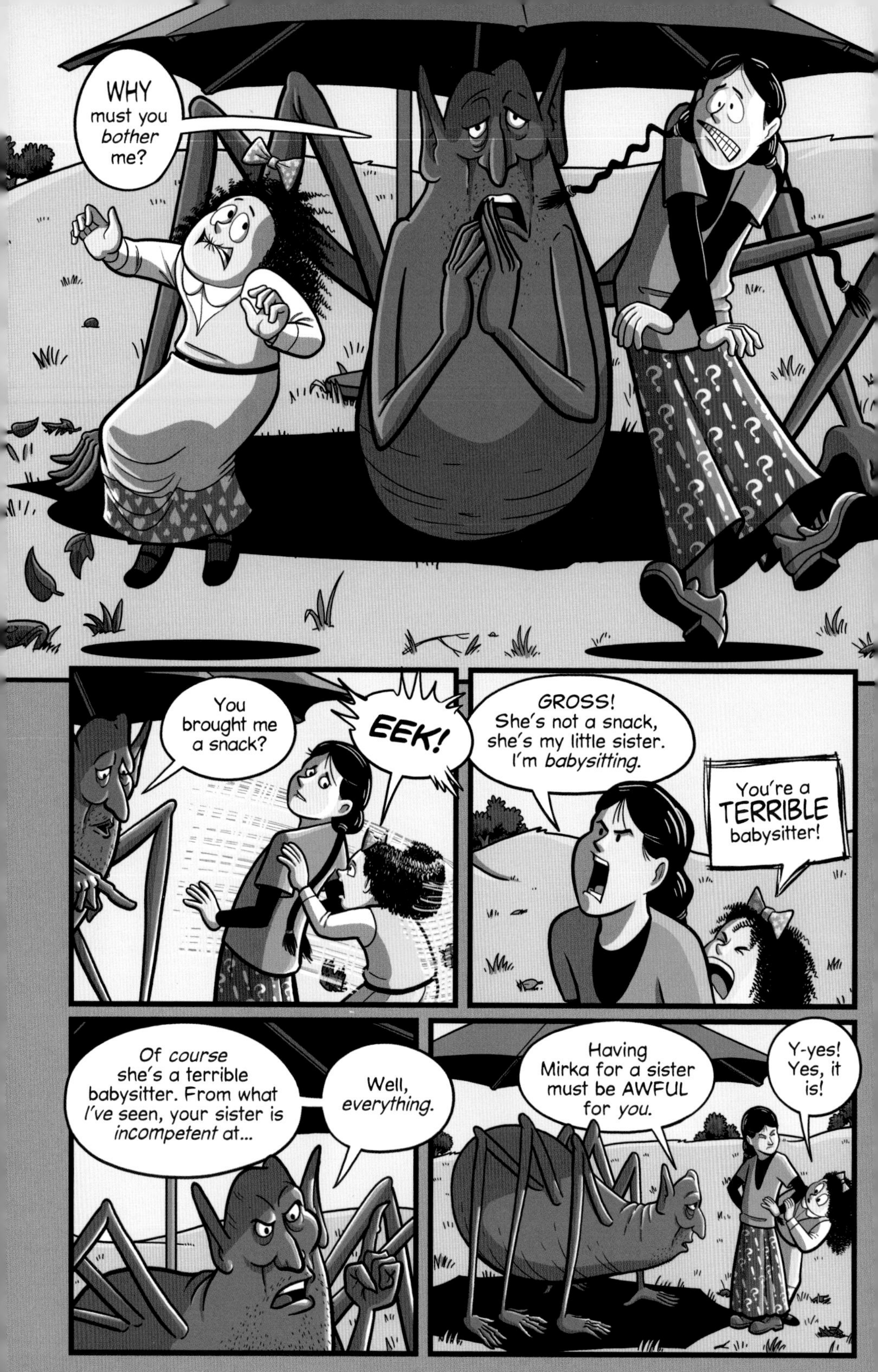

WHY must you *bother* me?
You brought me a snack?
EEK!
GROSS! She's not a snack, she's my little sister. I'm *babysitting*.
You're a TERRIBLE babysitter!
Of *course* she's a terrible babysitter. From what *I've* seen, your sister is *incompetent* at...
Well, *everything*.
Having Mirka for a sister must be AWFUL for *you*.
Y-yes! Yes, it is!

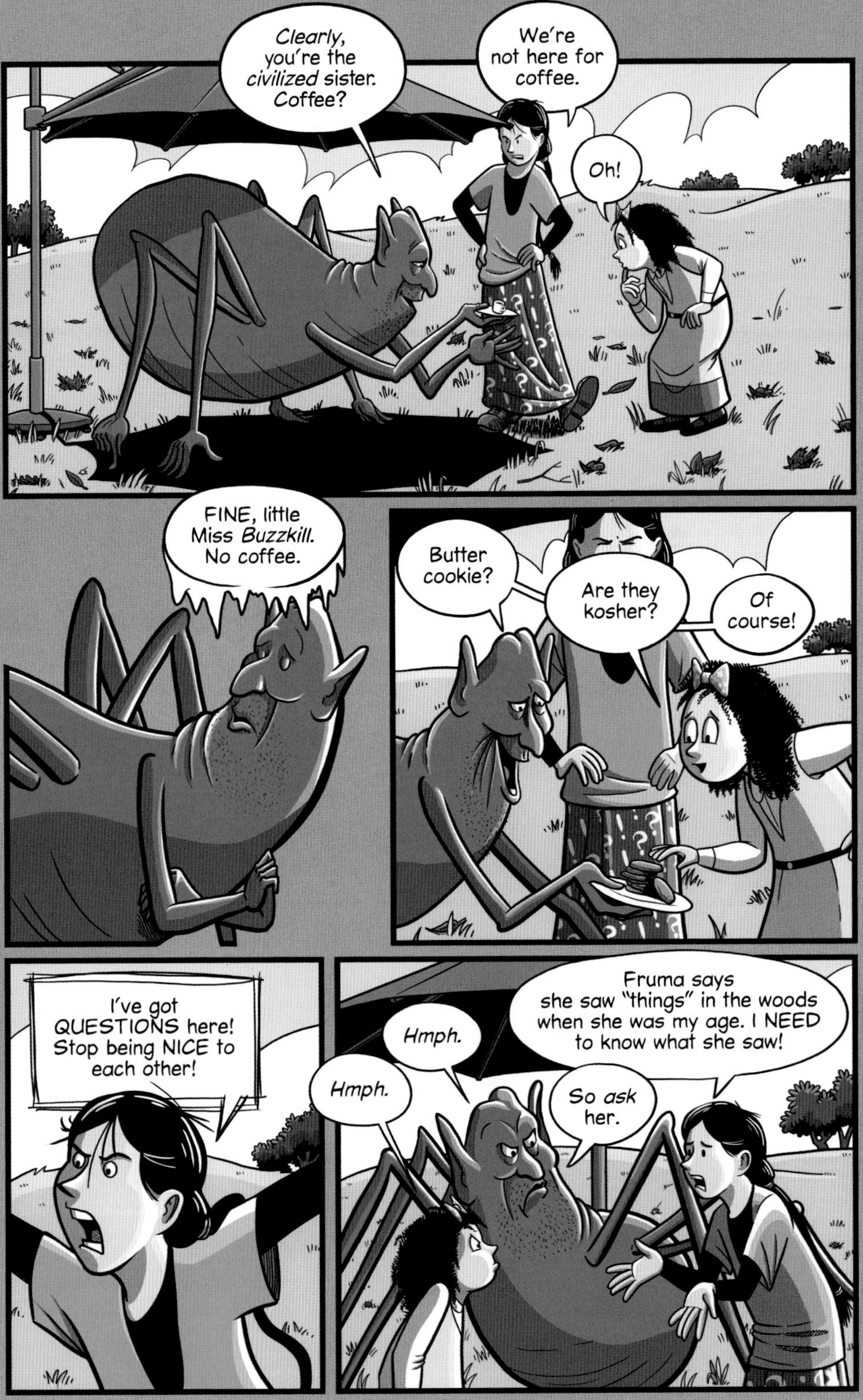
Clearly, you're the *civilized* sister. Coffee?
We're not here for coffee.
Oh!
FINE, little Miss *Buzzkill.* No coffee.
Butter cookie?
Are they kosher?
Of course!
I've got QUESTIONS here! Stop being NICE to each other!
Hmph.
Hmph.
Fruma says she saw "things" in the woods when she was my age. I NEED to know what she saw!
So ask her.

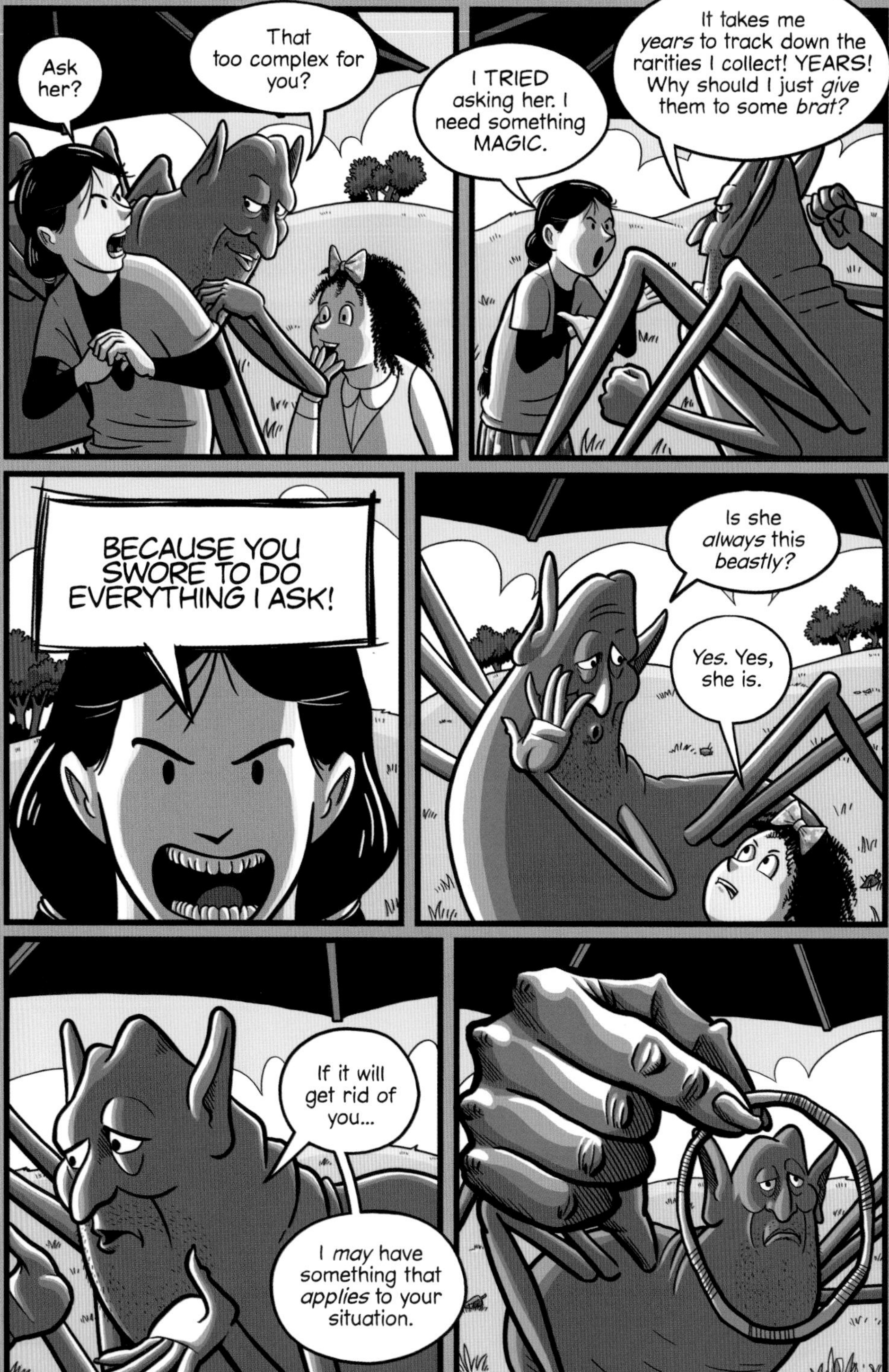
Ask her?
That too complex for you?
I TRIED asking her. I need something MAGIC.
It takes me *years* to track down the rarities I collect! YEARS! Why should I just *give* them to some *brat?*
BECAUSE YOU SWORE TO DO EVERYTHING I ASK!
Is she *always* this *beastly?*
Yes. Yes, she is.
If it will get rid of you...
I *may* have something that *applies* to your situation.

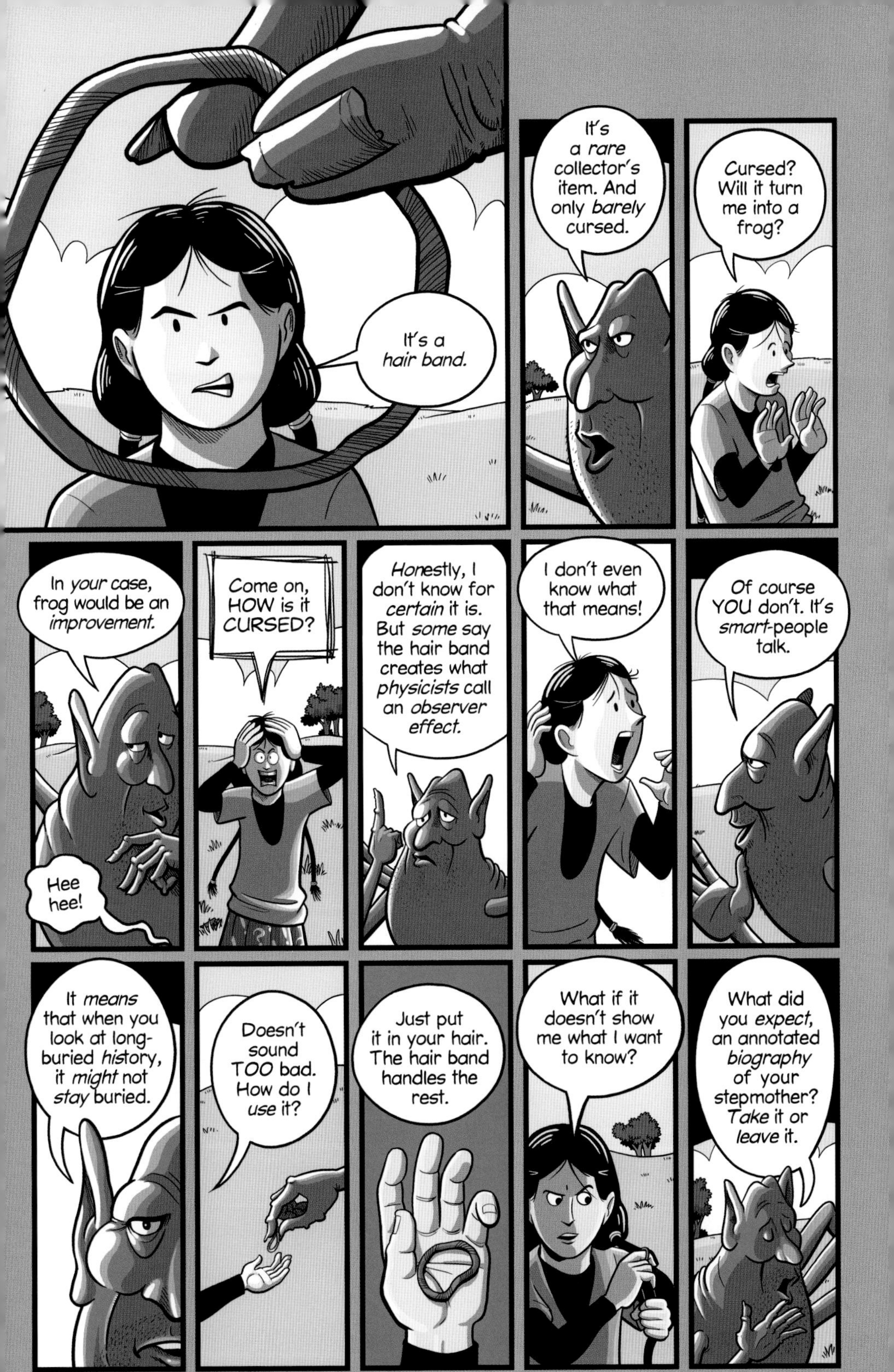
It's a *hair band.*
It's a *rare* collector's item. And only *barely* cursed.
Cursed? Will it turn me into a frog?
In *your case,* frog would be an *improvement.*
Hee hee!
Come on, HOW is it CURSED?
Honestly, I don't know for *certain* it is. But *some* say the hair band creates what *physicists* call an *observer effect.*
I don't even know what that means!
Of course YOU don't. It's *smart*-people talk.
It *means* that when you look at long-buried *history,* it *might* not *stay* buried.
Doesn't sound TOO bad. How do I *use* it?
Just put it in your hair. The hair band handles the rest.
What if it doesn't show me what I want to know?
What did you *expect,* an annotated *biography* of your stepmother? *Take* it or *leave* it.

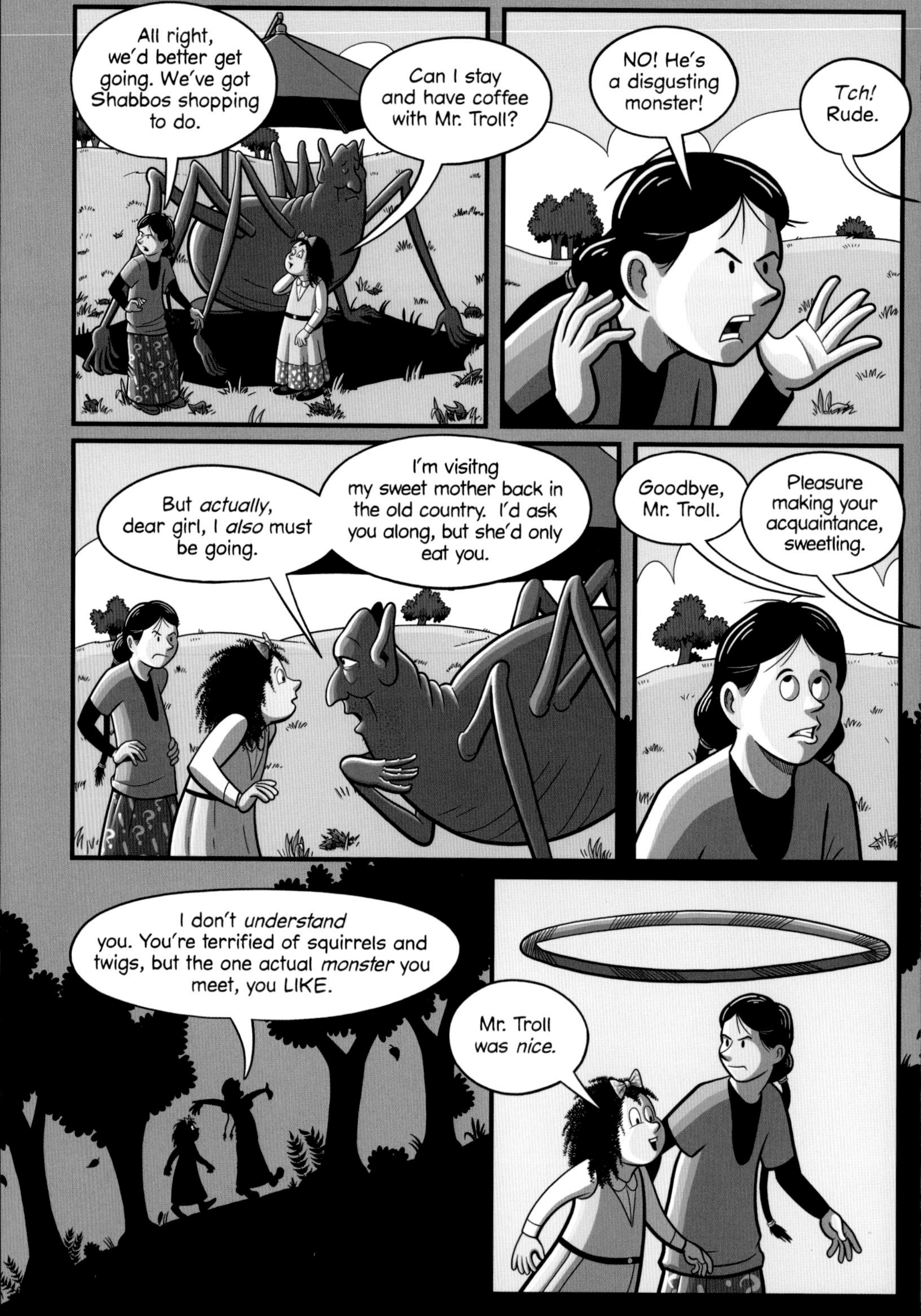
All right, we'd better get going. We've got Shabbos shopping to do.
Can I stay and have coffee with Mr. Troll?
NO! He's a disgusting monster!
Tch! Rude.
But *actually,* dear girl, I *also* must be going.
I'm visitng my sweet mother back in the old country. I'd ask you along, but she'd only eat you.
Goodbye, Mr. Troll.
Pleasure making your acquaintance, sweetling.
I don't *understand* you. You're terrified of squirrels and twigs, but the one actual *monster* you meet, you LIKE.
Mr. Troll was *nice.*

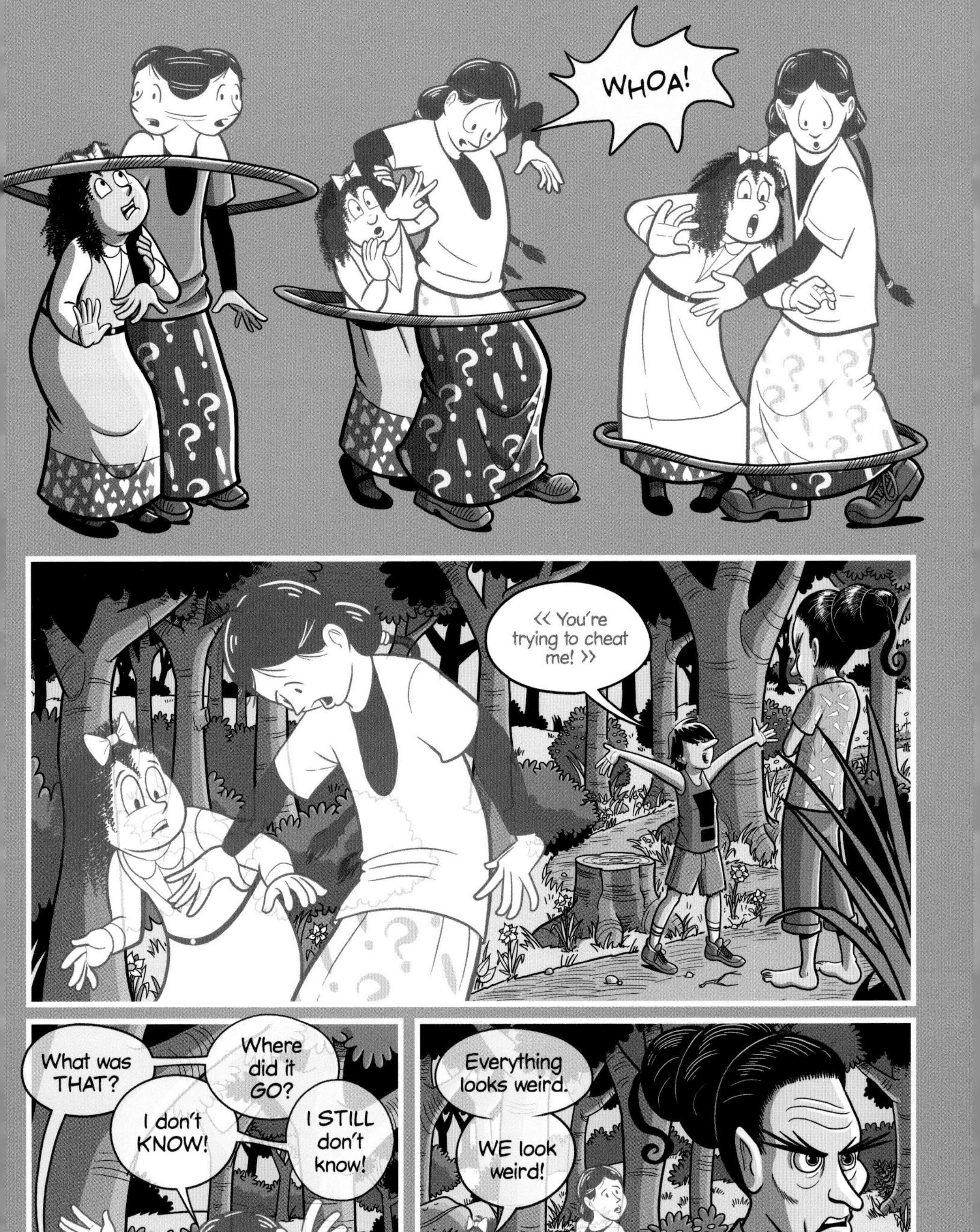
WHOA!
<< You're trying to cheat me! >>
What was THAT?
Where did it GO?
I don't KNOW!
I STILL don't know!
Everything looks weird.
WE look weird!
<< Why are you making this so *difficult*, brat? >>

Dialogue marked <<like this>> means they're speaking English instead of Yiddish.

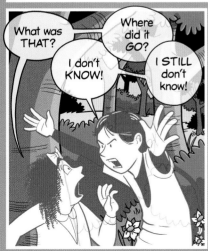

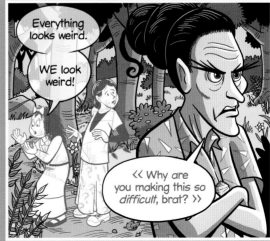

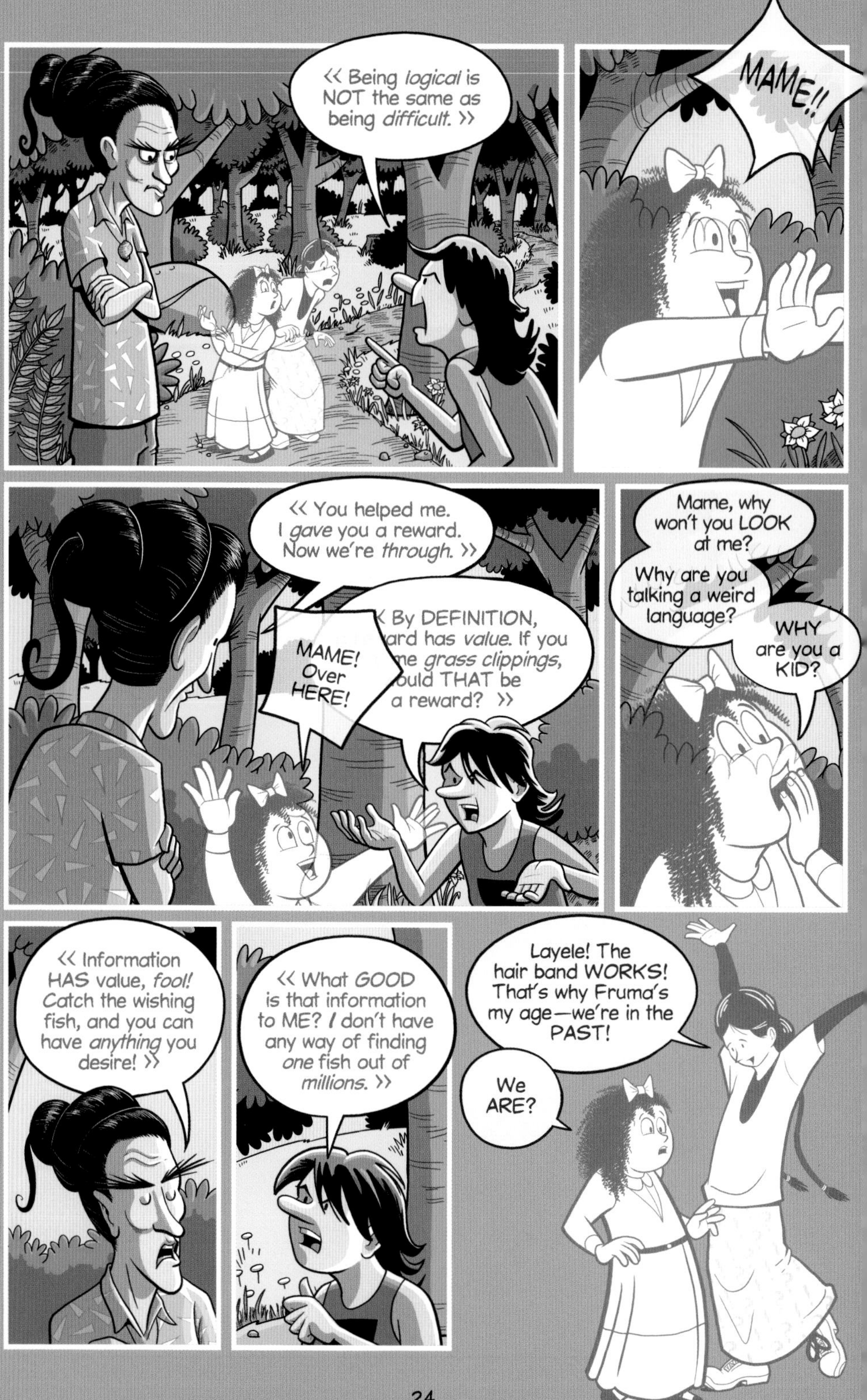

<< Being logical is NOT the same as being difficult. >>
MAME!!
<< You helped me. I gave you a reward. Now we're through. >>
MAME! Over HERE!
< By DEFINITION, ard has value. If you me grass clippings, ould THAT be a reward? >>
Mame, why won't you LOOK at me?
Why are you talking a weird language?
WHY are you a KID?
<< Information HAS value, fool! Catch the wishing fish, and you can have anything you desire! >>
<< What GOOD is that information to ME? I don't have any way of finding one fish out of millions. >>
Layele! The hair band WORKS! That's why Fruma's my age—we're in the PAST!
We ARE?

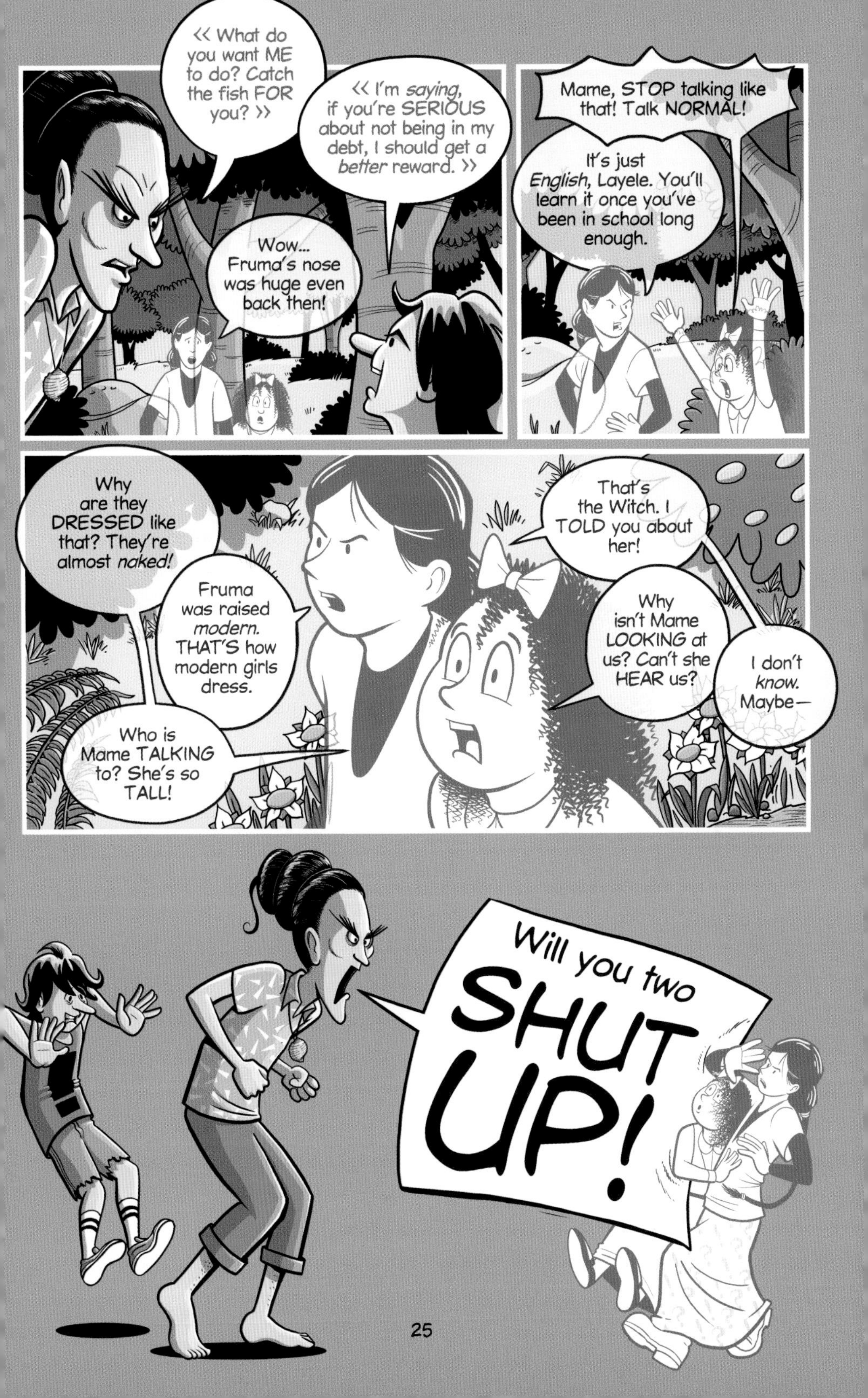

<< What do you want ME to do? Catch the fish FOR you? >>
<< I'm *saying*, if you're SERIOUS about not being in my debt, I should get a *better* reward. >>
Wow... Fruma's nose was huge even back then!
Mame, STOP talking like that! Talk NORMAL!
It's just *English*, Layele. You'll learn it once you've been in school long enough.
Why are they DRESSED like that? They're almost *naked!*
Fruma was raised *modern.* THAT'S how modern girls dress.
Who is Mame TALKING to? She's so TALL!
That's the Witch. I TOLD you about her!
Why isn't Mame LOOKING at us? Can't she HEAR us?
I don't *know.* Maybe—
Will you two SHUT UP!

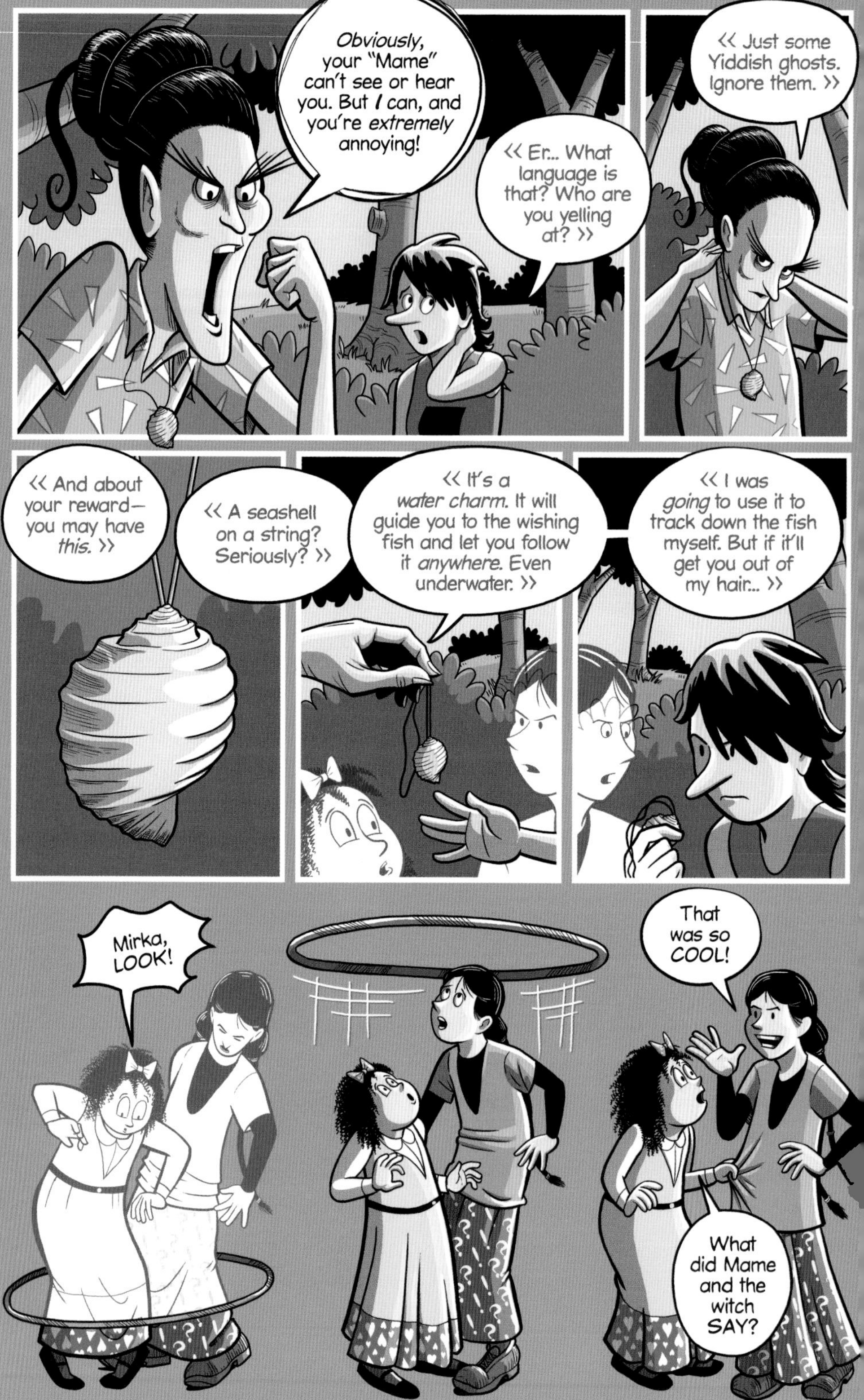
Obviously, your "Mame" can't see or hear you. But I can, and you're extremely annoying!
<< Er... What language is that? Who are you yelling at? >>
<< Just some Yiddish ghosts. Ignore them. >>
<< And about your reward—you may have this. >>
<< A seashell on a string? Seriously? >>
<< It's a water charm. It will guide you to the wishing fish and let you follow it anywhere. Even underwater. >>
<< I was going to use it to track down the fish myself. But if it'll get you out of my hair... >>
Mirka, LOOK!
That was so COOL!
What did Mame and the witch SAY?

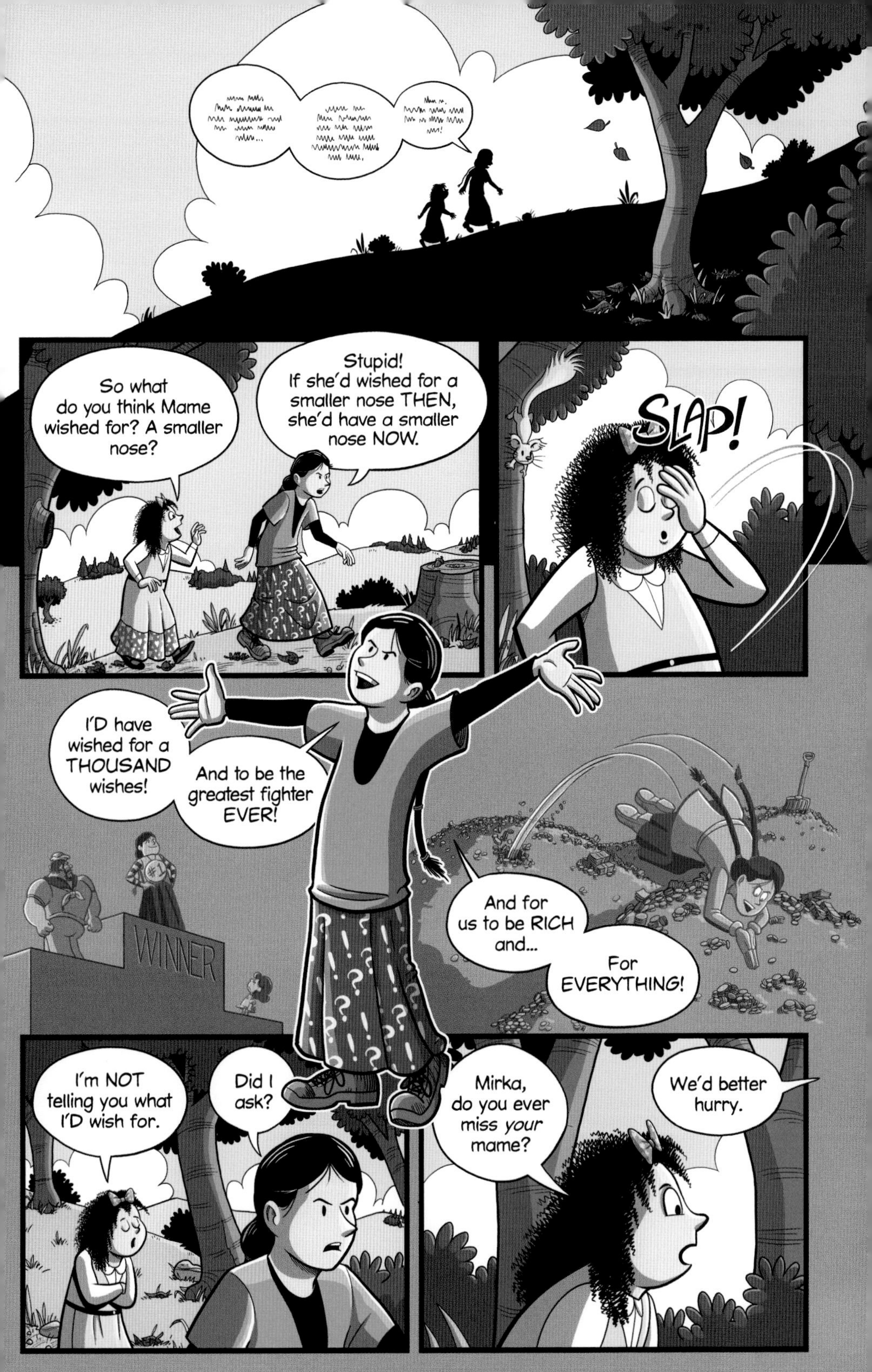
So what do you think Mame wished for? A smaller nose?
Stupid! If she'd wished for a smaller nose THEN, she'd have a smaller nose NOW.
SLAP!
I'D have wished for a THOUSAND wishes!
And to be the greatest fighter EVER!
WINNER
And for us to be RICH and...
For EVERYTHING!
I'm NOT telling you what I'D wish for.
Did I ask?
Mirka, do you ever miss *your* mame?
We'd better hurry.

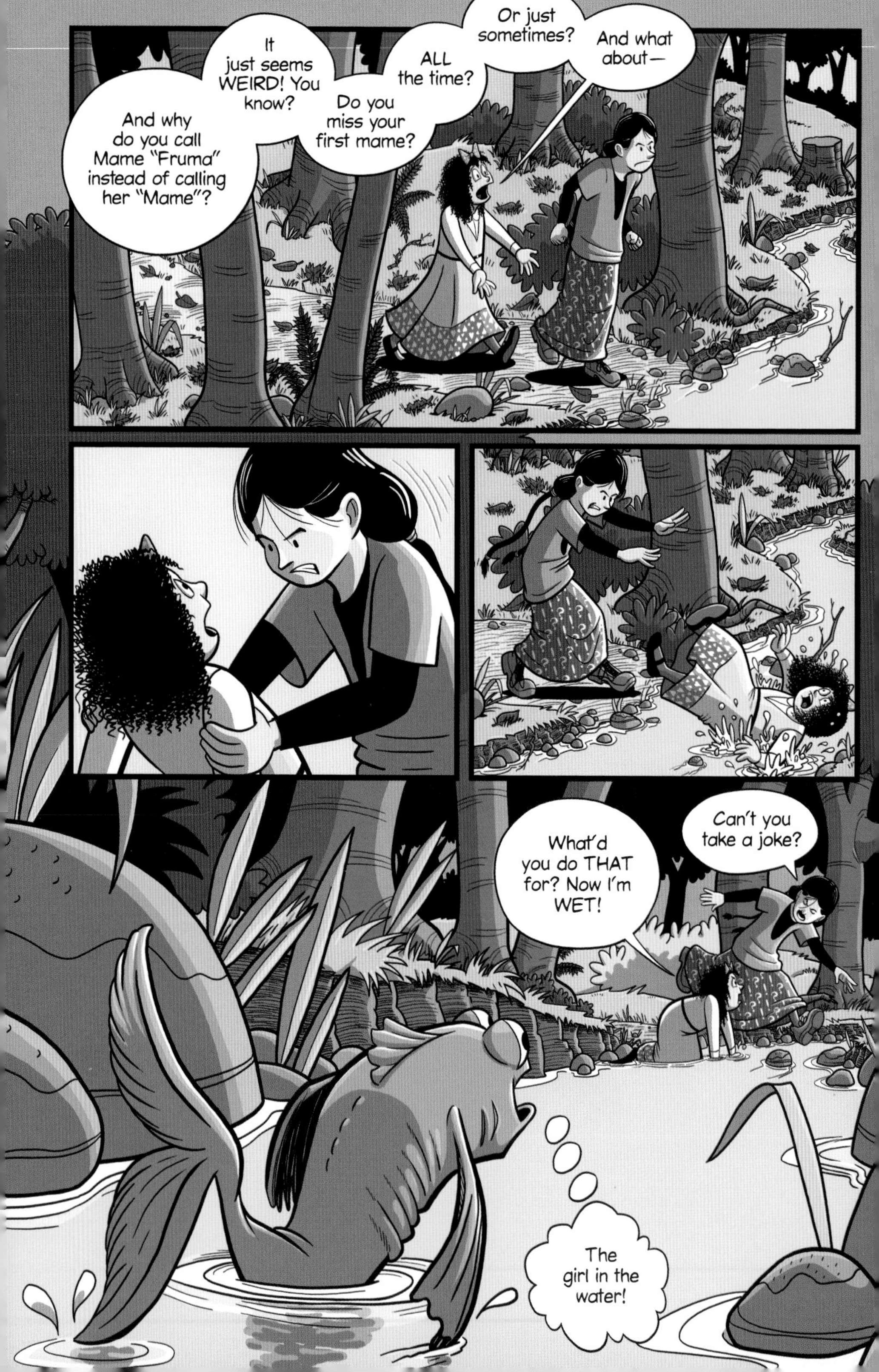
And why do you call Mame "Fruma" instead of calling her "Mame"?
It just seems WEIRD! You know?
Do you miss your first mame?
ALL the time?
Or just sometimes?
And what about—
What'd you do THAT for? Now I'm WET!
Can't you take a joke?
The girl in the water!

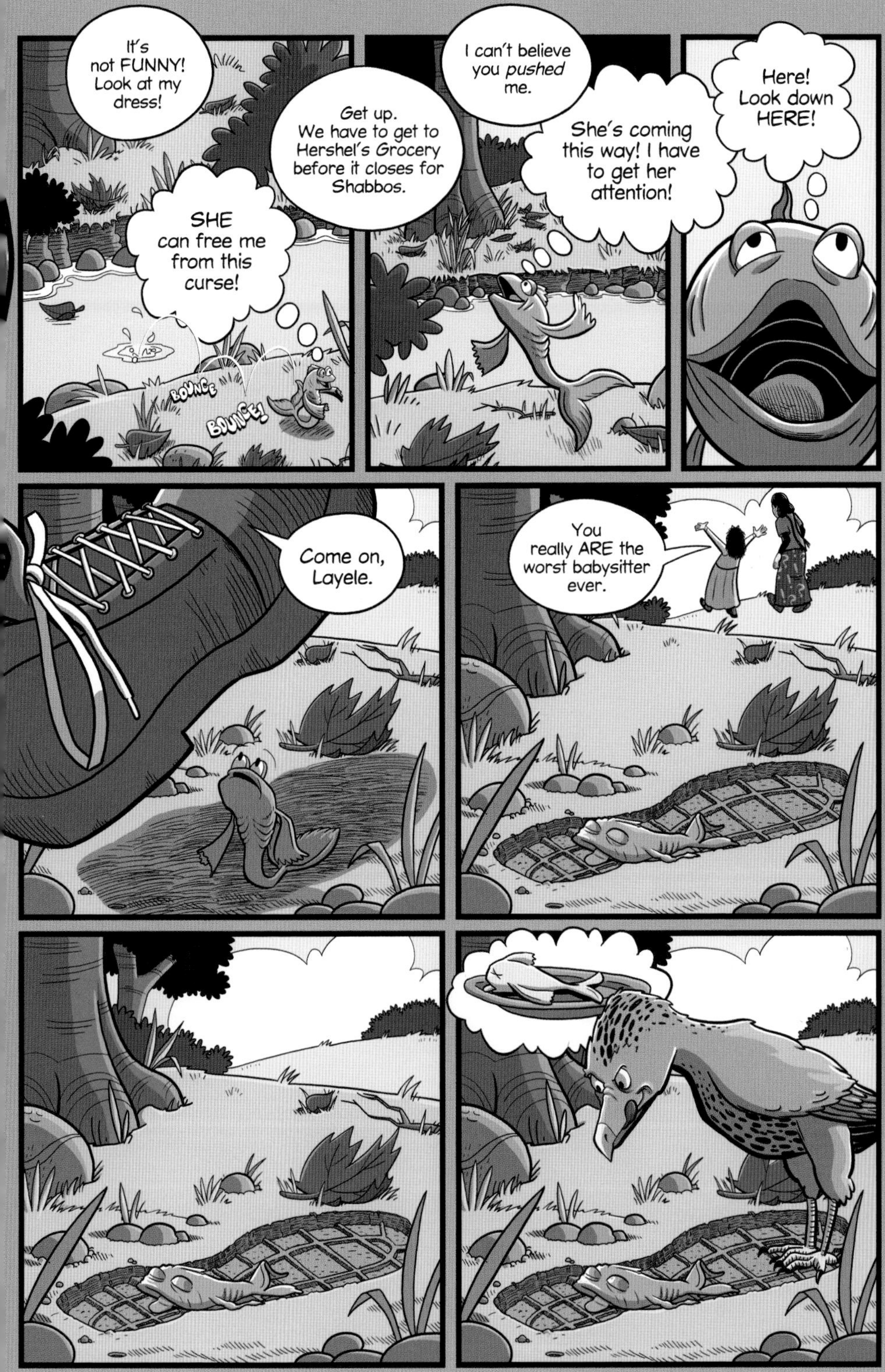
It's not FUNNY! Look at my dress!
SHE can free me from this curse!
BOUNCE
BOUNCE!
Get up. We have to get to Hershel's Grocery before it closes for Shabbos.
I can't believe you *pushed* me.
She's coming this way! I have to get her attention!
Here! Look down HERE!
Come on, Layele.
You really ARE the worst babysitter ever.

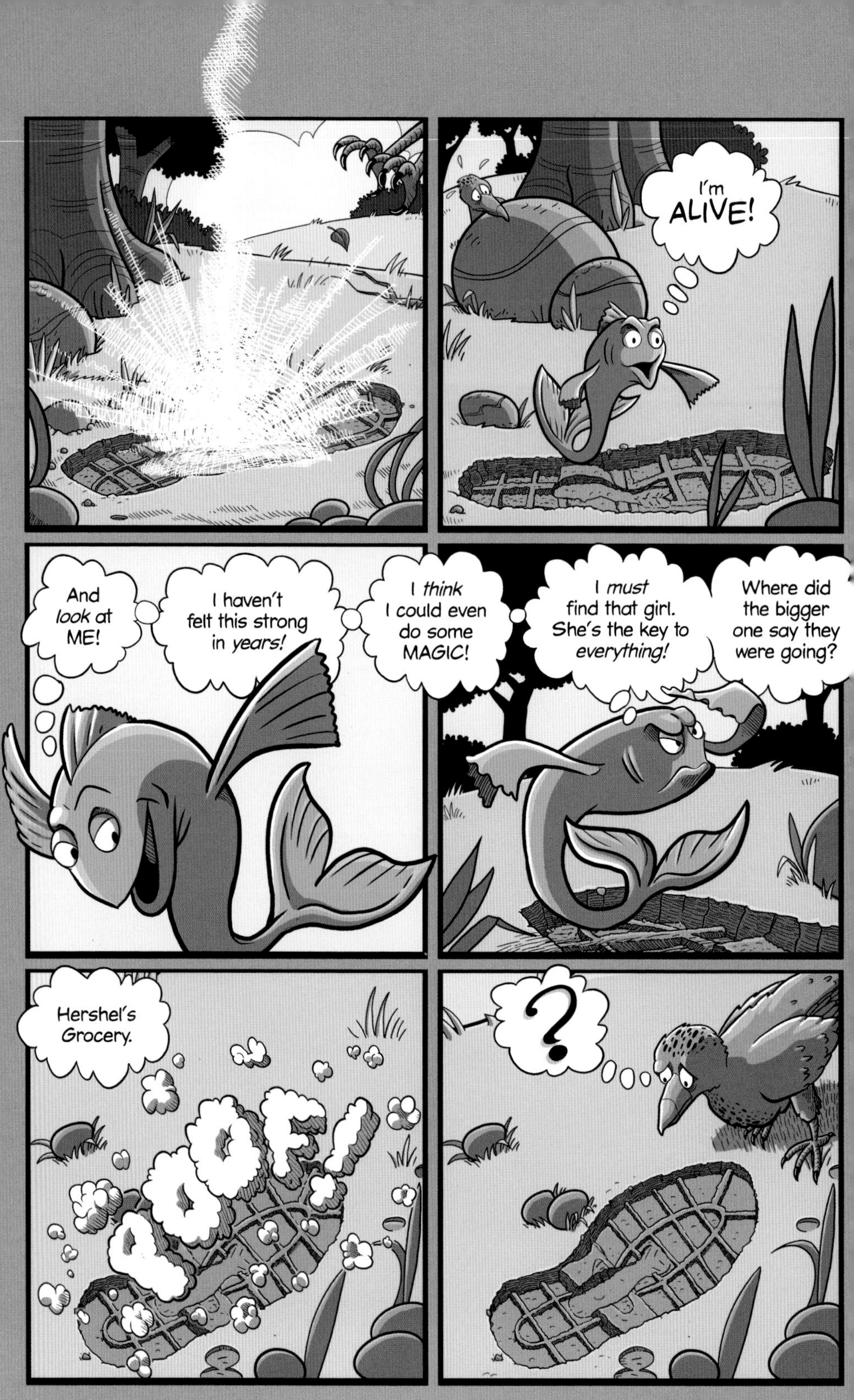
I'm ALIVE!
And *look* at ME!
I haven't felt this strong in *years!*
I *think* I could even do some MAGIC!
I *must* find that girl. She's the key to *everything!*
Where did the bigger one say they were going?
Hershel's Grocery.
POOF!
?

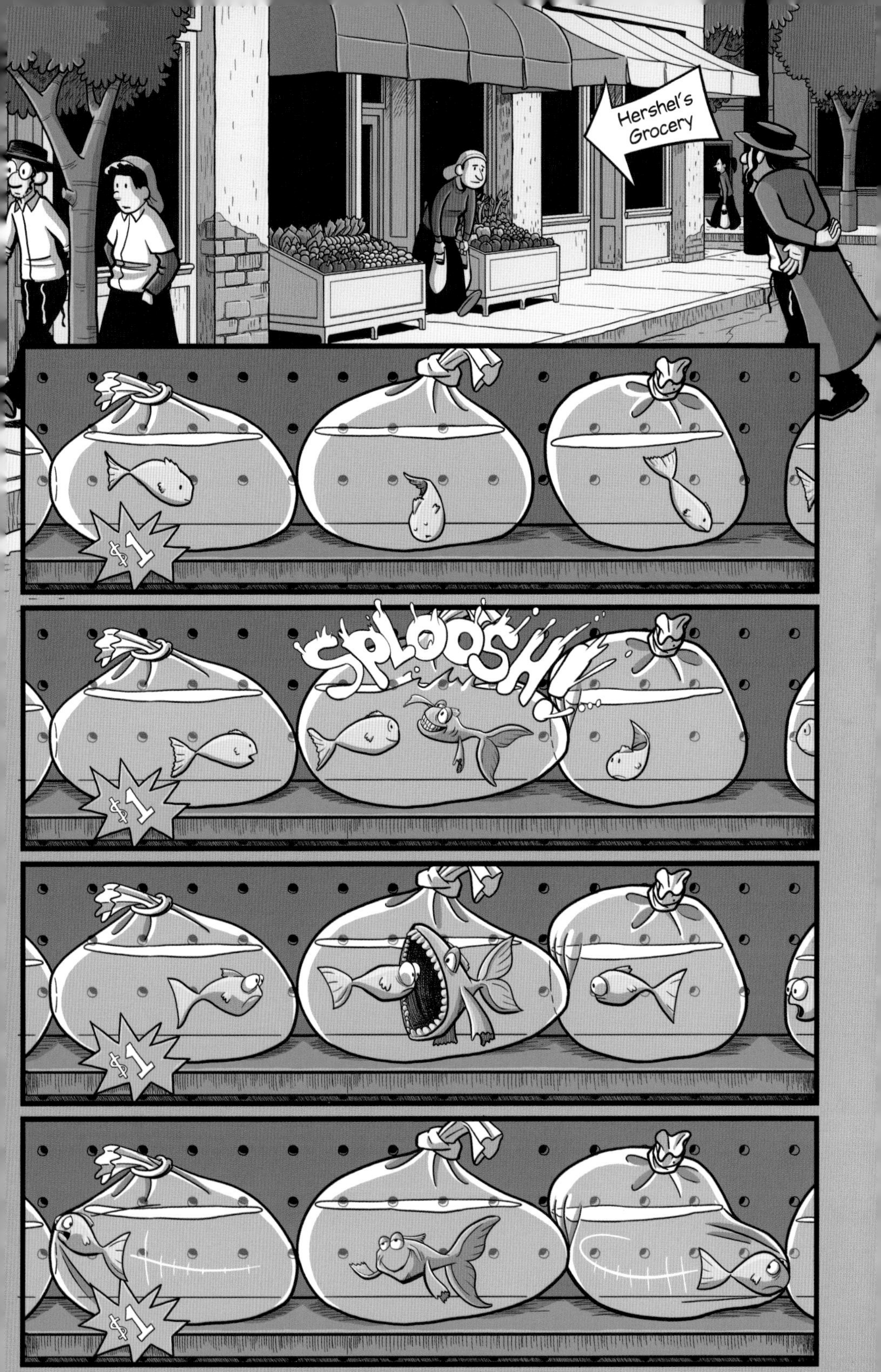
Hershel's Grocery
$1
SPLOOSH!
$1
$1
$1

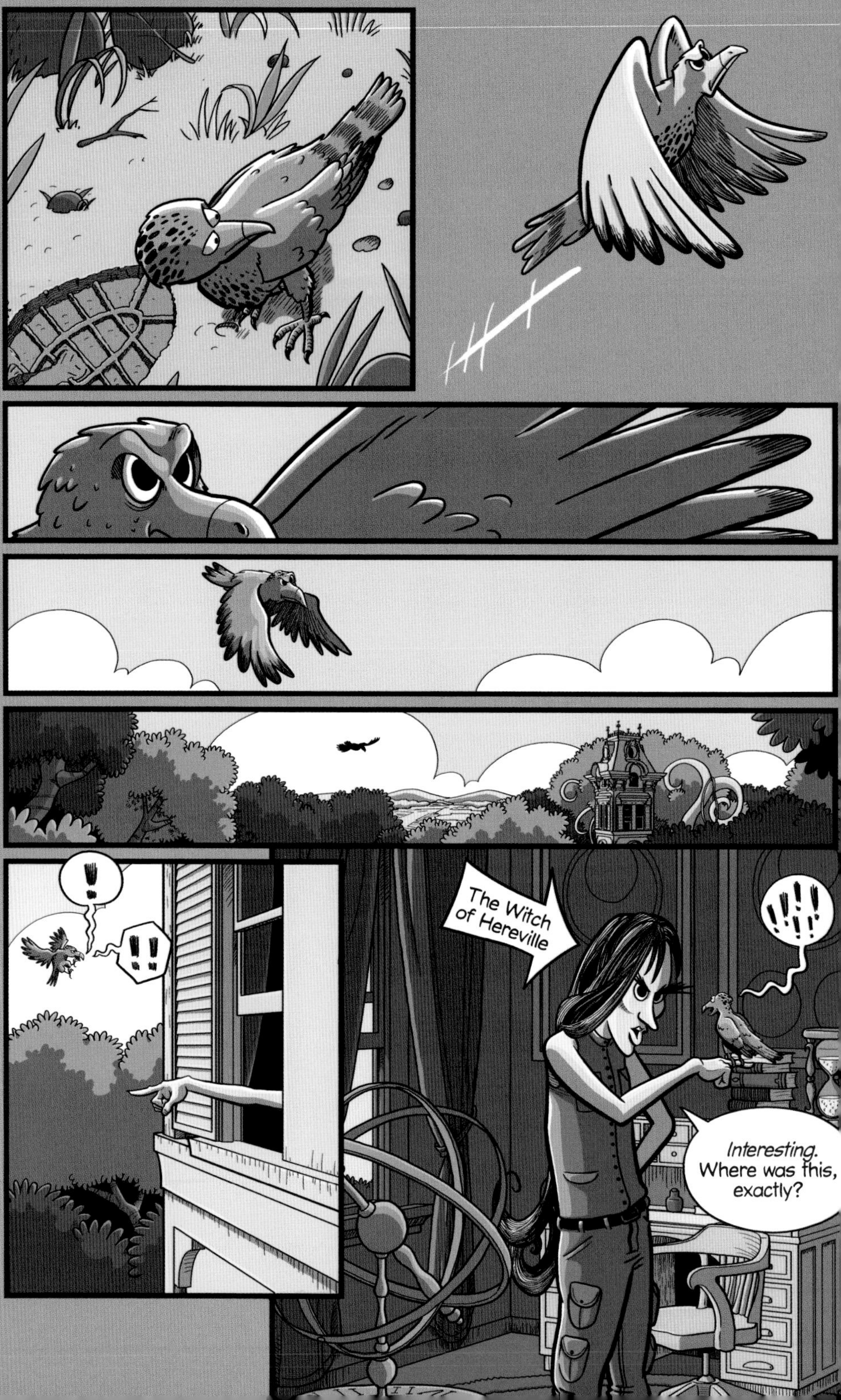
!
!!
The Witch of Hereville
!!!!!
Interesting. Where was this, exactly?

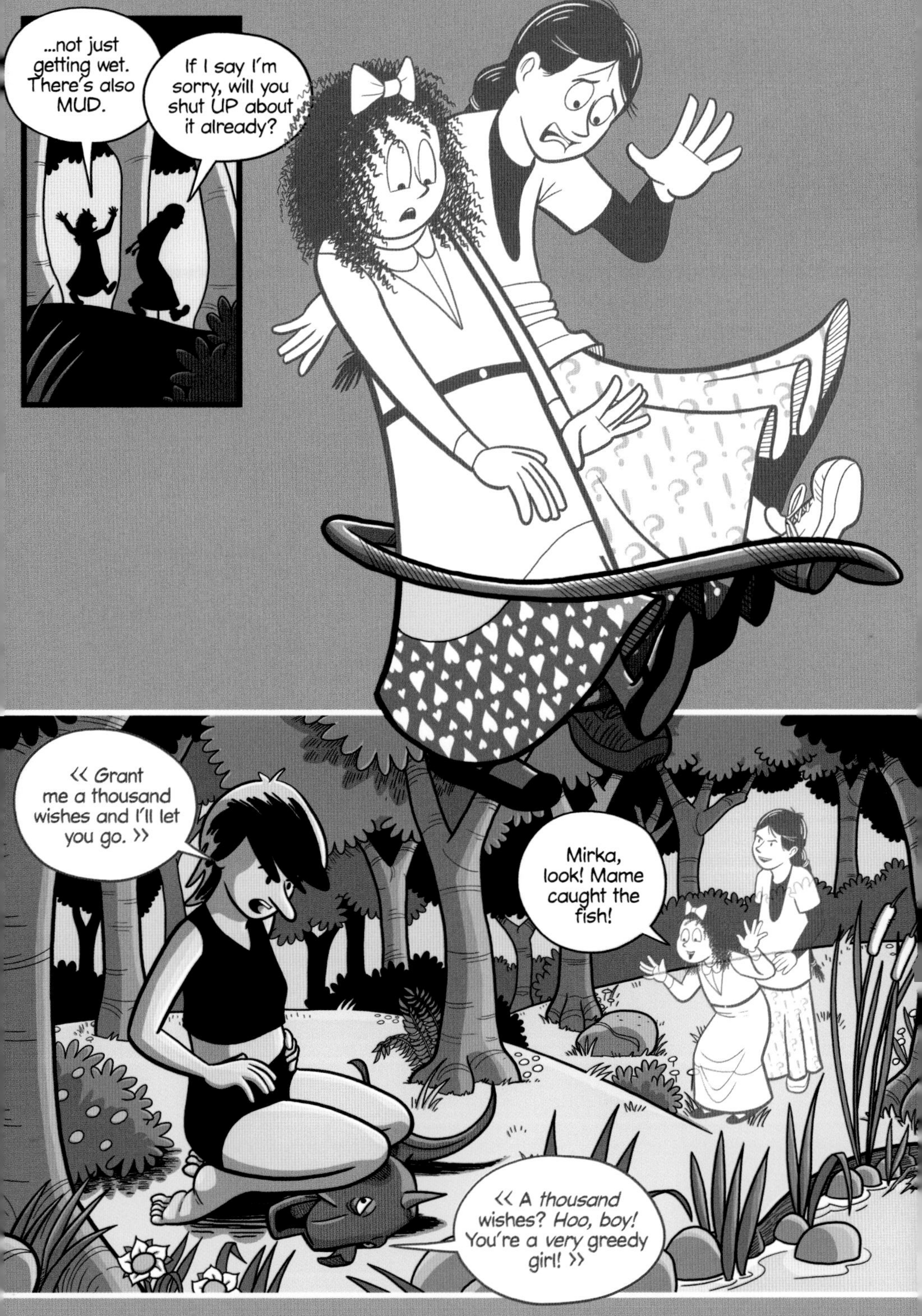
...not just getting wet. There's also MUD.
If I say I'm sorry, will you shut UP about it already?
<< Grant me a thousand wishes and I'll let you go. >>
Mirka, look! Mame caught the fish!
<< A *thousand* wishes? *Hoo, boy!* You're a *very* greedy girl! >>

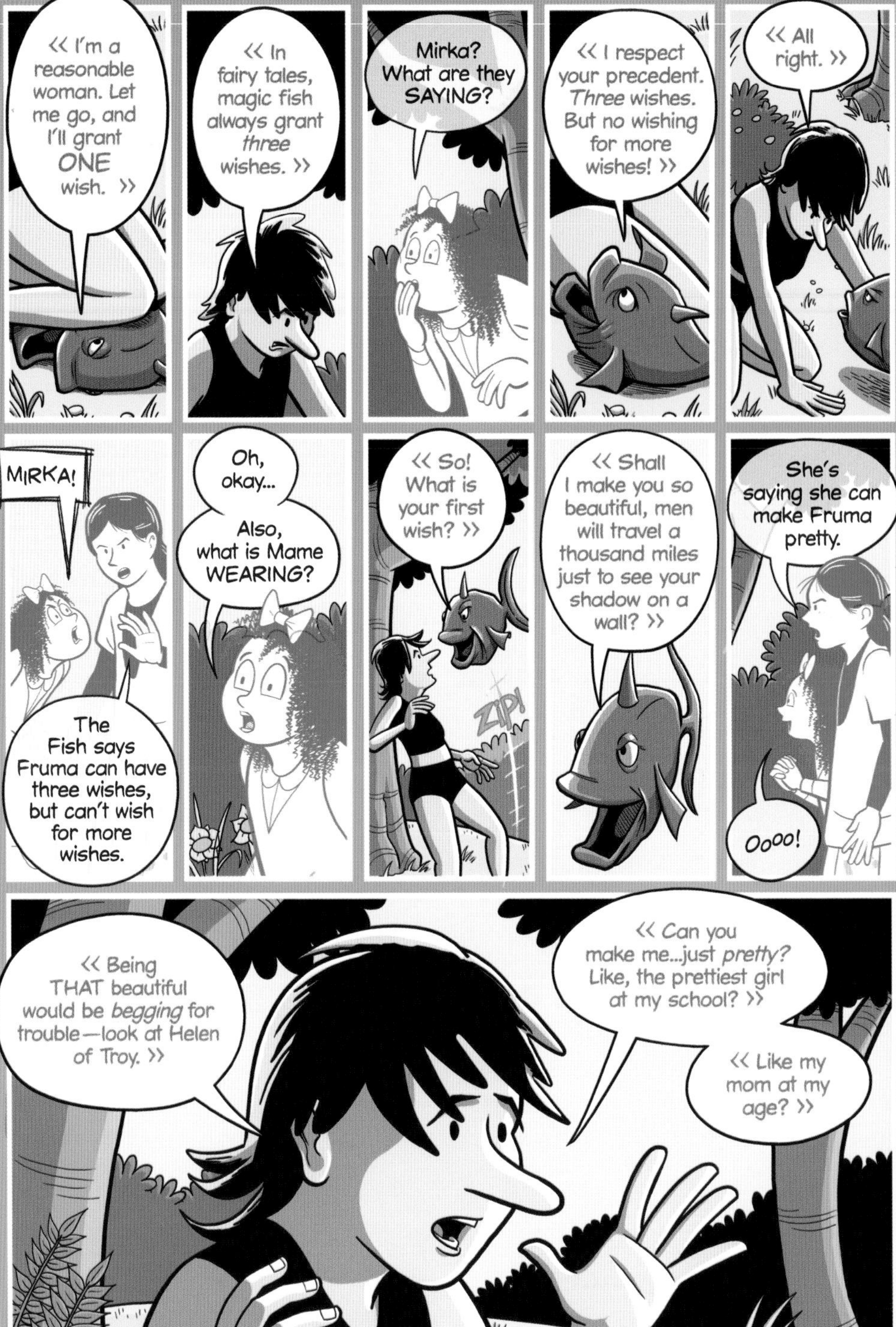

<< I'm a reasonable woman. Let me go, and I'll grant ONE wish. >>
<< In fairy tales, magic fish always grant *three* wishes. >>
Mirka? What are they SAYING?
<< I respect your precedent. *Three* wishes. But no wishing for more wishes! >>
<< All right. >>
MIRKA!
The Fish says Fruma can have three wishes, but can't wish for more wishes.
Oh, okay...
Also, what is Mame WEARING?
<< So! What is your first wish? >>
ZIP!
<< Shall I make you so beautiful, men will travel a thousand miles just to see your shadow on a wall? >>
She's saying she can make Fruma pretty.
Oooo!
<< Being THAT beautiful would be *begging* for trouble—look at Helen of Troy. >>
<< Can you make me...just *pretty?* Like, the prettiest girl at my school? >>
<< Like my mom at my age? >>

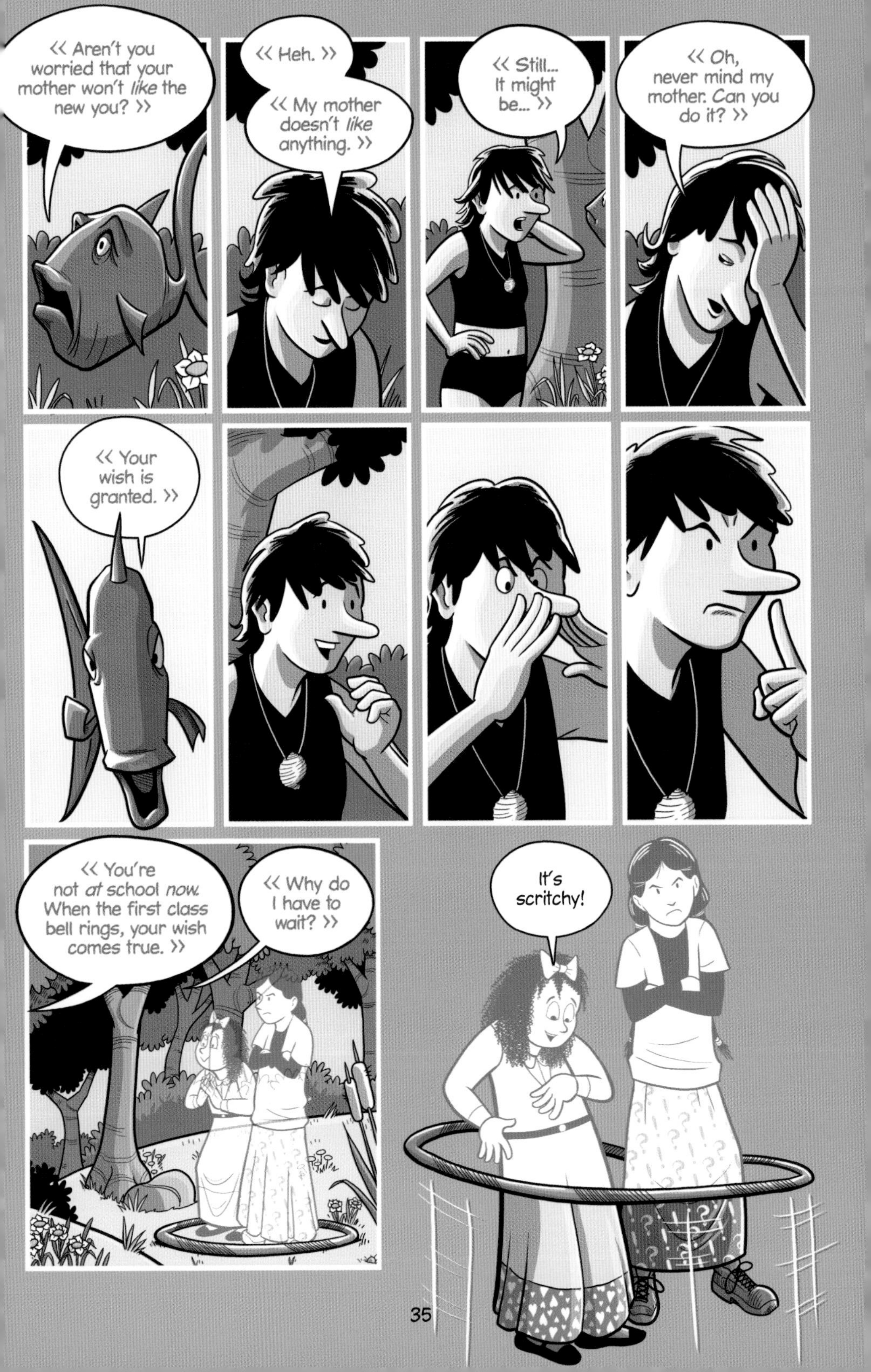

<< Aren't you worried that your mother won't *like* the new you? >>
<< Heh. >>
<< My mother doesn't *like* anything. >>
<< Still... It might be... >>
<< Oh, never mind my mother. Can you do it? >>
<< Your wish is granted. >>
<< You're not *at* school *now.* When the first class bell rings, your wish comes true. >>
<< Why do I have to wait? >>
It's scritchy!

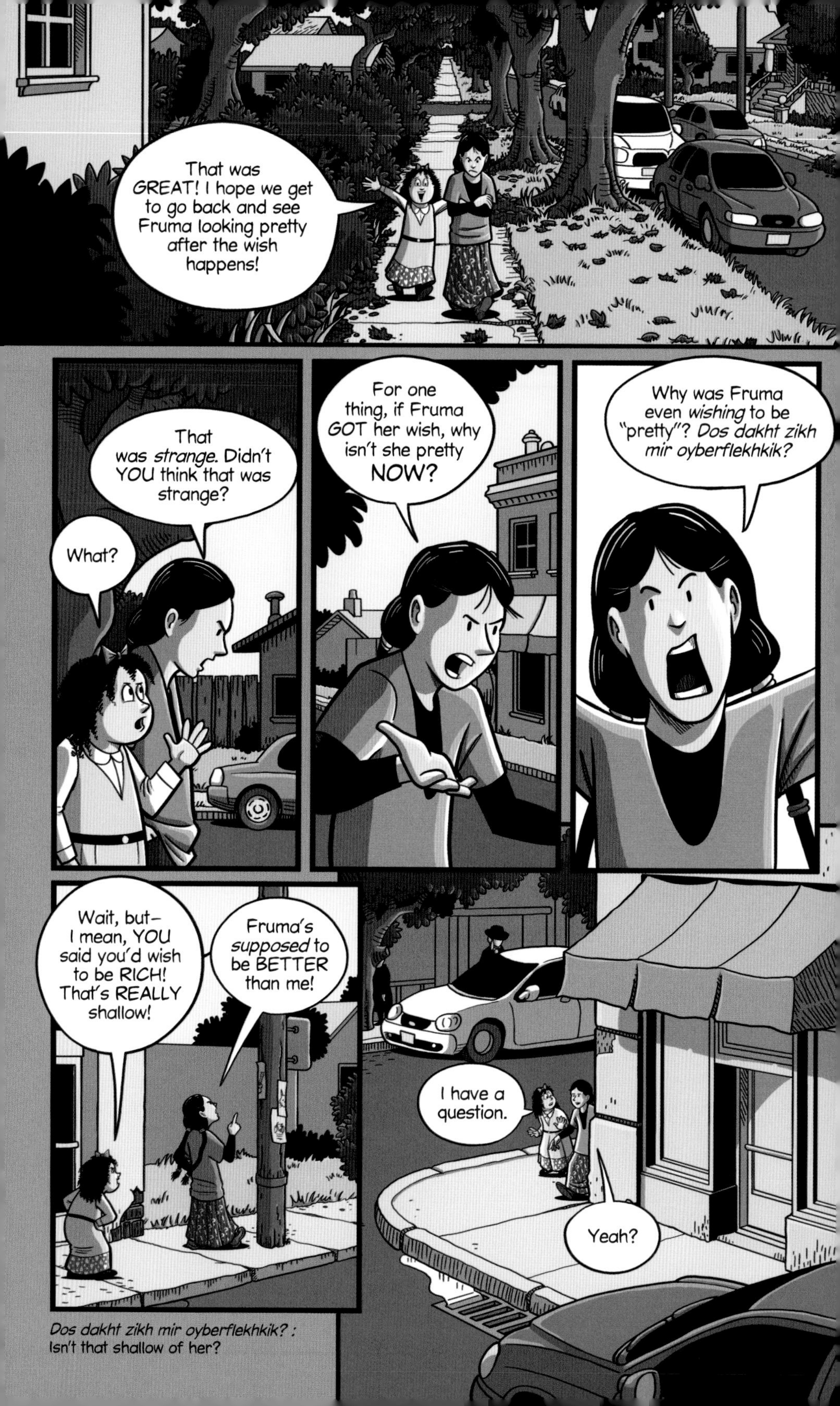
That was GREAT! I hope we get to go back and see Fruma looking pretty after the wish happens!
That was *strange*. Didn't YOU think that was strange?
What?
For one thing, if Fruma GOT her wish, why isn't she pretty NOW?
Why was Fruma even *wishing* to be "pretty"? *Dos dakht zikh mir oyberflekhkik?*
Wait, but— I mean, YOU said you'd wish to be RICH! That's REALLY shallow!
Fruma's *supposed* to be BETTER than me!
I have a question.
Yeah?

Dos dakht zikh mir oyberflekhkik? : Isn't that shallow of her?

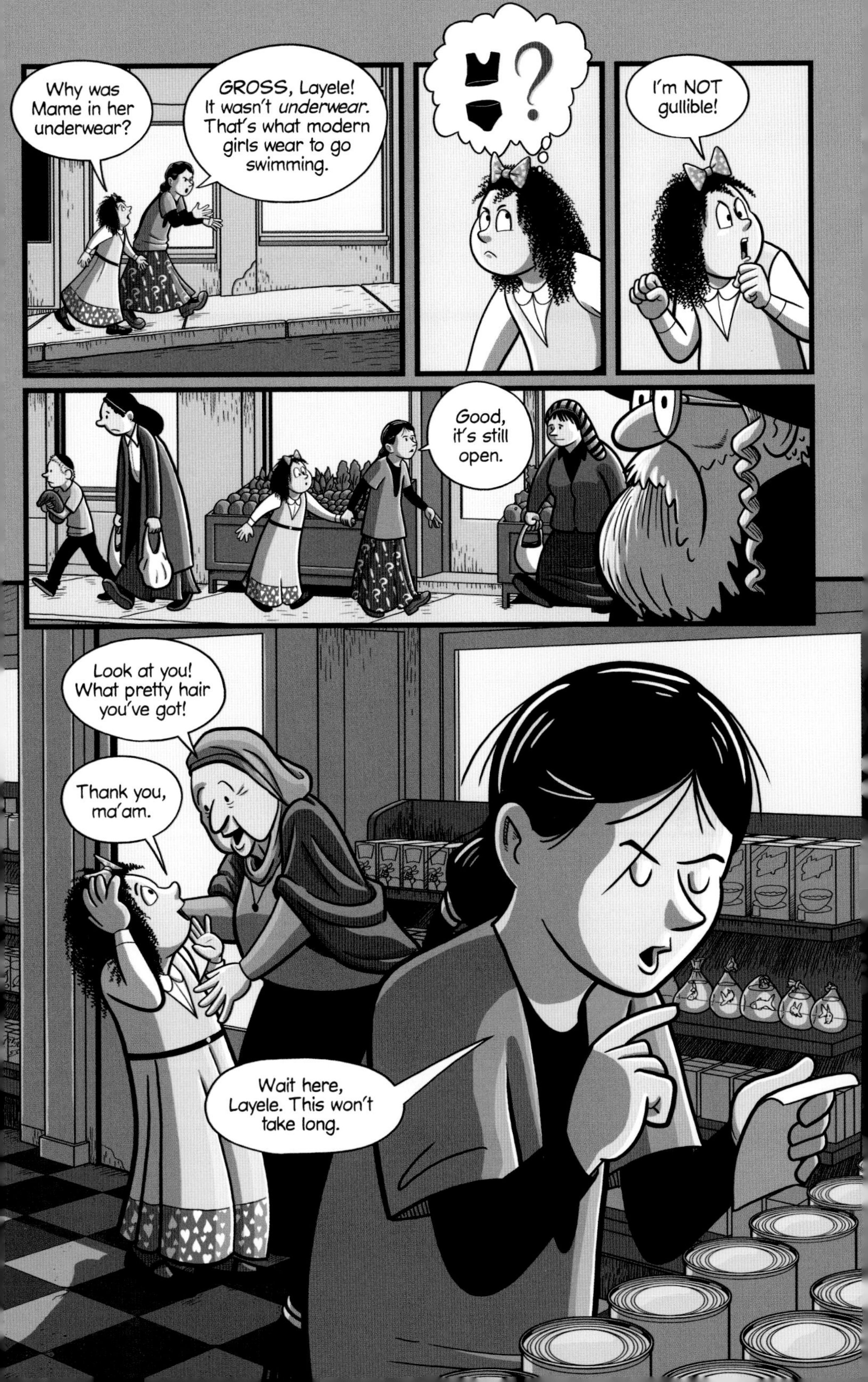
Why was Mame in her underwear?
GROSS, Layele! It wasn't *underwear*. That's what modern girls wear to go swimming.
?
I'm NOT gullible!
Good, it's still open.
Look at you! What pretty hair you've got!
Thank you, ma'am.
Wait here, Layele. This won't take long.

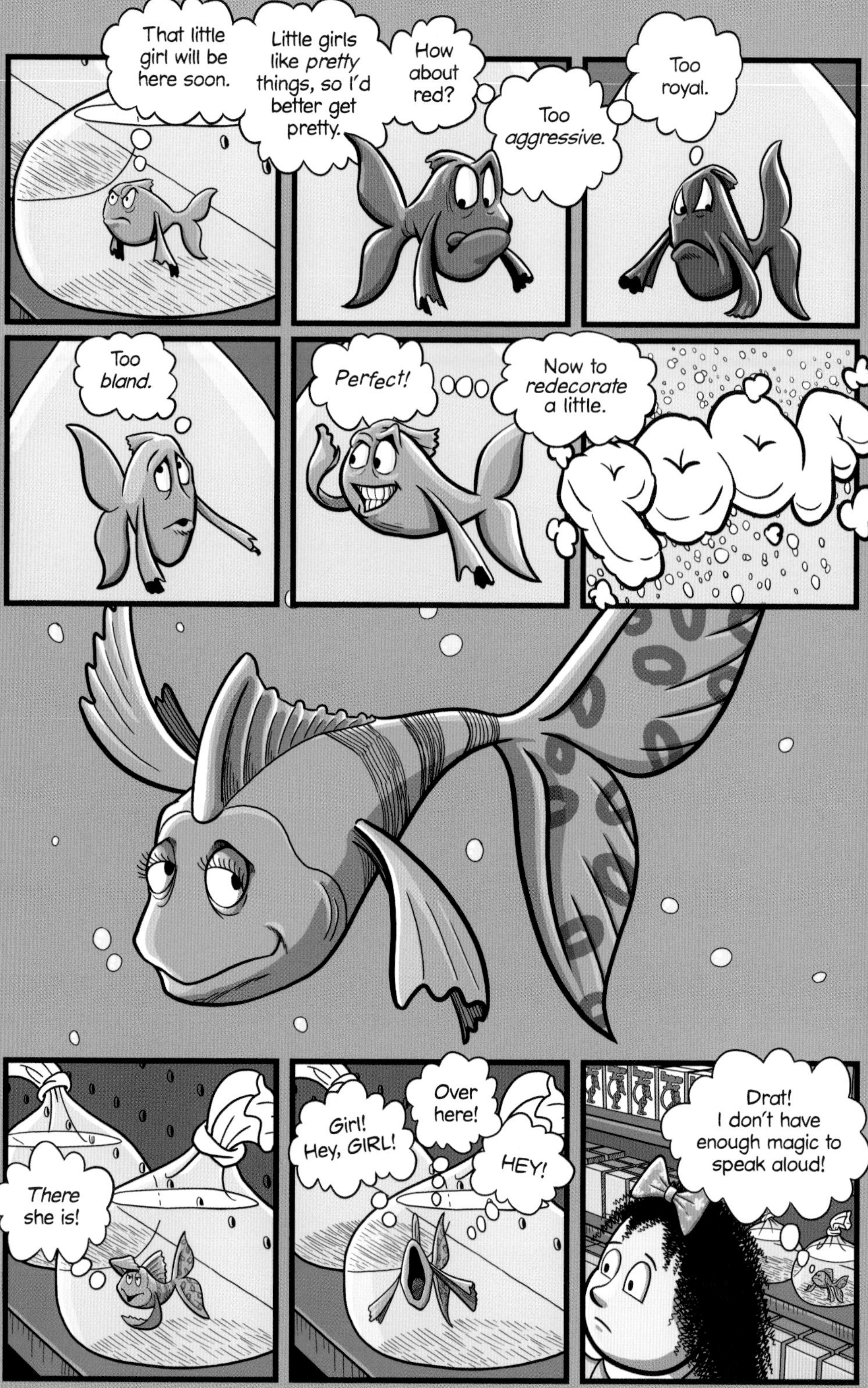
That little girl will be here soon.
Little girls like *pretty* things, so I'd better get pretty.
How about red?
Too *aggressive.*
Too royal.
Too *bland.*
Perfect!
Now to *redecorate* a little.
There she is!
Girl! Hey, GIRL!
Over here!
HEY!
Drat! I don't have enough magic to speak aloud!

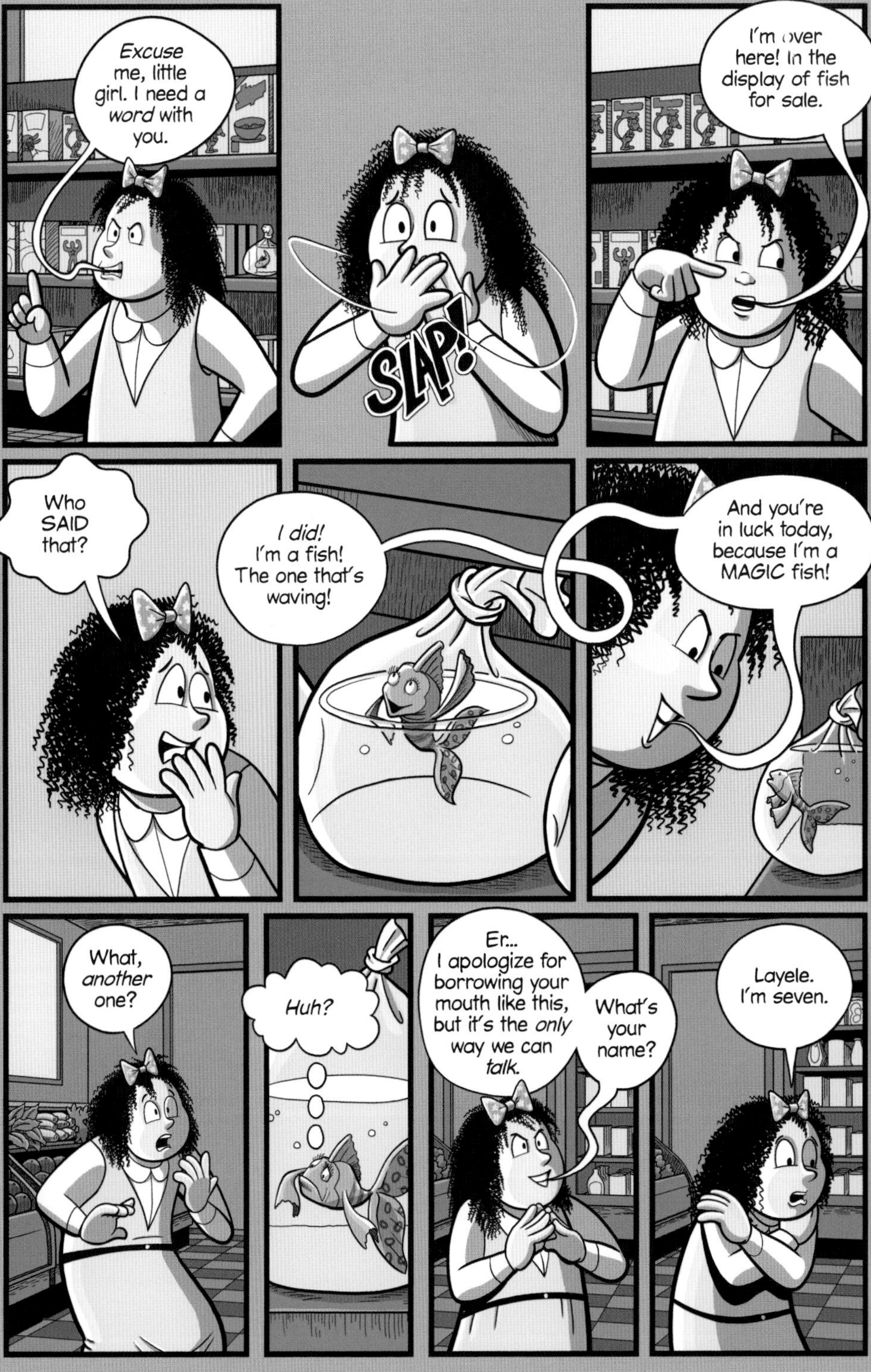
Excuse me, little girl. I need a *word* with you.
SLAP!
I'm over here! In the display of fish for sale.
Who SAID that?
I did! I'm a fish! The one that's waving!
And you're in luck today, because I'm a MAGIC fish!
What, *another* one?
Huh?
Er... I apologize for borrowing your mouth like this, but it's the *only* way we can *talk.*
What's your name?
Layele. I'm seven.

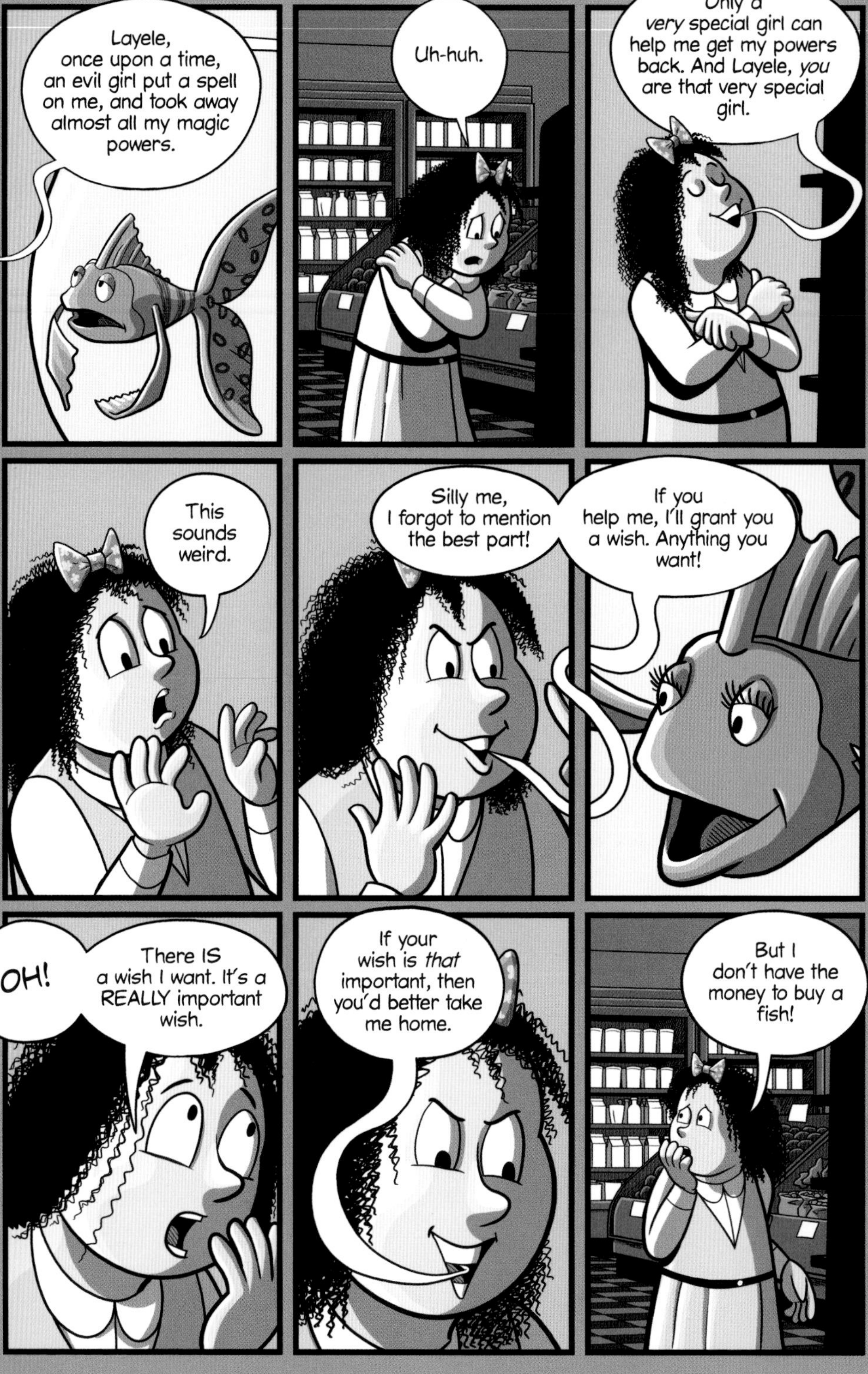

Layele, once upon a time, an evil girl put a spell on me, and took away almost all my magic powers.
Uh-huh.
Only a *very* special girl can help me get my powers back. And Layele, *you* are that very special girl.
This sounds weird.
Silly me, I forgot to mention the best part!
If you help me, I'll grant you a wish. Anything you want!
OH!
There IS a wish I want. It's a REALLY important wish.
If your wish is *that* important, then you'd better take me home.
But I don't have the money to buy a fish!

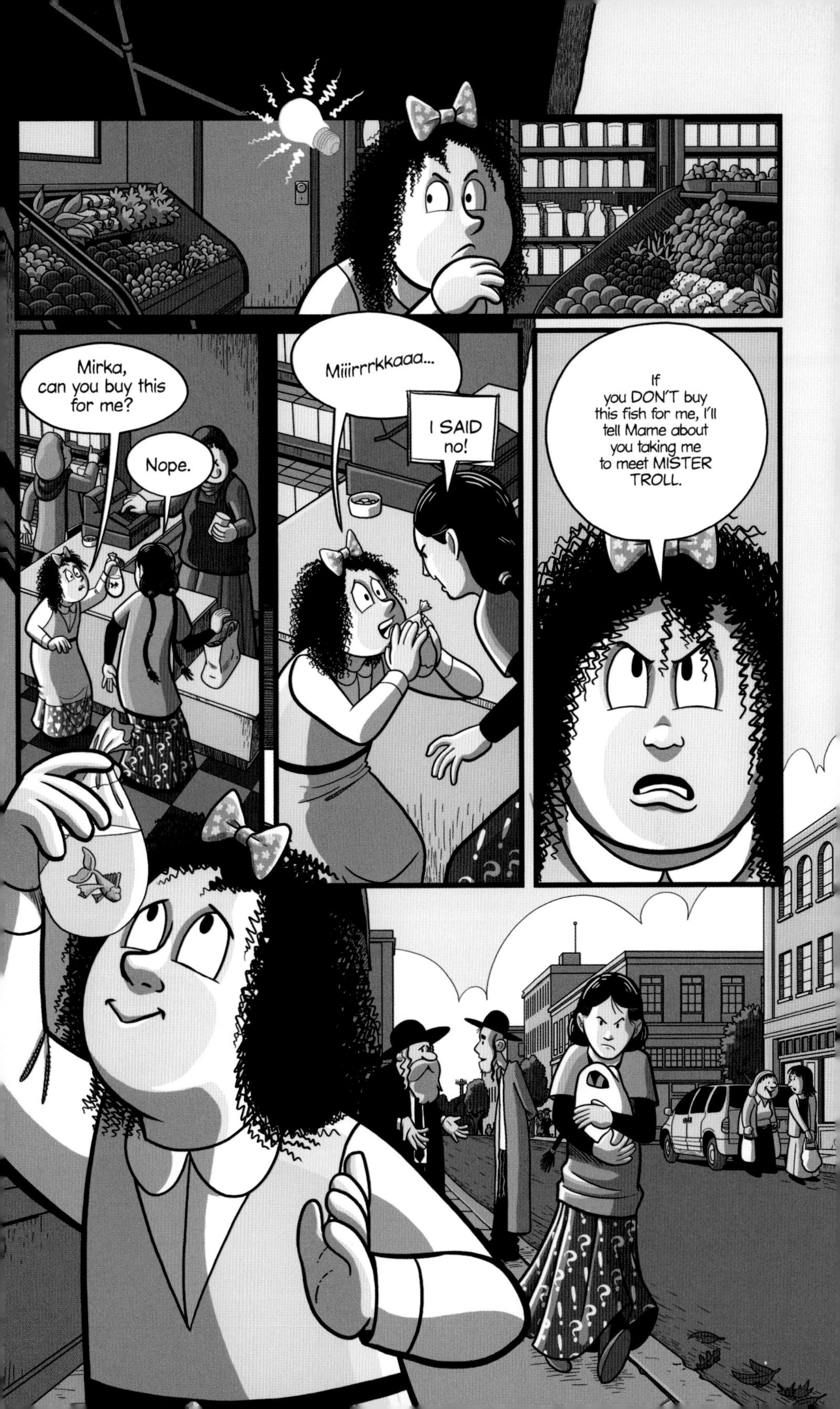

Mirka, can you buy this for me?
Nope.
Miiirrrkkaaa...
I SAID no!
If you DON'T buy this fish for me, I'll tell Mame about you taking me to meet MISTER TROLL.

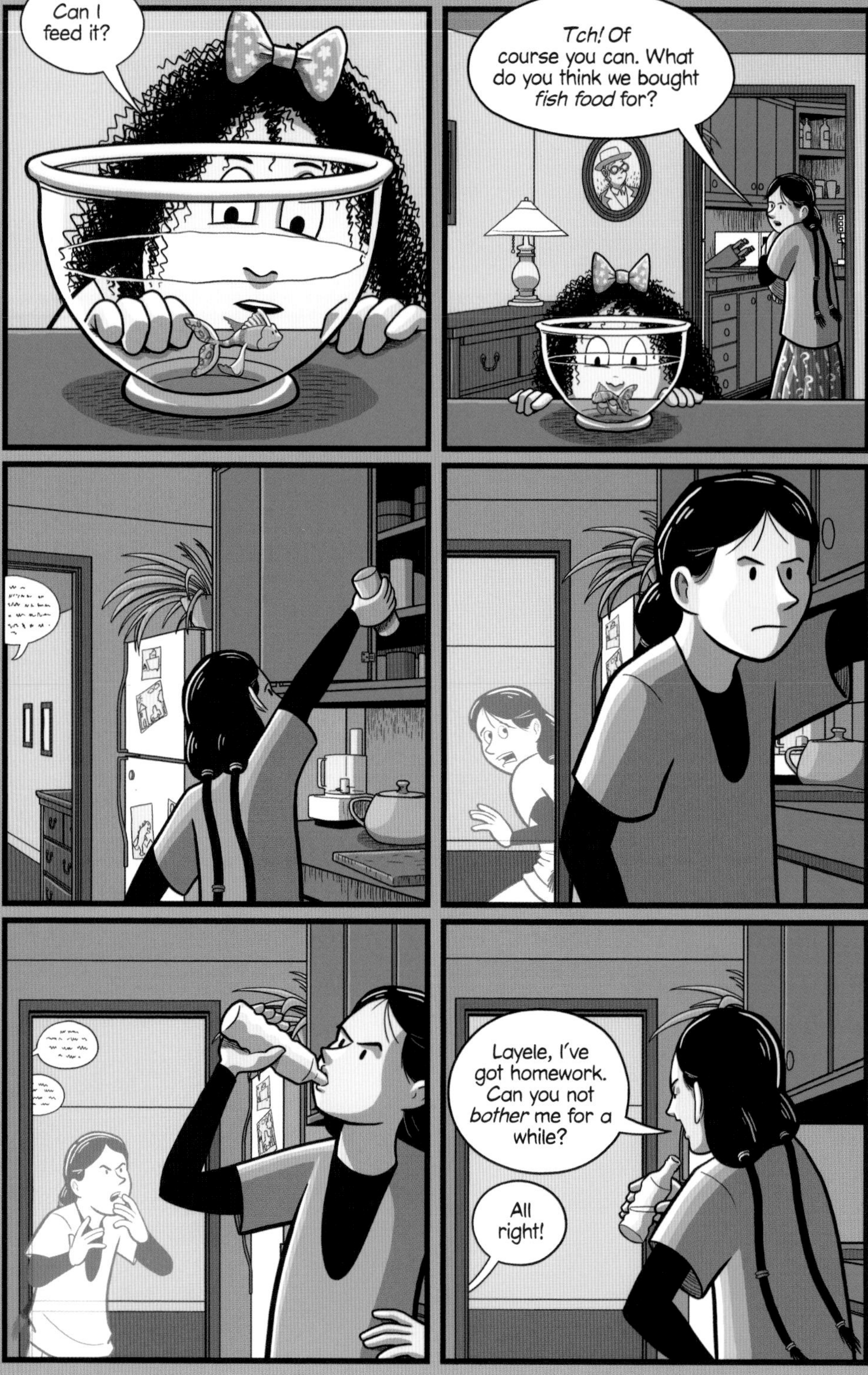
Can I feed it?
Tch! Of course you can. What do you think we bought *fish food* for?
Layele, I've got homework. Can you not *bother* me for a while?
All right!

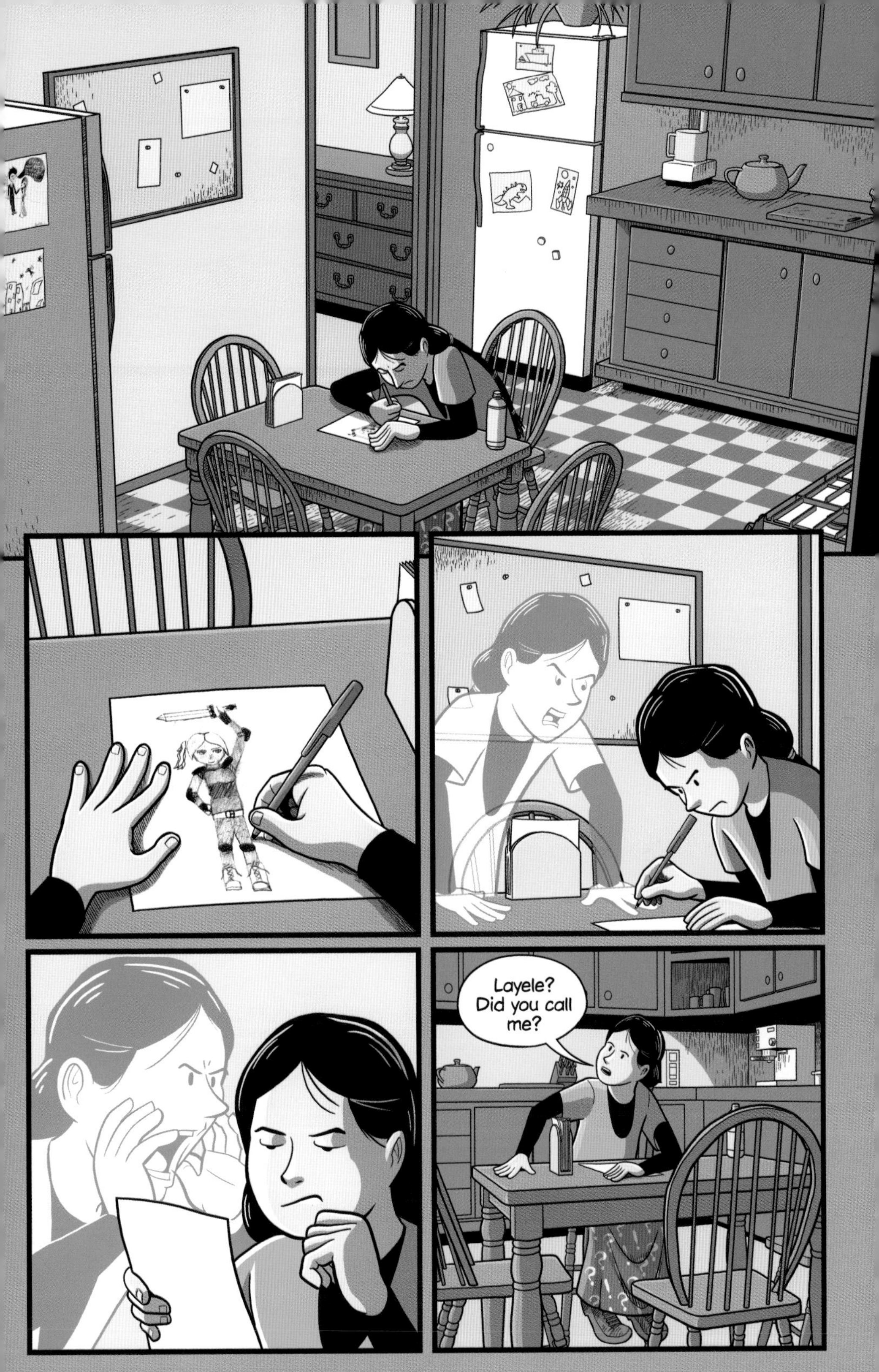
Layele?
Did you call
me?

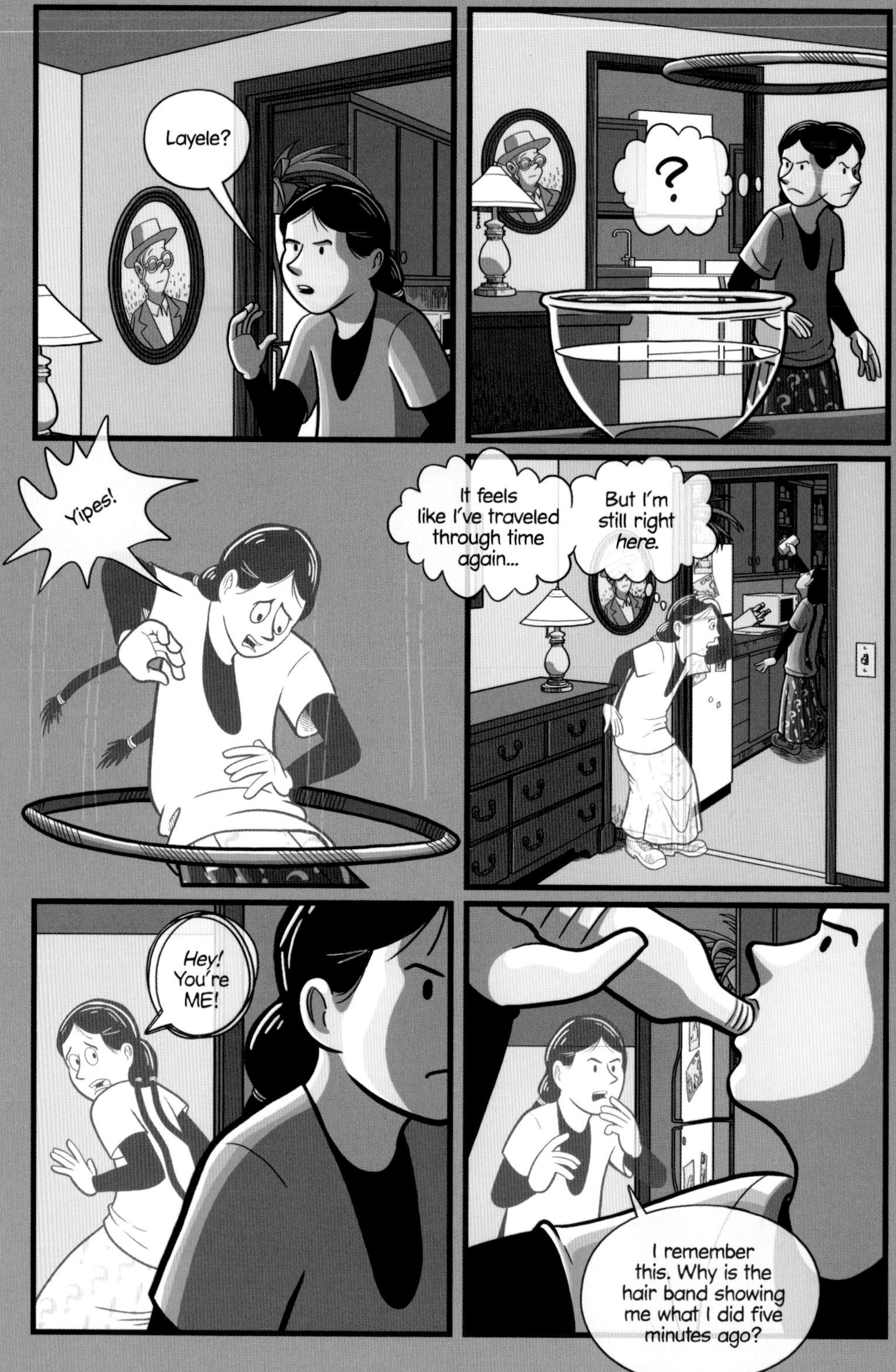
Layele?
?
Yipes!
It feels like I've traveled through time again...
But I'm still right *here.*
Hey! You're ME!
I remember this. Why is the hair band showing me what I did five minutes ago?

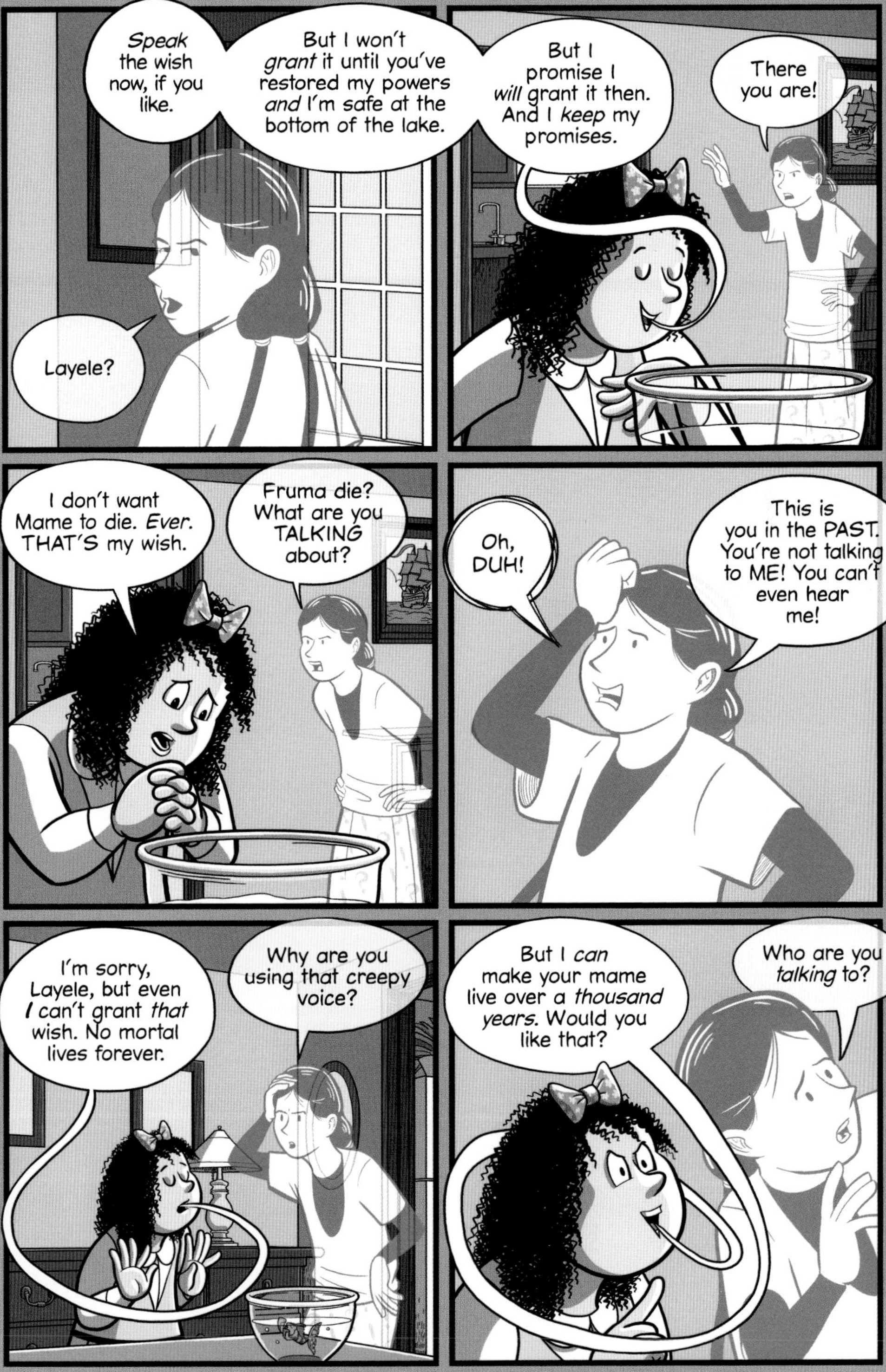
Speak the wish now, if you like.
But I won't grant it until you've restored my powers and I'm safe at the bottom of the lake.
Layele?
But I promise I will grant it then. And I keep my promises.
There you are!
I don't want Mame to die. Ever. THAT'S my wish.
Fruma die? What are you TALKING about?
Oh, DUH!
This is you in the PAST. You're not talking to ME! You can't even hear me!
I'm sorry, Layele, but even I can't grant that wish. No mortal lives forever.
Why are you using that creepy voice?
But I can make your mame live over a thousand years. Would you like that?
Who are you talking to?

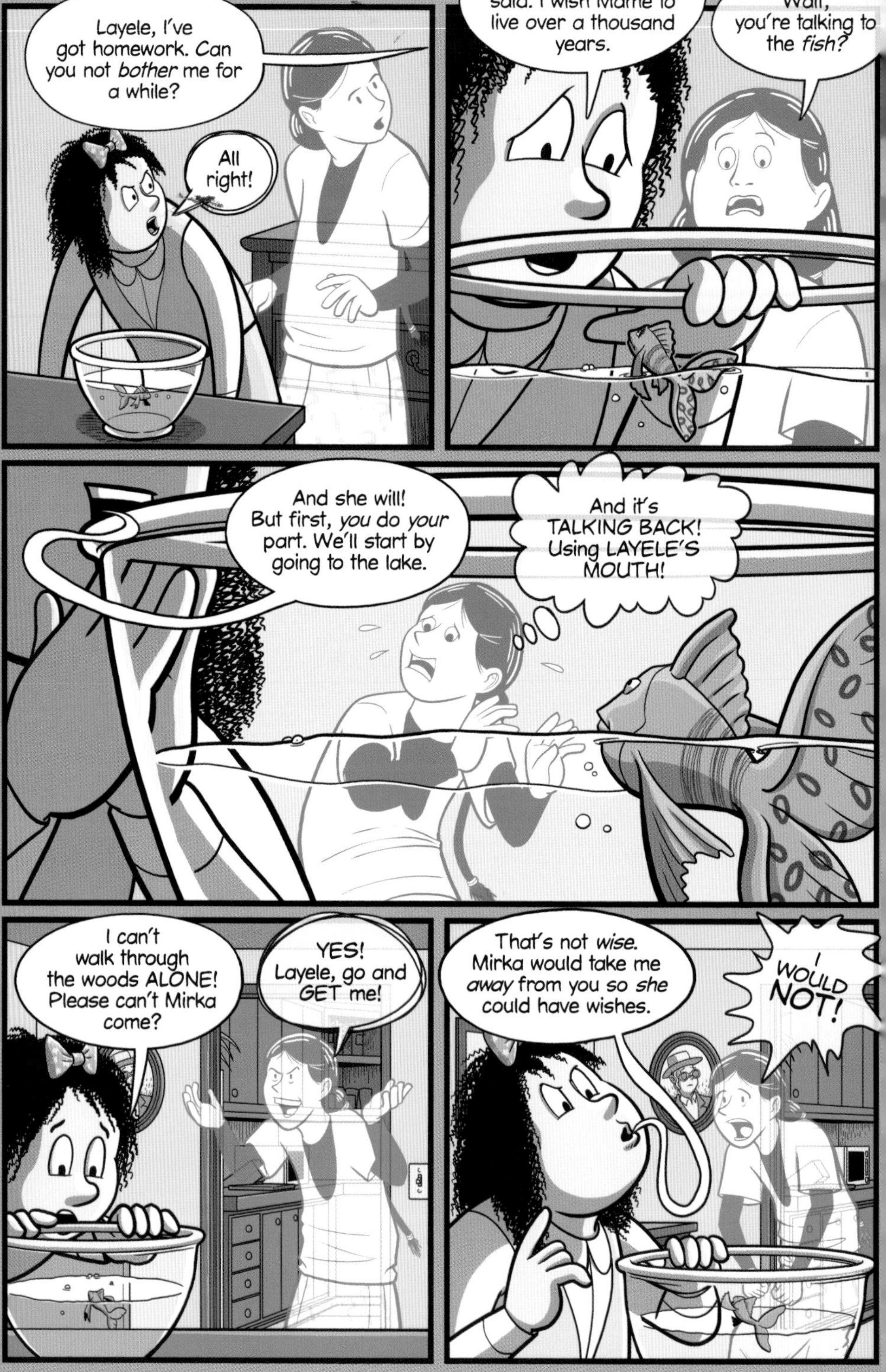
Layele, I've got homework. Can you not *bother* me for a while?
All right!
Ma'am, I want what *you* said. I wish Mame to live over a thousand years.
Wait, you're talking to the *fish?*
And she will! But first, *you* do *your* part. We'll start by going to the lake.
And it's TALKING BACK! Using LAYELE'S MOUTH!
I can't walk through the woods ALONE! Please can't Mirka come?
YES! Layele, go and GET me!
That's not *wise.* Mirka would take me *away* from you so *she* could have wishes.
I WOULD NOT!

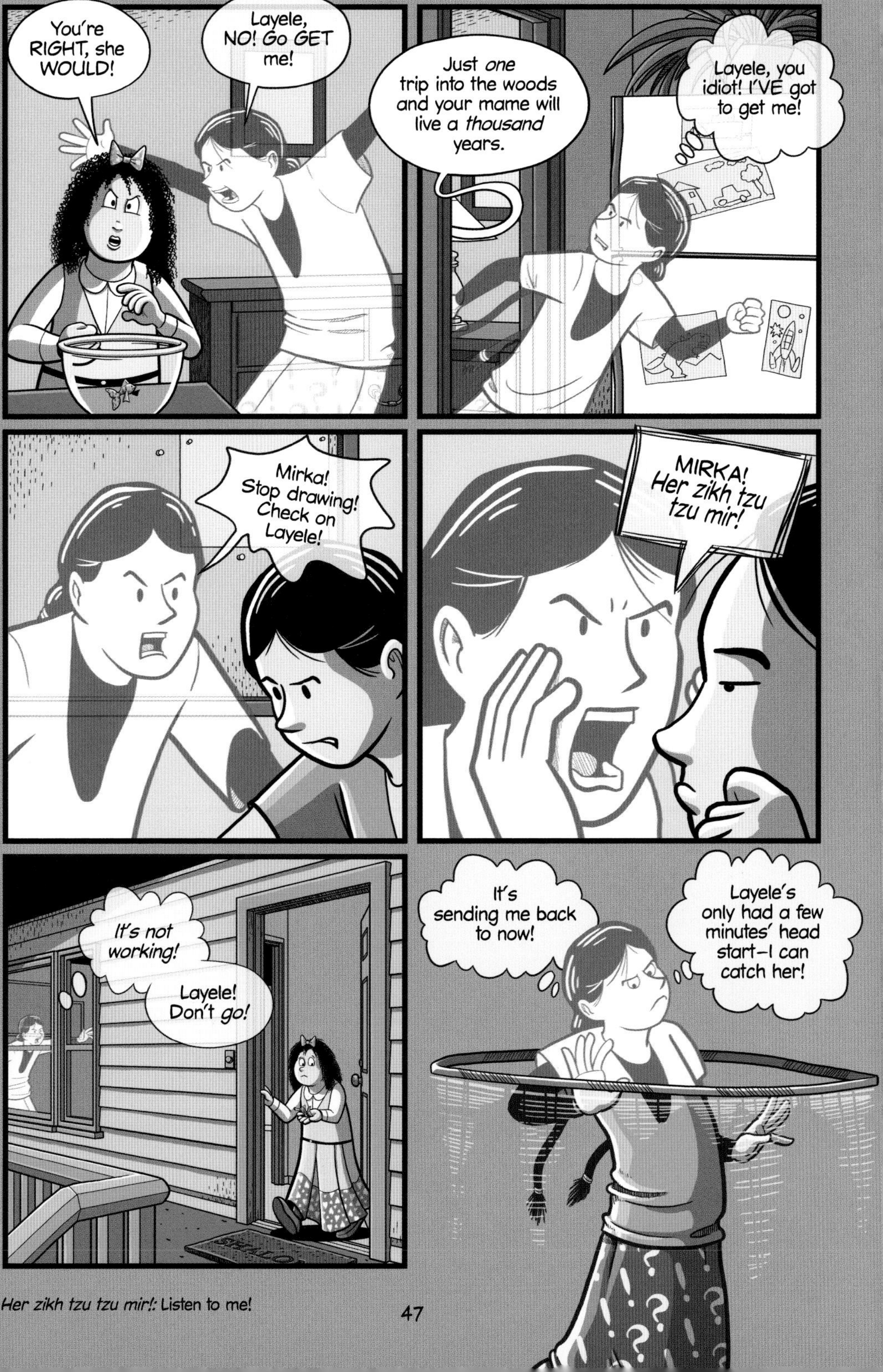
You're RIGHT, she WOULD!
Layele, NO! Go GET me!
Just *one* trip into the woods and your mame will live a *thousand* years.
Layele, you idiot! I'VE got to get me!
Mirka! Stop drawing! Check on Layele!
MIRKA! Her zikh tzu tzu mir!
It's not working!
Layele! Don't *go!*
It's sending me back to now!
Layele's only had a few minutes' head start—I can catch her!
SHALO

Her zikh tzu tzu mir!: Listen to me!

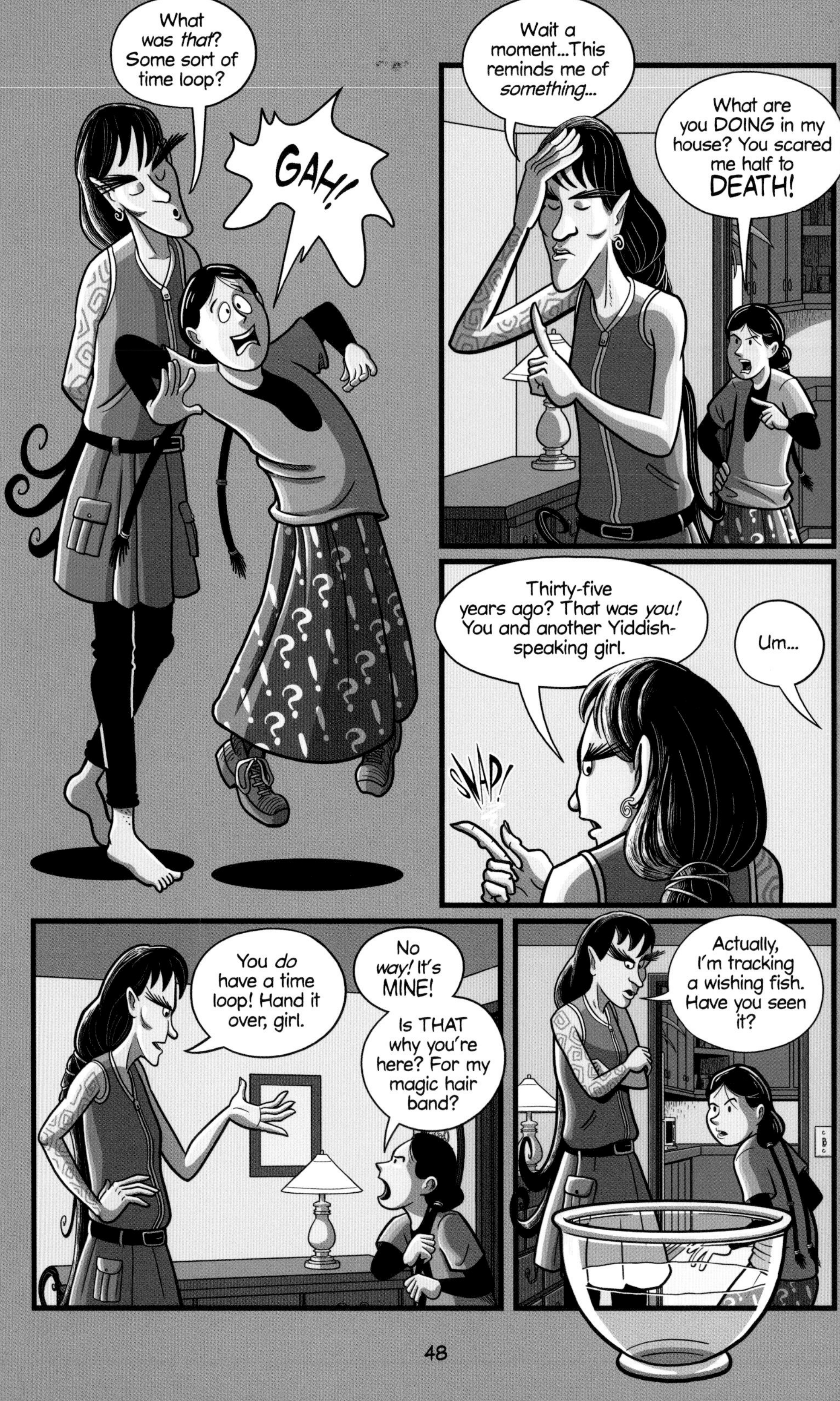
What was that? Some sort of time loop?
GAH!
Wait a moment...This reminds me of something...
What are you DOING in my house? You scared me half to DEATH!
Thirty-five years ago? That was you! You and another Yiddish-speaking girl.
SNAP!
Um...
You do have a time loop! Hand it over, girl.
No way! It's MINE!
Is THAT why you're here? For my magic hair band?
Actually, I'm tracking a wishing fish. Have you seen it?

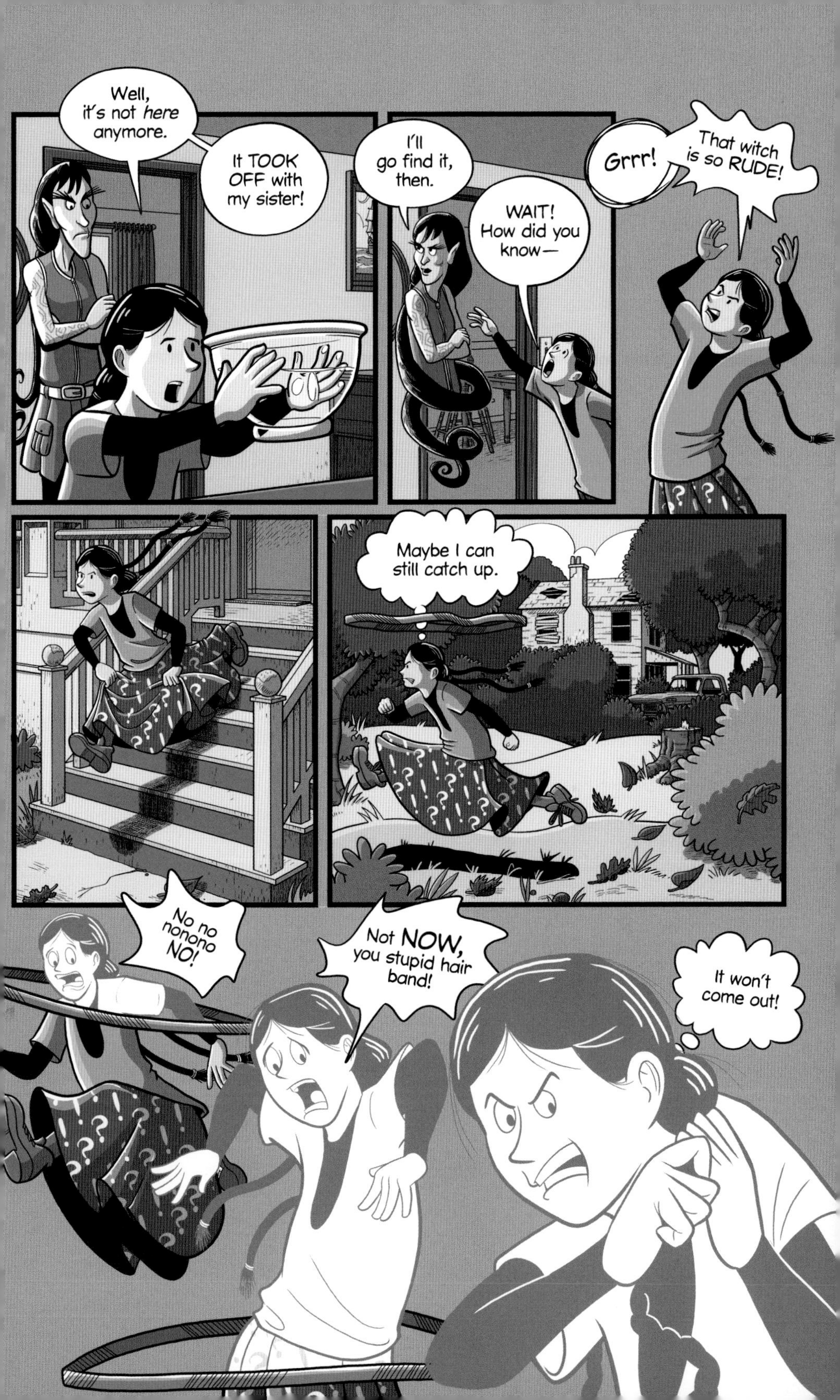
Well, it's not *here* anymore.
It TOOK OFF with my sister!
I'll go find it, then.
WAIT! How did you know—
Grrr!
That witch is so RUDE!
Maybe I can still catch up.
No no nonono NO!
Not NOW, you stupid hair band!
It won't come out!

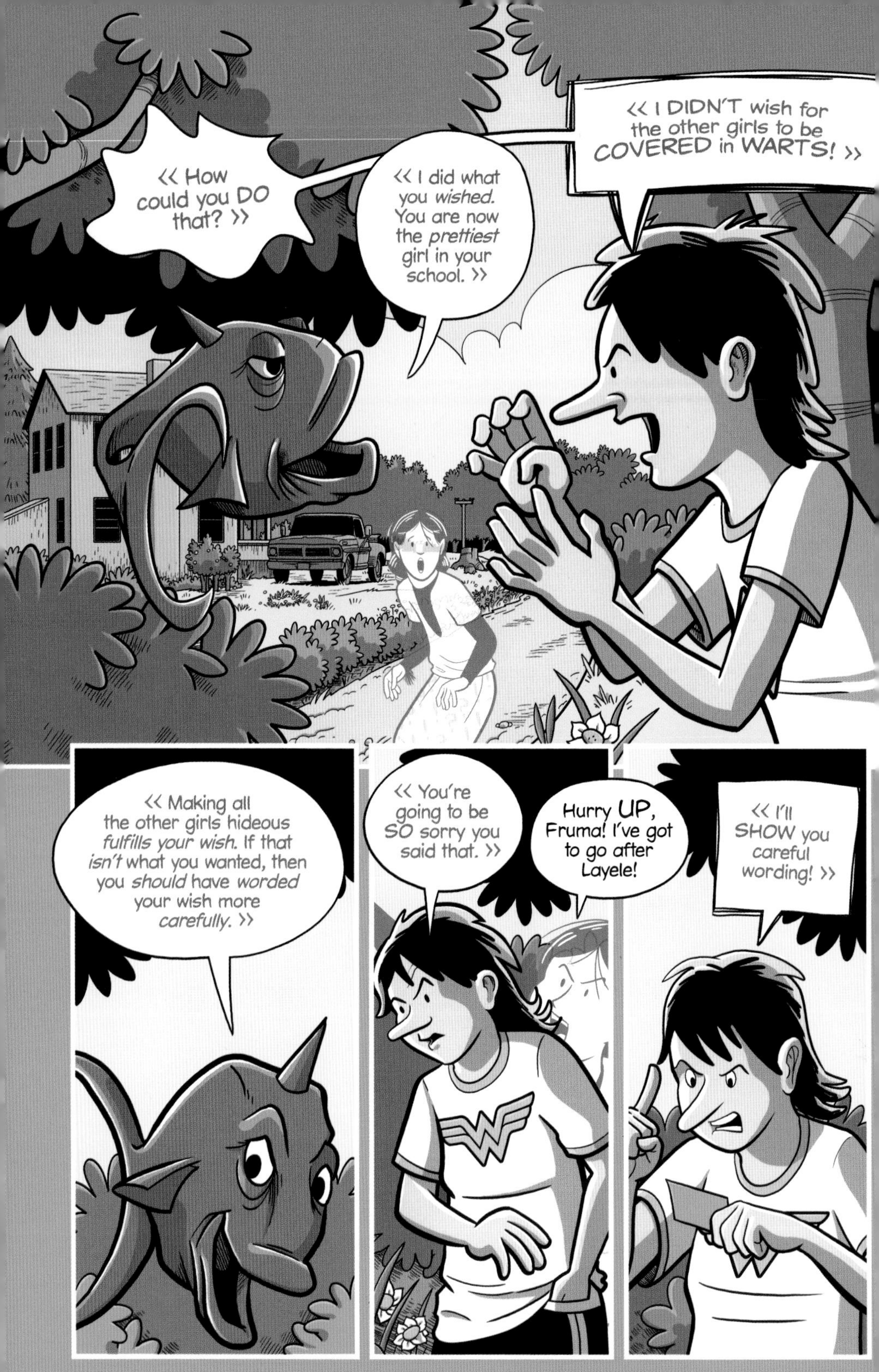

<< How could you DO that? >>
<< I did what you wished. You are now the prettiest girl in your school. >>
<< I DIDN'T wish for the other girls to be COVERED in WARTS! >>
<< Making all the other girls hideous fulfills your wish. If that isn't what you wanted, then you should have worded your wish more carefully. >>
<< You're going to be SO sorry you said that. >>
Hurry UP, Fruma! I've got to go after Layele!
<< I'll SHOW you careful wording! >>

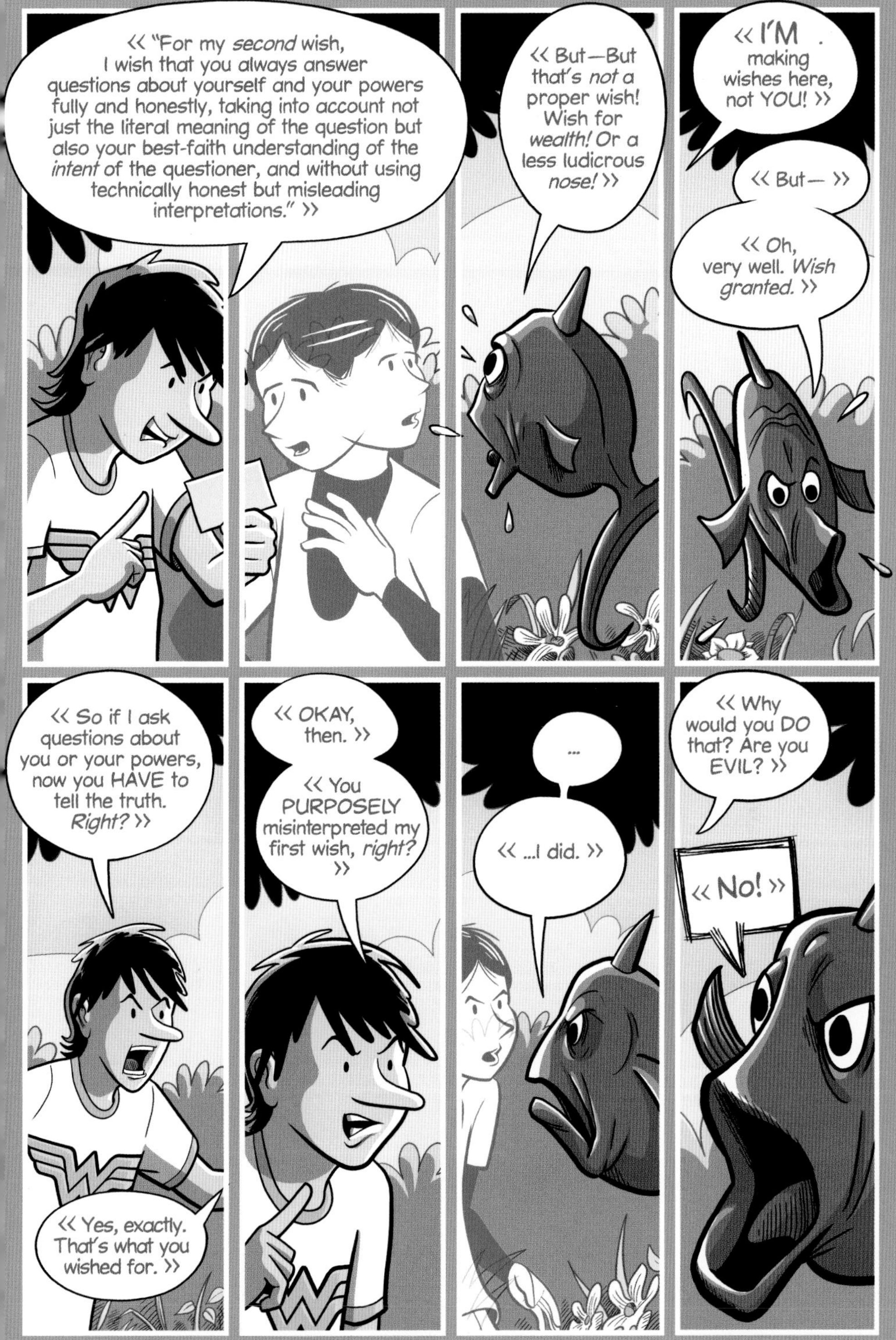

<< "For my *second* wish, I wish that you always answer questions about yourself and your powers fully and honestly, taking into account not just the literal meaning of the question but also your best-faith understanding of the *intent* of the questioner, and without using technically honest but misleading interpretations." >>
<< But—But that's *not* a proper wish! Wish for *wealth!* Or a less ludicrous *nose!* >>
<< I'M making wishes here, not YOU! >>
<< But— >>
<< Oh, very well. *Wish granted.* >>
<< So if I ask questions about you or your powers, now you HAVE to tell the truth. *Right?* >>
<< Yes, exactly. That's what you wished for. >>
<< OKAY, then. >>
<< You PURPOSELY misinterpreted my first wish, *right?* >>
...
<< ...I did. >>
<< Why would you DO that? Are you EVIL? >>
<< No! >>

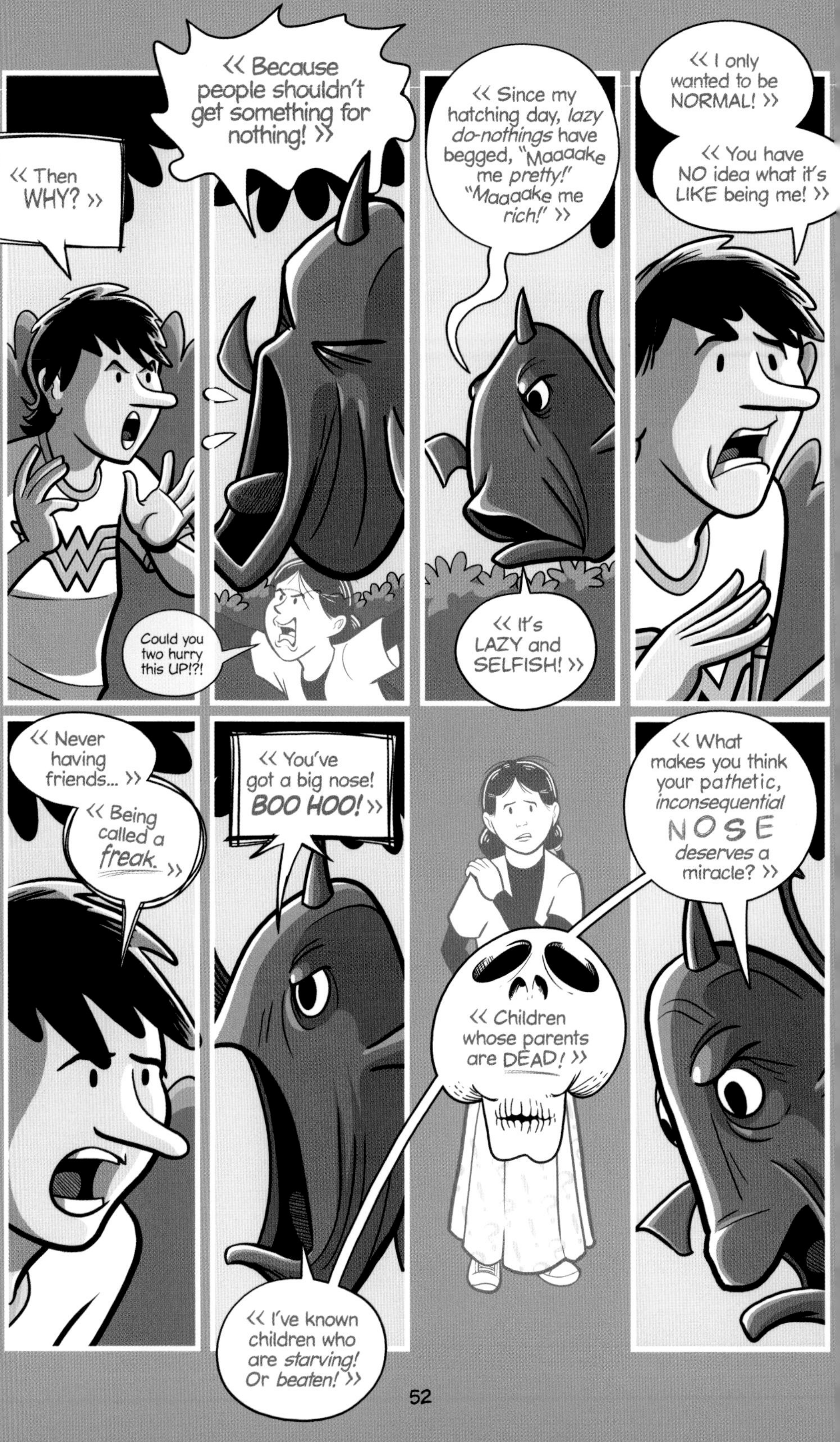

<< Then WHY? >>
<< Because people shouldn't get something for nothing! >>
Could you two hurry this UP!?!
<< Since my hatching day, *lazy do-nothings* have begged, "Maaaake me *pretty!*" "Maaaake me *rich!*" >>
<< It's LAZY and SELFISH! >>
<< I only wanted to be NORMAL! >>
<< You have NO idea what it's LIKE being me! >>
<< Never having friends... >>
<< Being called a *freak.* >>
<< You've got a big nose! ***BOO HOO!*** >>
<< I've known children who are *starving!* Or *beaten!* >>
<< Children whose parents are DEAD! >>
<< What makes you think your *pathetic, inconsequential* NOSE *deserves* a miracle? >>

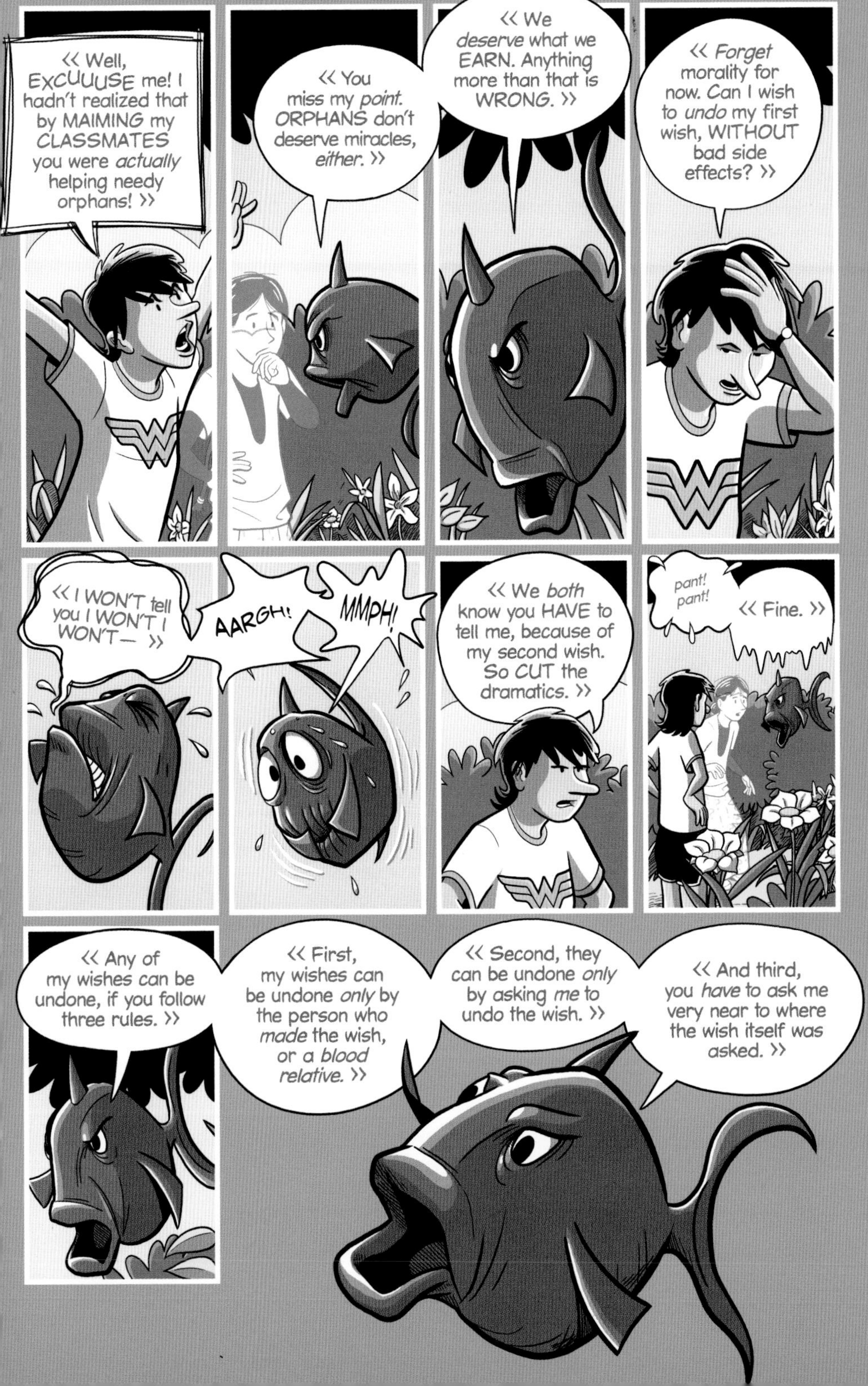

<< Well, EXCUUUSE me! I hadn't realized that by MAIMING my CLASSMATES you were *actually* helping needy orphans! >>
<< You miss my *point.* ORPHANS don't deserve miracles, *either.* >>
<< We *deserve* what we EARN. Anything more than that is WRONG. >>
<< *Forget* morality for now. Can I wish to *undo* my first wish, WITHOUT bad side effects? >>
<< I WON'T tell you I WON'T I WON'T— >>
AARGH!
MMPH!
<< We *both* know you HAVE to tell me, because of my second wish. So CUT the dramatics. >>
pant! pant!
<< Fine. >>
<< Any of my wishes can be undone, if you follow three rules. >>
<< First, my wishes can be undone *only* by the person who *made* the wish, or a *blood relative.* >>
<< Second, they can be undone *only* by asking *me* to undo the wish. >>
<< And third, you *have* to ask me very near to where the wish itself was asked. >>

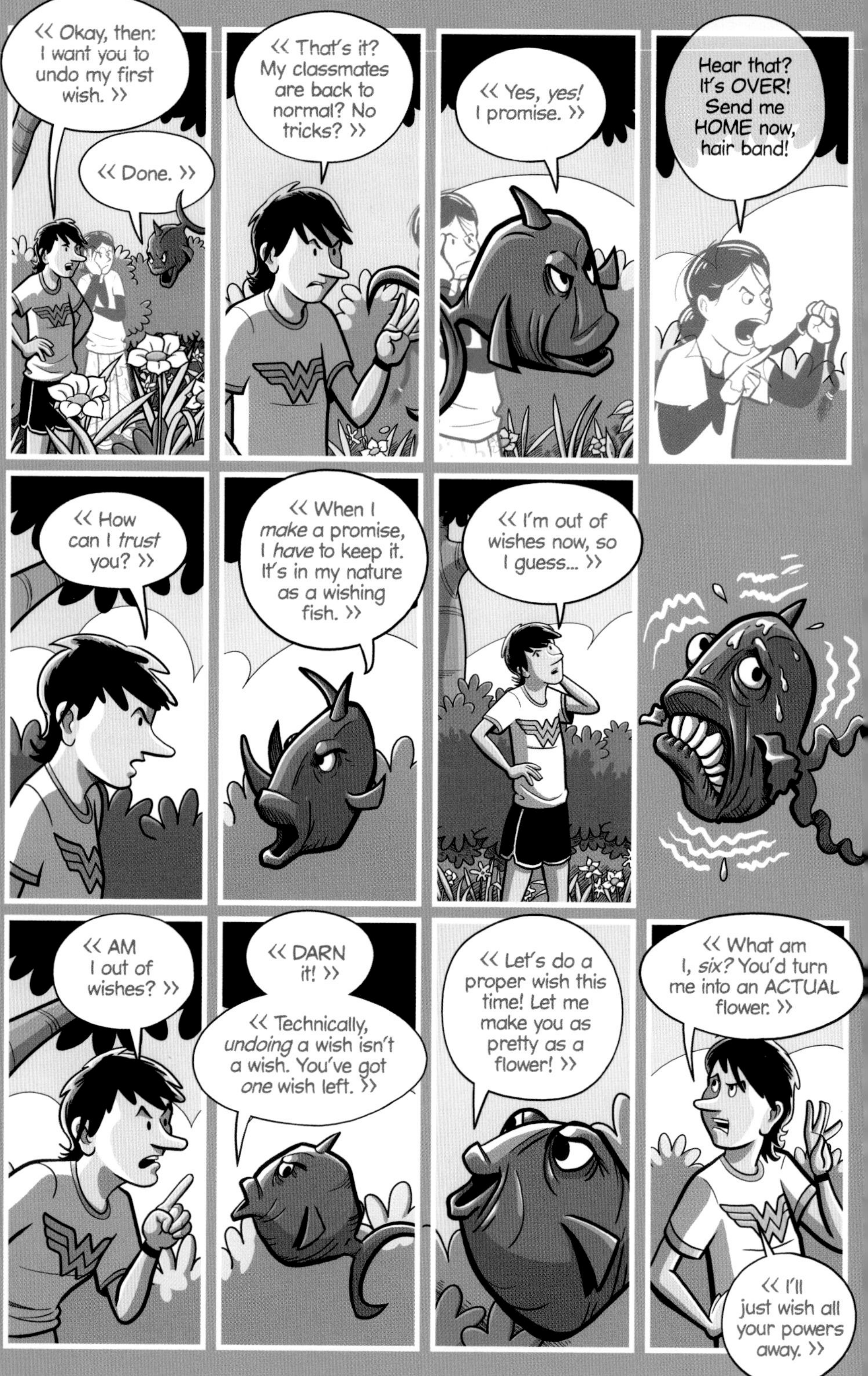

<< Okay, then: I want you to undo my first wish. >>
<< Done. >>
<< That's it? My classmates are back to normal? No tricks? >>
<< Yes, *yes!* I promise. >>
Hear that? It's OVER! Send me HOME now, hair band!
<< How can I *trust* you? >>
<< When I *make* a promise, I *have* to keep it. It's in my nature as a wishing fish. >>
<< I'm out of wishes now, so I guess... >>
<< AM I out of wishes? >>
<< DARN it! >>
<< Technically, *undoing* a wish isn't a wish. You've got *one* wish left. >>
<< Let's do a proper wish this time! Let me make you as pretty as a flower! >>
<< What am I, *six?* You'd turn me into an ACTUAL flower. >>
<< I'll just wish all your powers away. >>

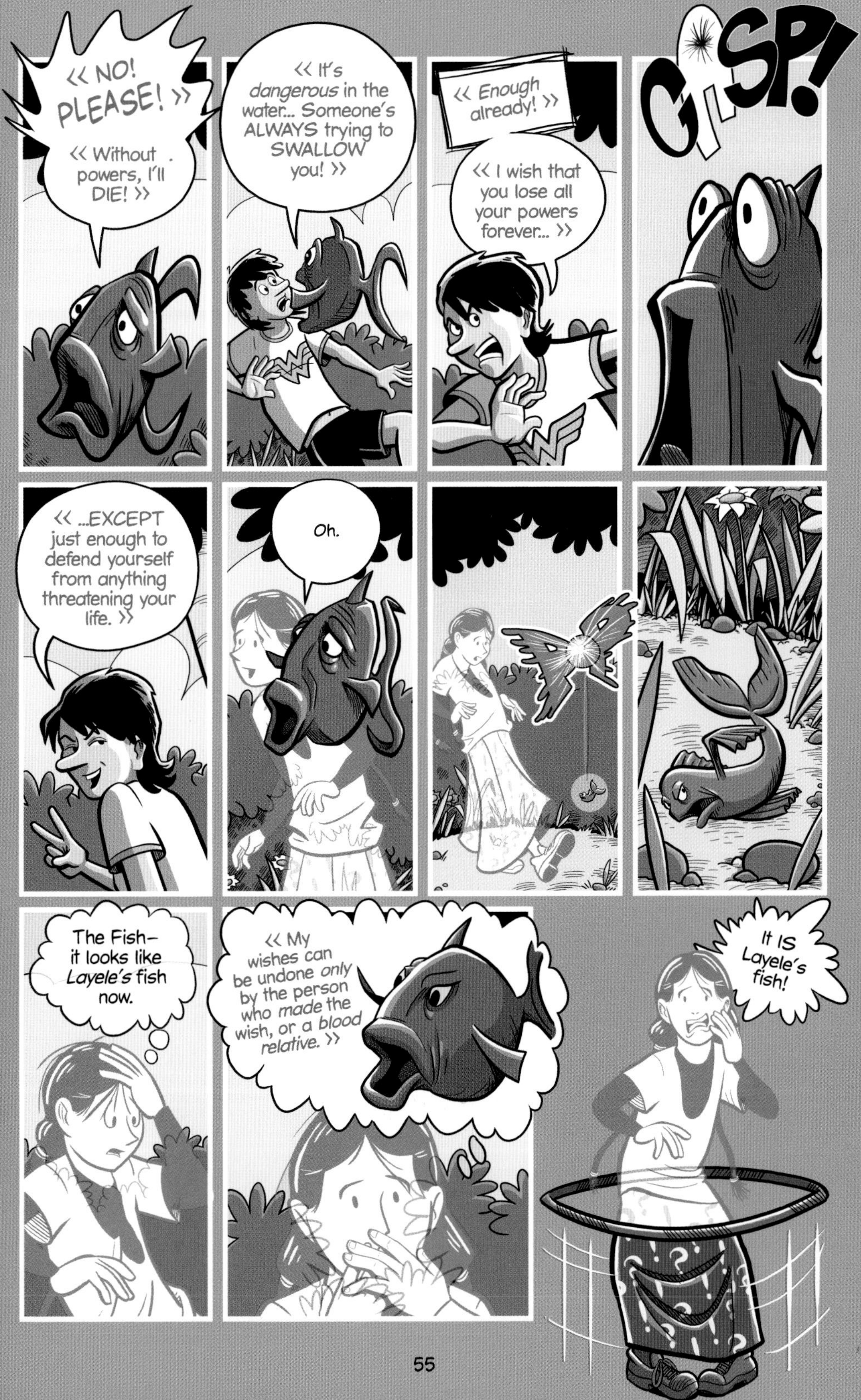

<< NO! PLEASE! >>
<< Without powers, I'll DIE! >>
<< It's *dangerous* in the water... Someone's ALWAYS trying to SWALLOW you! >>
<< Enough already! >>
<< I wish that you lose all your powers forever... >>
GASP!
<< ...EXCEPT just enough to defend yourself from anything threatening your life. >>
Oh.
The Fish— it looks like *Layele's* fish now.
<< My wishes can be undone *only* by the person who *made* the wish, or a *blood relative.* >>
It IS Layele's fish!

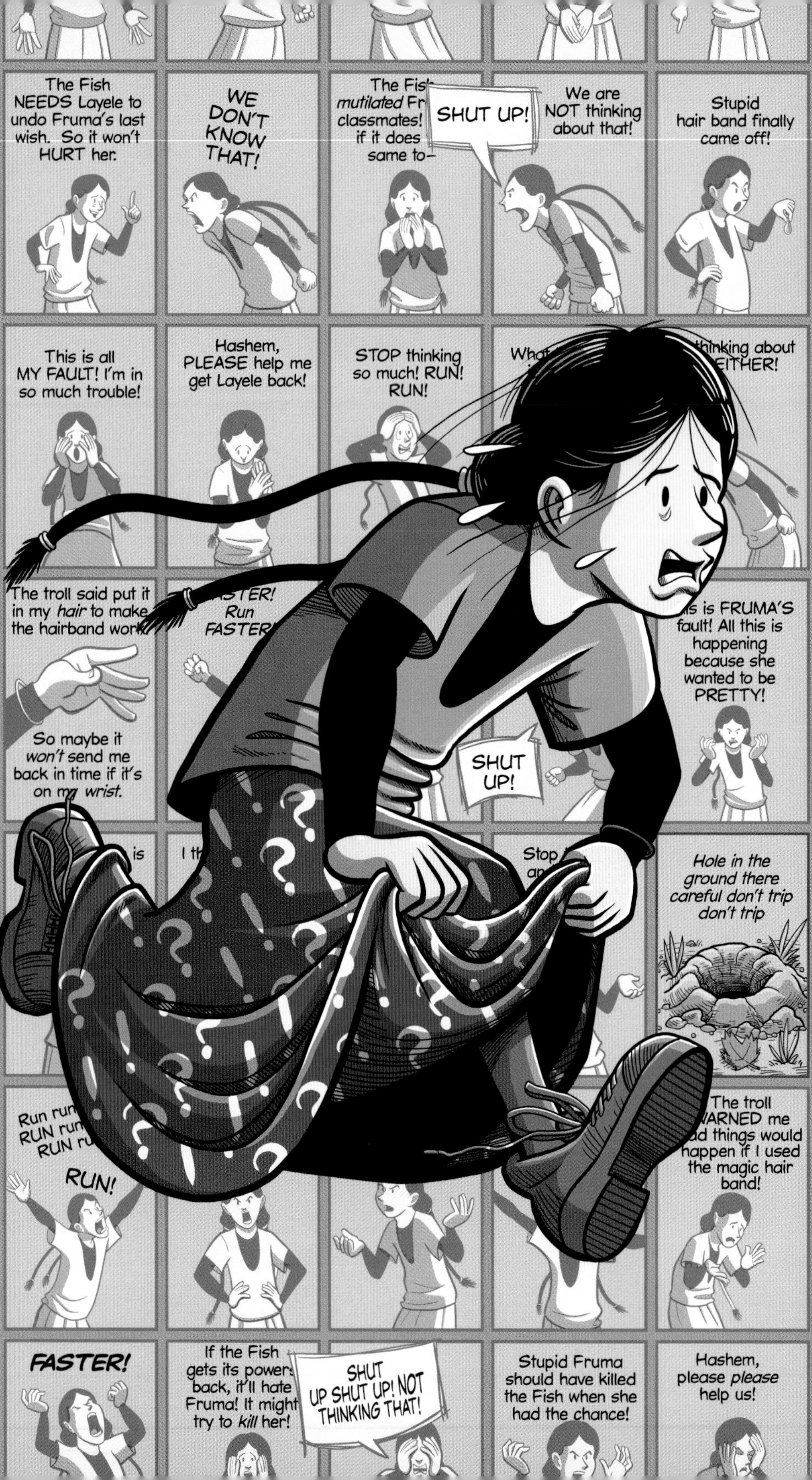

The Fish NEEDS Layele to undo Fruma's last wish. So it won't HURT her.
WE DON'T KNOW THAT!
The Fish mutilated Fr classmates! if it does same to—
SHUT UP!
We are NOT thinking about that!
Stupid hair band finally came off!
This is all MY FAULT! I'm in so much trouble!
Hashem, PLEASE help me get Layele back!
STOP thinking so much! RUN! RUN!
thinking about EITHER!
The troll said put it in my hair to make the hairband work.
So maybe it won't send me back in time if it's on my wrist.
Run FASTER
is FRUMA'S fault! All this is happening because she wanted to be PRETTY!
SHUT UP!
Hole in the ground there careful don't trip don't trip
Run run RUN run RUN r
RUN!
The troll WARNED me ad things would happen if I used the magic hair band!
FASTER!
If the Fish gets its powers back, it'll hate Fruma! It might try to kill her!
SHUT UP SHUT UP! NOT THINKING THAT!
Stupid Fruma should have killed the Fish when she had the chance!
Hashem, please please help us!

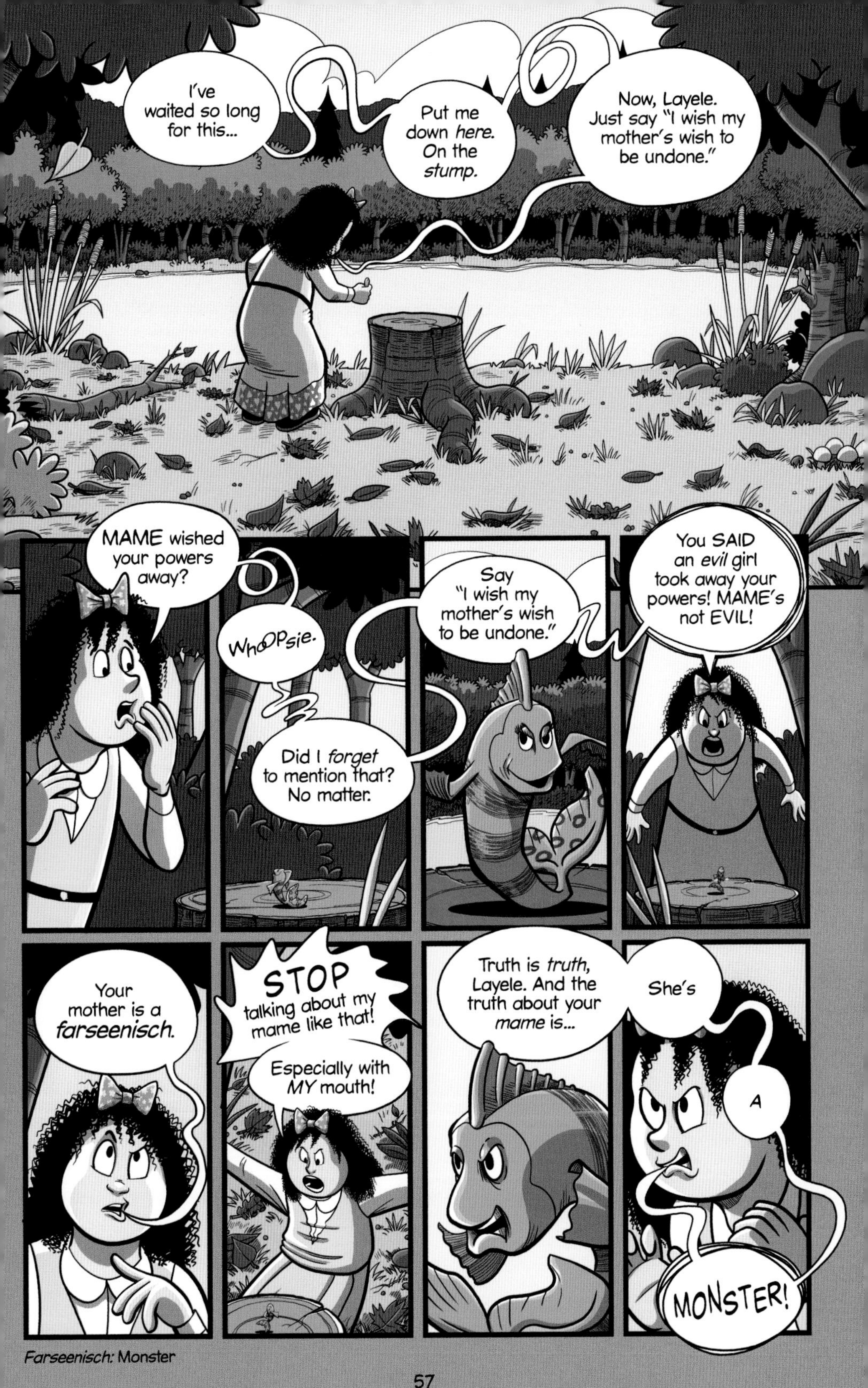
I've waited so long for this...
Put me down *here*. On the *stump*.
Now, Layele. Just say "I wish my mother's wish to be undone."
MAME wished your powers away?
WhOOPsie.
Did I *forget* to mention that? No matter.
Say "I wish my mother's wish to be undone."
You SAID an *evil* girl took away your powers! MAME's not EVIL!
Your mother is a *farseenisch*.
STOP talking about my mame like that!
Especially with *MY* mouth!
Truth is *truth*, Layele. And the truth about your *mame* is...
She's
A
MONSTER!

Farseenisch: Monster

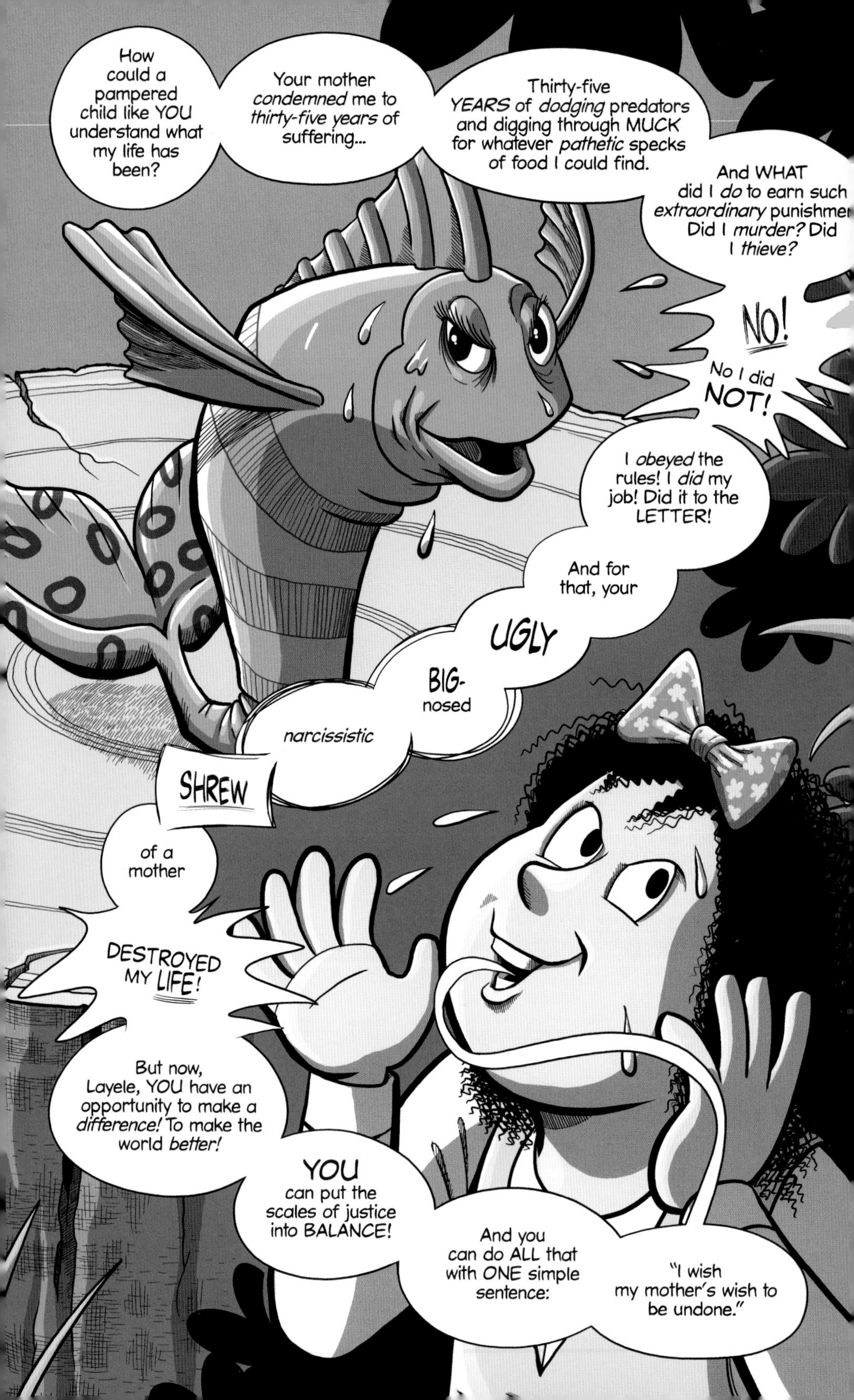
How could a pampered child like YOU understand what my life has been?
Your mother *condemned* me to *thirty-five years* of suffering...
Thirty-five *YEARS* of *dodging* predators and digging through MUCK for whatever *pathetic* specks of food I could find.
And WHAT did I *do* to earn such *extraordinary* punishme
Did I *murder?* Did I *thieve?*
NO!
No I did NOT!
I *obeyed* the rules! I *did* my job! Did it to the LETTER!
And for that, your
UGLY
BIG-nosed
narcissistic
SHREW
of a mother
DESTROYED MY LIFE!
But now, Layele, YOU have an opportunity to make a *difference!* To make the world *better!*
YOU can put the scales of justice into BALANCE!
And you can do ALL that with ONE simple sentence:
"I wish my mother's wish to be undone."

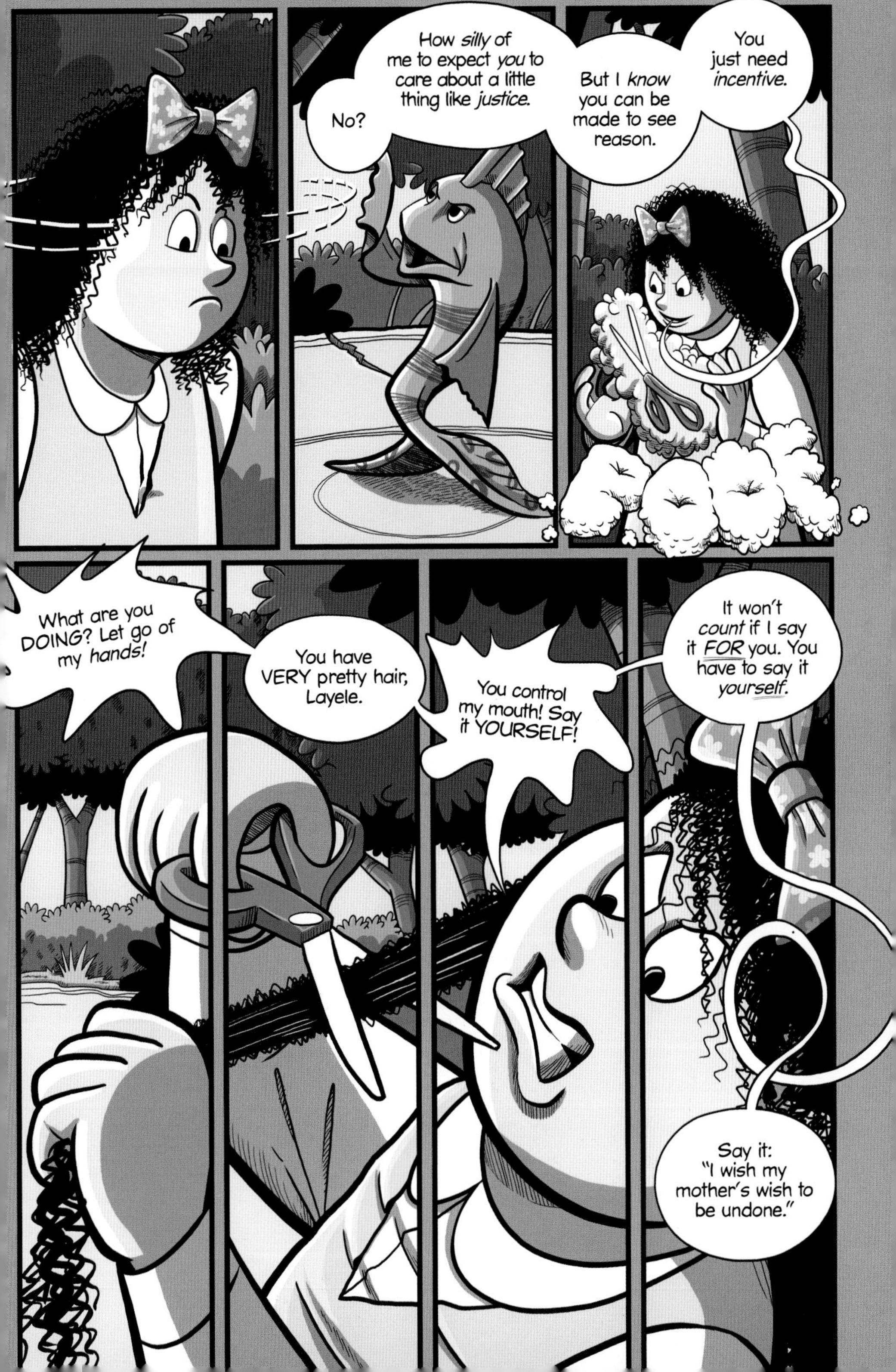

No?
How *silly* of me to expect *you* to care about a little thing like *justice*.
But I *know* you can be made to see reason.
You just need *incentive*.
What are you DOING? Let go of my *hands!*
You have VERY pretty hair, Layele.
You control my mouth! Say it YOURSELF!
It won't *count* if I say it FOR you. You have to say it *yourself*.
Say it: "I wish my mother's wish to be undone."

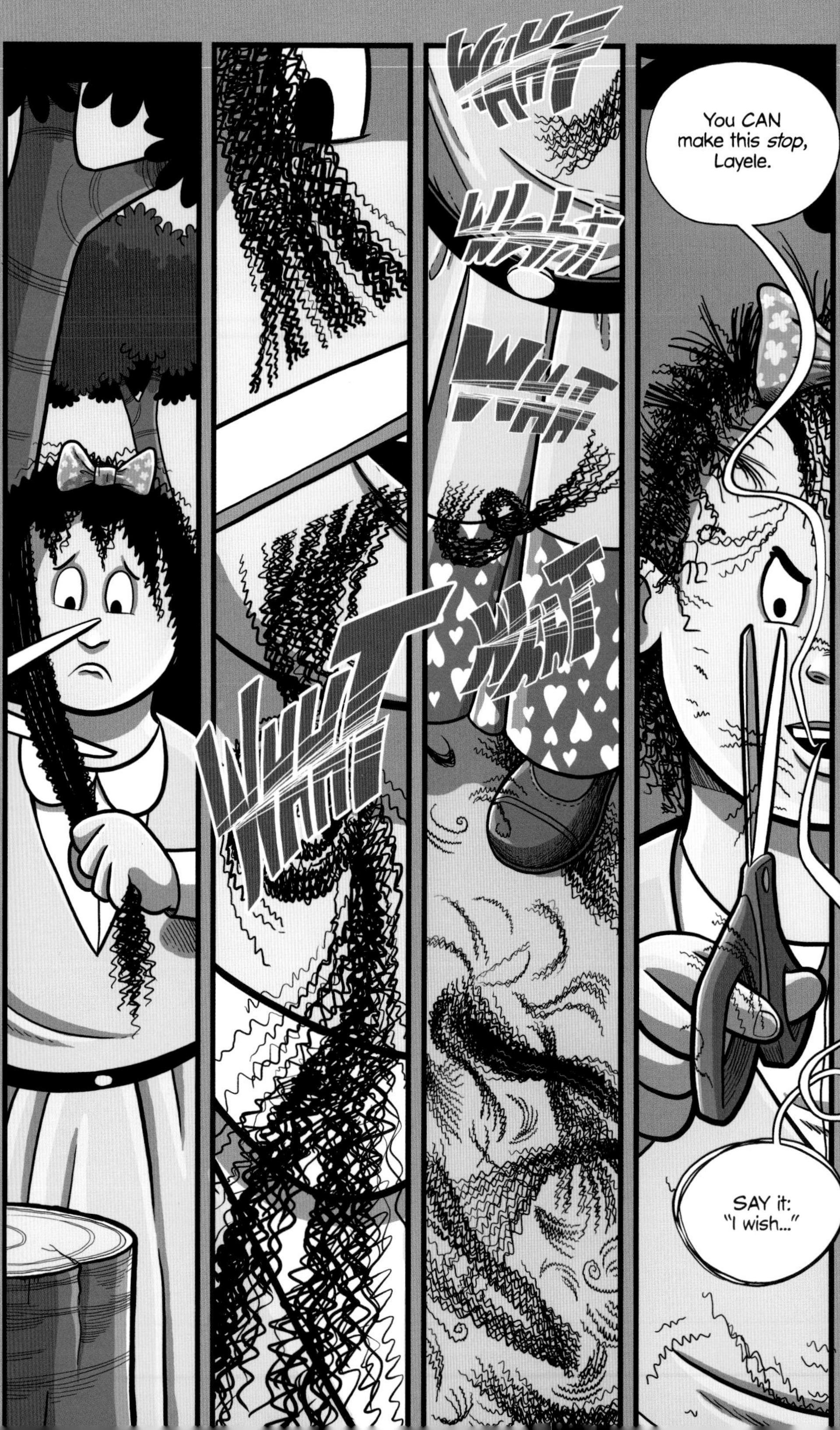
You CAN make this *stop*, Layele.
SAY it: "I wish..."

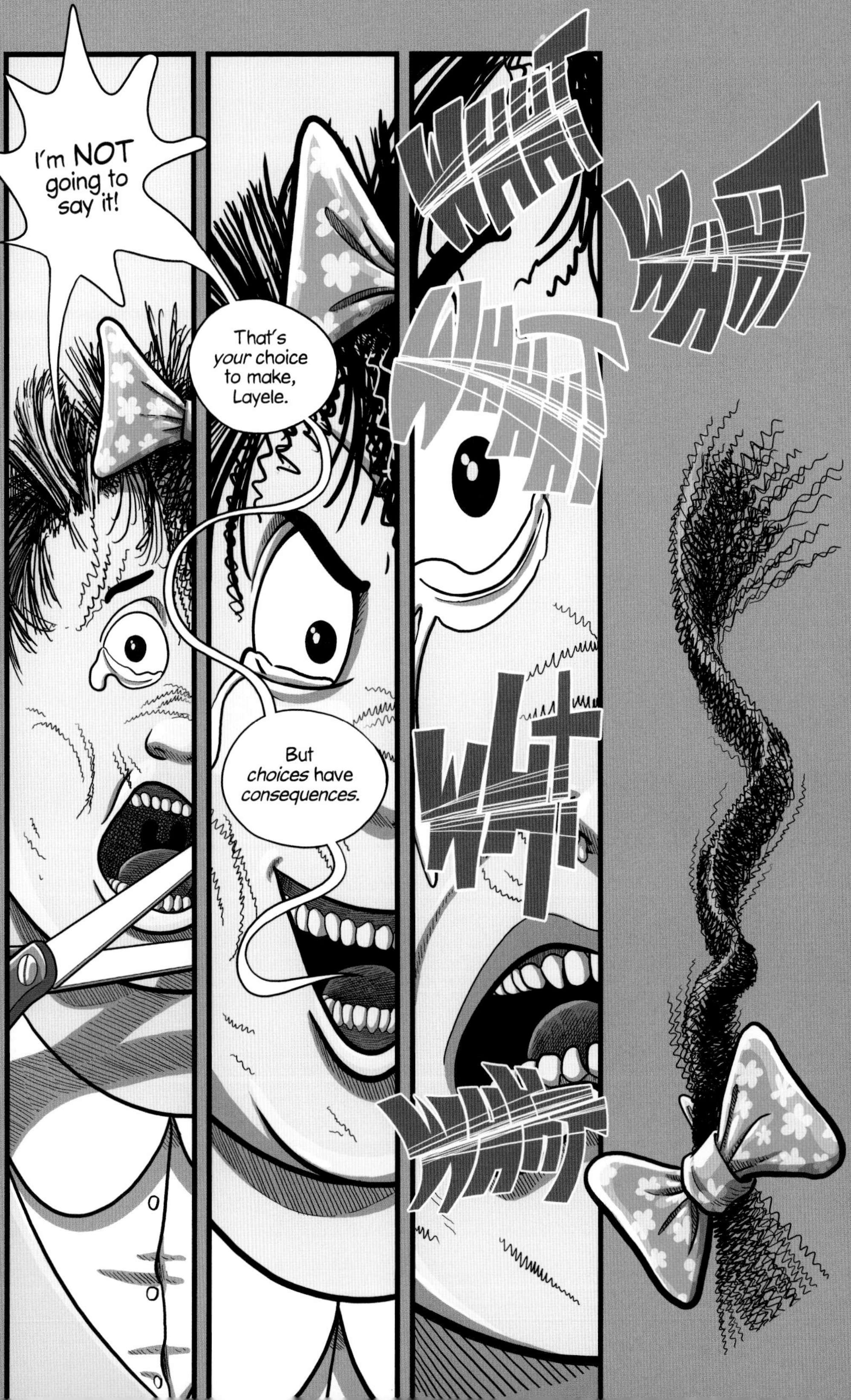
I'm NOT going to say it!
That's *your* choice to make, Layele.
But *choices* have *consequences.*

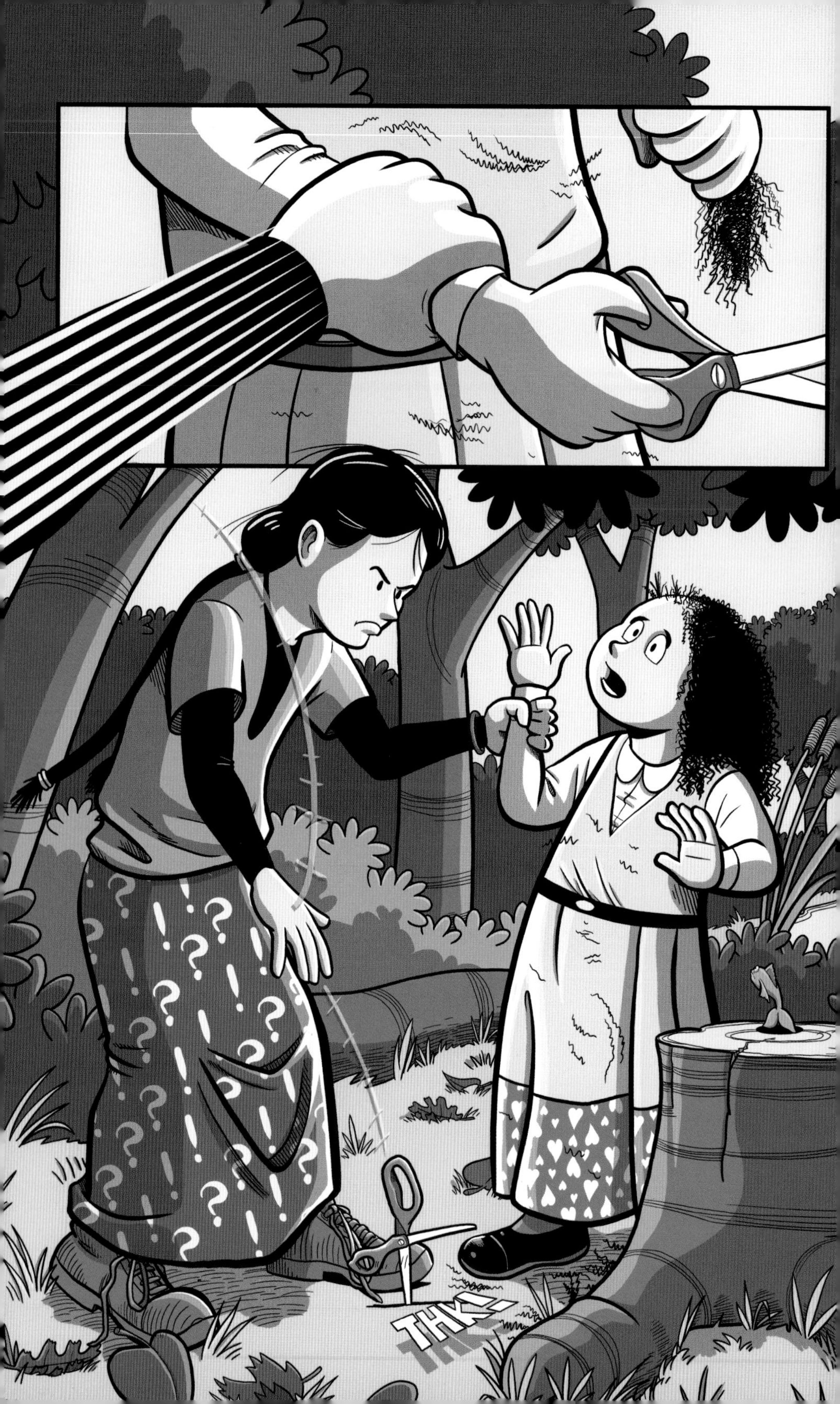
THK!

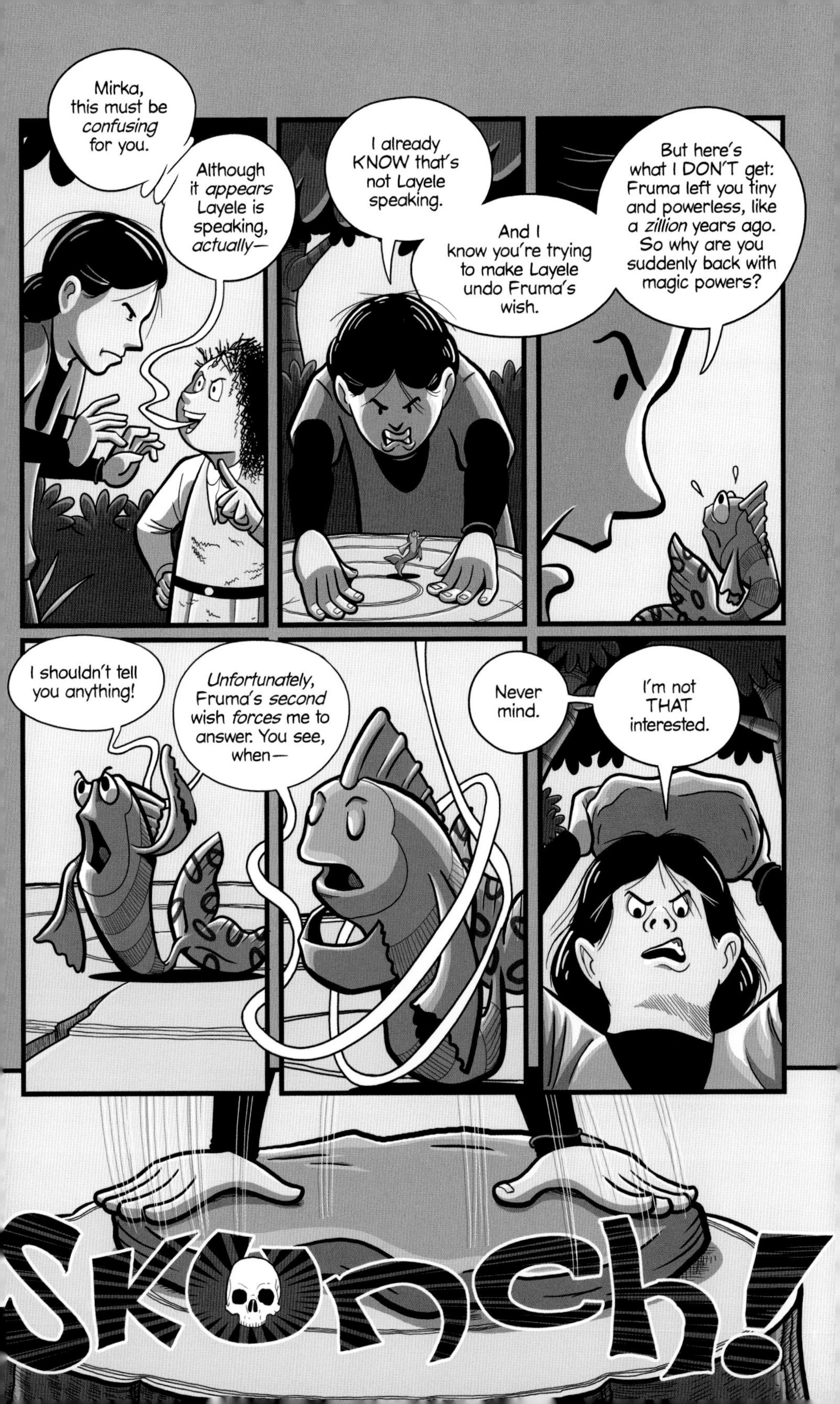

Mirka, this must be *confusing* for you.
Although it *appears* Layele is speaking, *actually*—
I already KNOW that's not Layele speaking.
And I know you're trying to make Layele undo Fruma's wish.
But here's what I DON'T get: Fruma left you tiny and powerless, like a *zillion* years ago. So why are you suddenly back with magic powers?
I shouldn't tell you anything!
Unfortunately, Fruma's *second* wish *forces* me to answer. You see, when—
Never mind.
I'm not THAT interested.
SKUNCH!

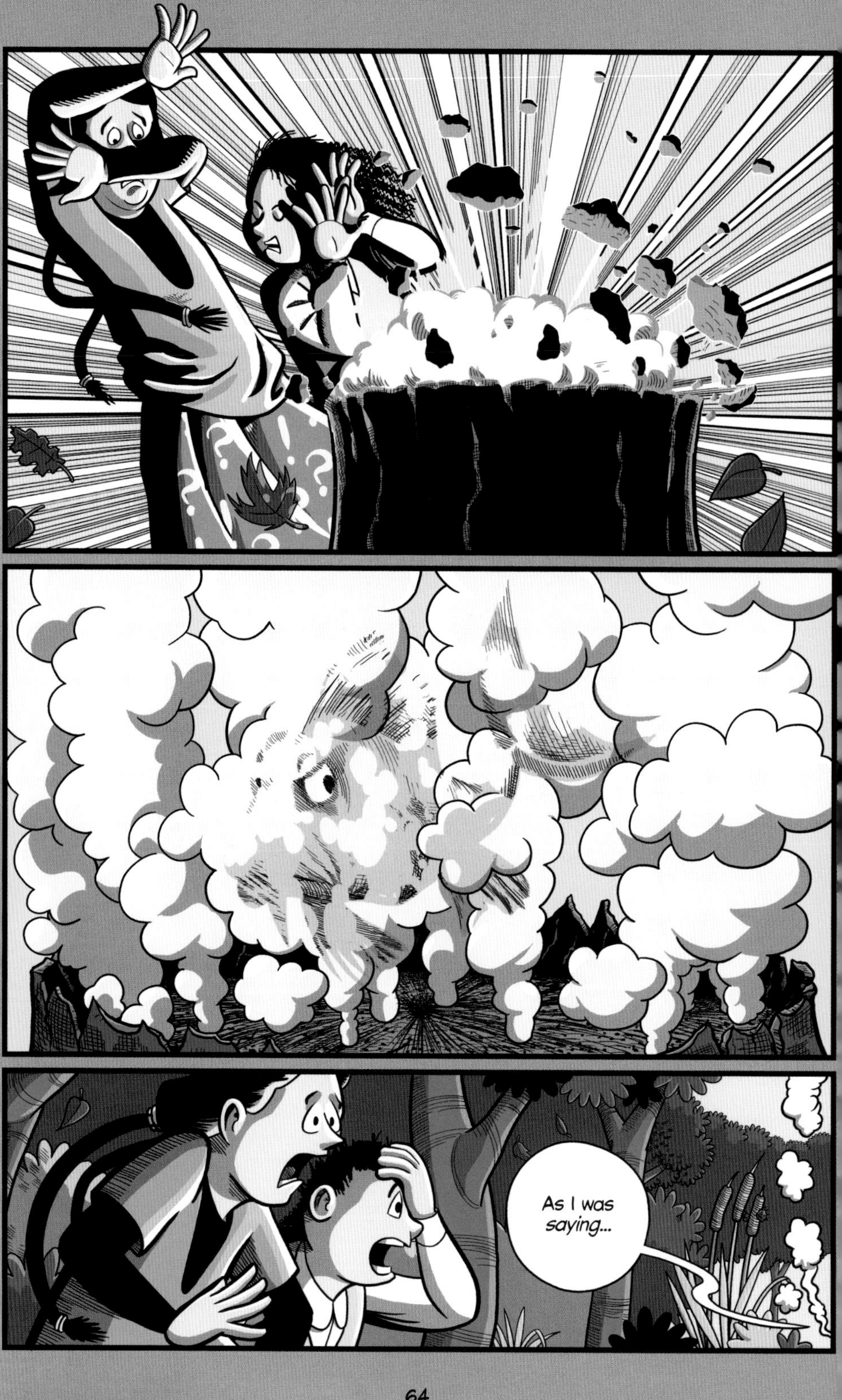
As I was saying...

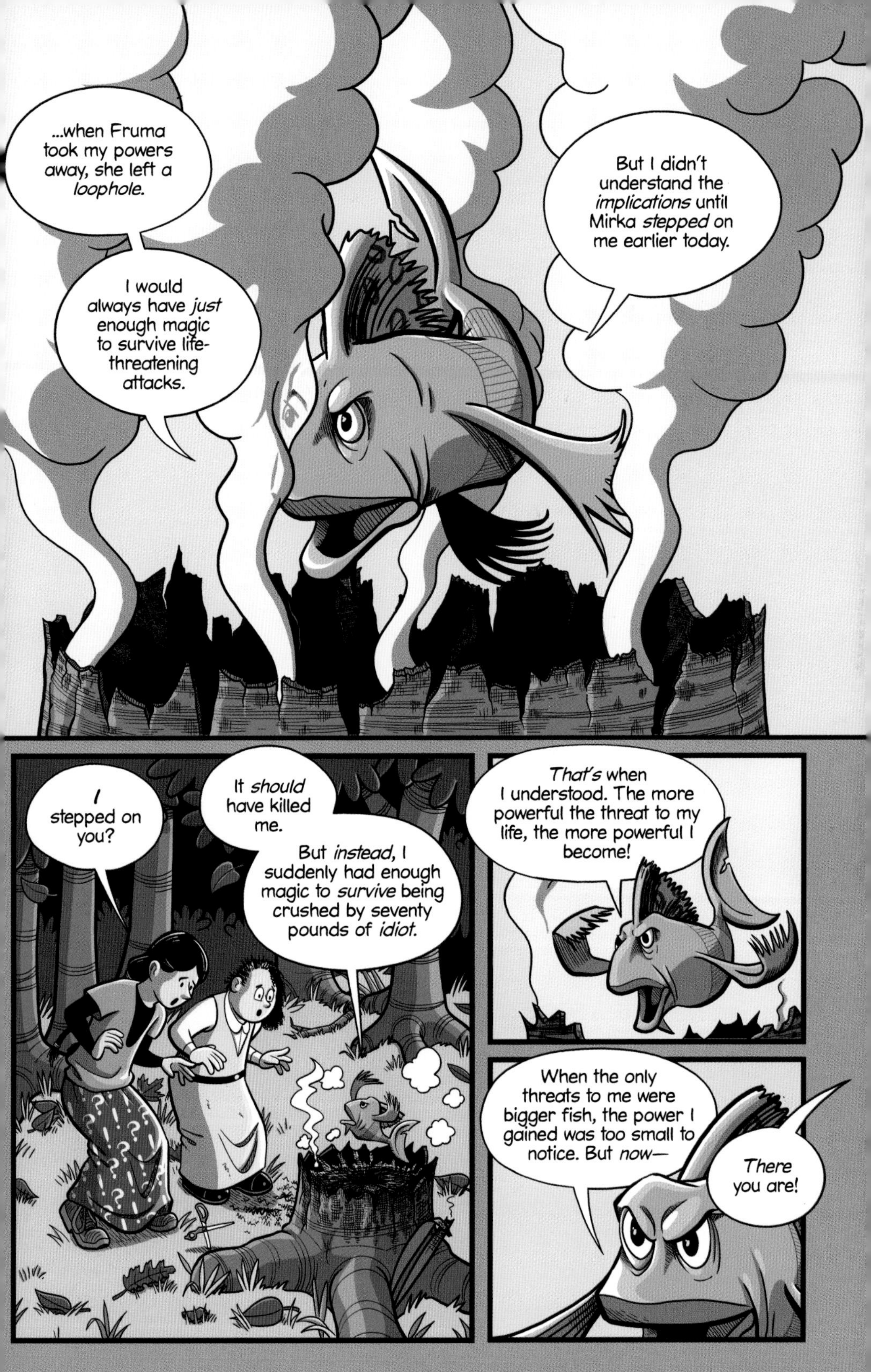
...when Fruma took my powers away, she left a *loophole.*
I would always have *just* enough magic to survive life-threatening attacks.
But I didn't understand the *implications* until Mirka *stepped* on me earlier today.
I stepped on you?
It *should* have killed me.
But *instead*, I suddenly had enough magic to *survive* being crushed by seventy pounds of *idiot.*
That's when I understood. The more powerful the threat to my life, the more powerful I become!
When the only threats to me were bigger fish, the power I gained was too small to notice. But *now*—
There you are!

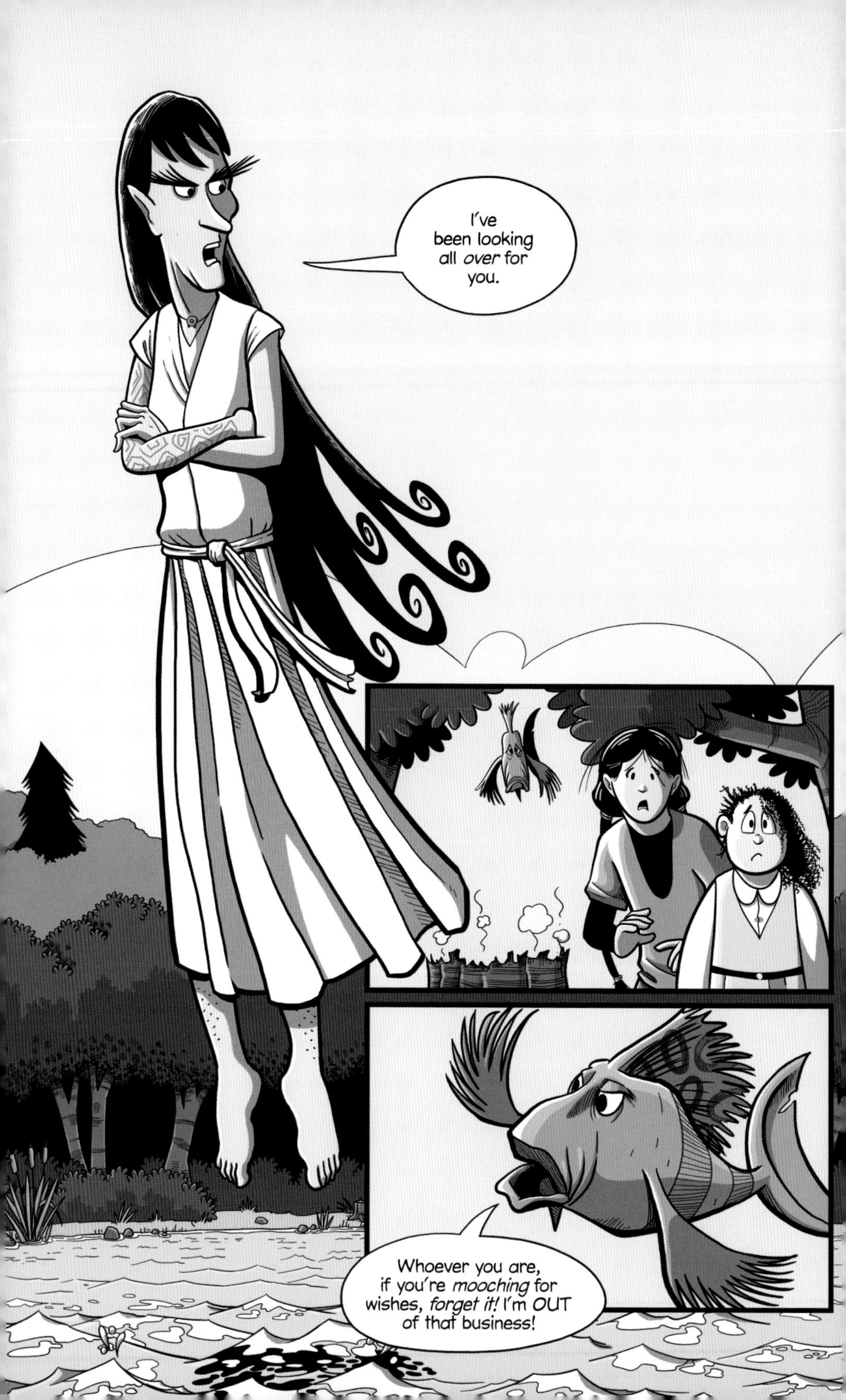
I've been looking all *over* for you.
Whoever you are, if you're *mooching* for wishes, *forget it!* I'm OUT of that business!

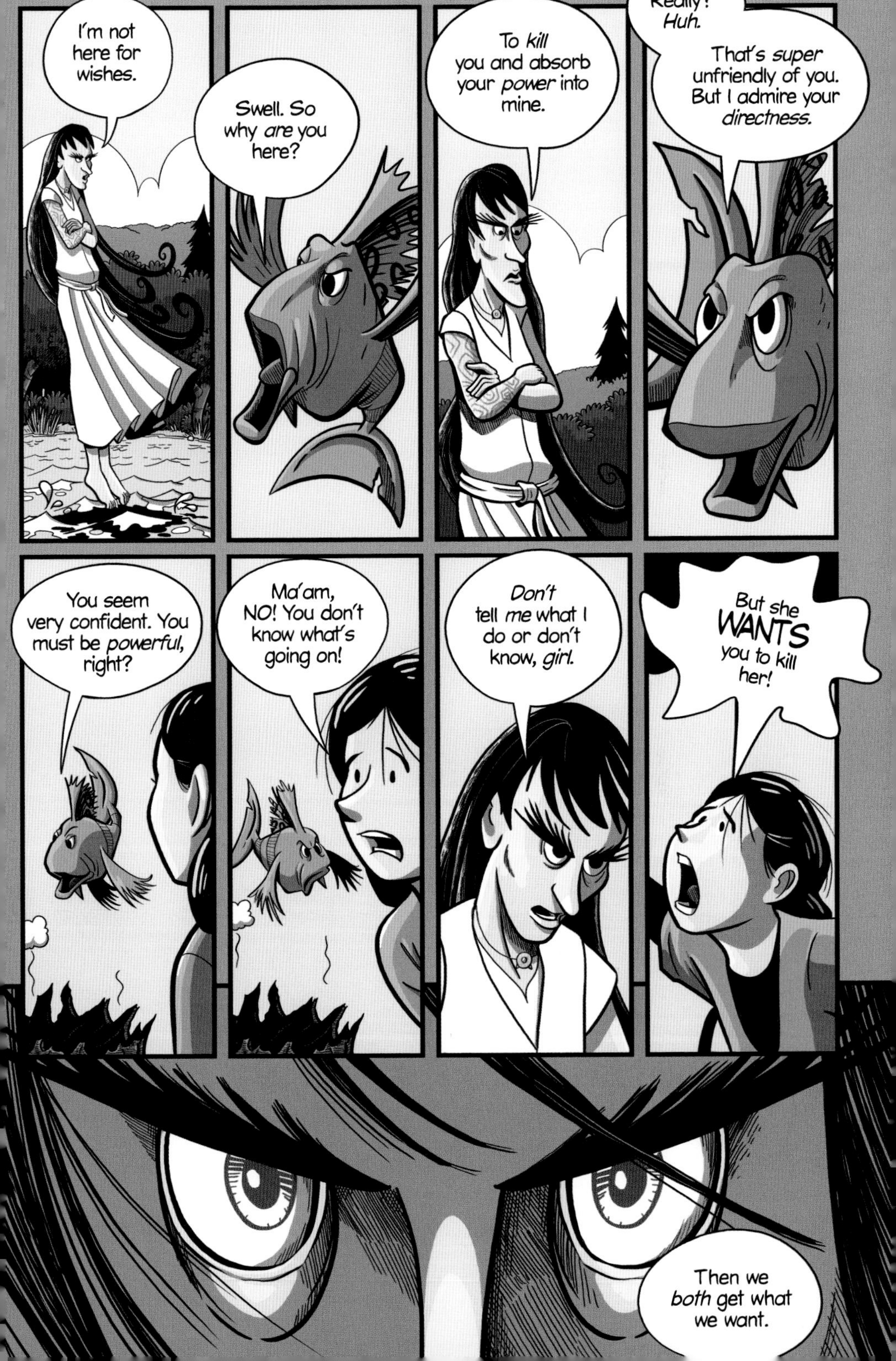
I'm not here for wishes.
Swell. So why *are* you here?
To *kill* you and absorb your *power* into mine.
Really? *Huh.*
That's *super* unfriendly of you. But I admire your *directness.*
You seem very confident. You must be *powerful,* right?
Ma'am, NO! You don't know what's going on!
Don't tell *me* what I do or don't know, *girl.*
But she **WANTS** you to kill her!
Then we *both* get what we want.

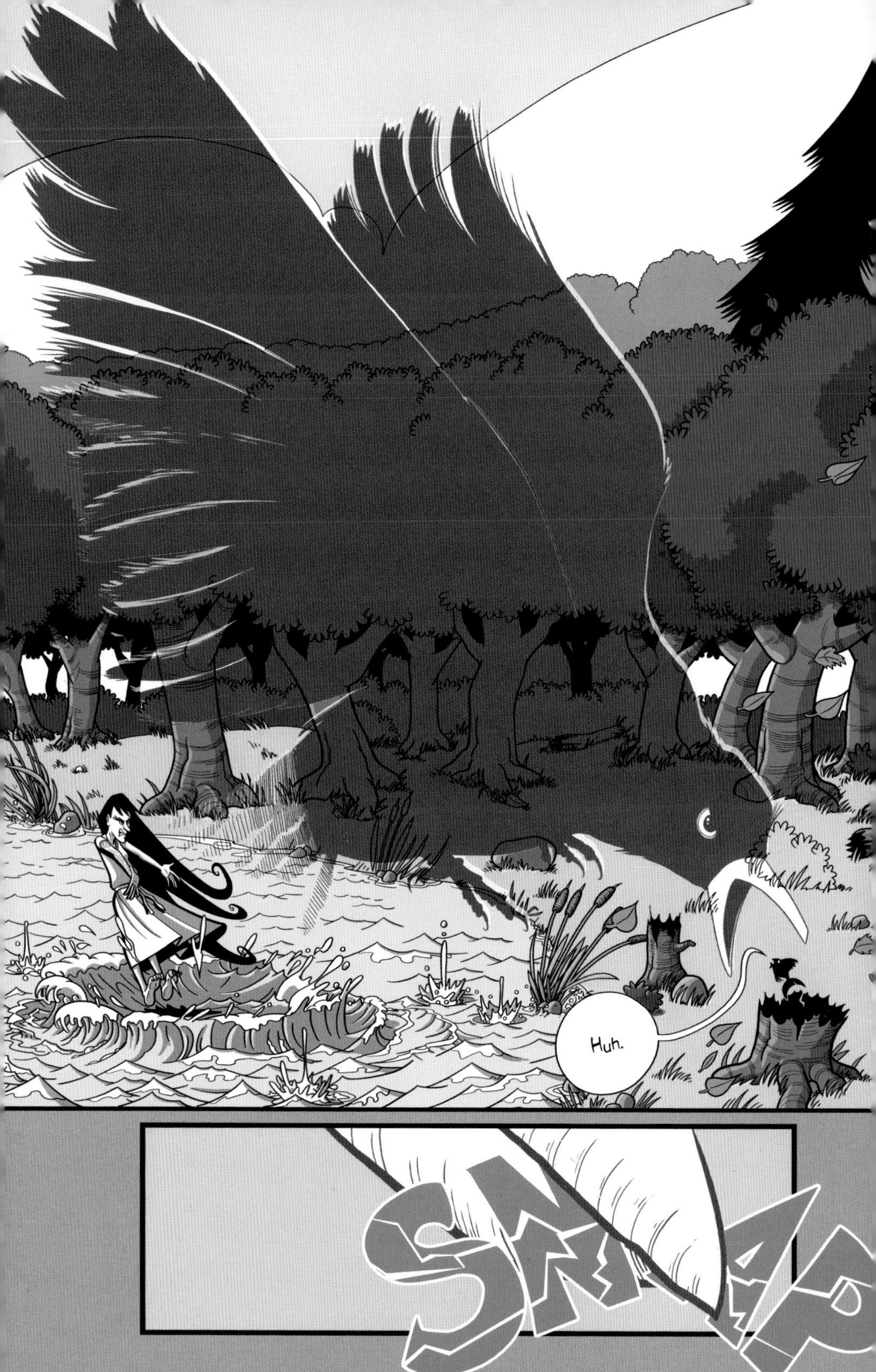
Huh.
SNAP

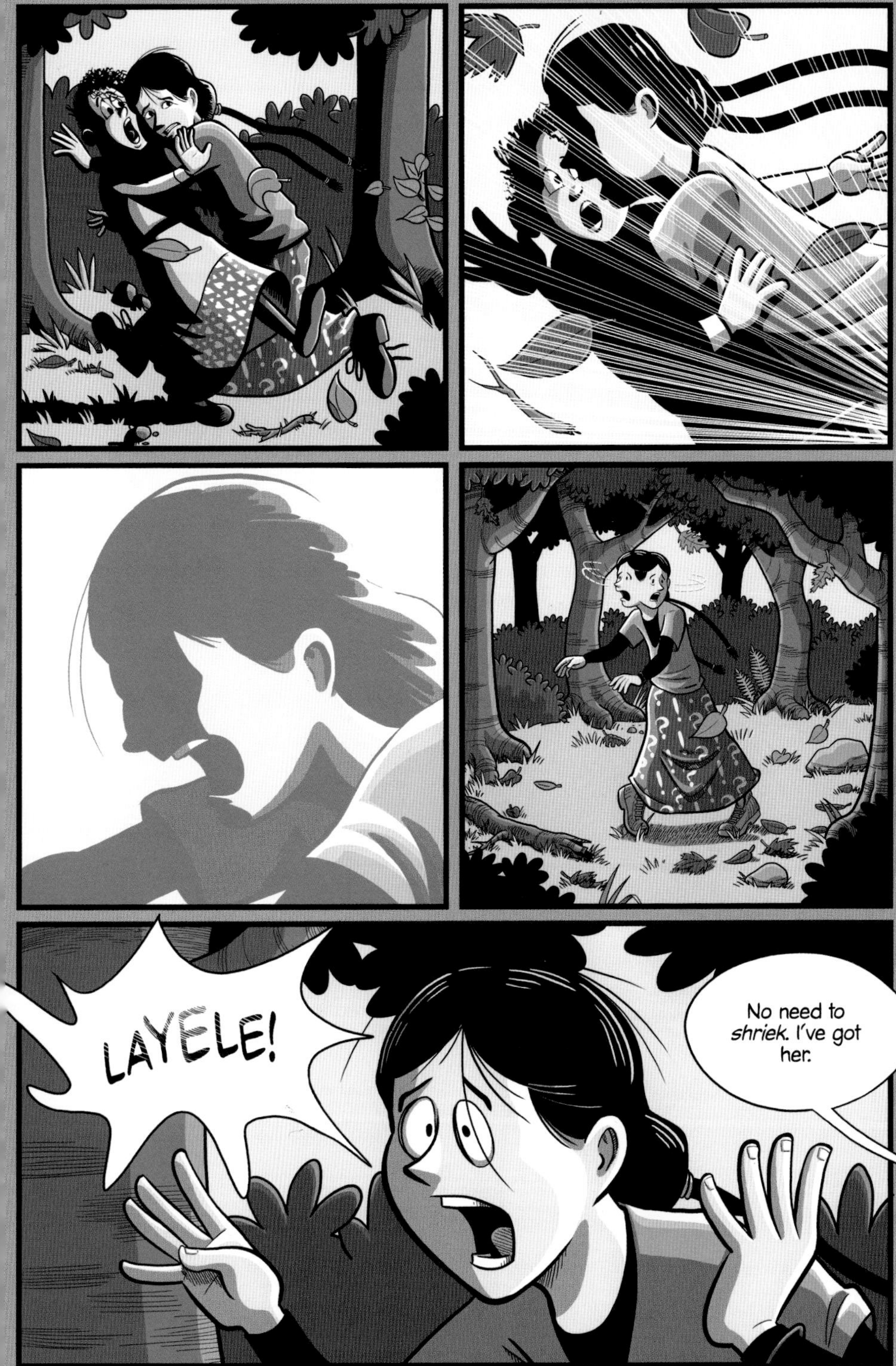
LAYELE!
No need to *shriek*. I've got her.

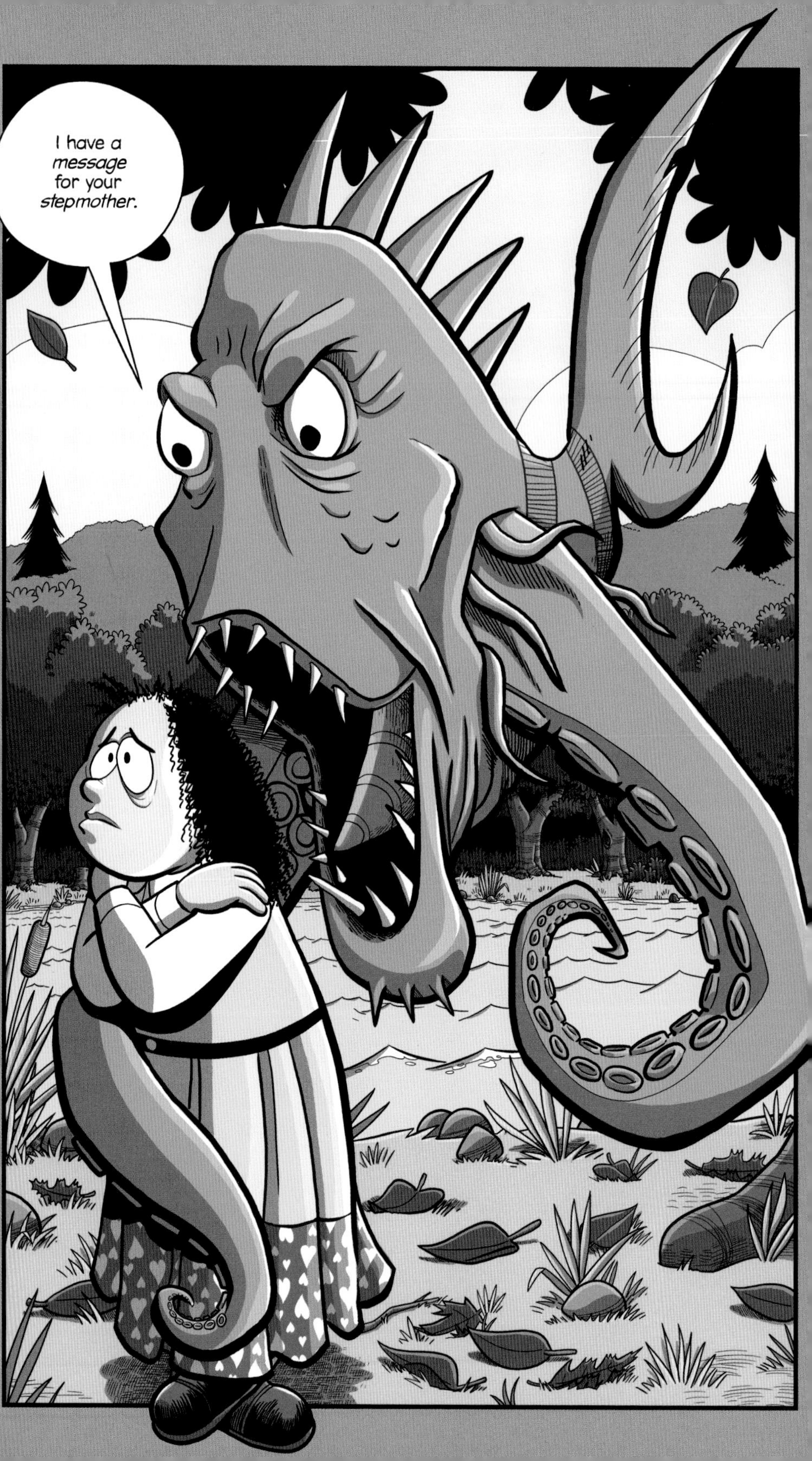
I have a *message* for your *stepmother.*

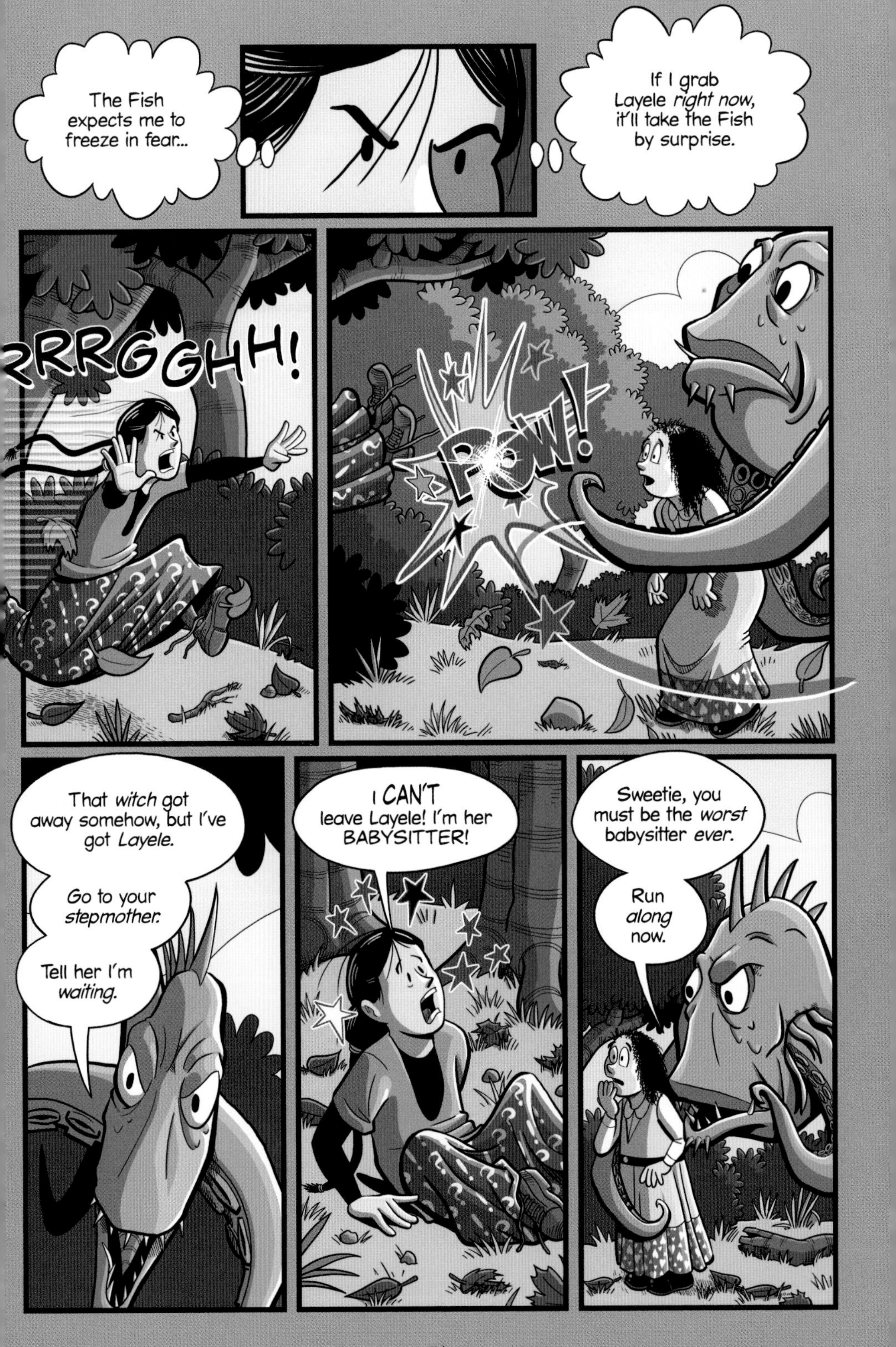
The Fish expects me to freeze in fear...
If I grab Layele *right now*, it'll take the Fish by surprise.
RRRGGHH!
POW!
That *witch* got away somehow, but I've got *Layele*.
Go to your *stepmother*.
Tell her I'm *waiting*.
I CAN'T leave Layele! I'm her BABYSITTER!
Sweetie, you must be the *worst* babysitter *ever*.
Run *along* now.

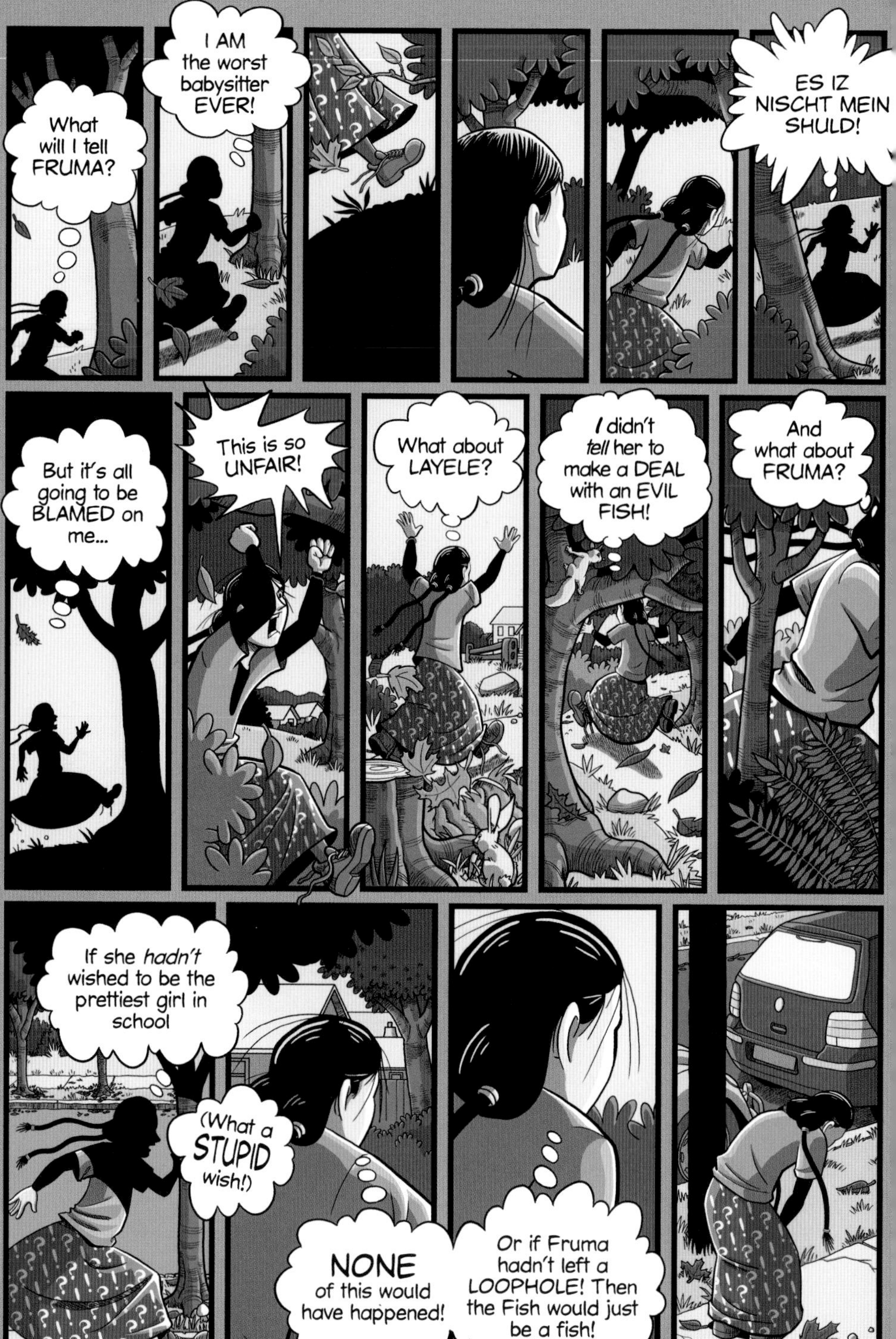
What will I tell FRUMA?
I AM the worst babysitter EVER!
ES IZ NISCHT MEIN SHULD!
But it's all going to be BLAMED on me...
This is so UNFAIR!
What about LAYELE?
I didn't tell her to make a DEAL with an EVIL FISH!
And what about FRUMA?
If she hadn't wished to be the prettiest girl in school
(What a STUPID wish!)
NONE of this would have happened!
Or if Fruma hadn't left a LOOPHOLE! Then the Fish would just be a fish!

Es iz nischt mein shuld!: This isn't all my fault!

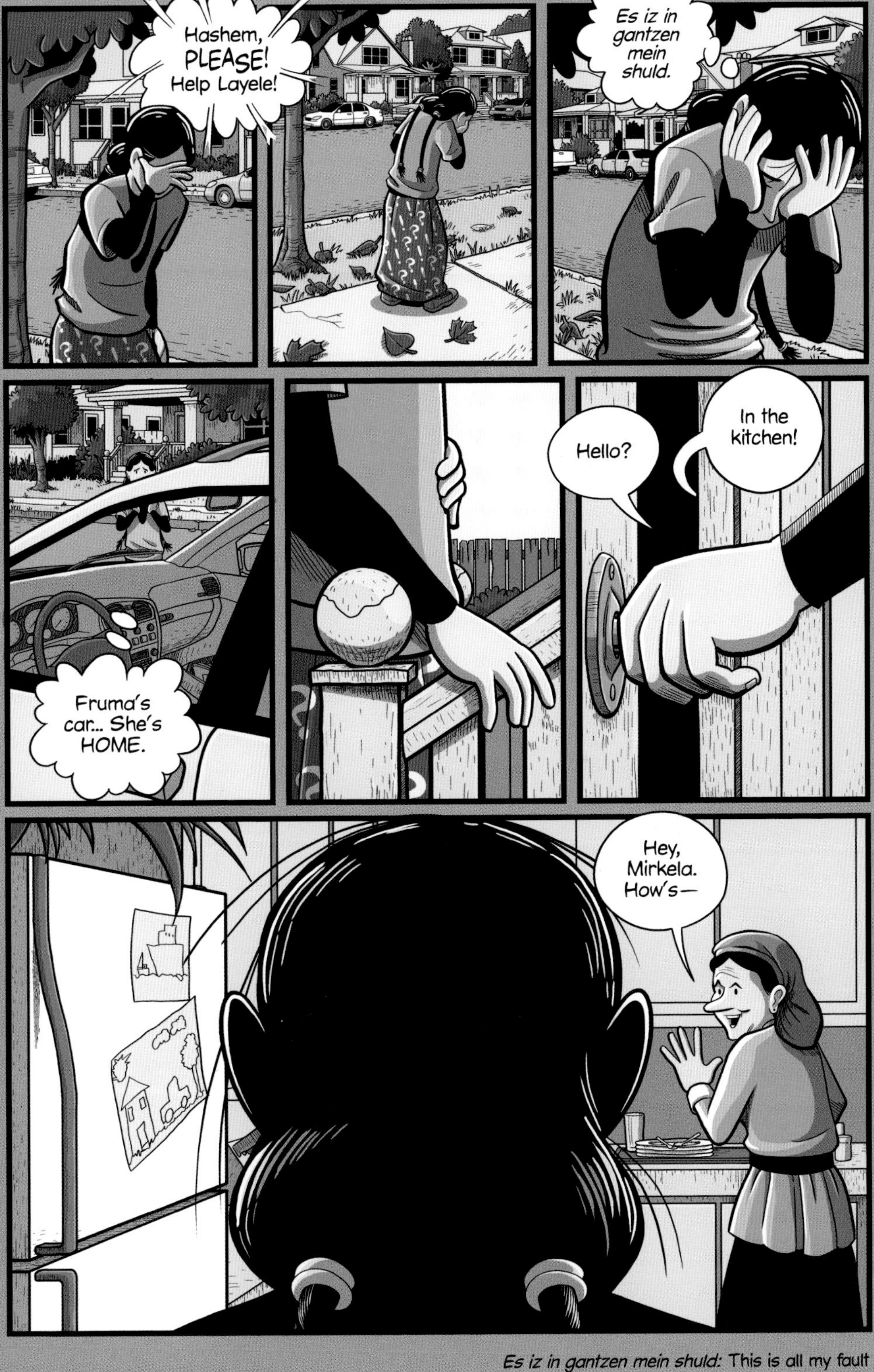
Hashem, PLEASE! Help Layele!
Es iz in gantzen mein shuld.
Fruma's car... She's HOME.
Hello?
In the kitchen!
Hey, Mirkela. How's—

Es iz in gantzen mein shuld: This is all my fault

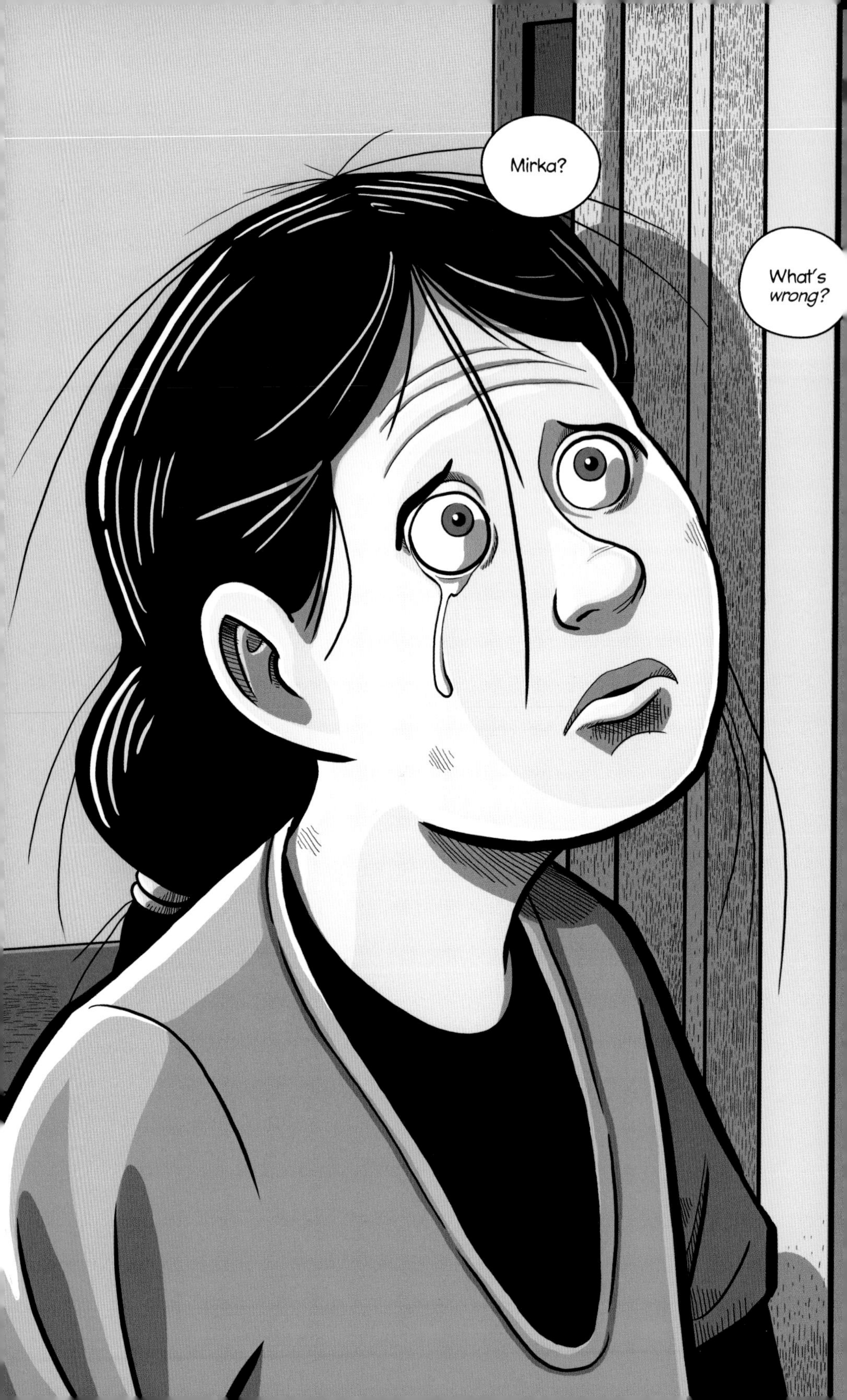
Mirka?
What's wrong?

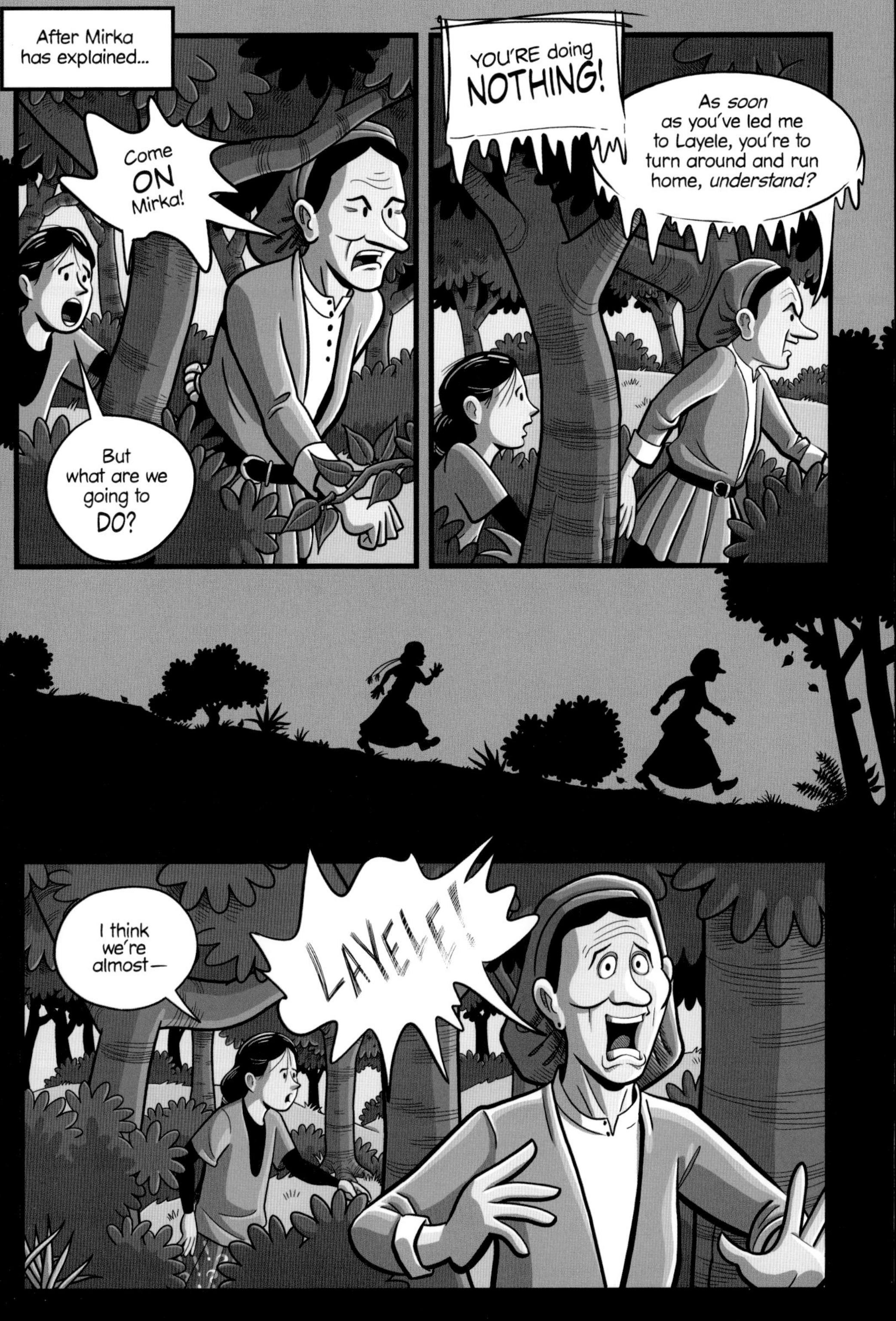
After Mirka has explained...
Come ON Mirka!
But what are we going to DO?
YOU'RE doing NOTHING!
As *soon* as you've led me to Layele, you're to turn around and run home, *understand?*
I think we're almost—
LAYELE!

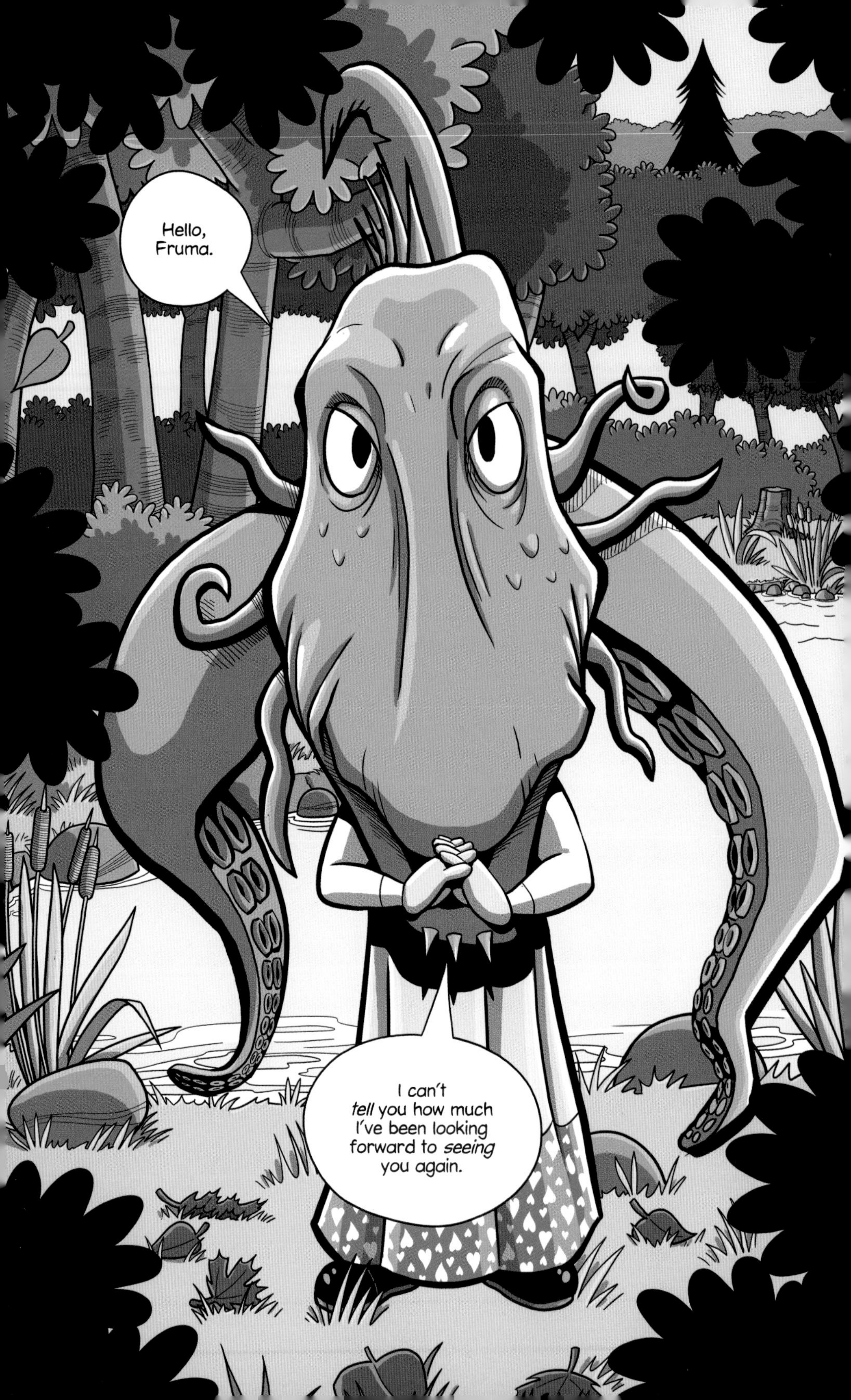
Hello, Fruma.
I can't *tell* you how much I've been looking forward to *seeing* you again.

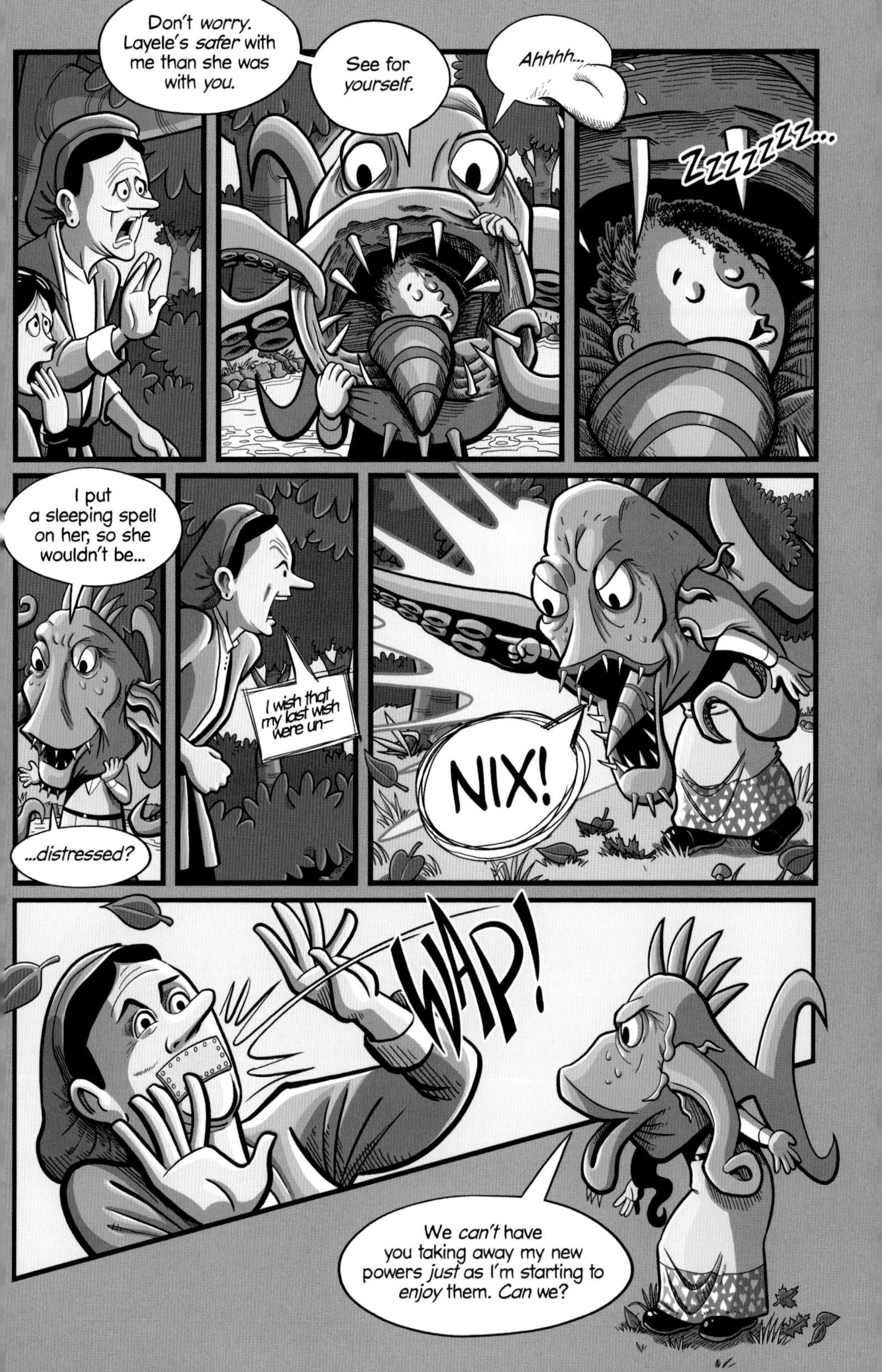
Don't *worry.* Layele's *safer* with me than she was with *you.*
See for *yourself.*
Ahhhh...
Zzzzzzz...
I put a sleeping spell on her, so she wouldn't be...
...*distressed?*
I wish that my last wish were un—
NIX!
WAP!
We *can't* have you taking away my new powers *just* as I'm starting to *enjoy* them. *Can* we?

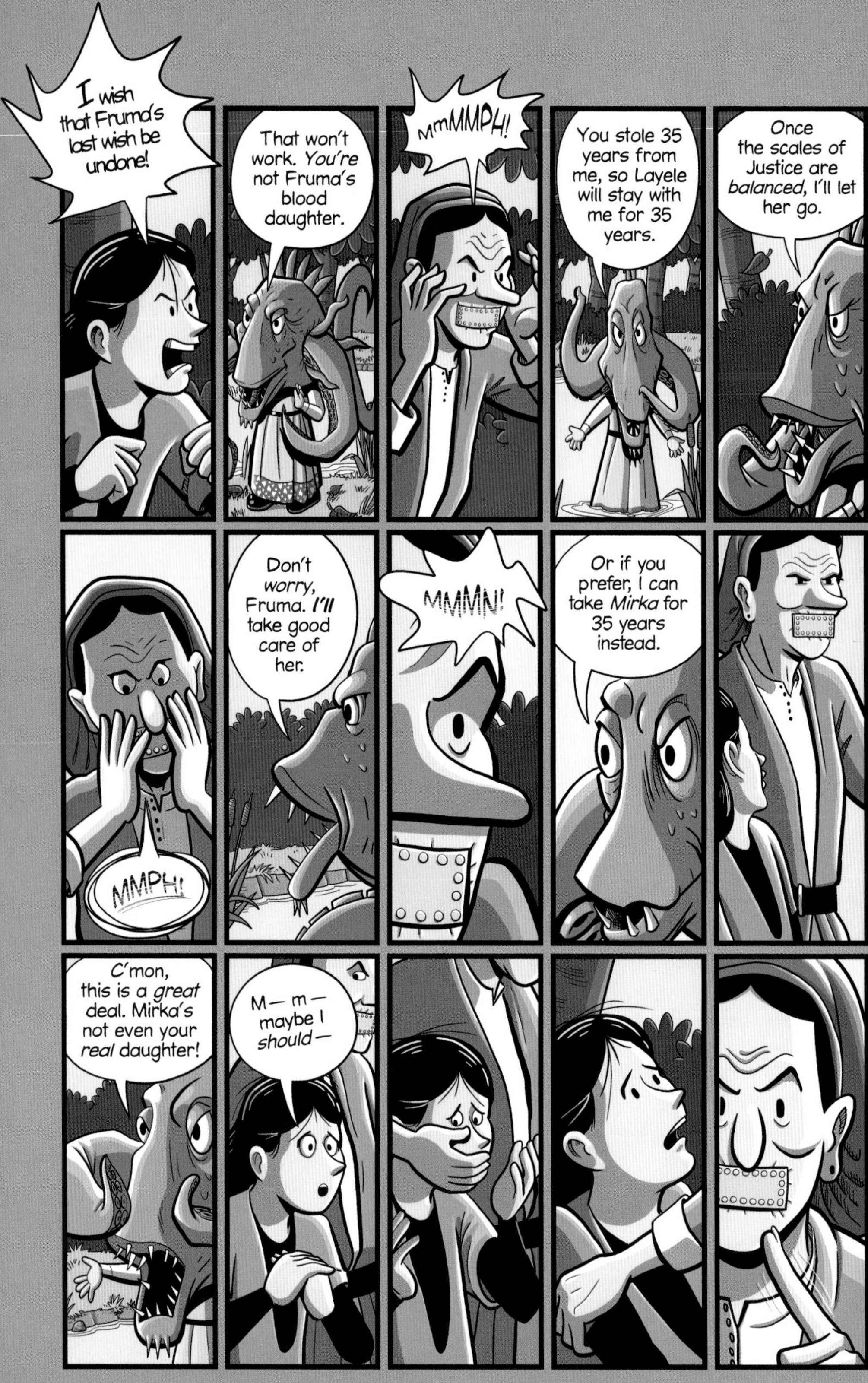
I wish that Fruma's last wish be undone!
That won't work. *You're* not Fruma's blood daughter.
MmMMPH!
You stole 35 years from me, so Layele will stay with me for 35 years.
Once the scales of Justice are *balanced*, I'll let her go.
MMPH!
Don't *worry*, Fruma. *I'll* take good care of her.
MMMN!
Or if you prefer, I can take *Mirka* for 35 years instead.
C'mon, this is a *great* deal. Mirka's not even your *real* daughter!
M— m— maybe I *should*—

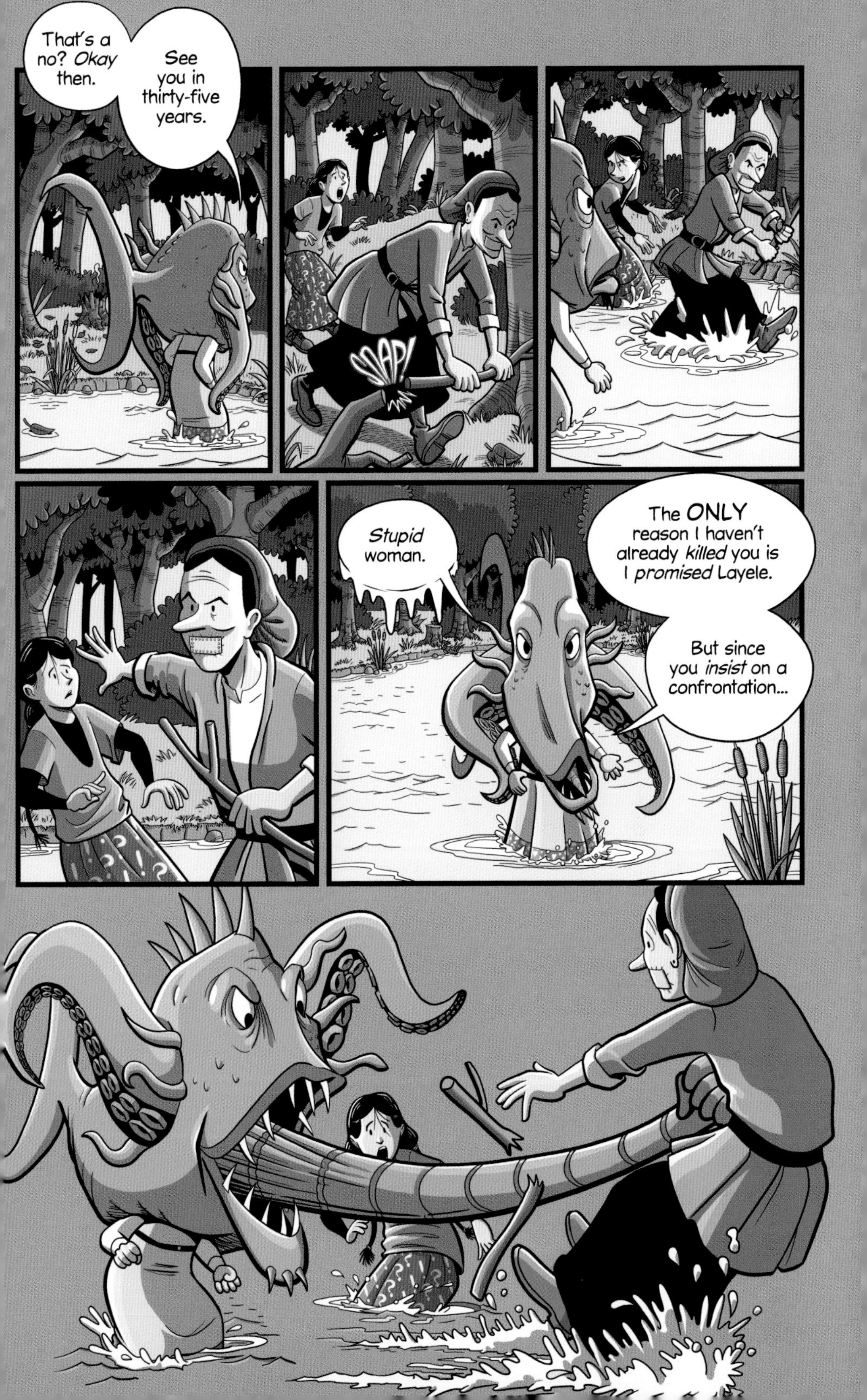

That's a no? *Okay* then.
See you in thirty-five years.
SNAP!
Stupid woman.
The ONLY reason I haven't already *killed* you is I *promised* Layele.
But since you *insist* on a confrontation...

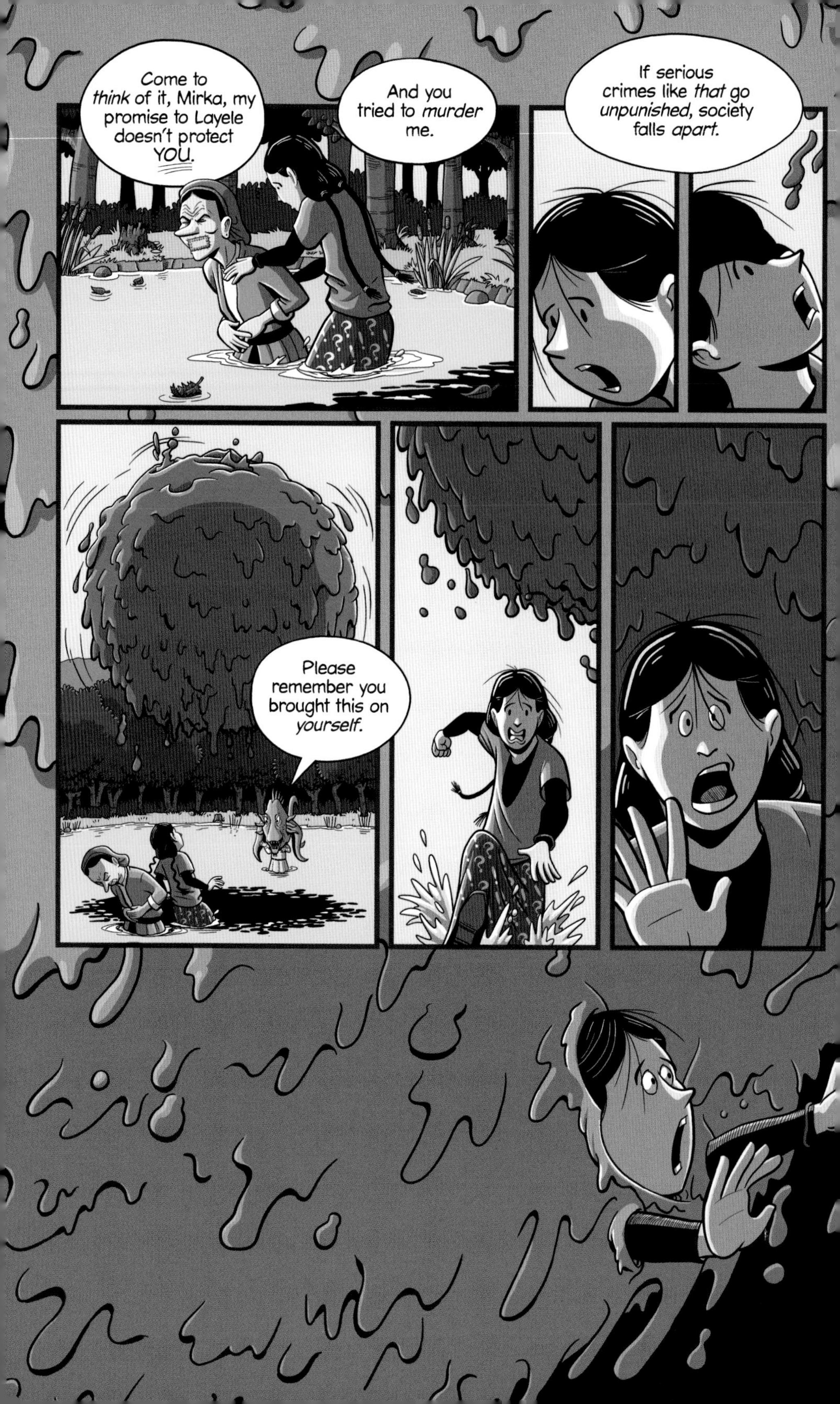
Come to think of it, Mirka, my promise to Layele doesn't protect YOU.
And you tried to murder me.
If serious crimes like that go unpunished, society falls apart.
Please remember you brought this on yourself.

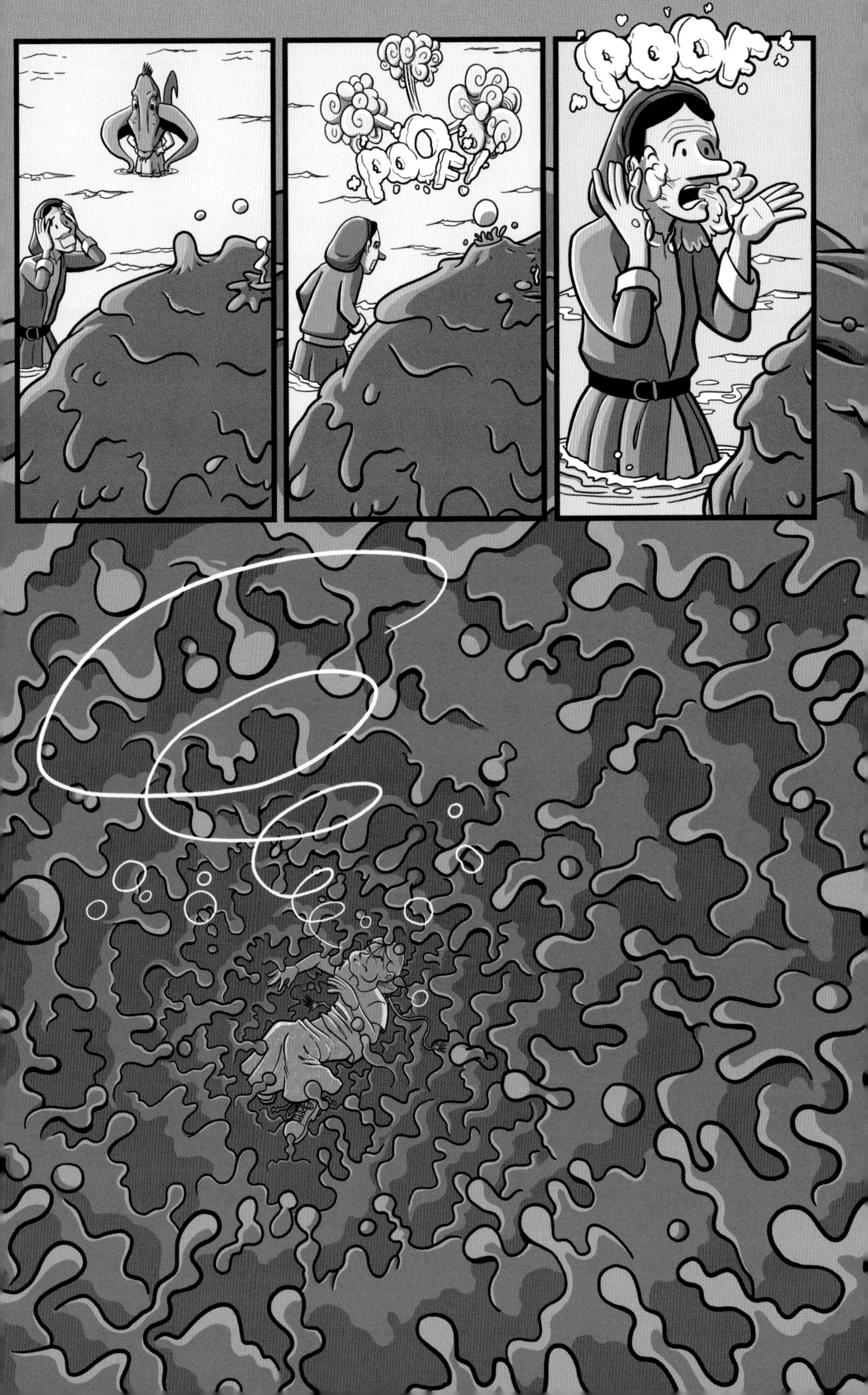
POOF!
POOF!

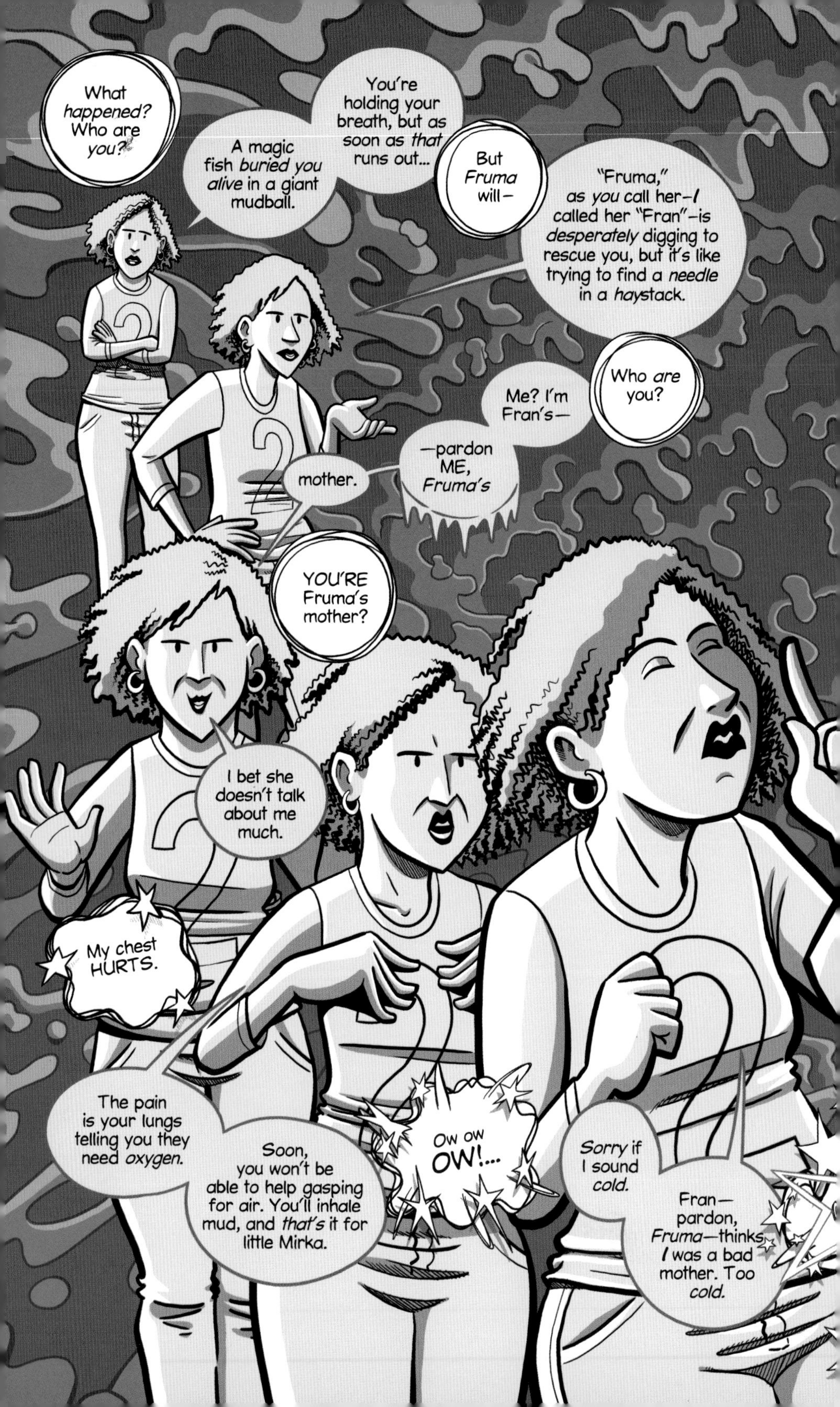

What happened? Who are you?
A magic fish buried you alive in a giant mudball.
You're holding your breath, but as soon as that runs out...
But Fruma will—
"Fruma," as you call her—I called her "Fran"—is desperately digging to rescue you, but it's like trying to find a needle in a haystack.
Who are you?
Me? I'm Fran's—
—pardon ME, Fruma's
mother.
YOU'RE Fruma's mother?
I bet she doesn't talk about me much.
My chest HURTS.
The pain is your lungs telling you they need oxygen.
Soon, you won't be able to help gasping for air. You'll inhale mud, and that's it for little Mirka.
Ow ow OW!...
Sorry if I sound cold.
Fran—pardon, Fruma—thinks I was a bad mother. Too cold.

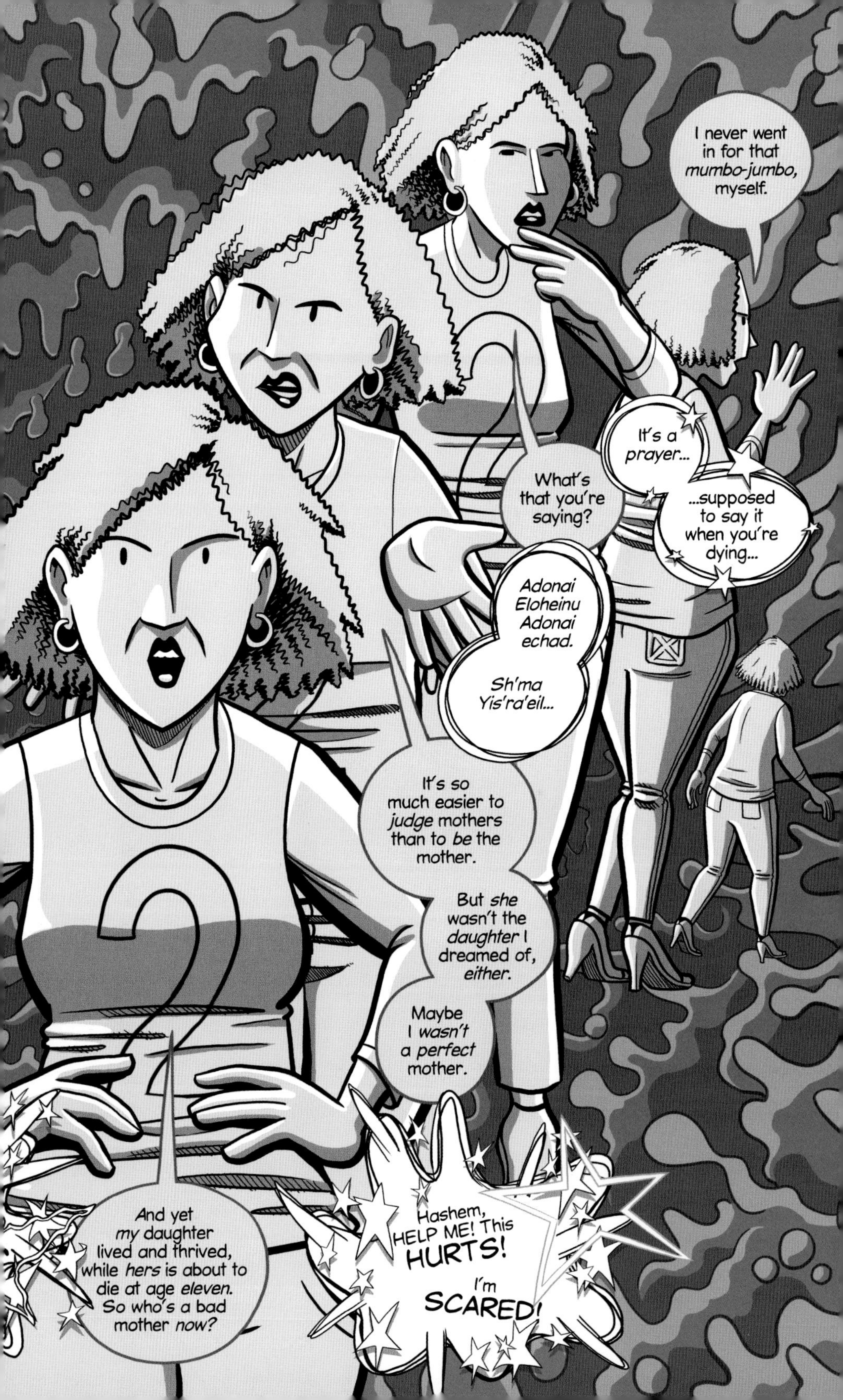

I never went in for that *mumbo-jumbo,* myself.
It's a *prayer*...
...supposed to say it when you're dying...
What's that you're saying?
Adonai Eloheinu Adonai echad.
Sh'ma Yis'ra'eil...
It's so much easier to *judge* mothers than to *be* the mother.
But *she* wasn't the *daughter* I dreamed of, *either.*
Maybe I *wasn't* a *perfect* mother.
And yet *my* daughter lived and thrived, while *hers* is about to die at age *eleven.* So who's a bad mother *now?*
Hashem, HELP ME! This HURTS!
I'm SCARED!

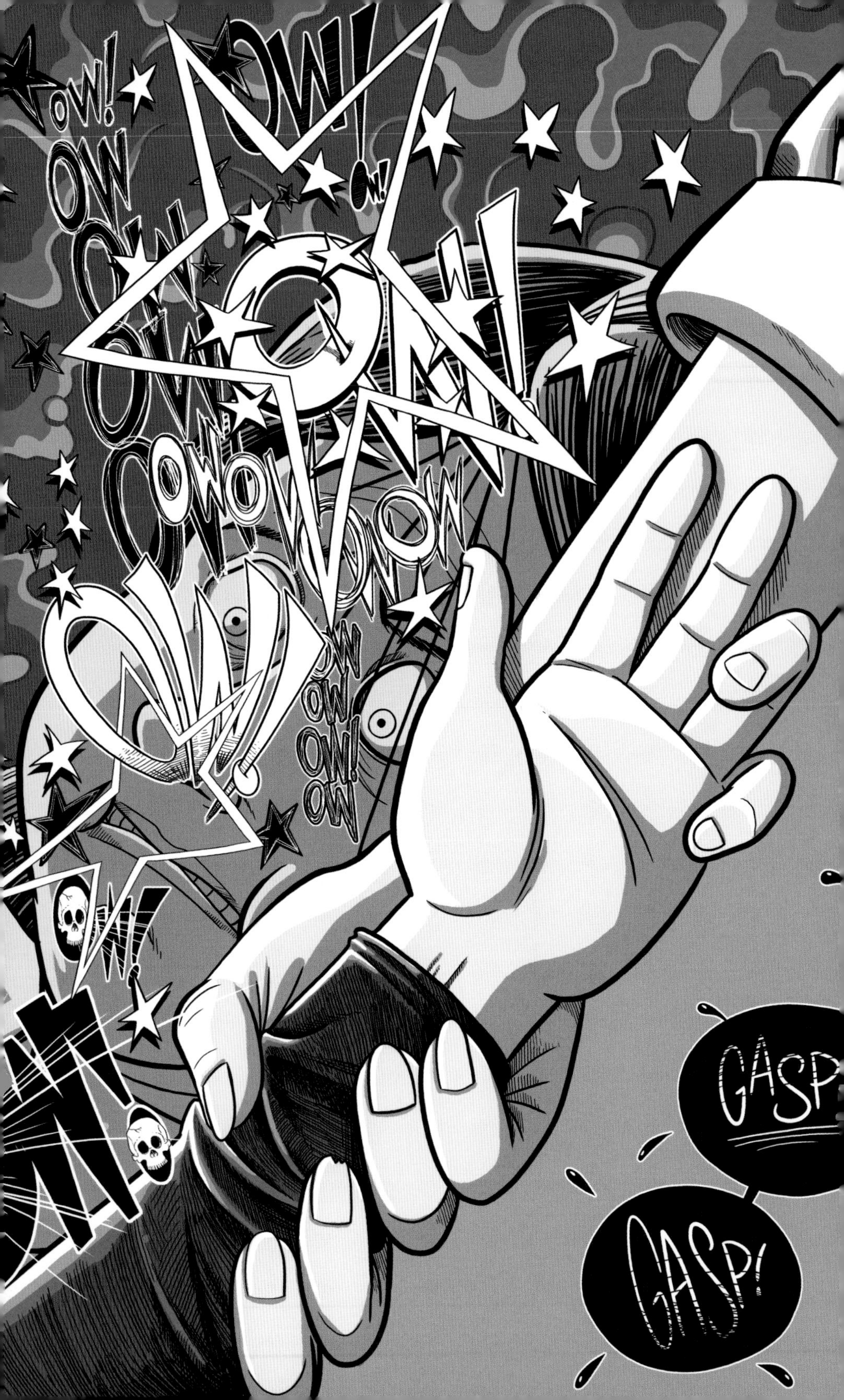
OW!
OW
OW!
OW!
OW!
OWOWOWOW
OW OW OW! OW
OW!
GASP
GASP!

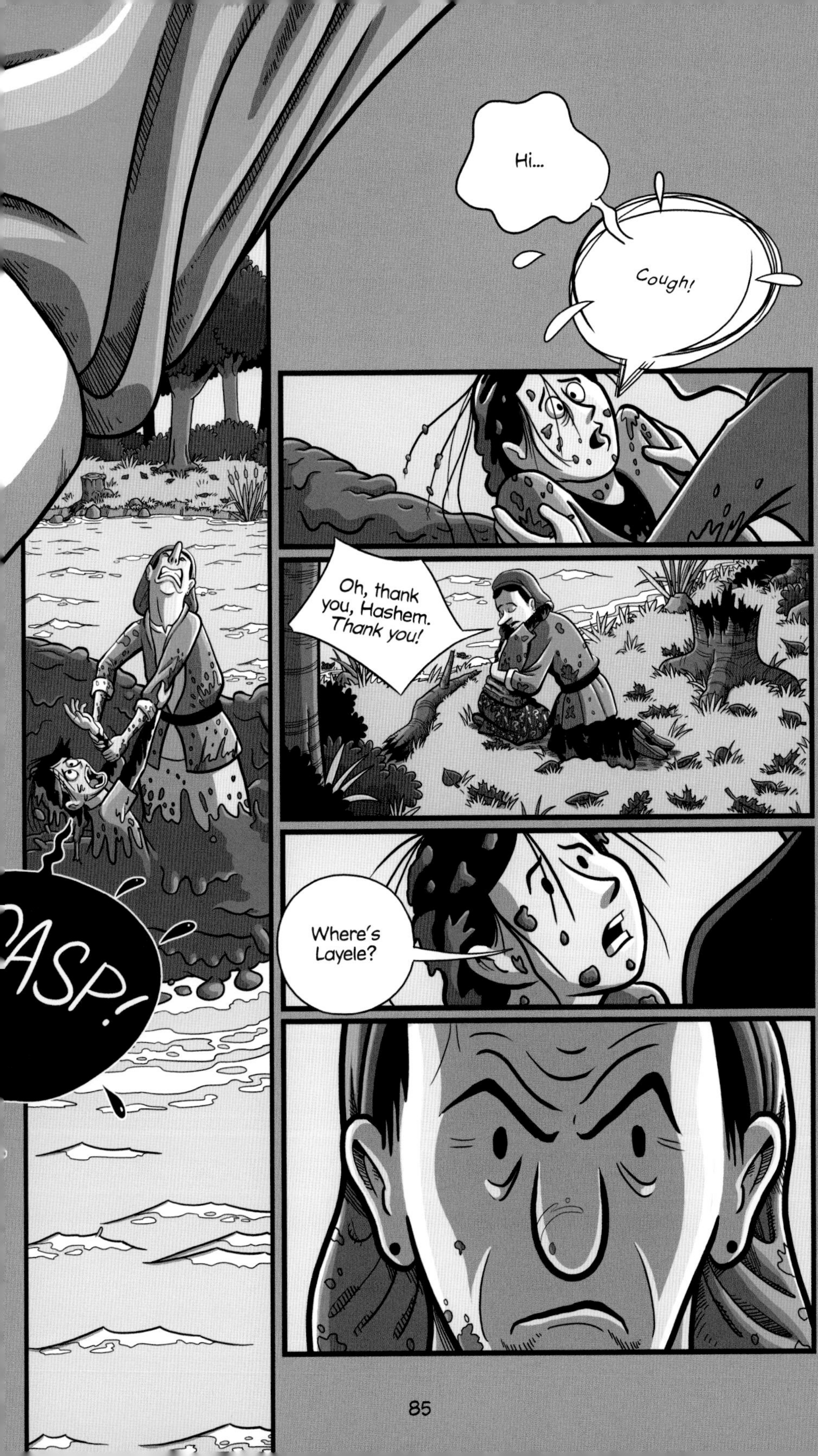
GASP!
Hi...
Cough!
Oh, thank you, Hashem. Thank you!
Where's Layele?

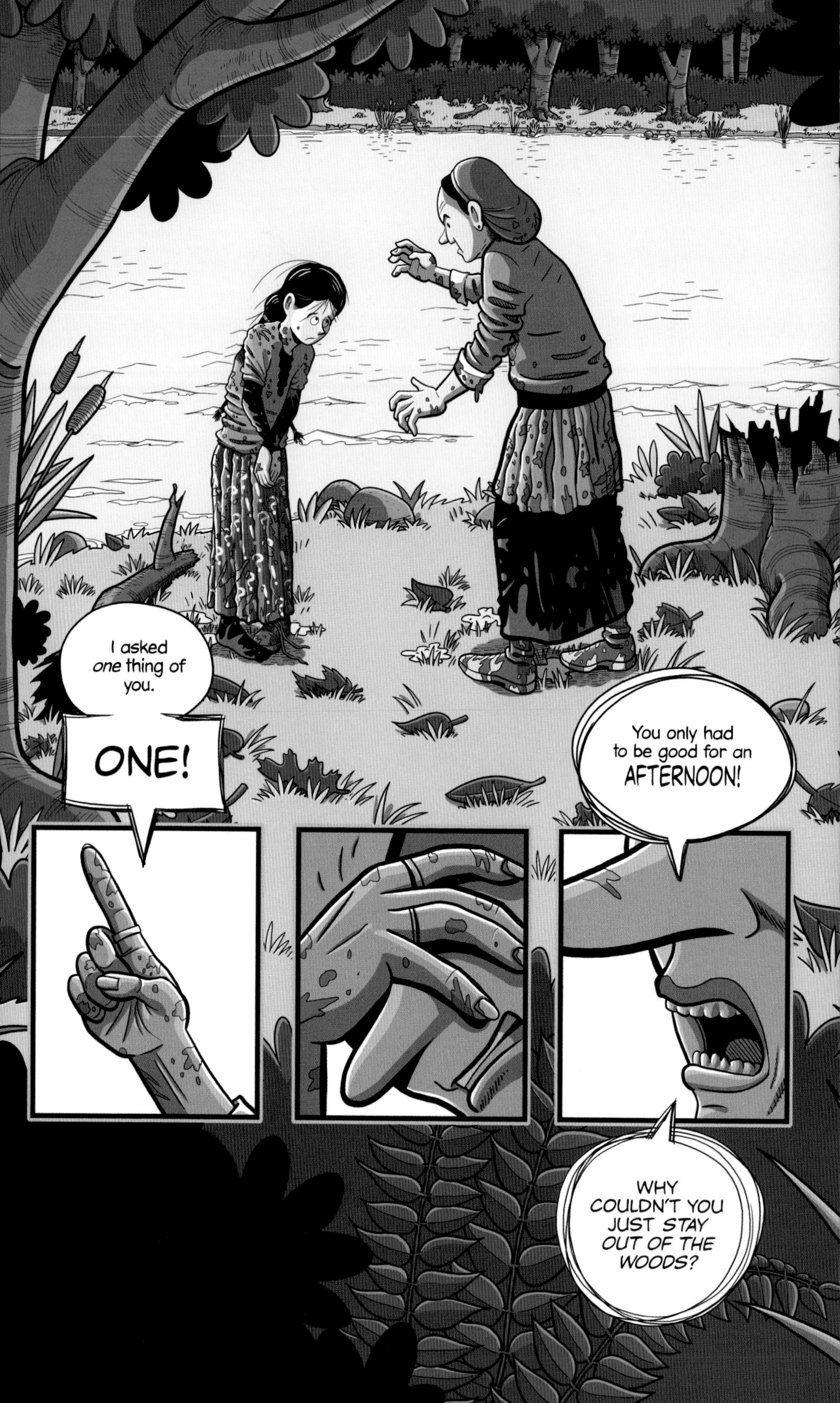
I asked *one* thing of you.
ONE!
You only had to be good for an AFTERNOON!
WHY COULDN'T YOU JUST *STAY OUT OF THE WOODS?*

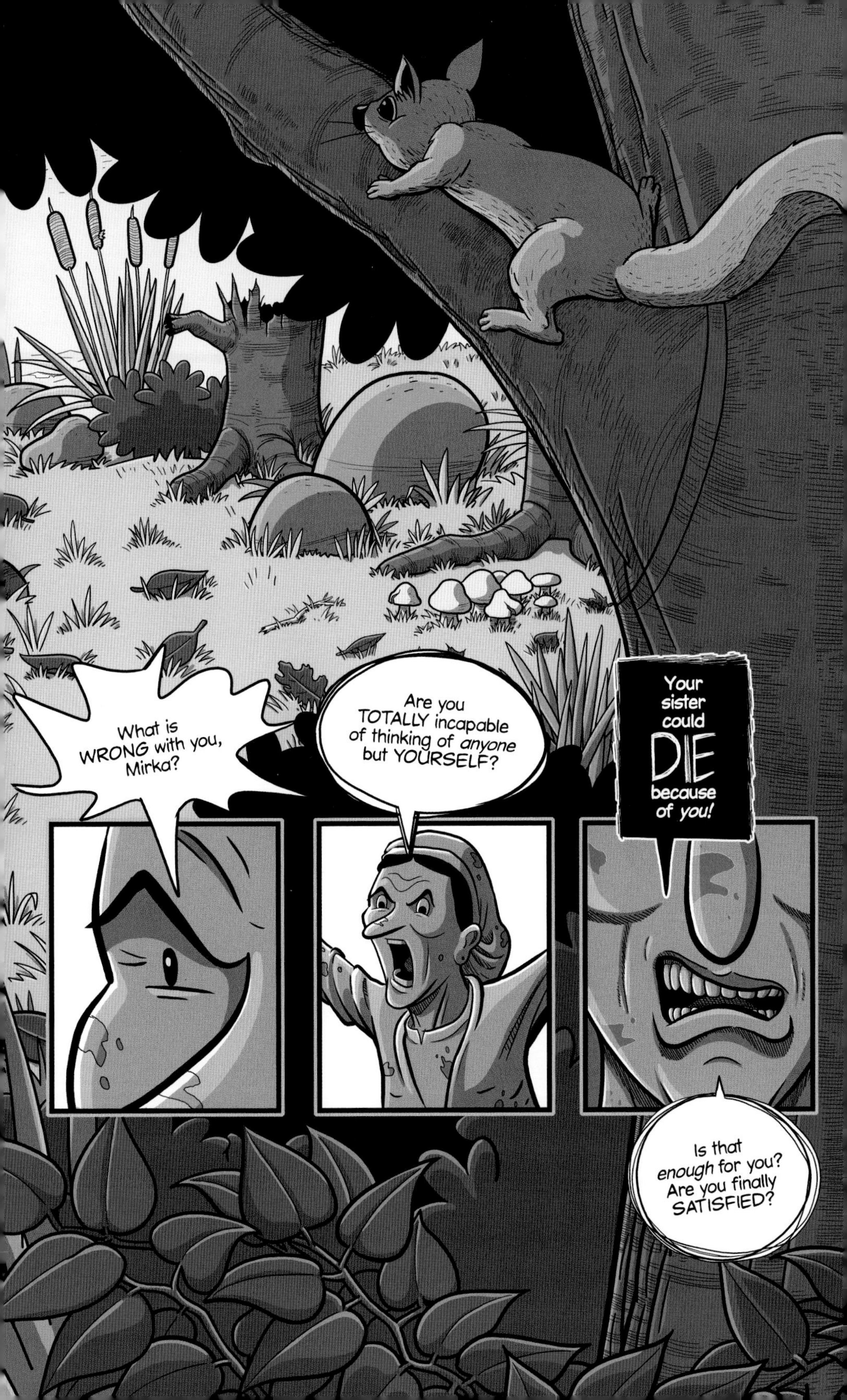
What is WRONG with you, Mirka?
Are you TOTALLY incapable of thinking of *anyone* but YOURSELF?
Your sister could DIE because of *you!*
Is that *enough* for you? Are you finally SATISFIED?

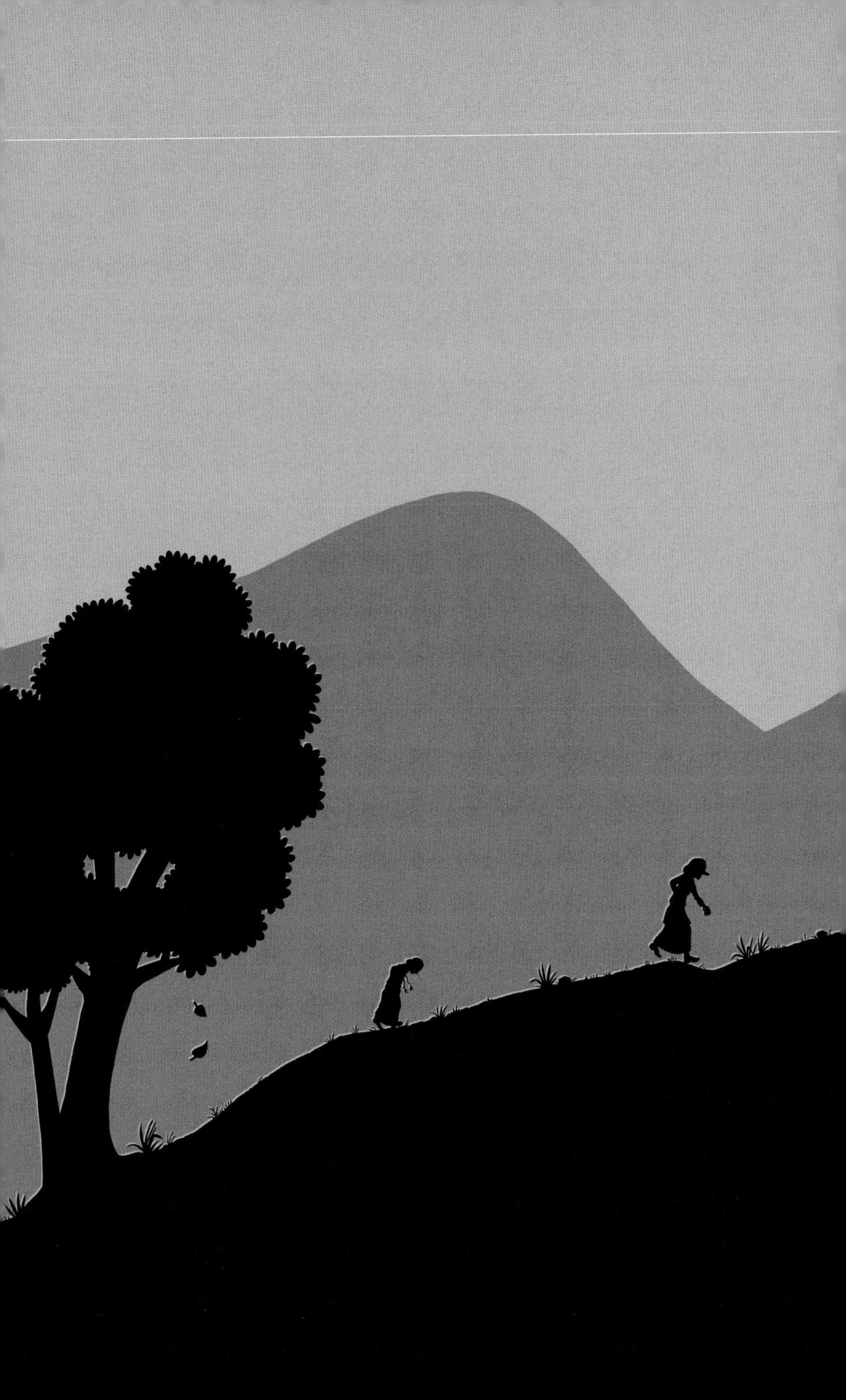

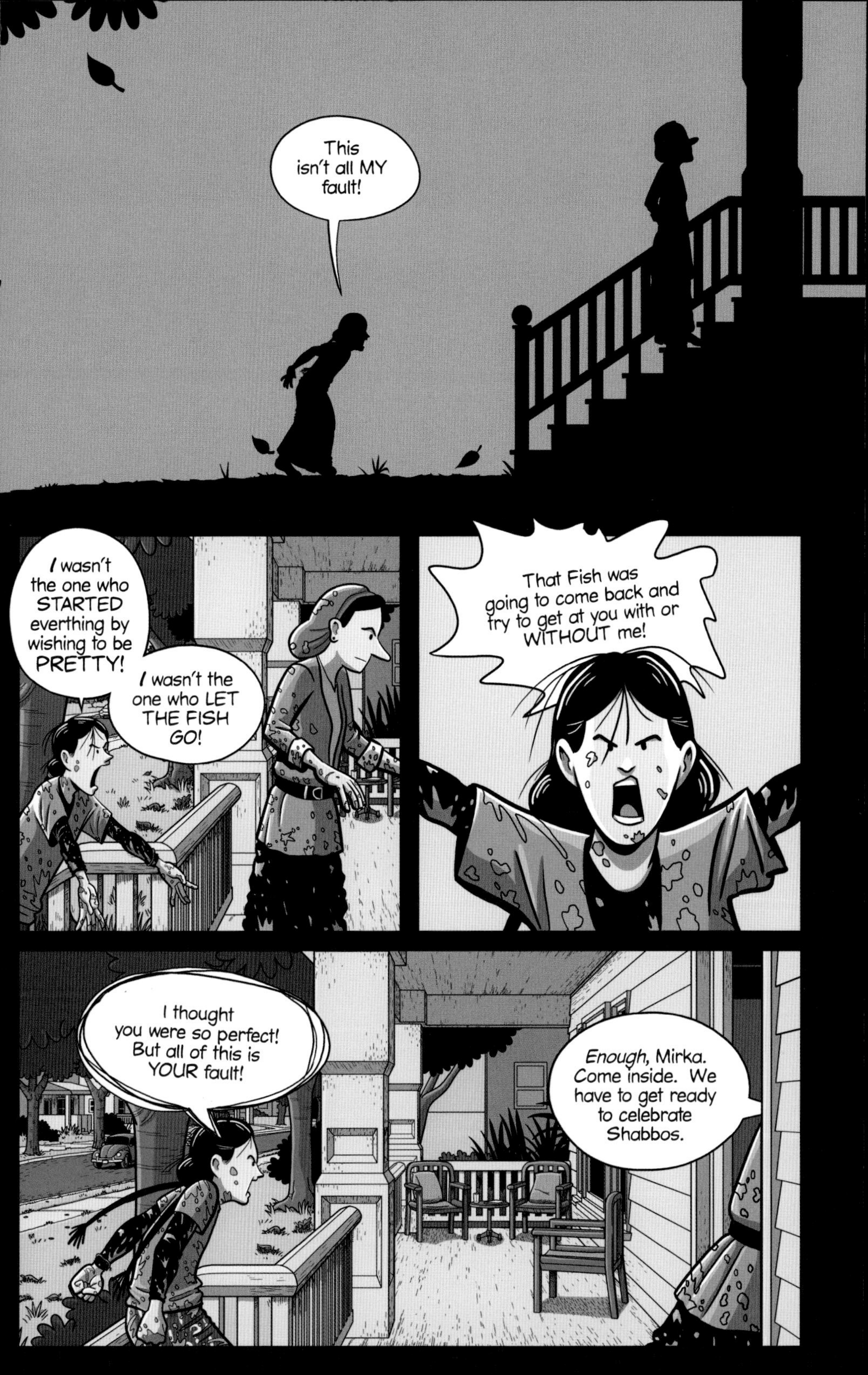

This isn't all MY fault!
I wasn't the one who STARTED everthing by wishing to be PRETTY!
I wasn't the one who LET THE FISH GO!
That Fish was going to come back and try to get at you with or WITHOUT me!
I thought you were so perfect! But all of this is YOUR fault!
Enough, Mirka. Come inside. We have to get ready to celebrate Shabbos.

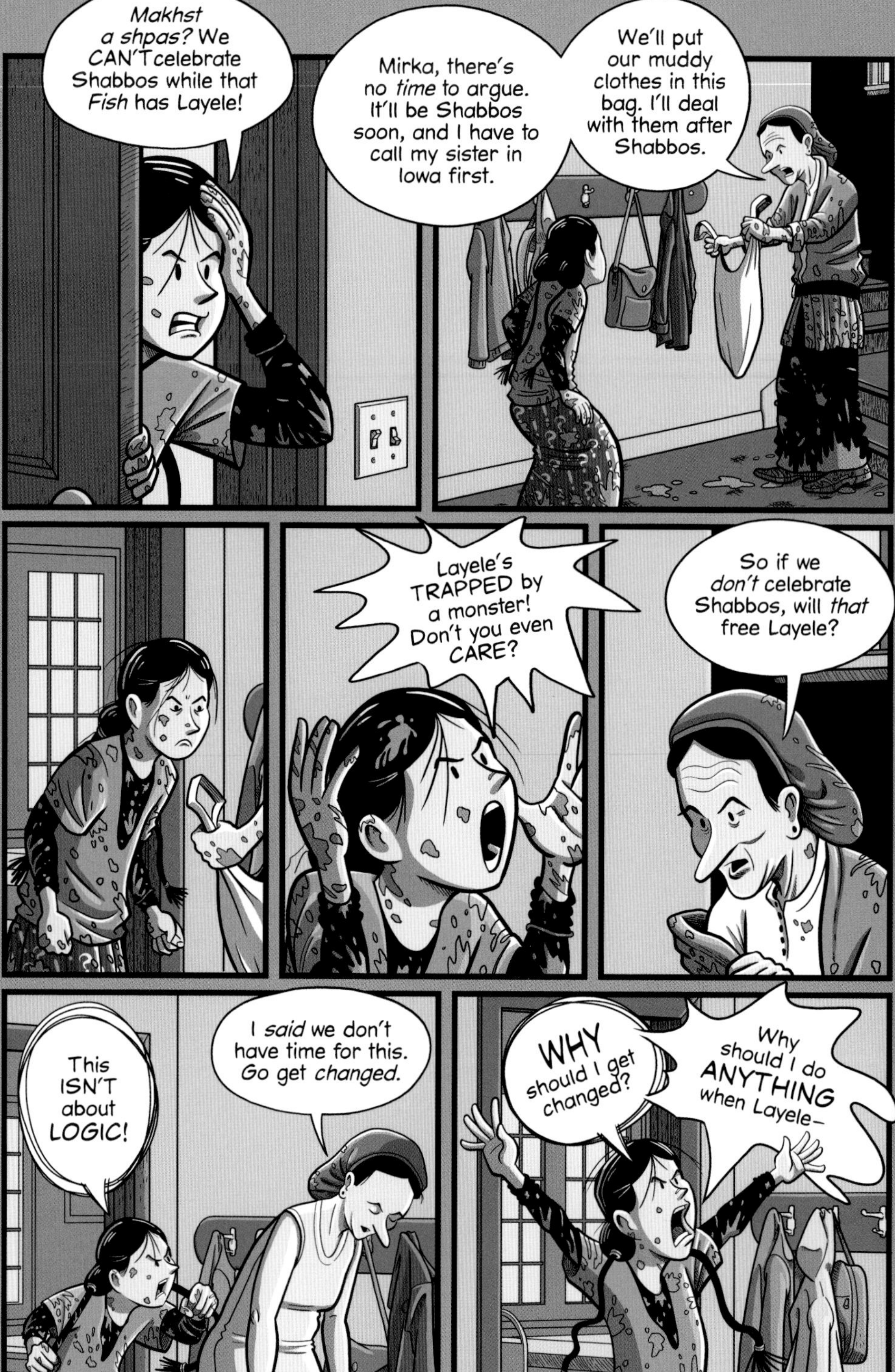
Makhst a shpas? We CAN'T celebrate Shabbos while that *Fish* has Layele!
Mirka, there's no *time* to argue. It'll be Shabbos soon, and I have to call my sister in Iowa first.
We'll put our muddy clothes in this bag. I'll deal with them after Shabbos.
Layele's TRAPPED by a monster! Don't you even CARE?
So if we *don't* celebrate Shabbos, will *that* free Layele?
This ISN'T about LOGIC!
I *said* we don't have time for this. Go get *changed*.
WHY should I get changed?
Why should I do ANYTHING when Layele–

Makhst a shpas?: Are you kidding?

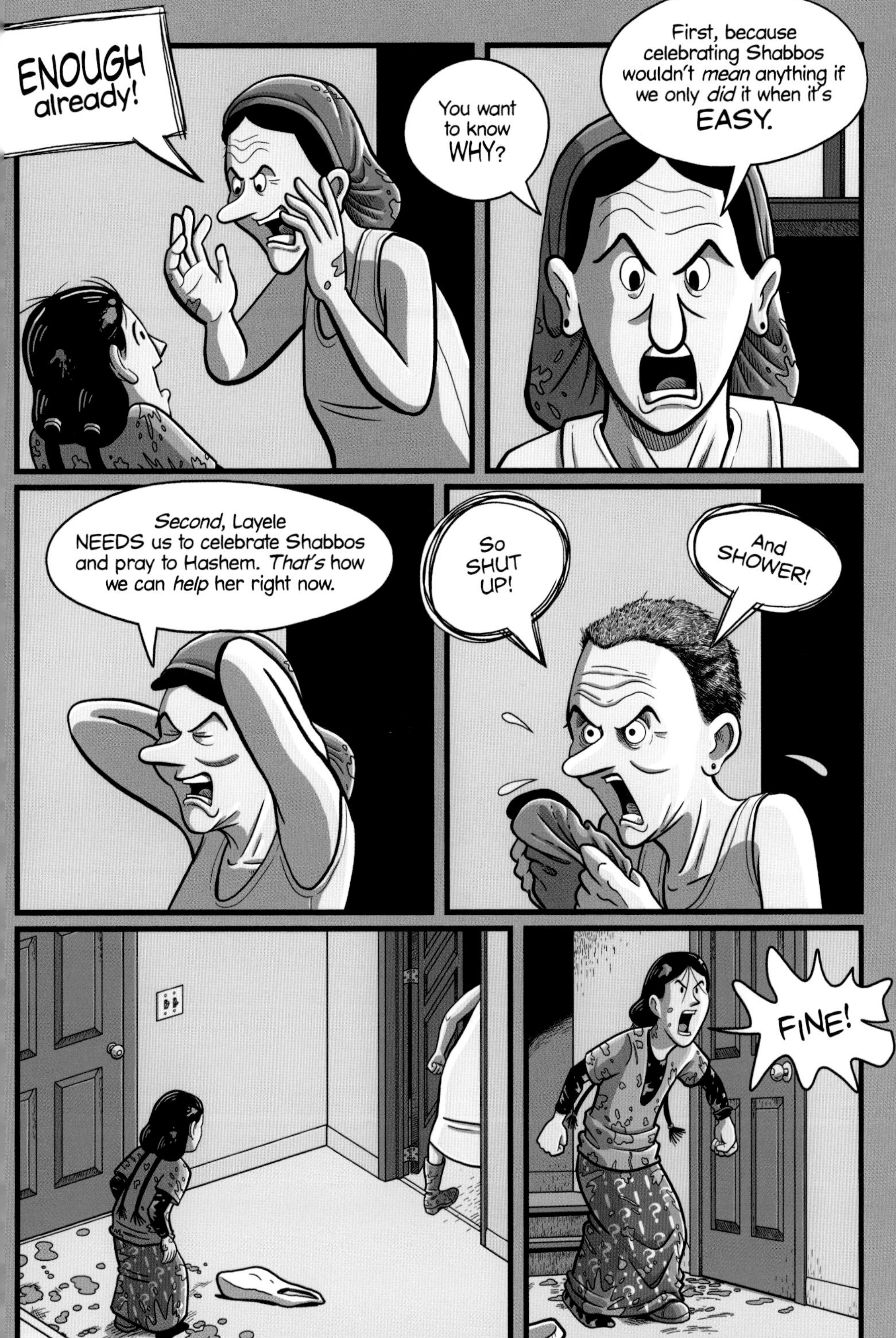
ENOUGH already!
You want to know WHY?
First, because celebrating Shabbos wouldn't *mean* anything if we only *did* it when it's EASY.
Second, Layele NEEDS us to celebrate Shabbos and pray to Hashem. *That's* how we can *help* her right now.
So SHUT UP!
And SHOWER!
FINE!

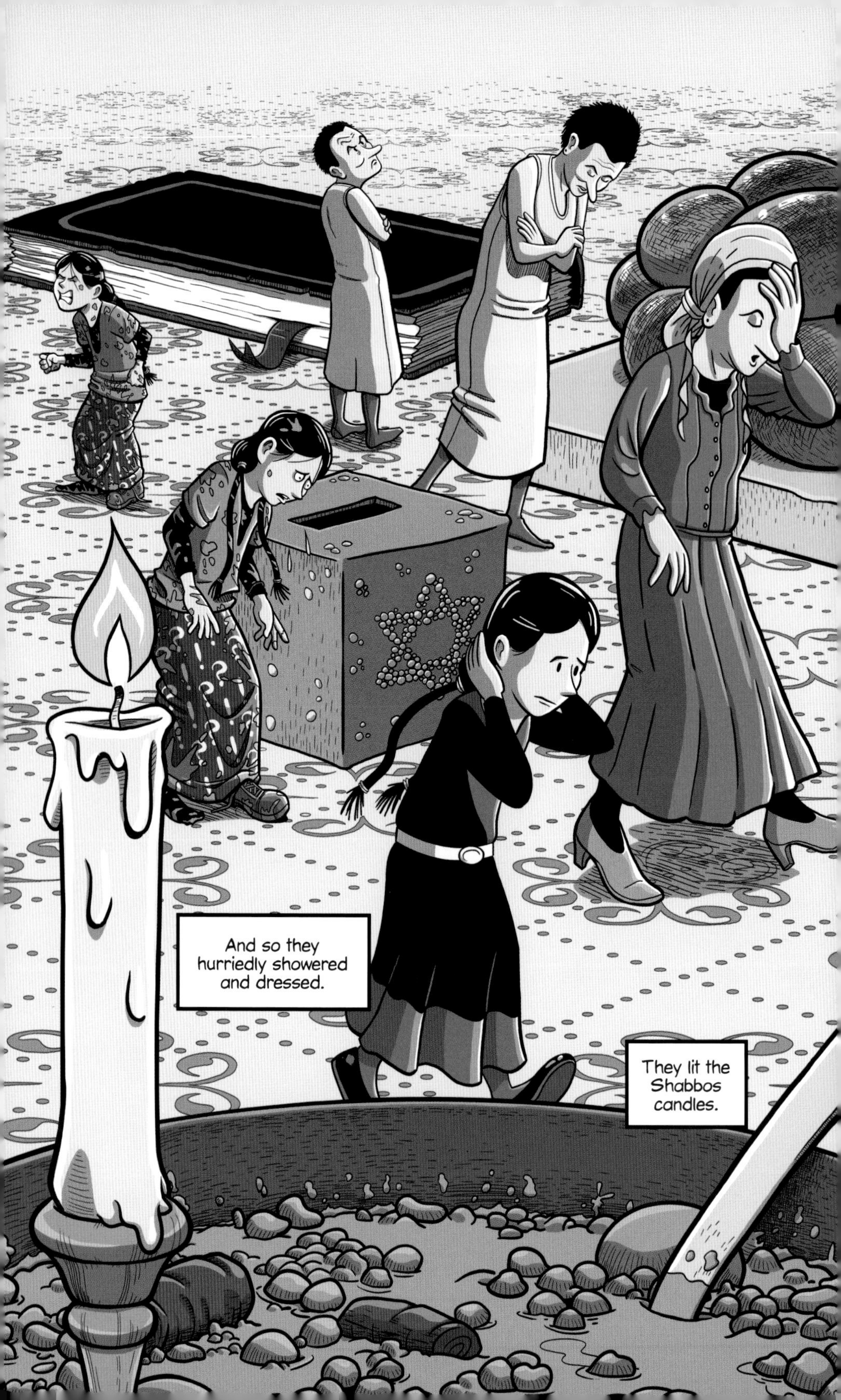
And so they hurriedly showered and dressed.
They lit the Shabbos candles.

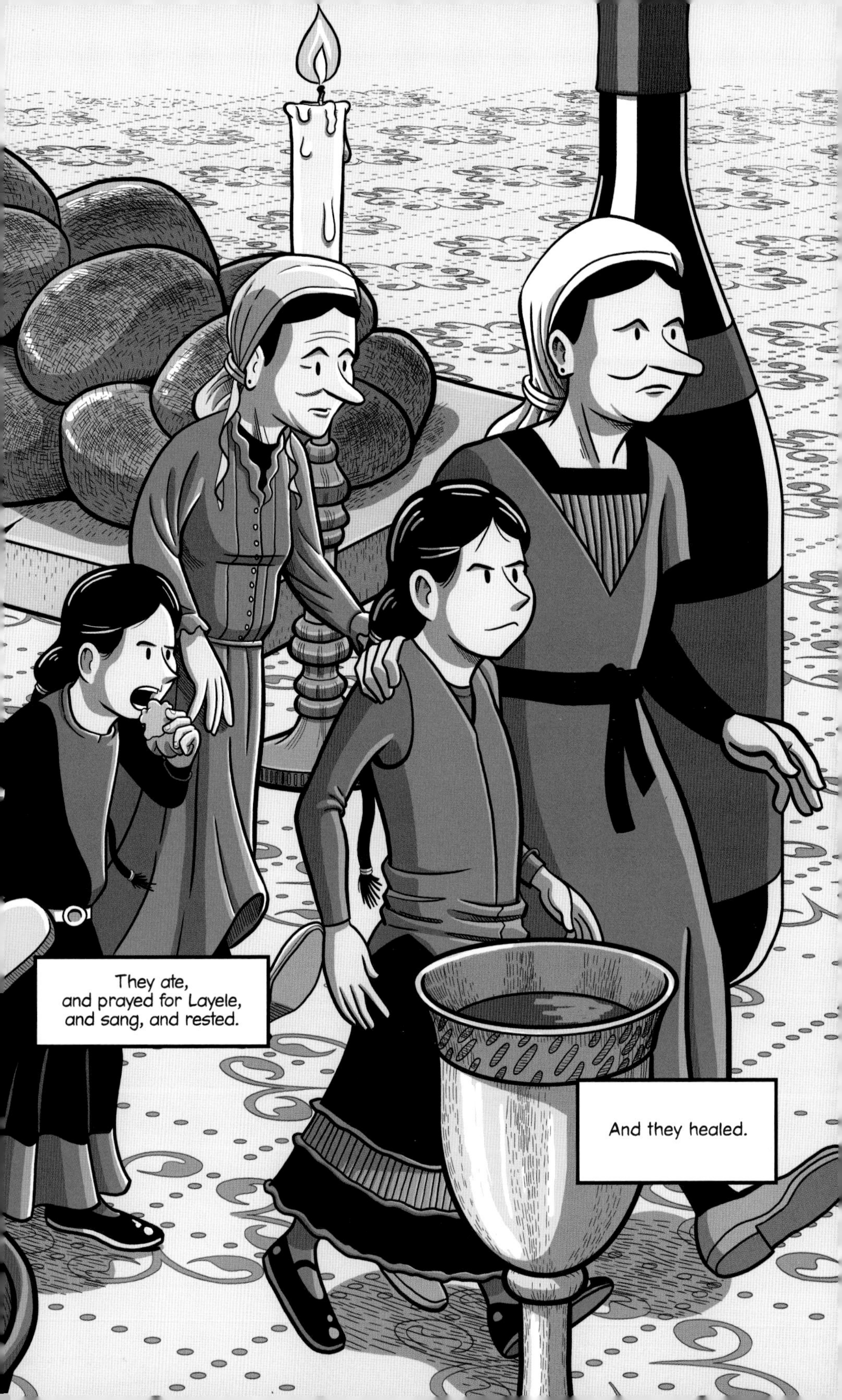
They ate,
and prayed for Layele,
and sang, and rested.
And they healed.

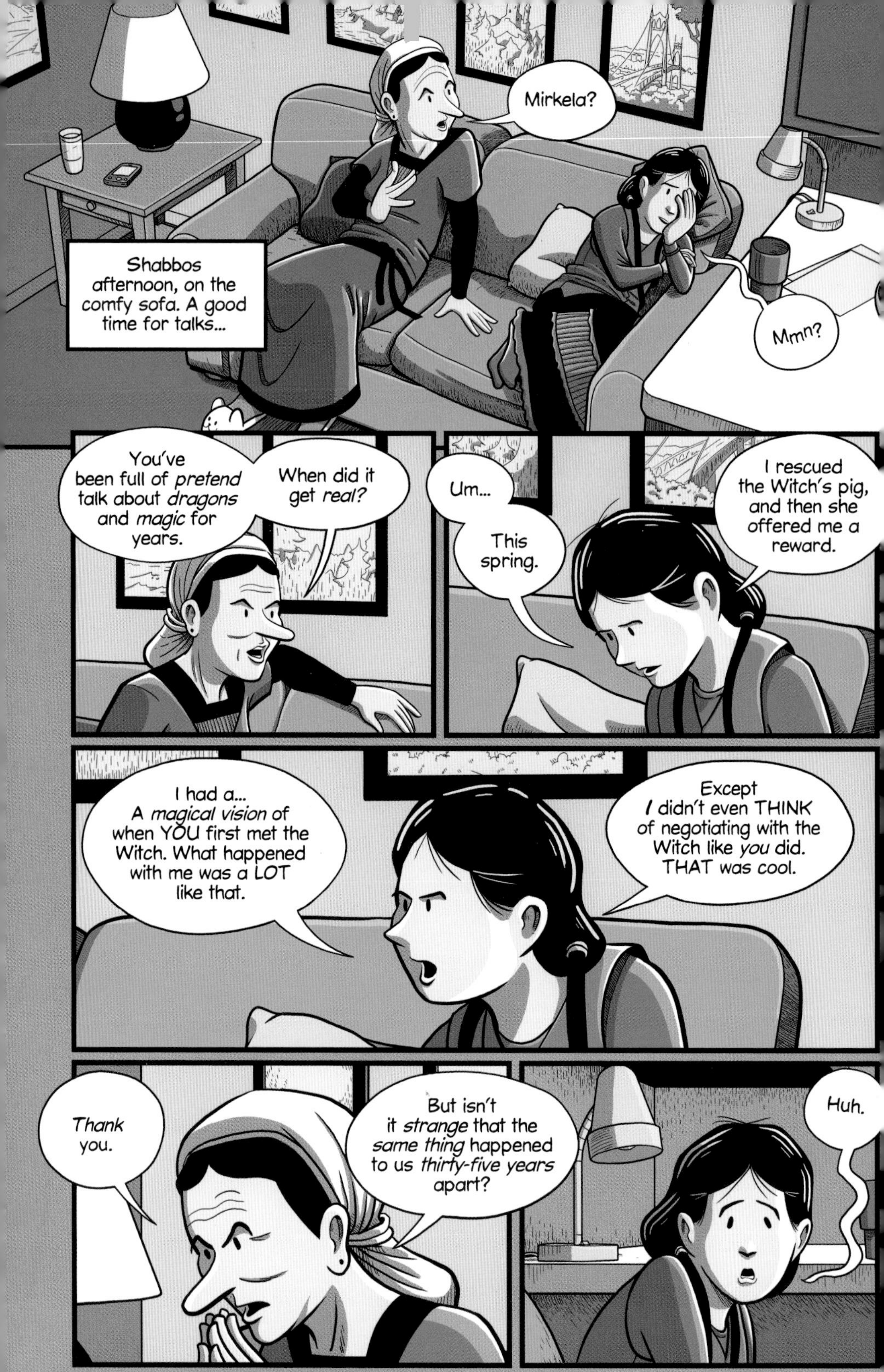

Mirkela?
Shabbos afternoon, on the comfy sofa. A good time for talks...
Mmn?
You've been full of *pretend* talk about *dragons* and *magic* for years.
When did it get *real?*
Um...
This spring.
I rescued the Witch's pig, and then she offered me a reward.
I had a... A *magical vision* of when YOU first met the Witch. What happened with me was a LOT like that.
Except *I* didn't even THINK of negotiating with the Witch like *you* did. THAT was cool.
Thank you.
But isn't it *strange* that the *same thing* happened to us *thirty-five years* apart?
Huh.

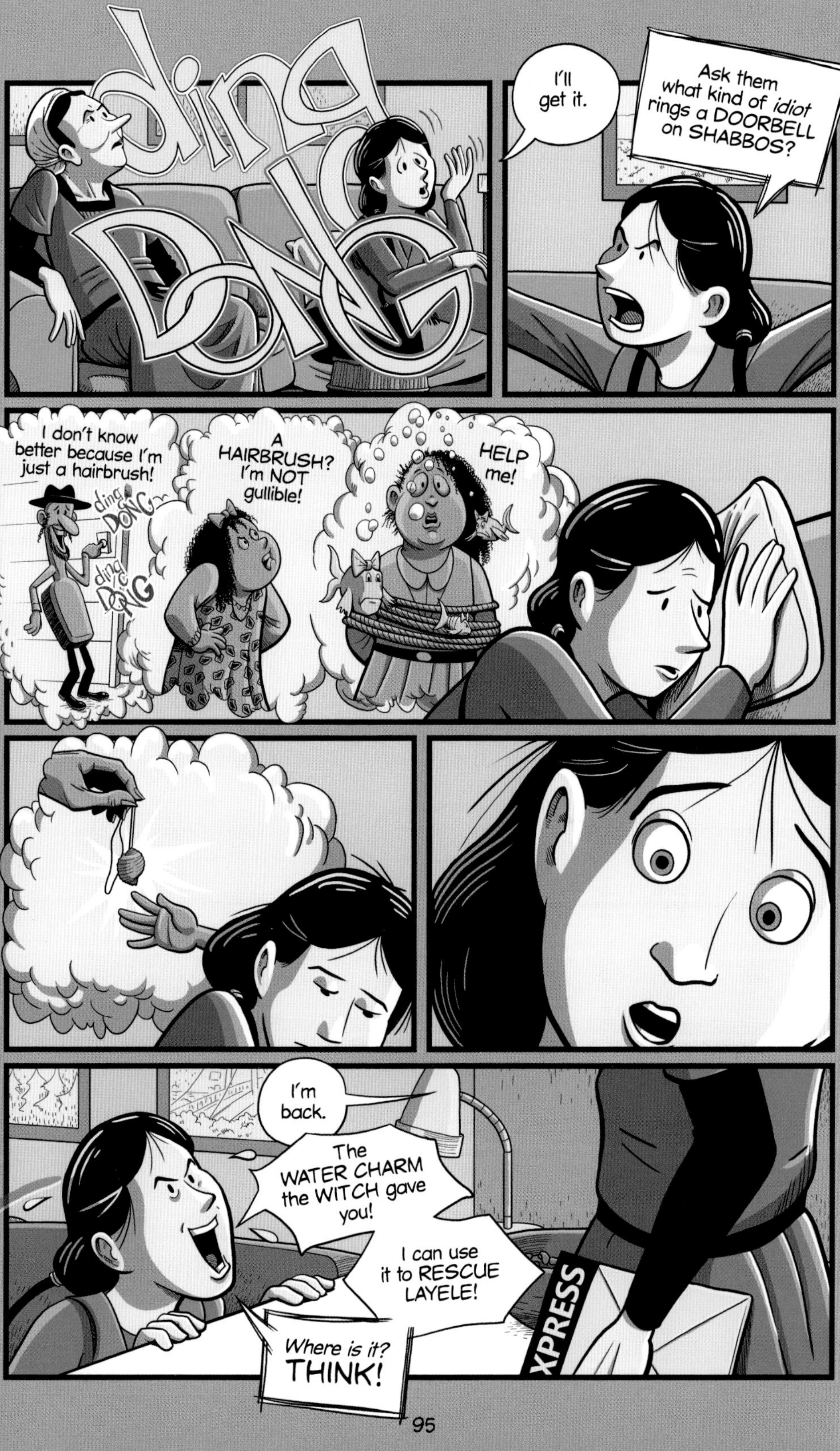
ding
DONG
I'll get it.
Ask them what kind of *idiot* rings a DOORBELL on SHABBOS?
I don't know better because I'm just a hairbrush!
ding DONG
ding DONG
A HAIRBRUSH? I'm NOT gullible!
HELP me!
I'm back.
The WATER CHARM the WITCH gave you!
I can use it to RESCUE LAYELE!
Where is it? THINK!
XPRESS

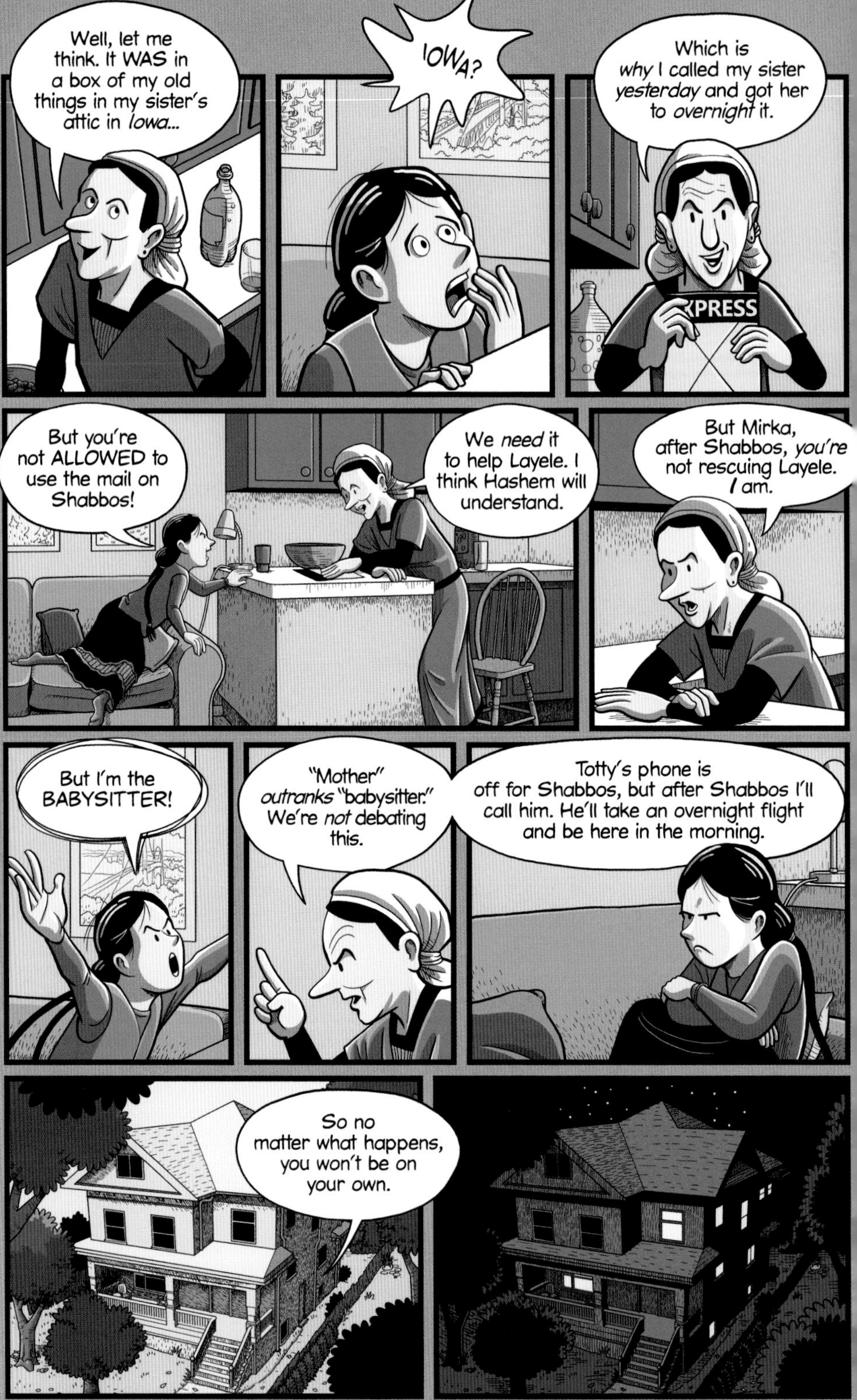
Well, let me think. It WAS in a box of my old things in my sister's attic in *Iowa*...
IOWA?
Which is *why* I called my sister *yesterday* and got her to *overnight* it.
XPRESS
But you're not ALLOWED to use the mail on Shabbos!
We *need* it to help Layele. I think Hashem will understand.
But Mirka, after Shabbos, *you're* not rescuing Layele. *I* am.
But I'm the BABYSITTER!
"Mother" *outranks* "babysitter." We're *not* debating this.
Totty's phone is off for Shabbos, but after Shabbos I'll call him. He'll take an overnight flight and be here in the morning.
So no matter what happens, you won't be on your own.

Totty: Dad

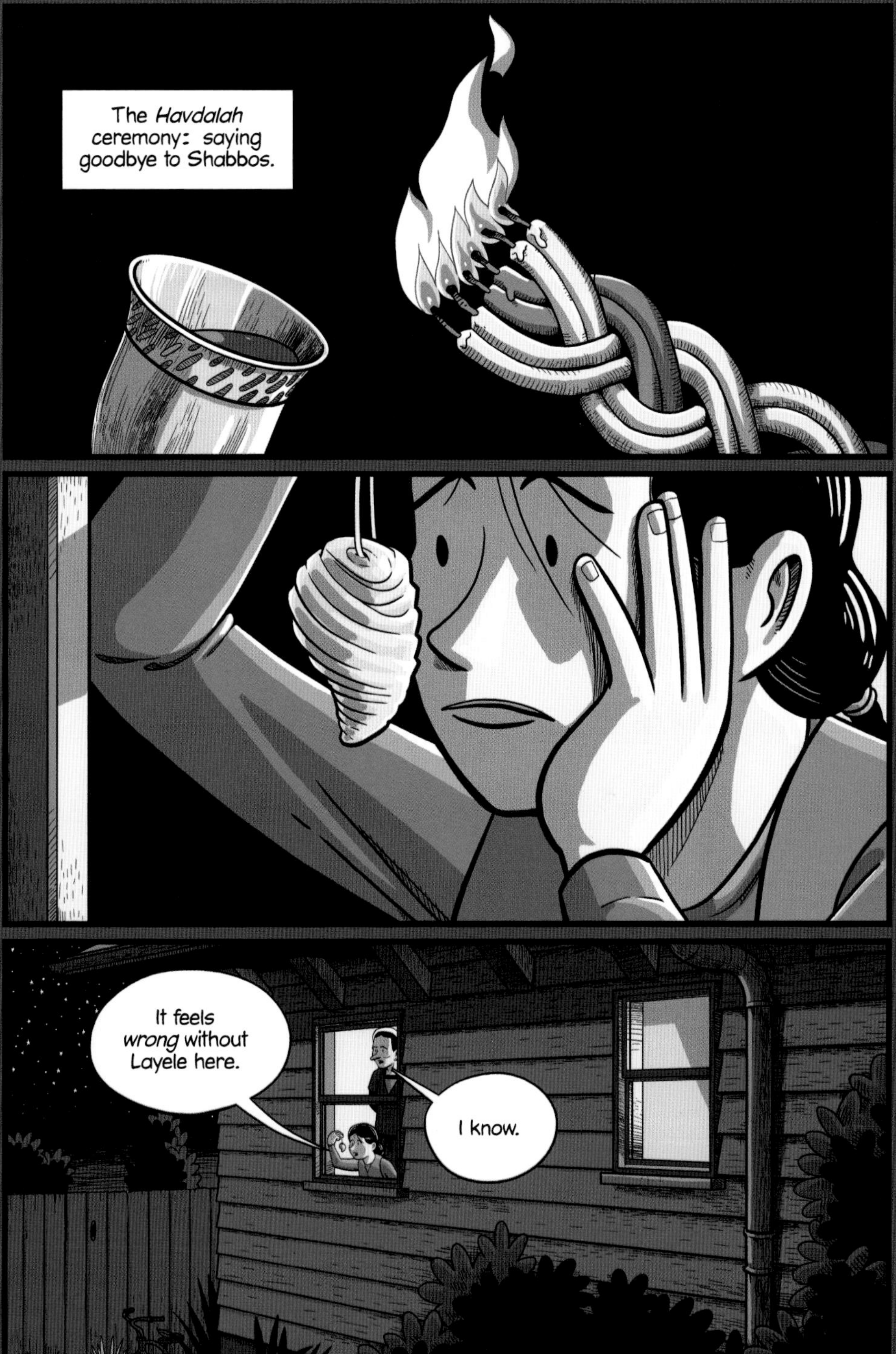
The *Havdalah* ceremony: saying goodbye to Shabbos.
It feels *wrong* without Layele here.
I know.

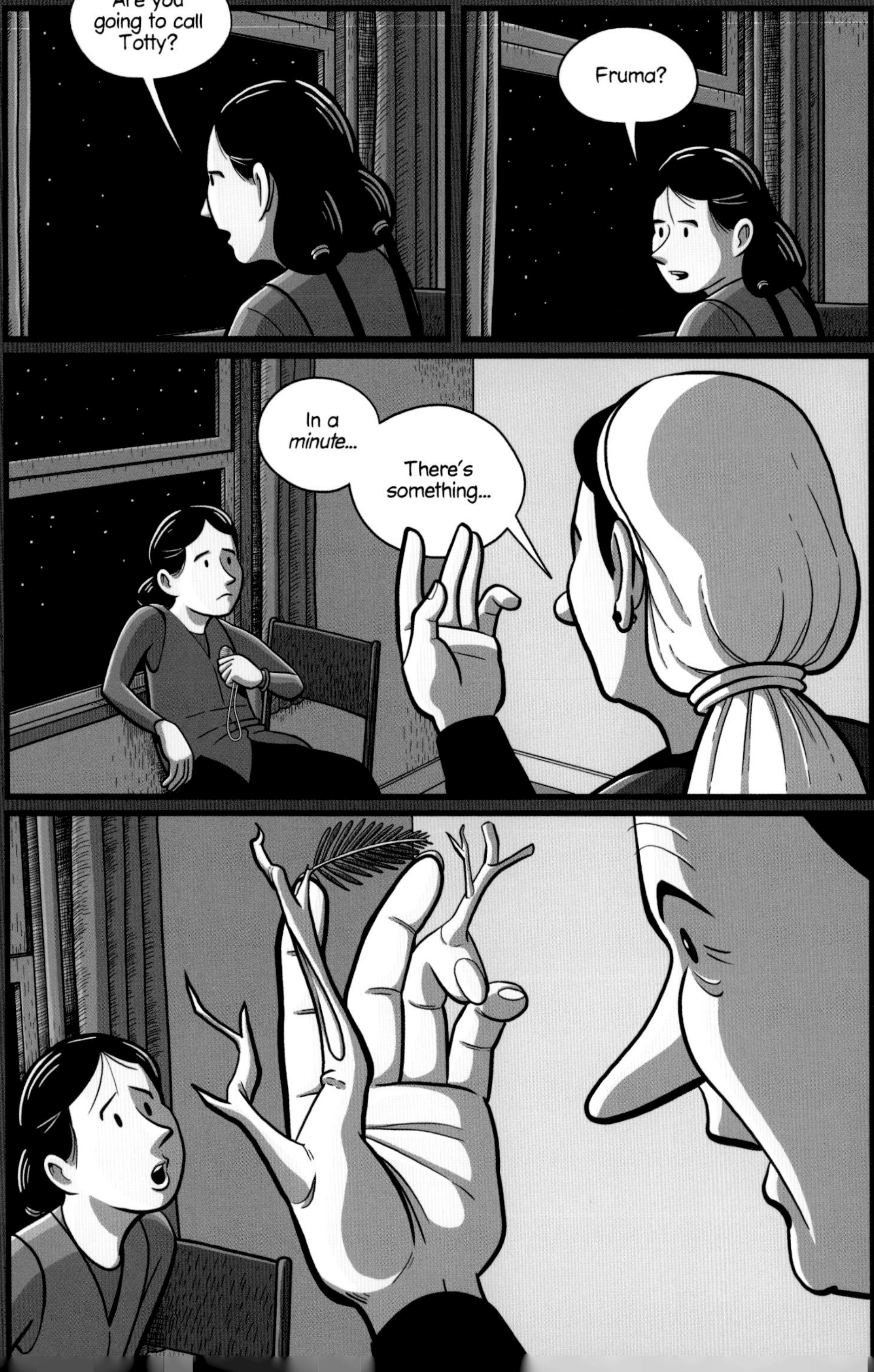
Are you going to call Totty?
Fruma?
In a *minute*...
There's something...

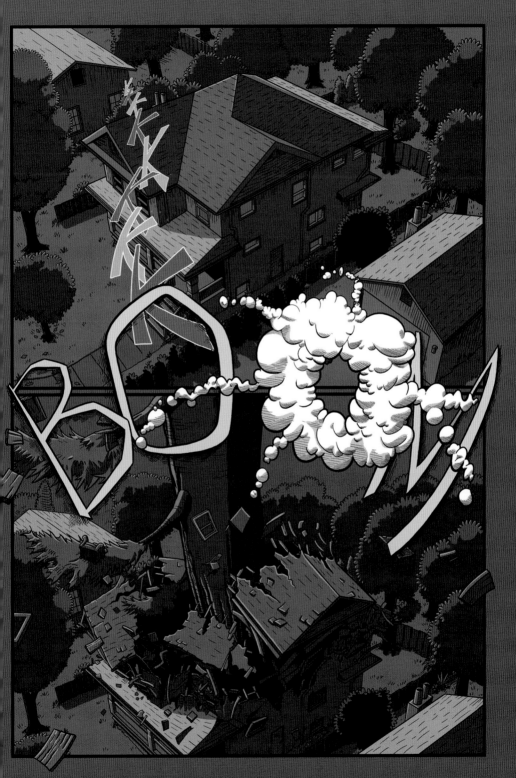

99

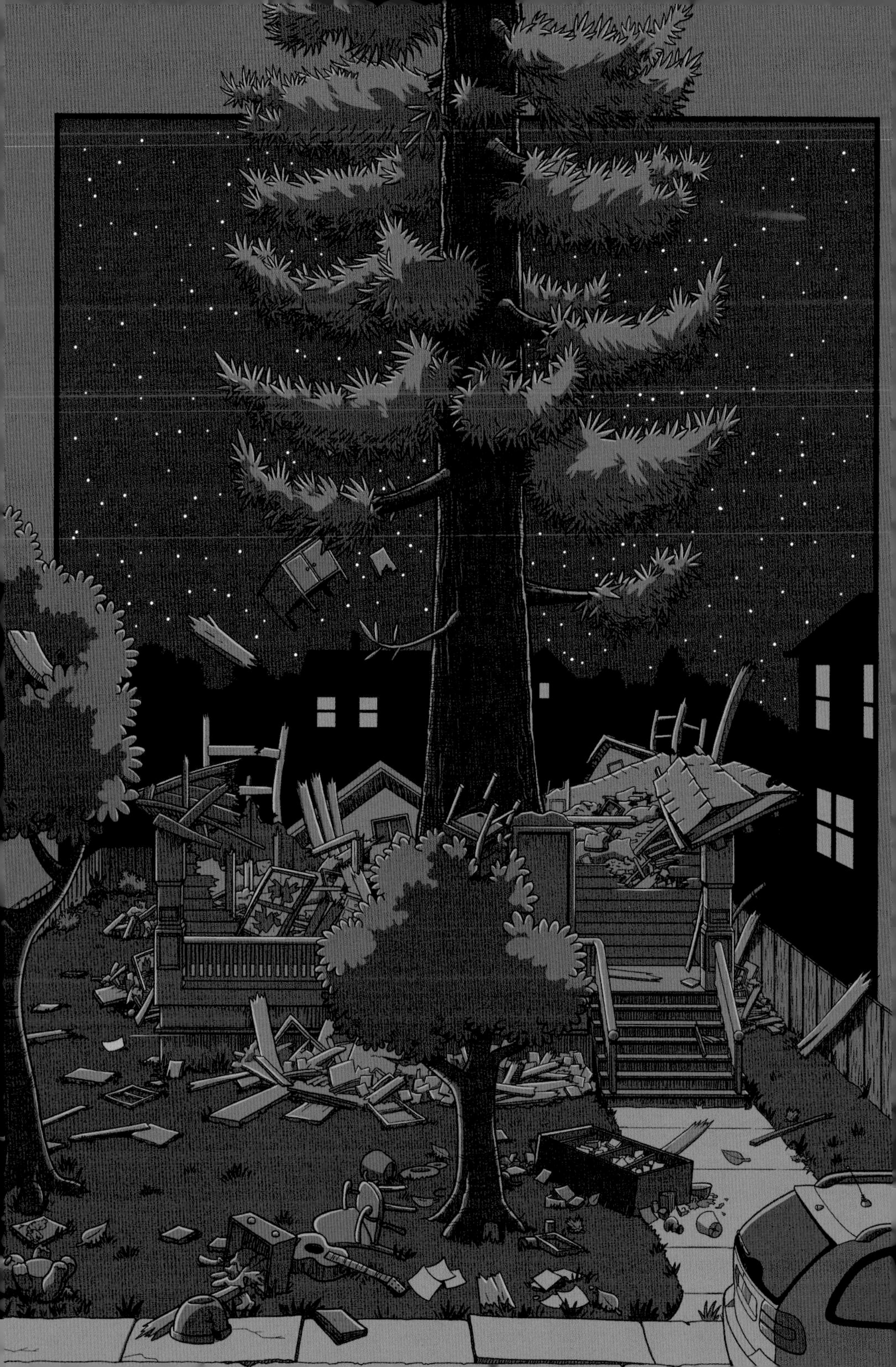

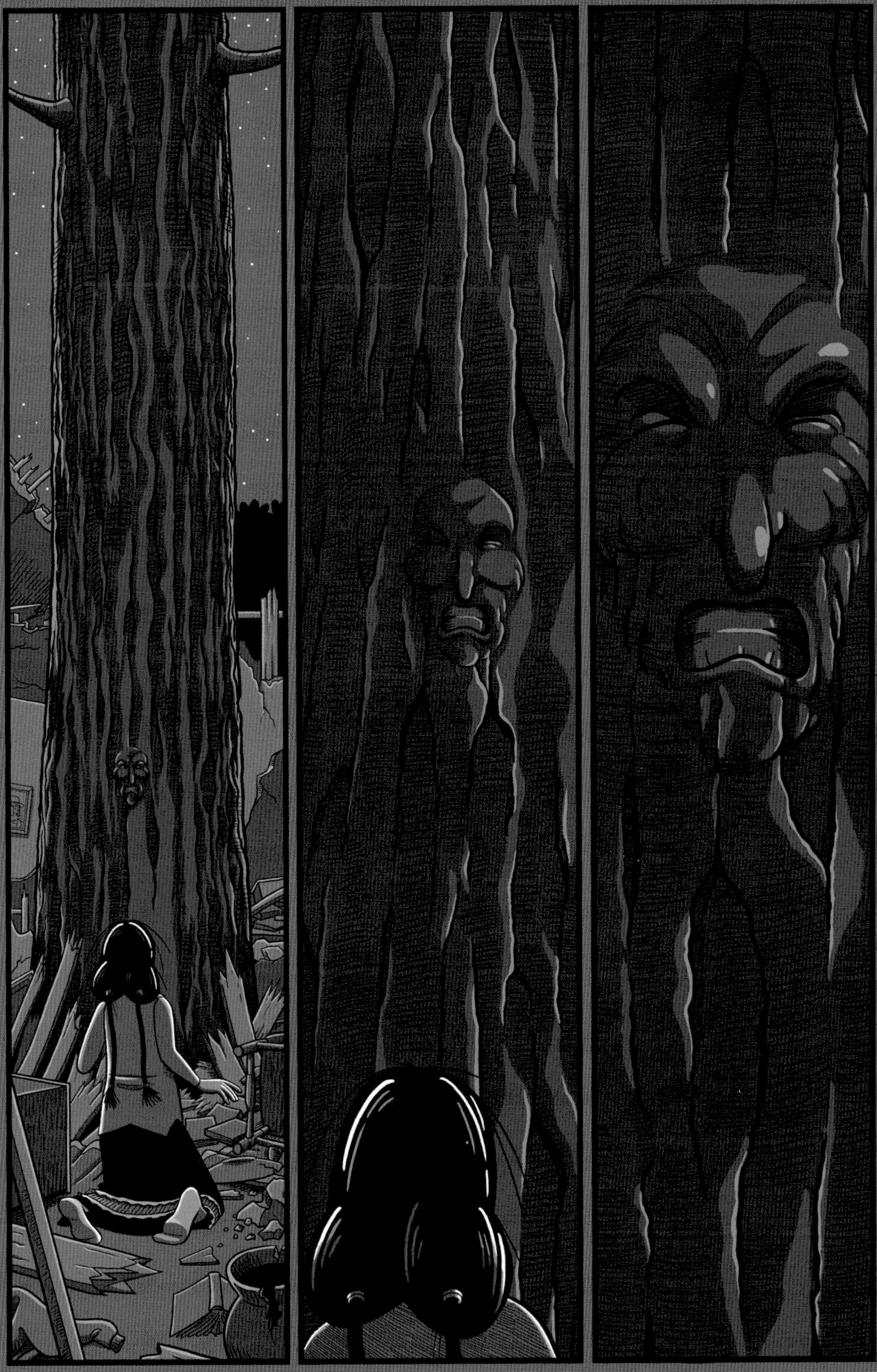

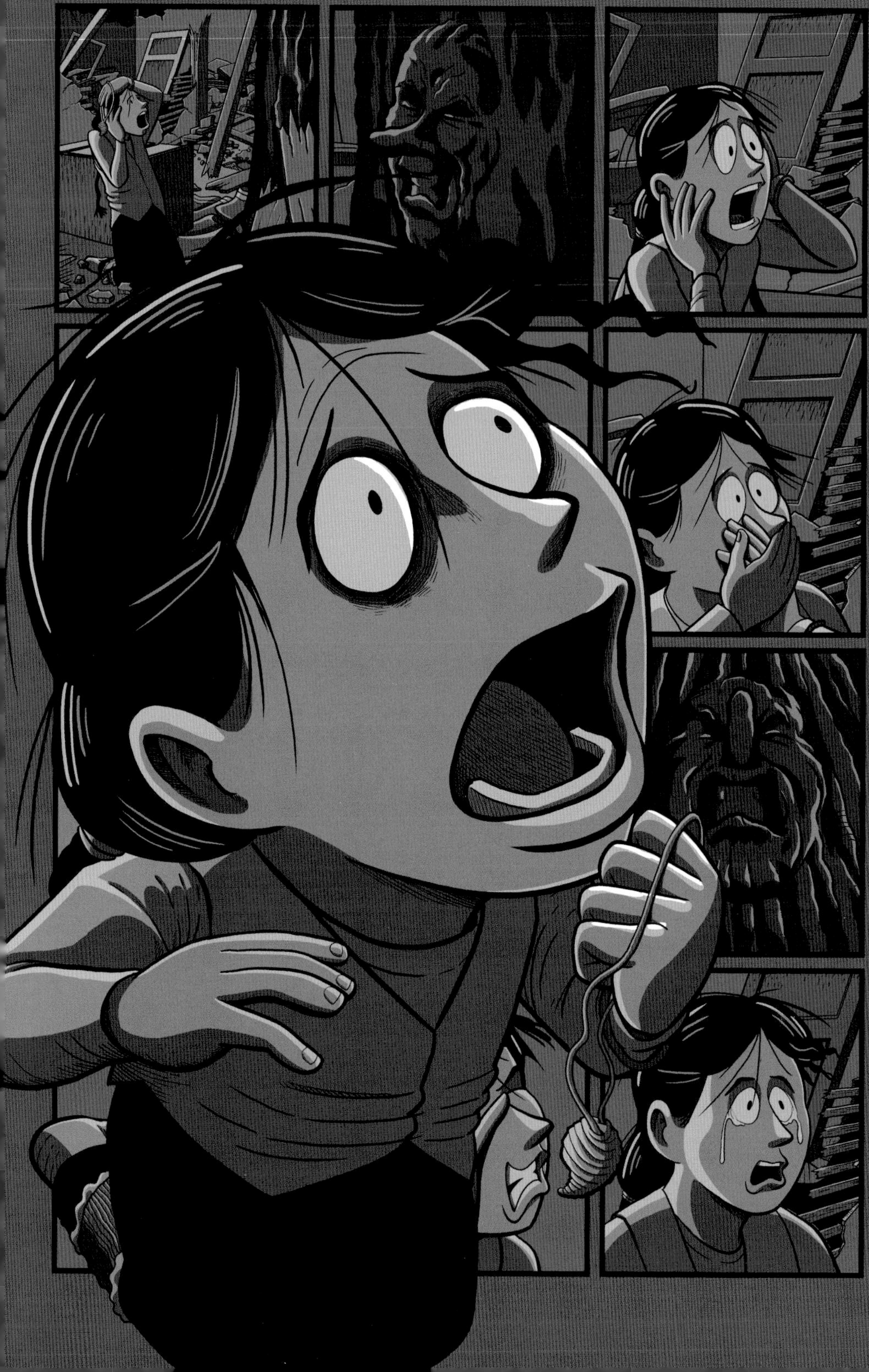

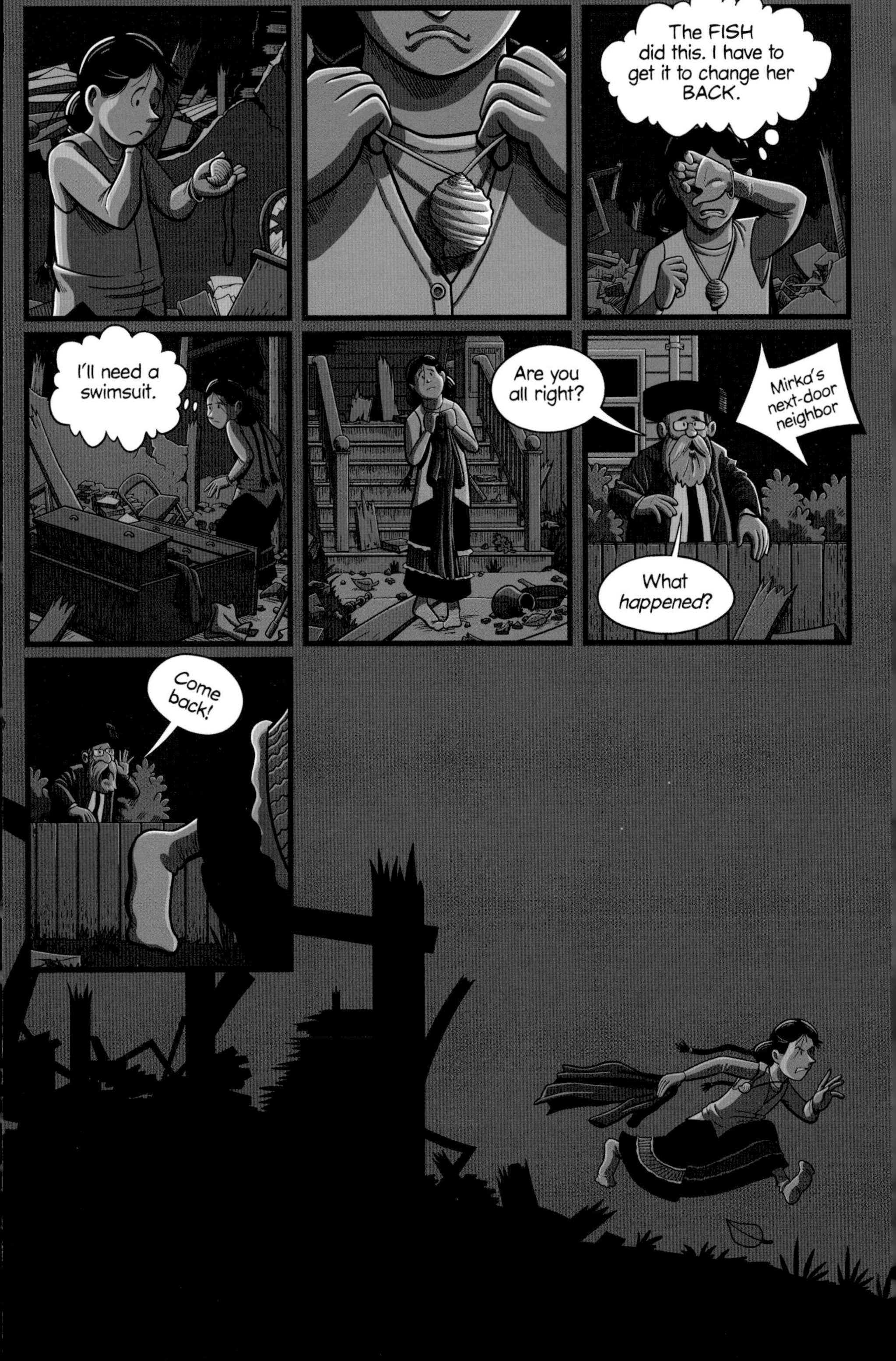

The FISH did this. I have to get it to change her BACK.
I'll need a swimsuit.
Are you all right?
Mirka's next-door neighbor
What happened?
Come back!

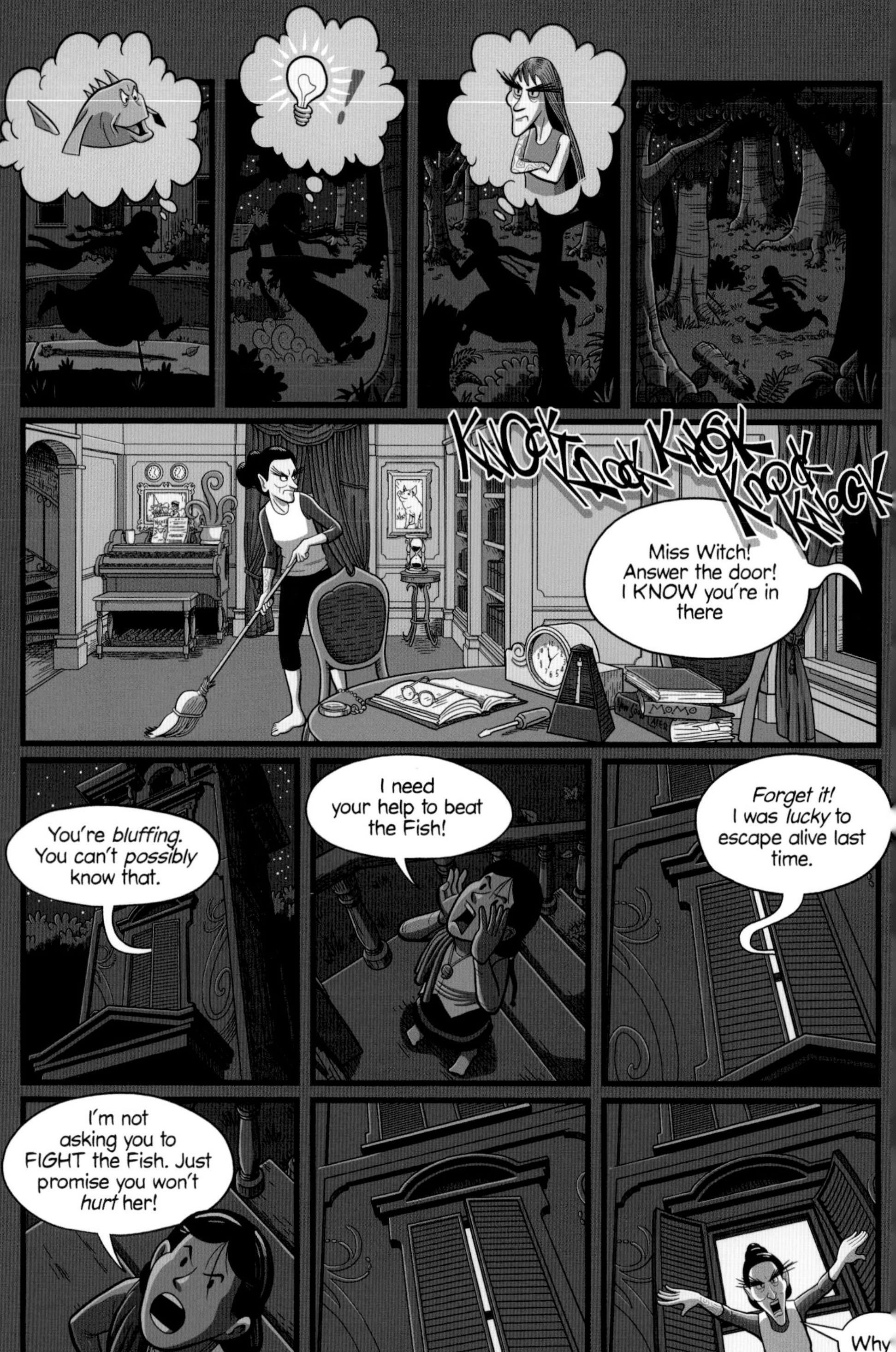
!
KNOCK KNOCK KNOCK KNOCK KNOCK KNOCK
Miss Witch! Answer the door! I KNOW you're in there
MOMO
You're *bluffing.* You can't *possibly* know that.
I need your help to beat the Fish!
Forget it! I was *lucky* to escape alive last time.
I'm not asking you to FIGHT the Fish. Just promise you won't *hurt* her!
Why

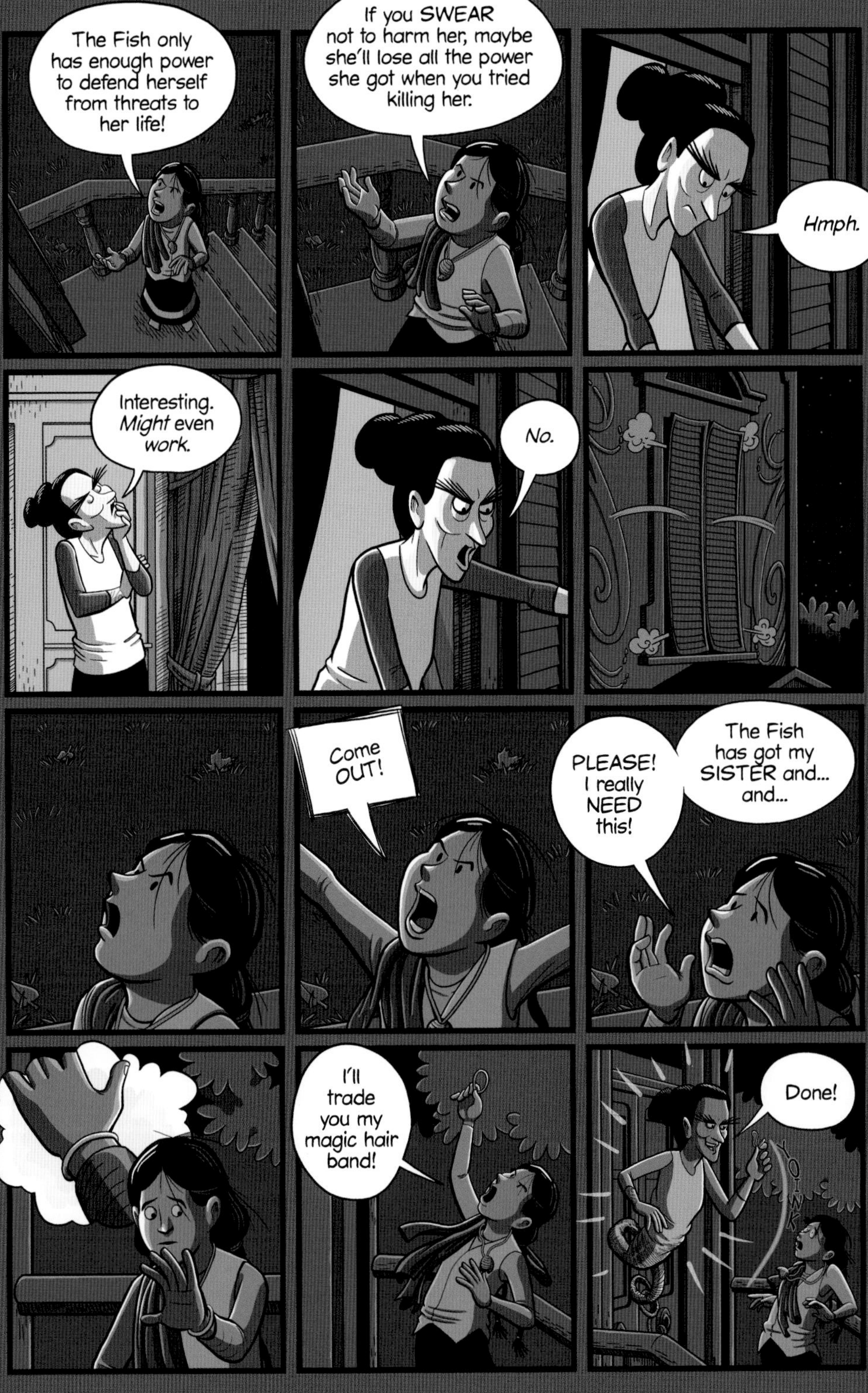

The Fish only has enough power to defend herself from threats to her life!
If you SWEAR not to harm her, maybe she'll lose all the power she got when you tried killing her.
Hmph.
Interesting. Might even work.
No.
Come OUT!
PLEASE! I really NEED this!
The Fish has got my SISTER and... and...
I'll trade you my magic hair band!
Done!
YOINK

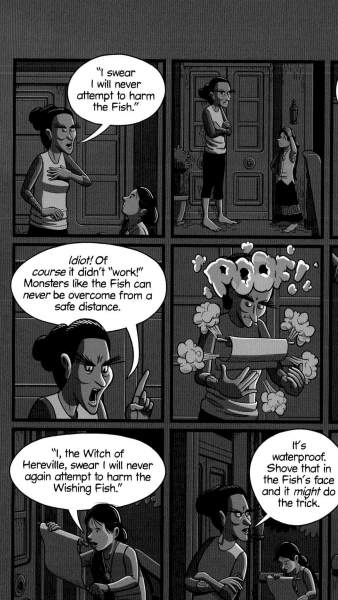

"I swear I will never attempt to harm the Fish."

Did it work?

Idiot! Of *course* it didn't "work!" Monsters like the Fish can *never* be overcome from a safe distance.

POOF!

Here.

"I, the Witch of Hereville, swear I will never again attempt to harm the Wishing Fish."

It's waterproof. Shove that in the Fish's face and it *might* do the trick.

No guarantees.

Thank you, ma'am.

Why are *you* still here?

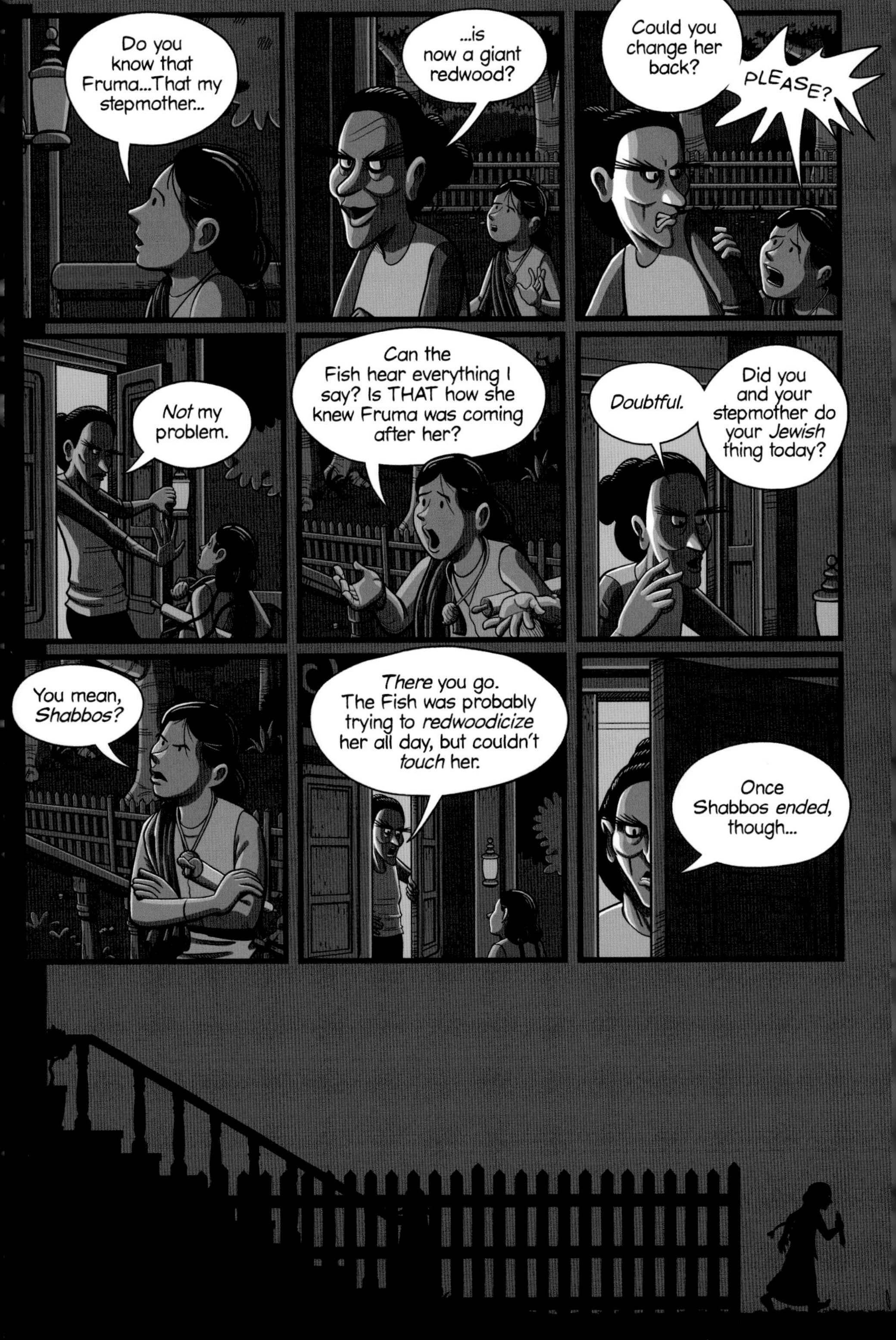
Do you know that Fruma...That my stepmother...
...is now a giant redwood?
Could you change her back?
PLEASE?
Not my problem.
Can the Fish hear everything I say? Is THAT how she knew Fruma was coming after her?
Doubtful.
Did you and your stepmother do your *Jewish* thing today?
You mean, *Shabbos?*
There you go. The Fish was probably trying to *redwoodicize* her all day, but couldn't *touch* her.
Once Shabbos *ended,* though...

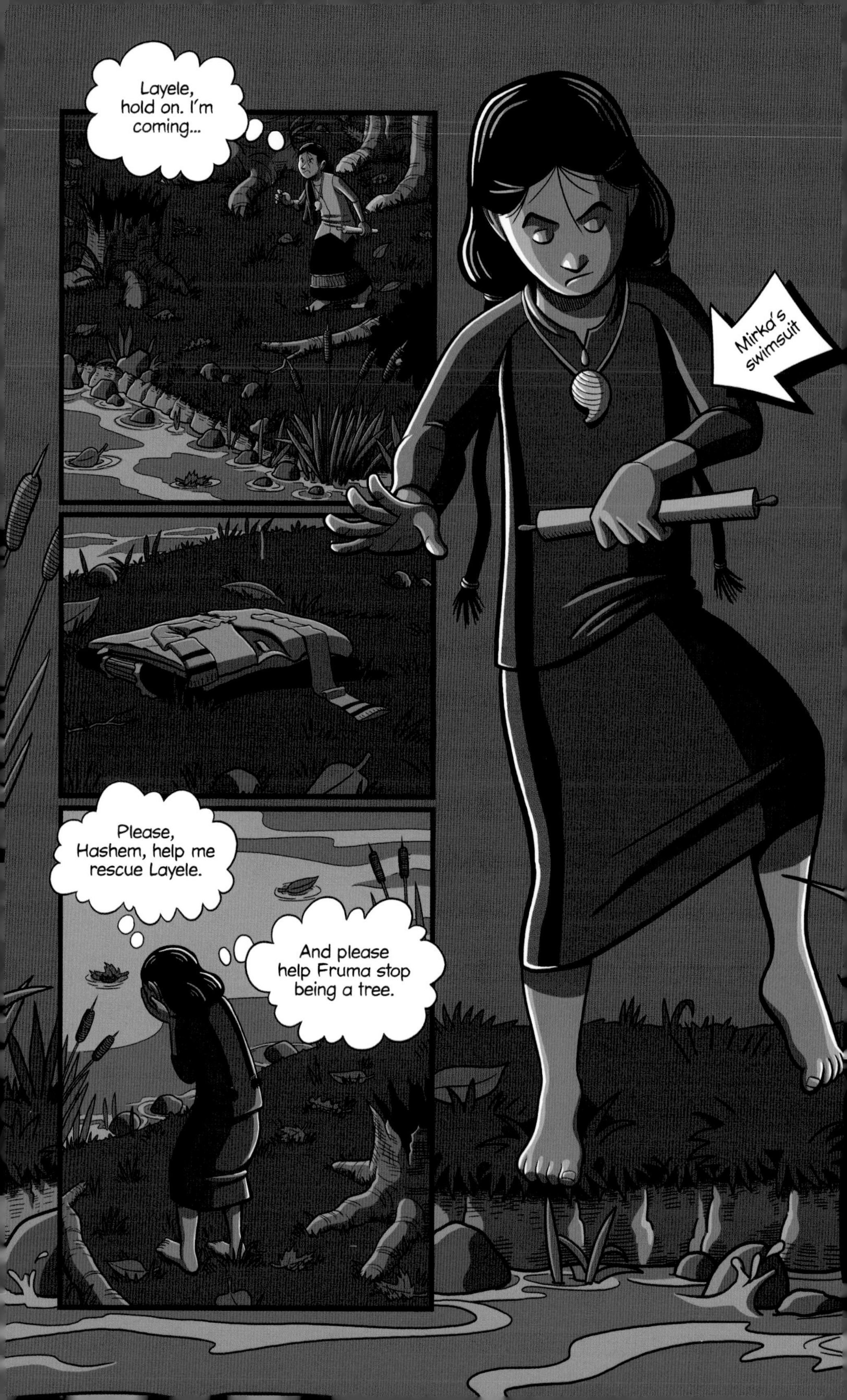
Layele, hold on. I'm coming...
Mirka's swimsuit
Please, Hashem, help me rescue Layele.
And please help Fruma stop being a tree.

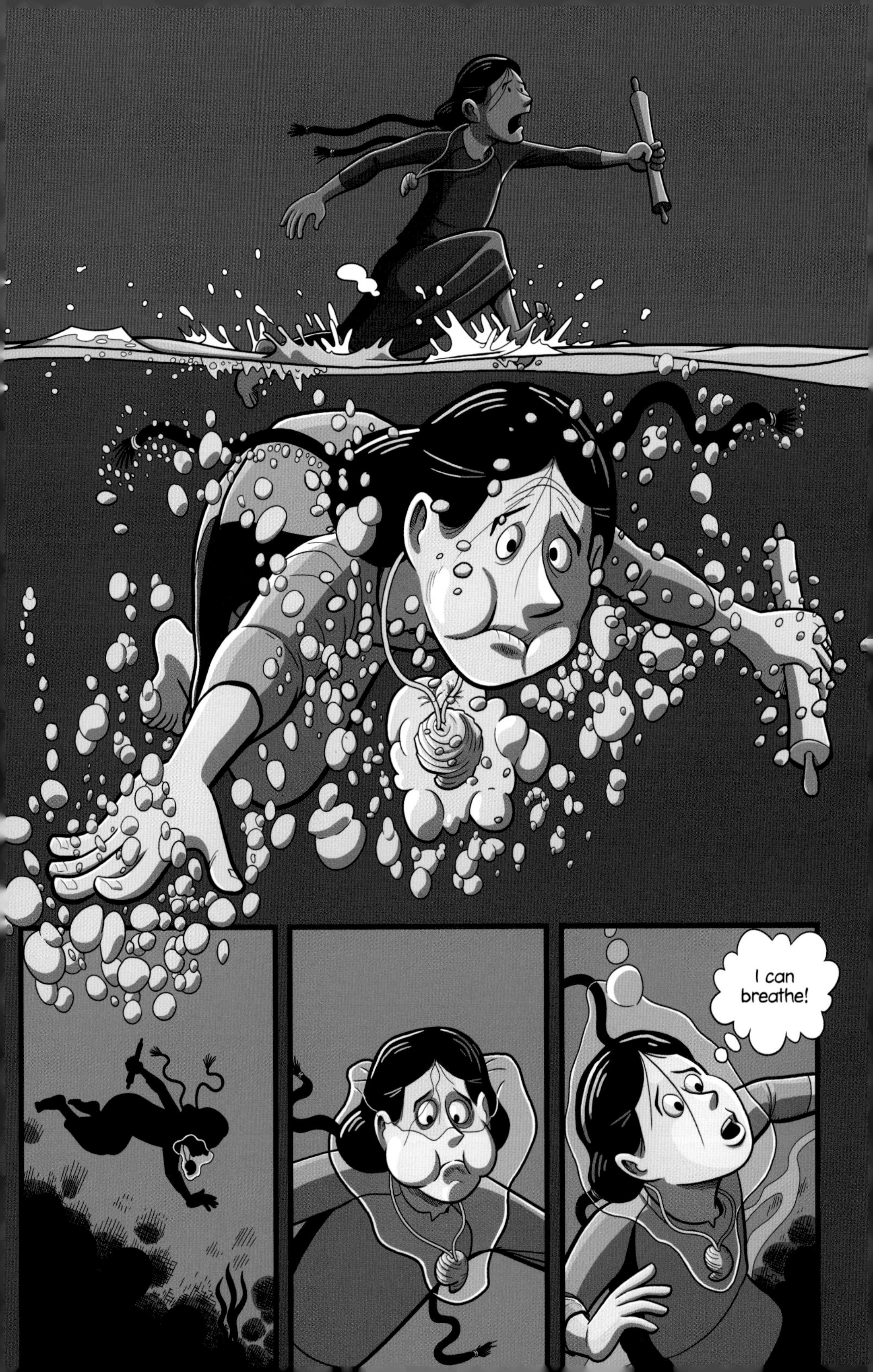
I can
breathe!

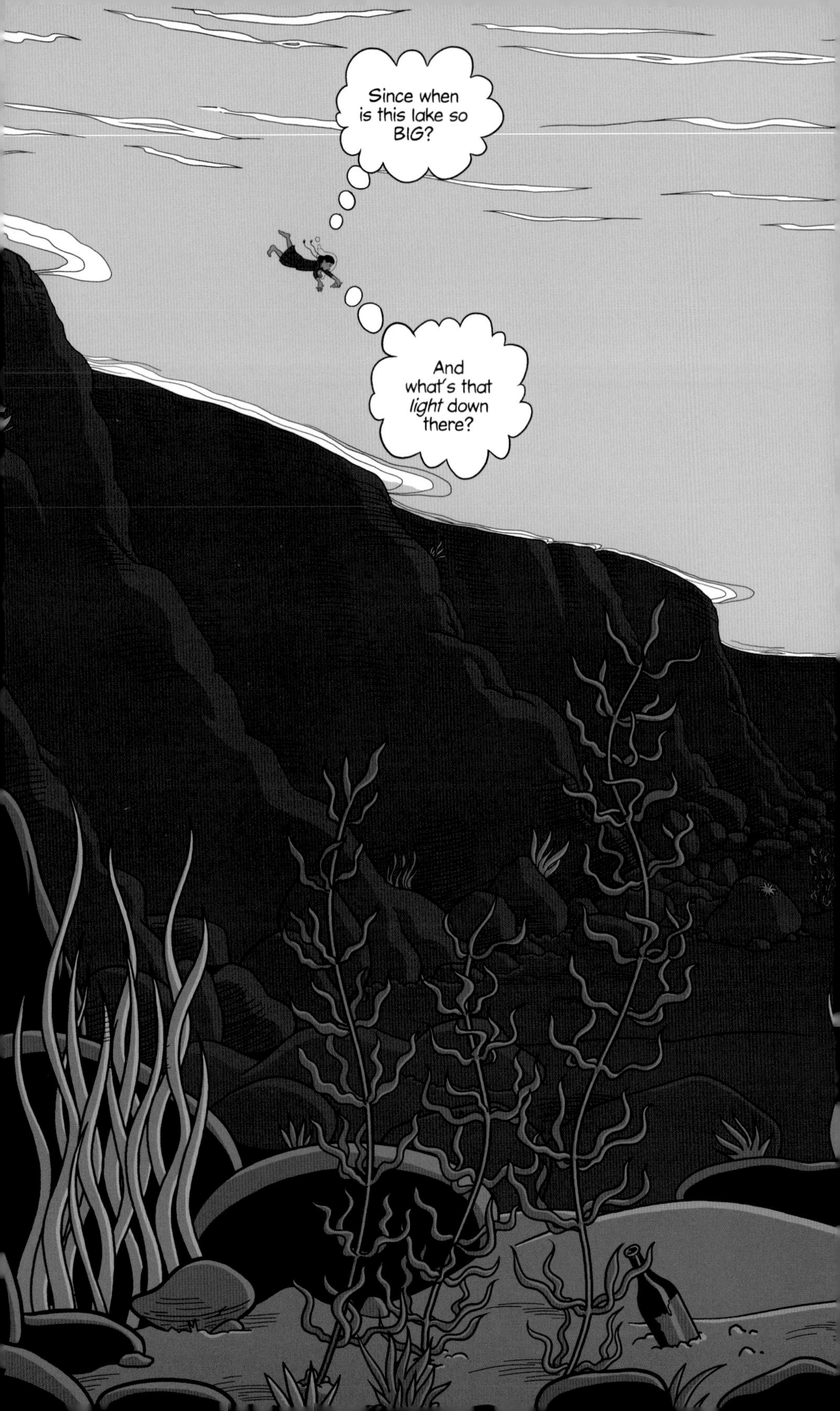
Since when is this lake so BIG?
And what's that *light* down there?

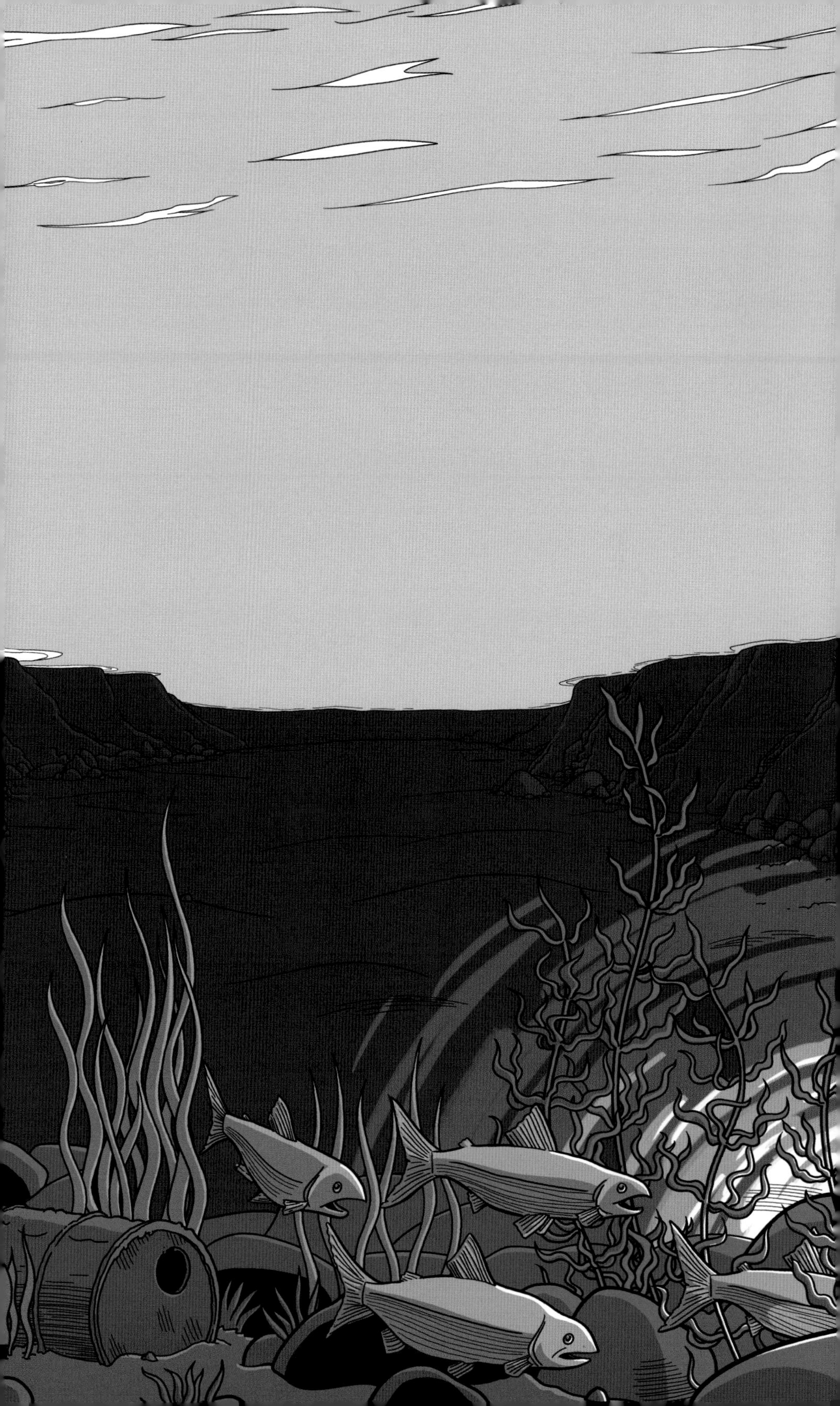

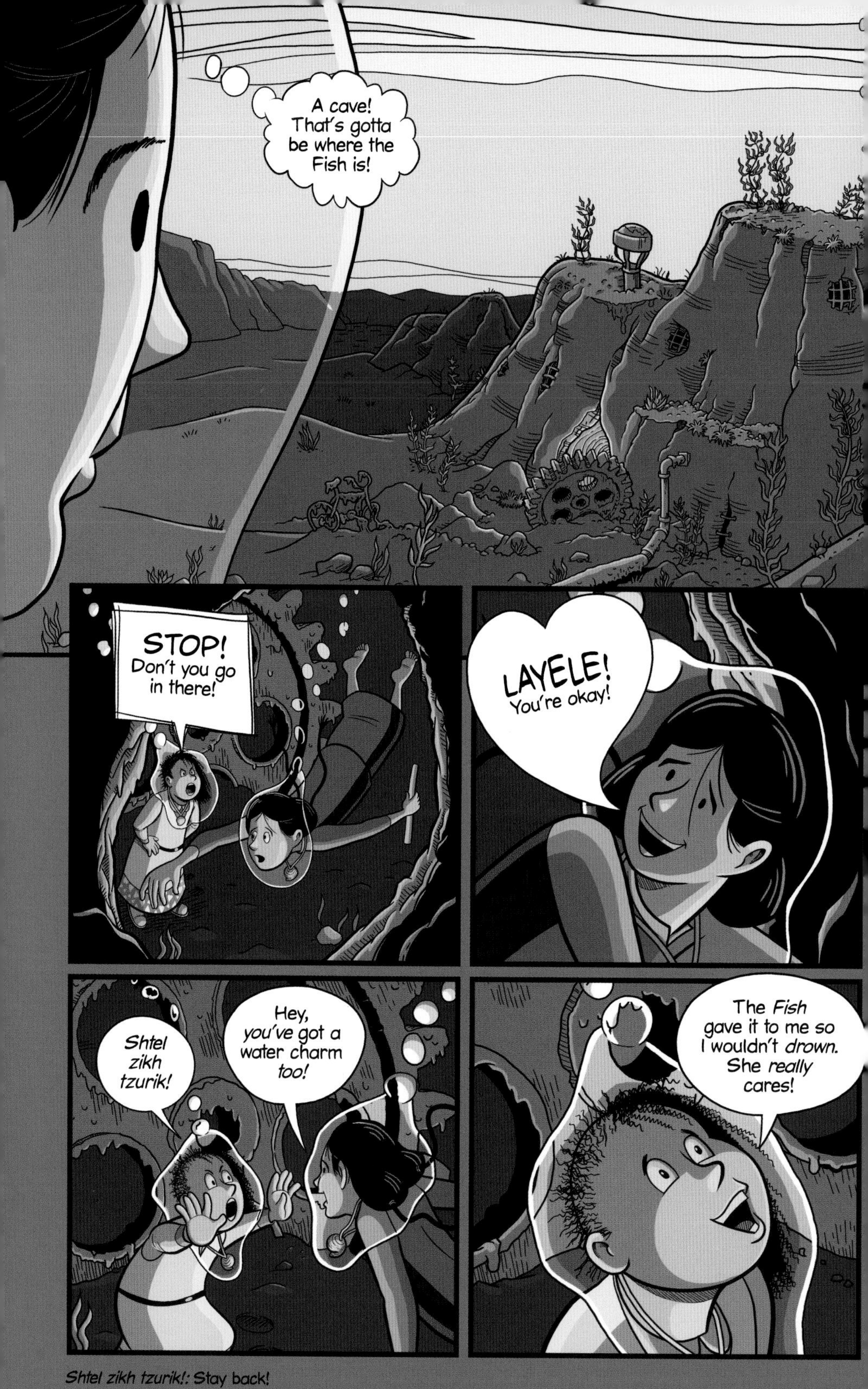

A cave! That's gotta be where the Fish is!
STOP! Don't you go in there!
LAYELE! You're okay!
Shtel zikh tzurik!
Hey, you've got a water charm too!
The Fish gave it to me so I wouldn't drown. She really cares!

Shtel zikh tzurik!: Stay back!

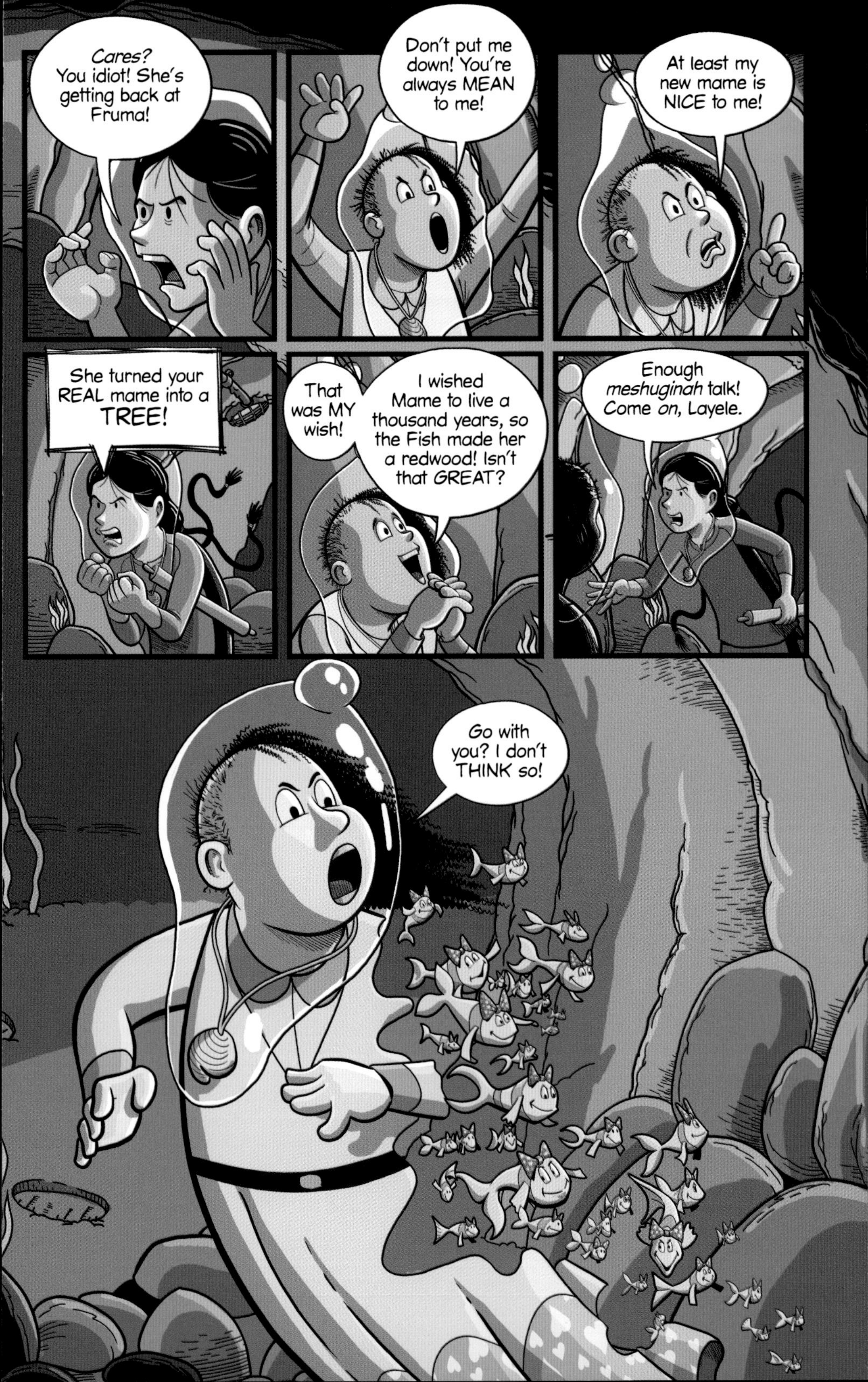
Cares? You idiot! She's getting back at Fruma!
Don't put me down! You're always MEAN to me!
At least my new mame is NICE to me!
She turned your REAL mame into a TREE!
That was MY wish!
I wished Mame to live a thousand years, so the Fish made her a redwood! Isn't that GREAT?
Enough meshuginah talk! Come on, Layele.
Go with you? I don't THINK so!

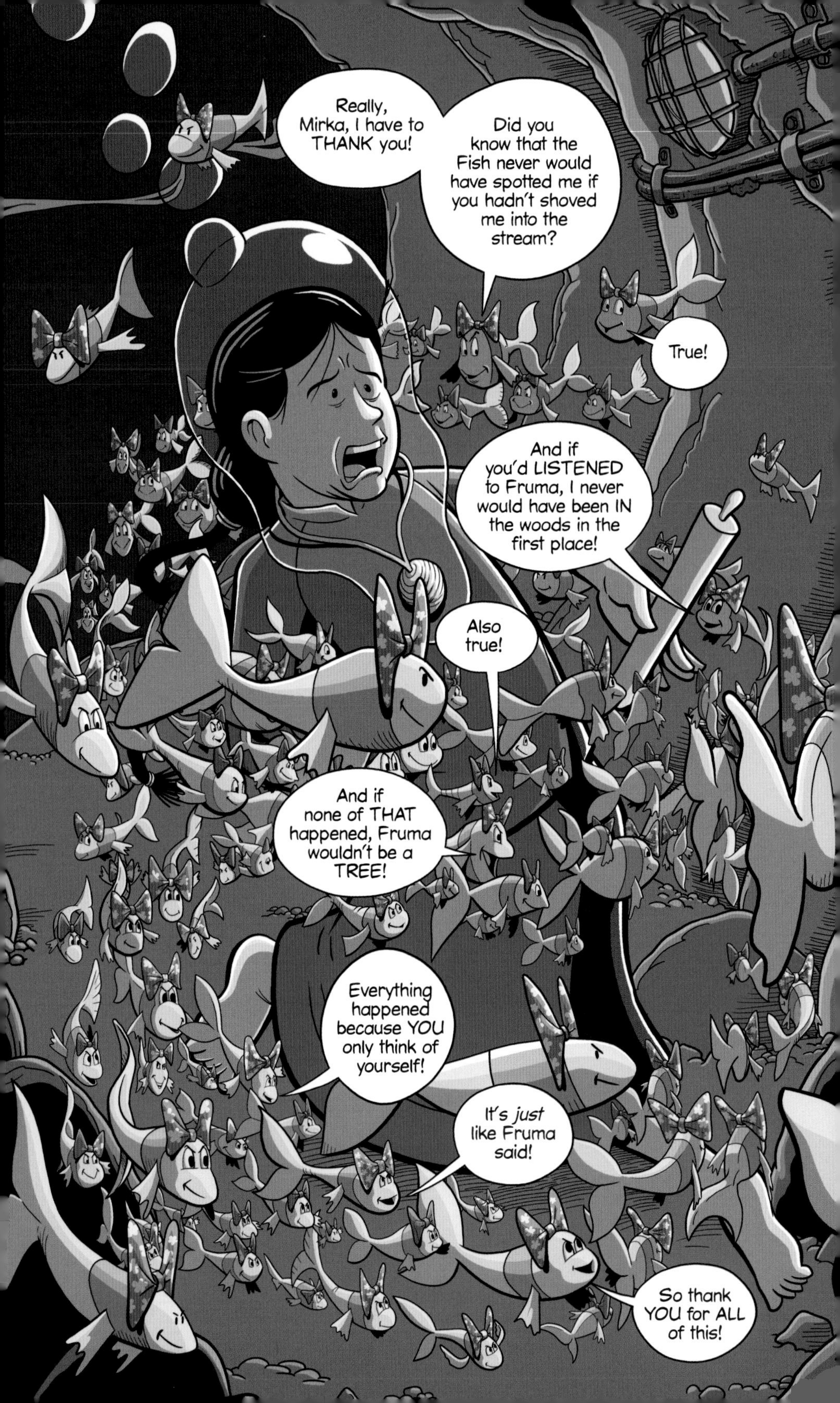

Really, Mirka, I have to THANK you!
Did you know that the Fish never would have spotted me if you hadn't shoved me into the stream?
True!
And if you'd LISTENED to Fruma, I never would have been IN the woods in the first place!
Also true!
And if none of THAT happened, Fruma wouldn't be a TREE!
Everything happened because YOU only think of yourself!
It's *just* like Fruma said!
So thank YOU for ALL of this!

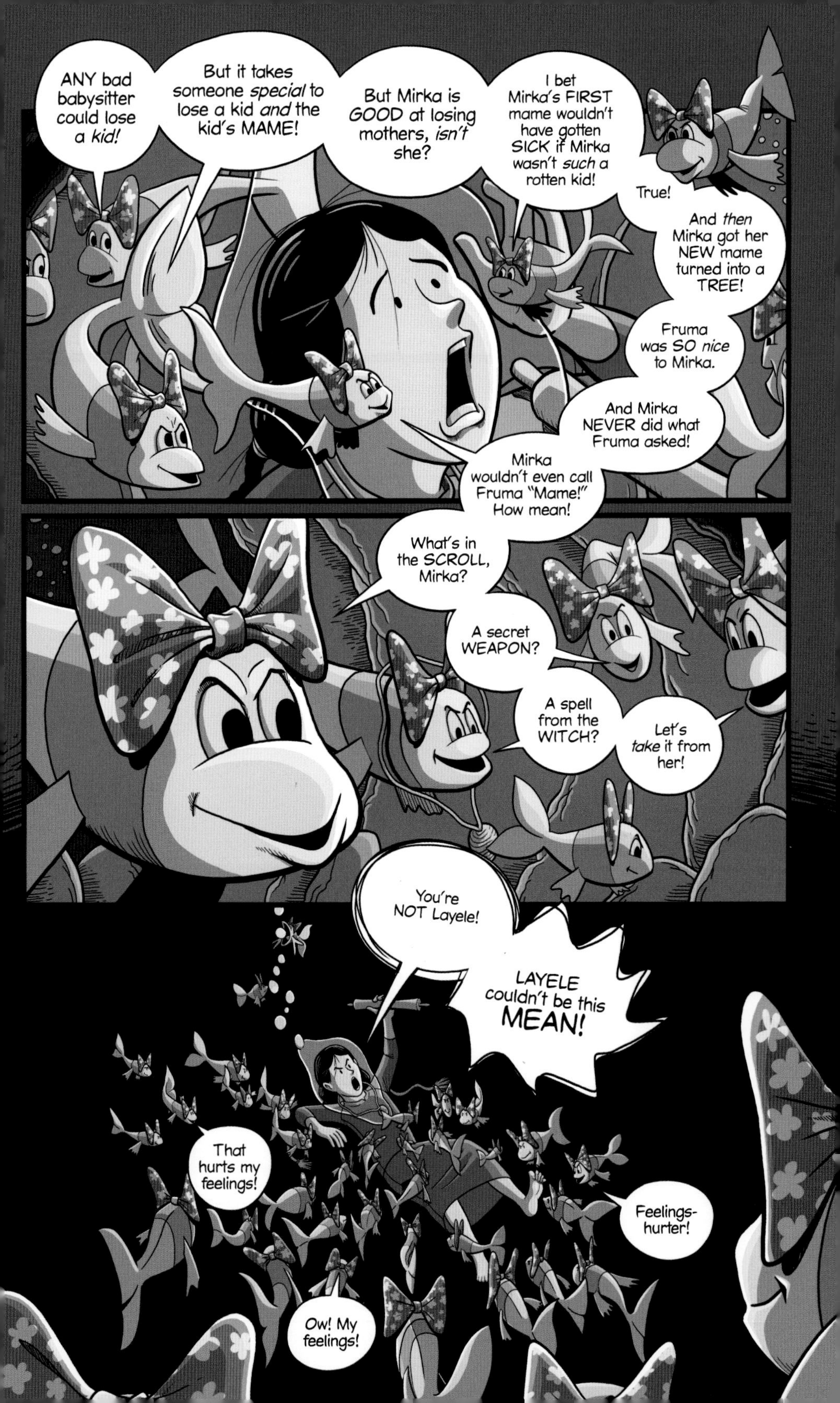
ANY bad babysitter could lose a *kid!*
But it takes someone *special* to lose a kid *and* the kid's MAME!
But Mirka is GOOD at losing mothers, *isn't* she?
I bet Mirka's FIRST mame wouldn't have gotten SICK if Mirka wasn't *such* a rotten kid!
True!
And *then* Mirka got her NEW mame turned into a TREE!
Fruma was SO *nice* to Mirka.
And Mirka NEVER did what Fruma asked!
Mirka wouldn't even call Fruma "Mame!" How mean!
What's in the SCROLL, Mirka?
A secret WEAPON?
A spell from the WITCH?
Let's *take* it from her!
You're NOT Layele!
LAYELE couldn't be this MEAN!
That hurts my feelings!
Feelings-hurter!
Ow! My feelings!

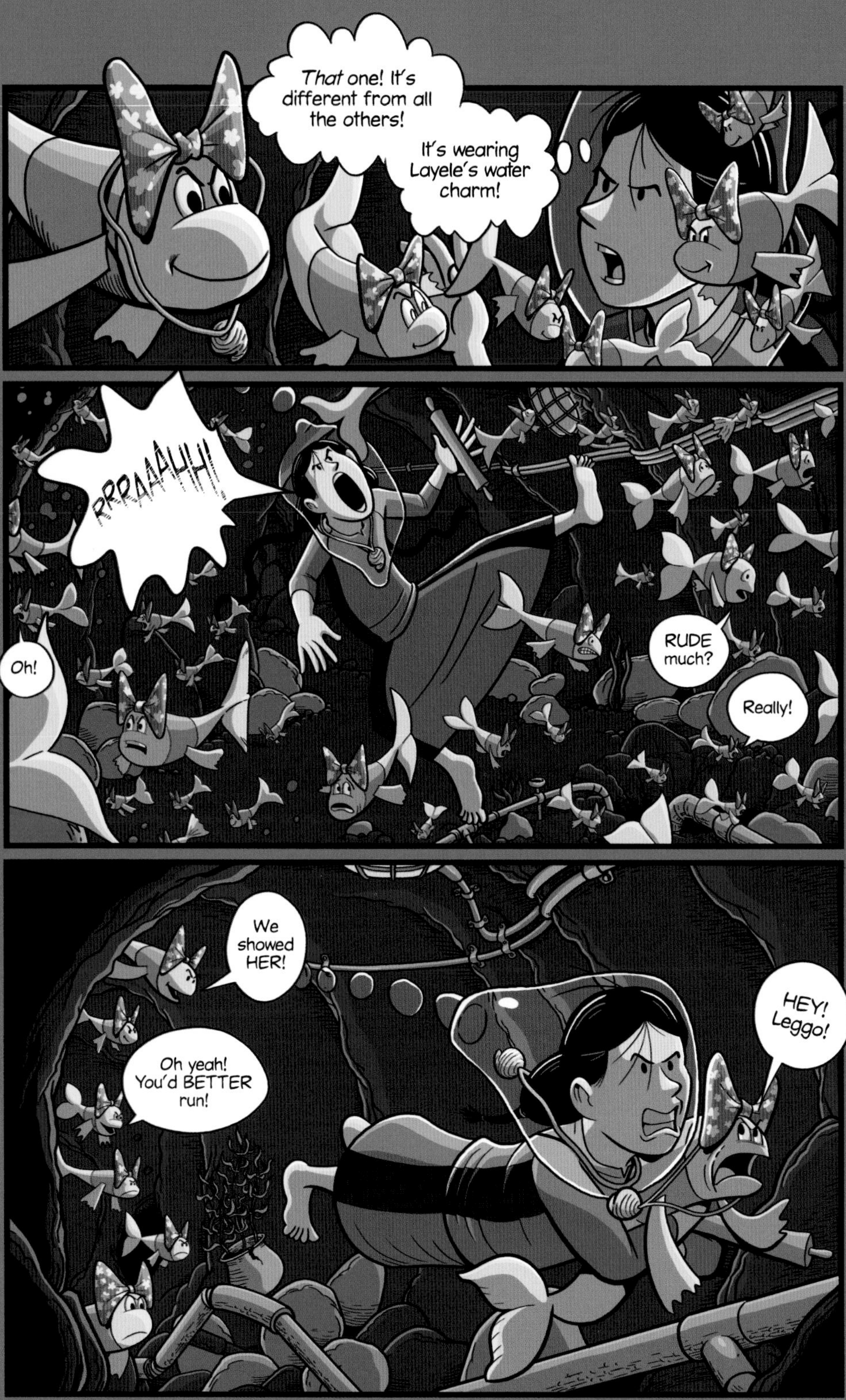
That one! It's different from all the others!
It's wearing Layele's water charm!
RRRAAAHH!
Oh!
RUDE much?
Really!
We showed HER!
Oh yeah! You'd BETTER run!
HEY! Leggo!

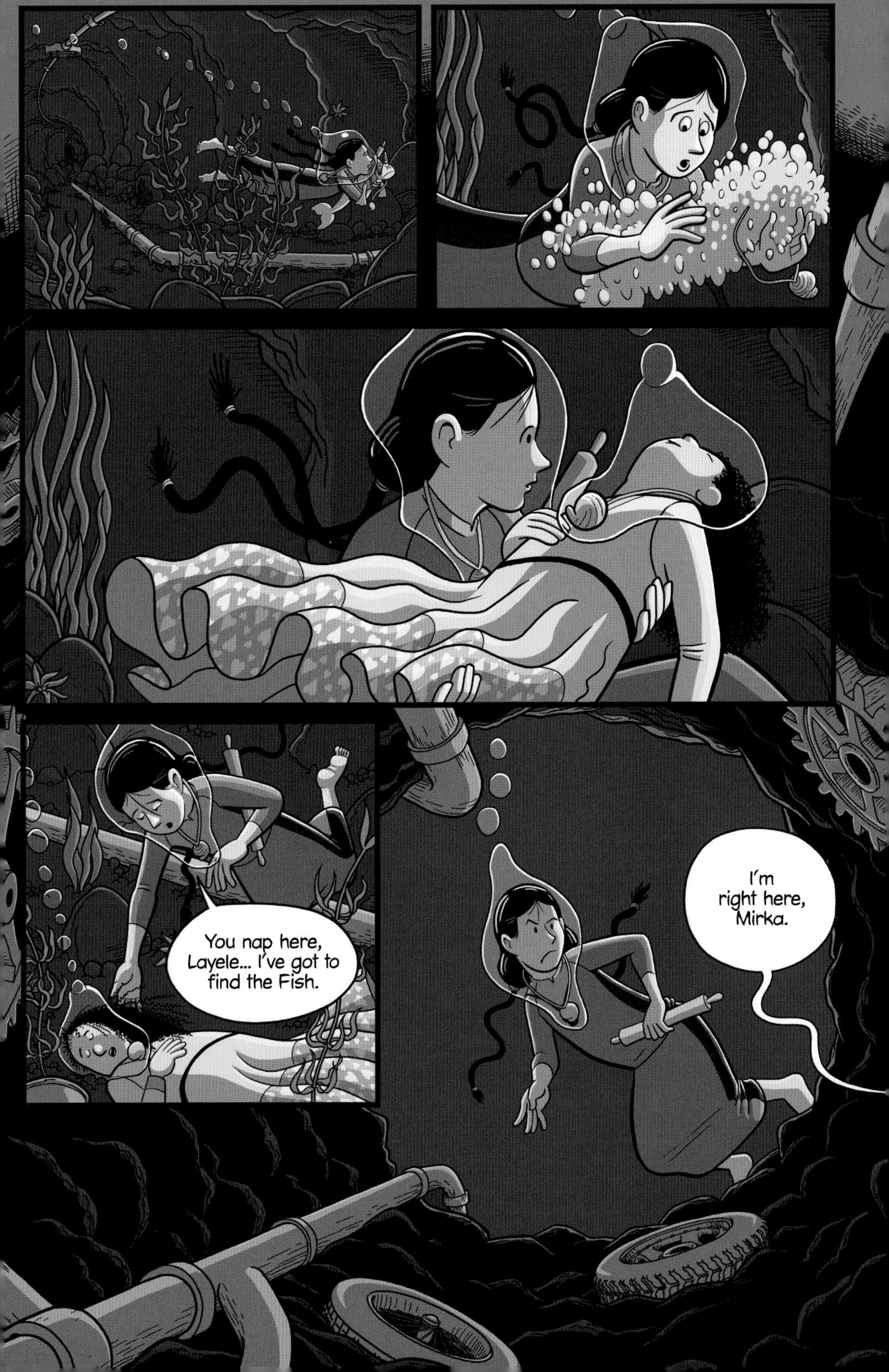
You nap here, Layele... I've got to find the Fish.
I'm right here, Mirka.

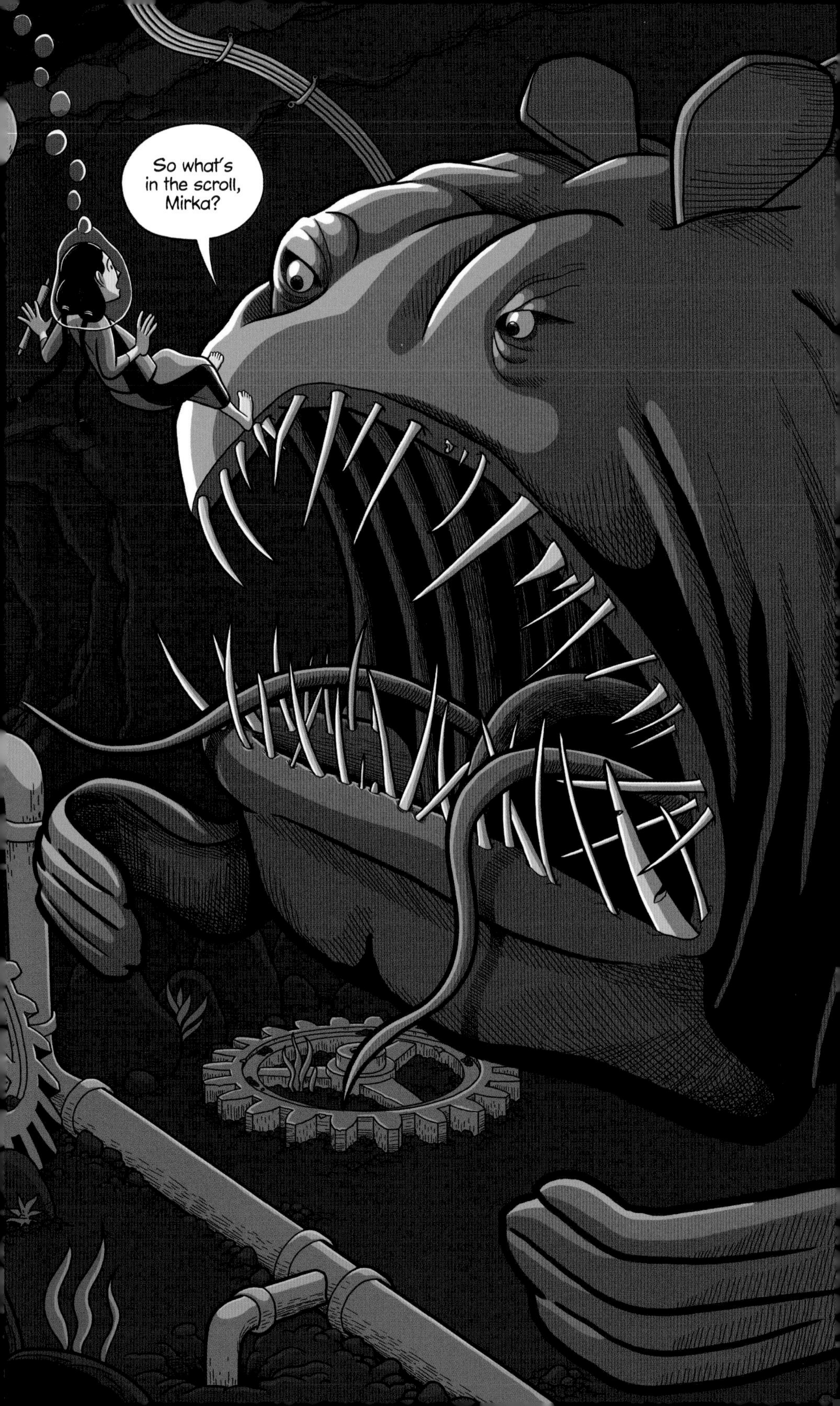
So what's in the scroll, Mirka?

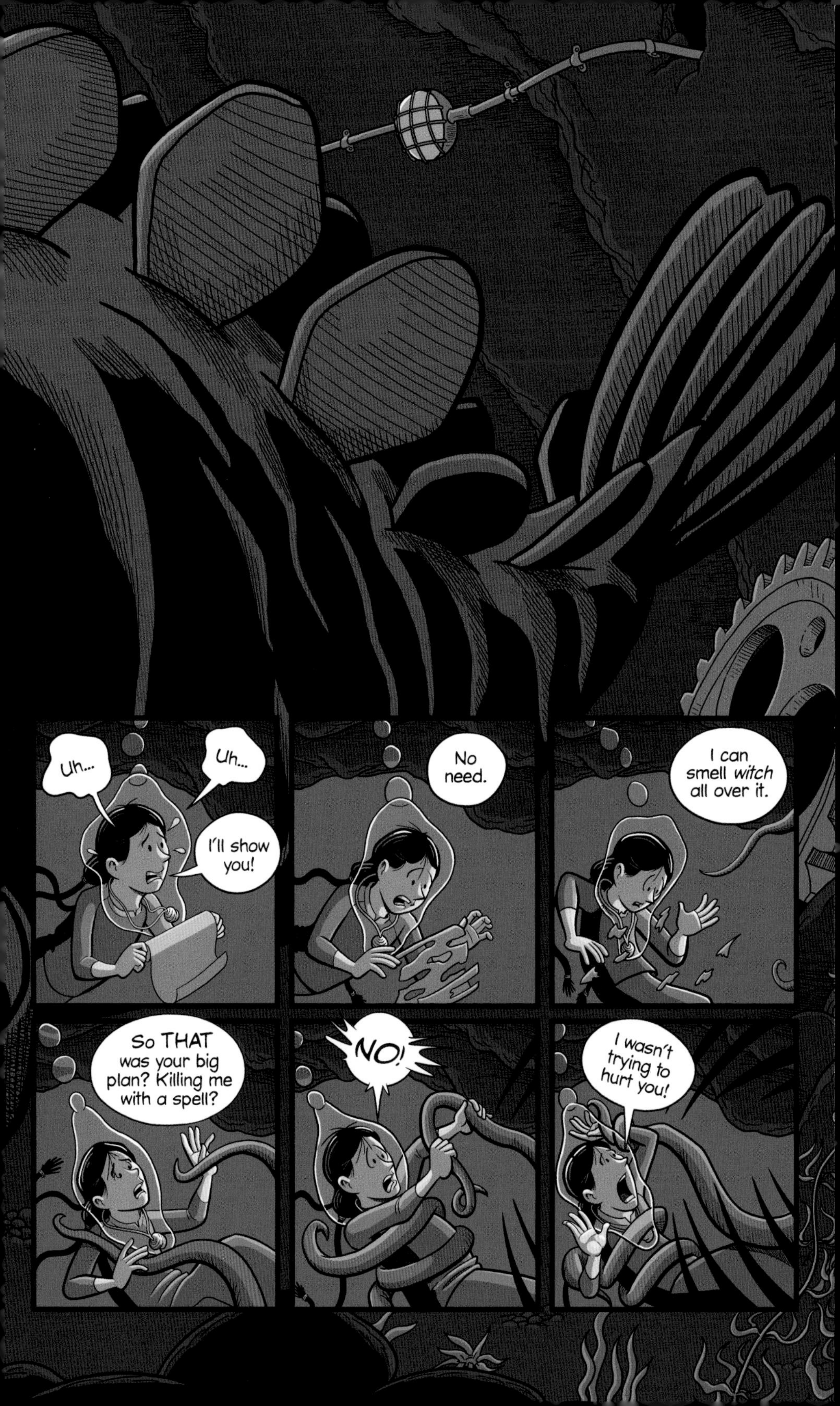
Uh...
Uh...
I'll show you!
No need.
I can smell *witch* all over it.
So THAT was your big plan? Killing me with a spell?
NO!
I wasn't trying to hurt you!

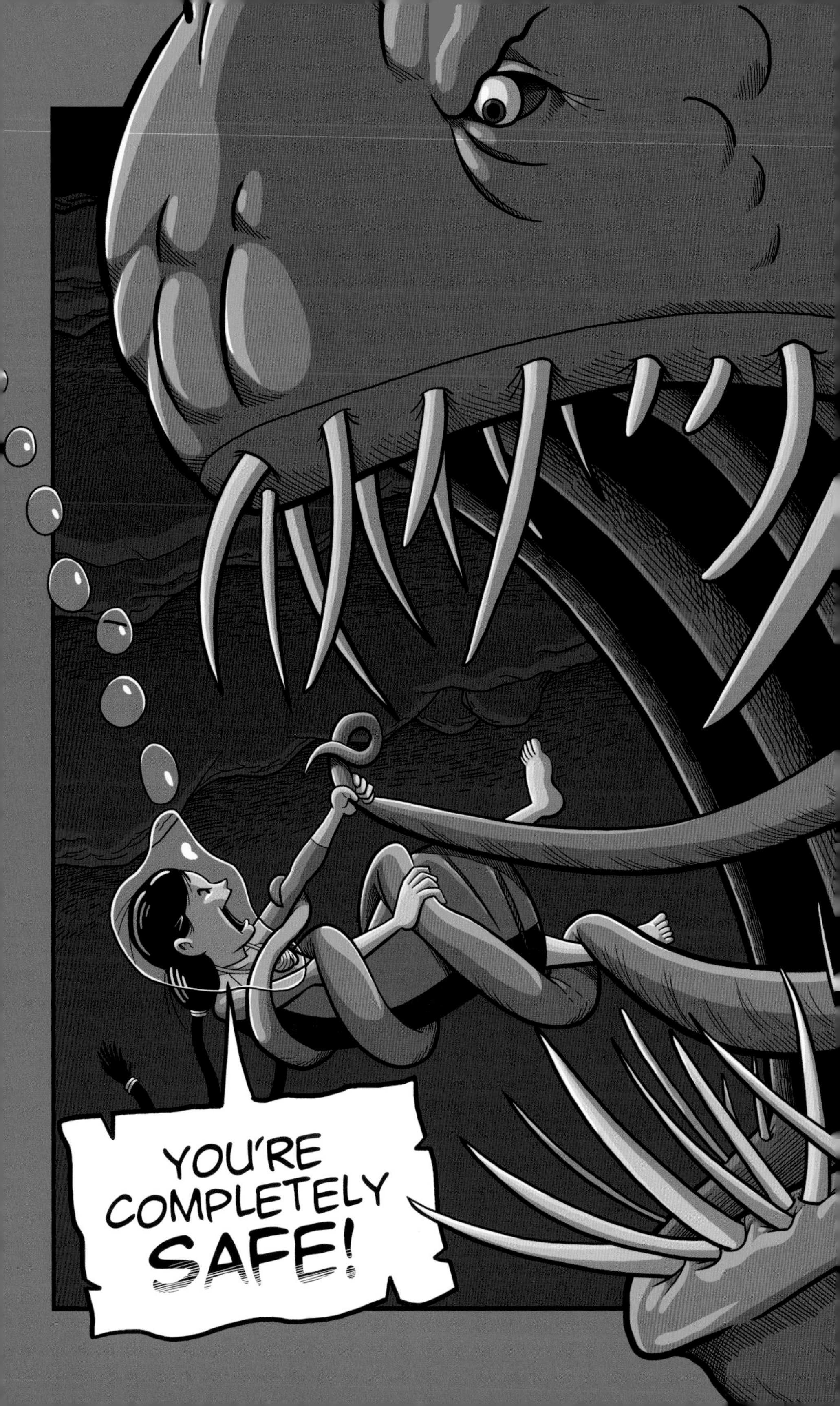
YOU'RE COMPLETELY SAFE!

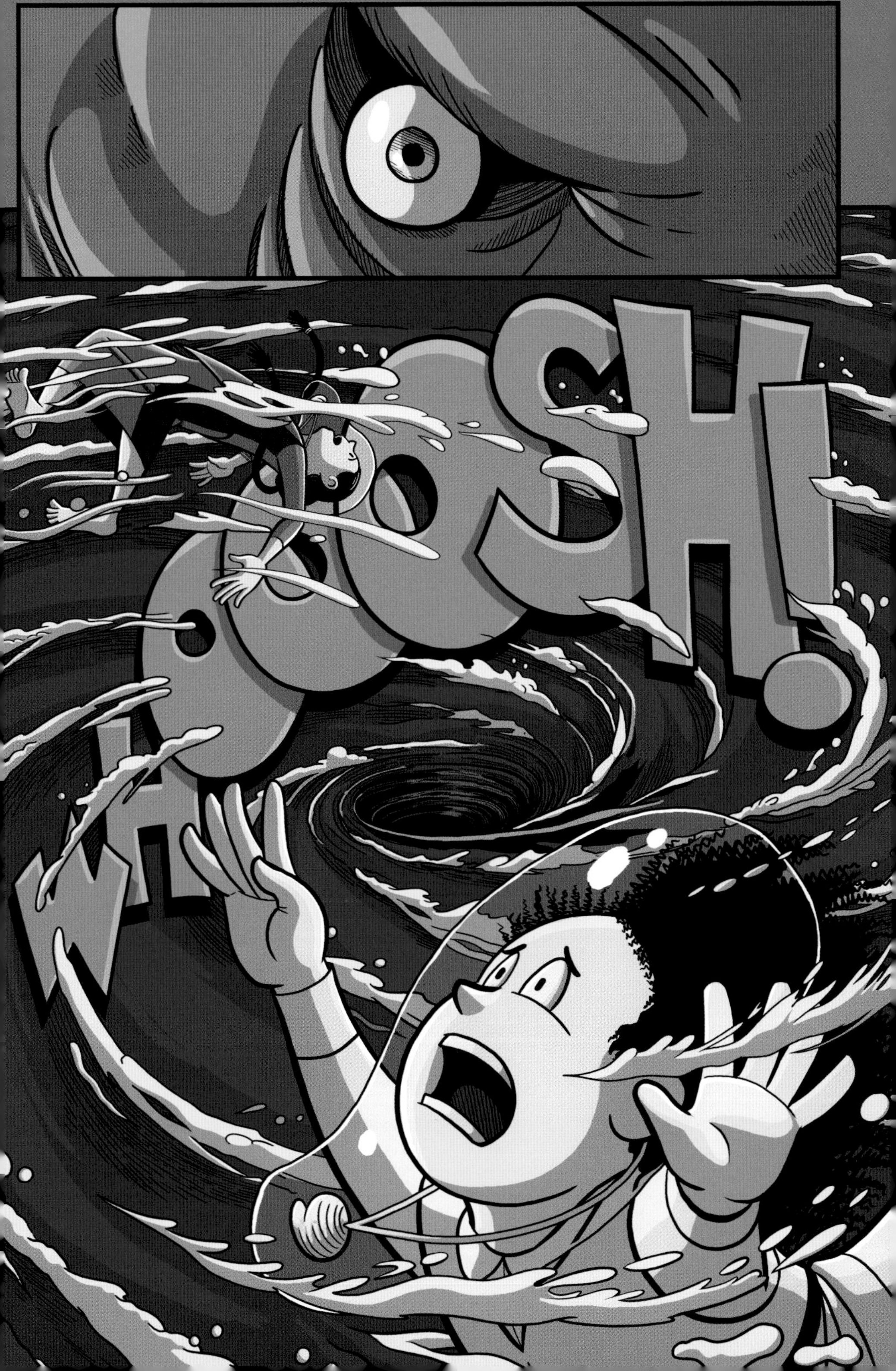
WHOOSH!

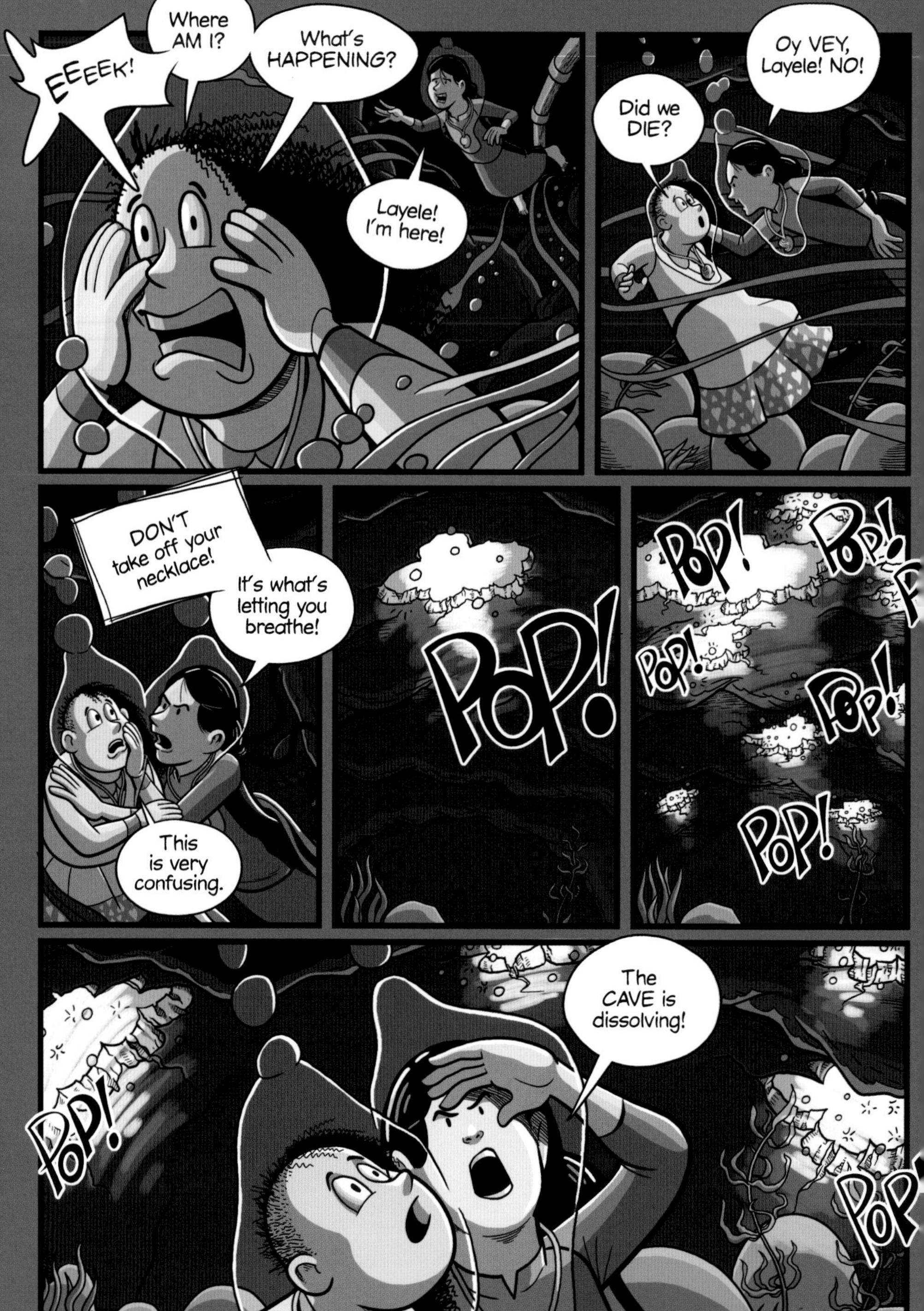
EEEEK!
Where AM I?
What's HAPPENING?
Layele! I'm here!
Did we DIE?
Oy VEY, Layele! NO!
DON'T take off your necklace!
It's what's letting you breathe!
This is very confusing.
POP!
POP!
POP!
POP!
POP!
POP!
The CAVE is dissolving!
POP!

Oy vey: Sheesh

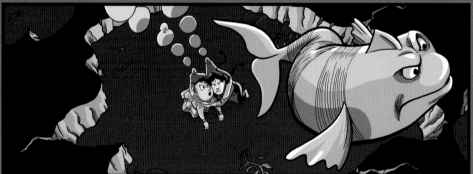

I'll be right back!

What? NO! Don't LEAVE me!

You're a TERRIBLE BABYSITTER!

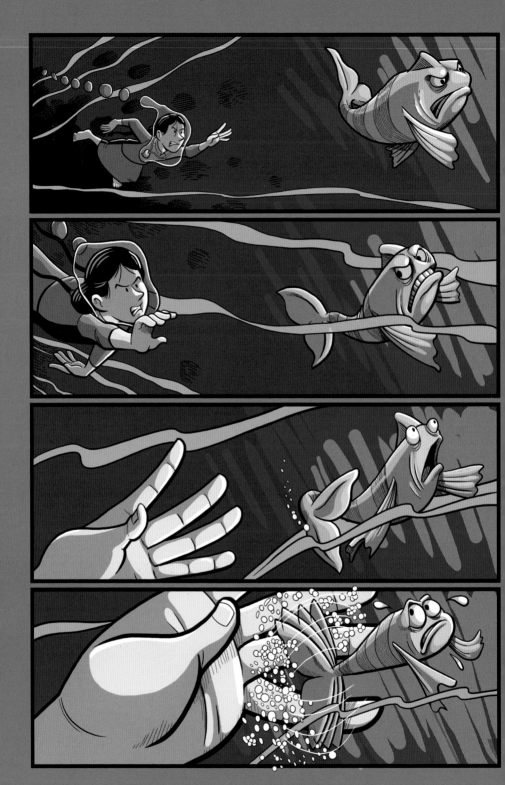

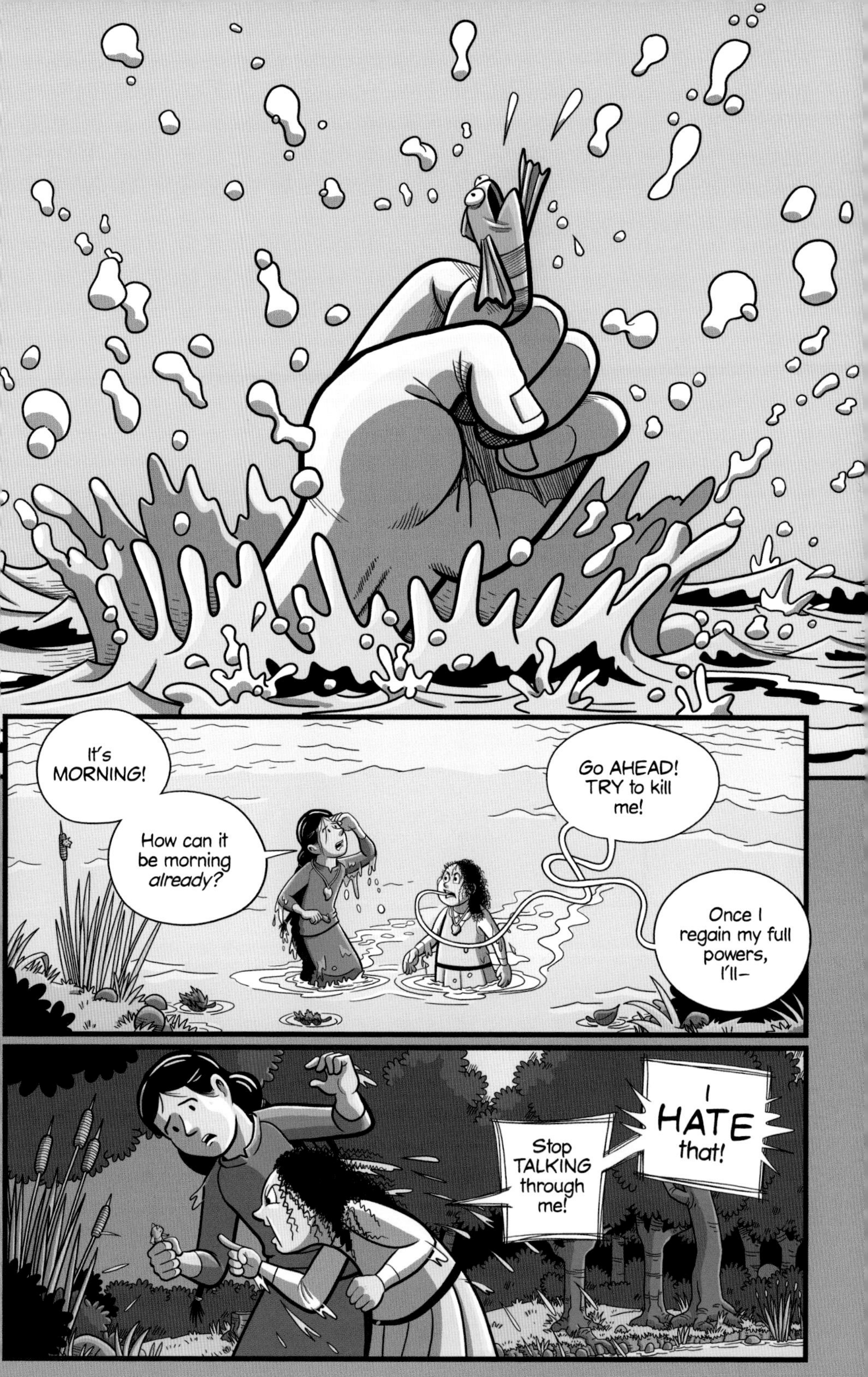
It's MORNING!
How can it be morning *already*?
Go AHEAD! TRY to kill me!
Once I regain my full powers, I'll–
Stop TALKING through me!
I HATE that!

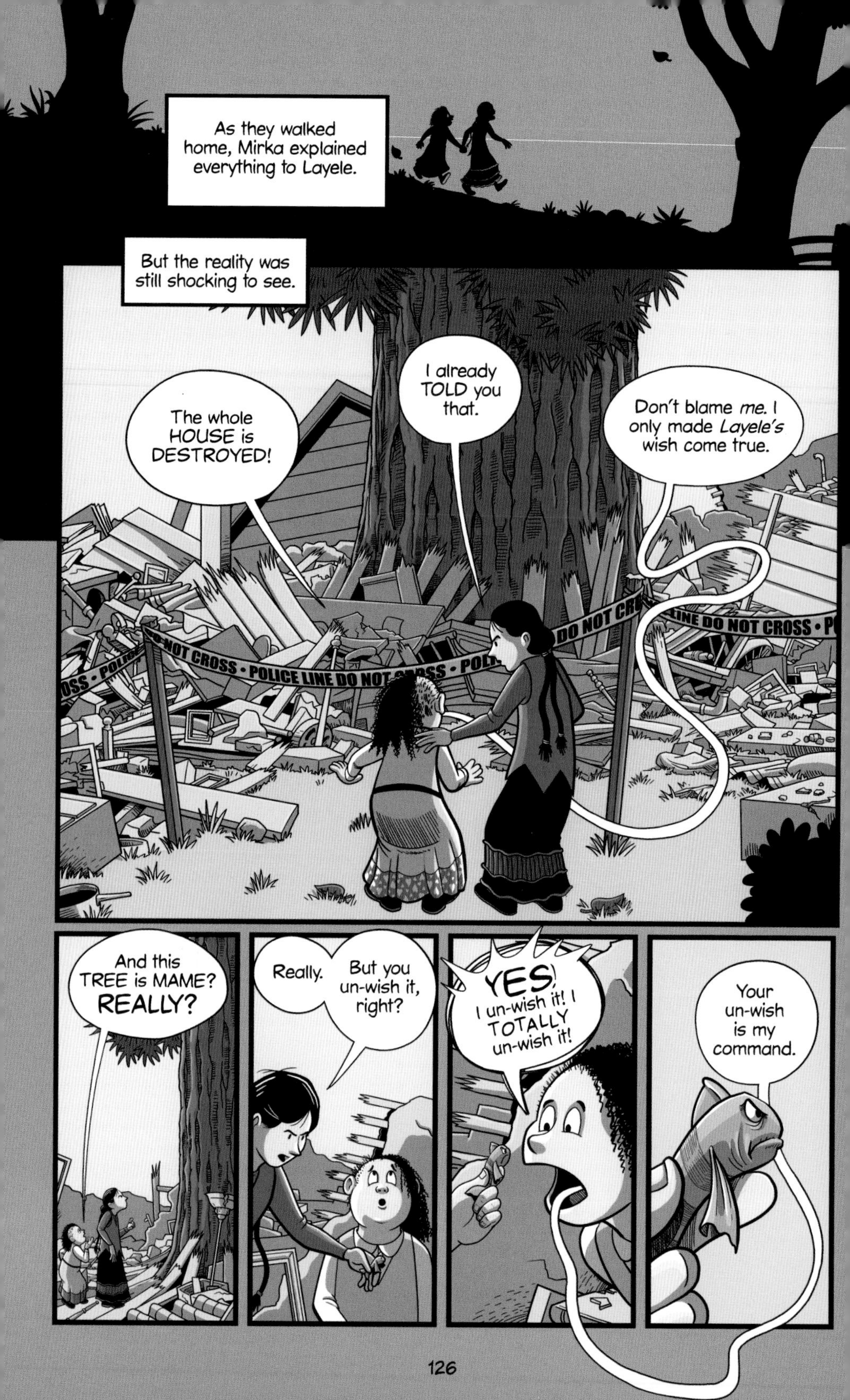

As they walked home, Mirka explained everything to Layele.
But the reality was still shocking to see.
The whole HOUSE is DESTROYED!
I already TOLD you that.
Don't blame *me*. I only made *Layele's* wish come true.
DO NOT CROSS • POLICE LINE DO NOT CROSS • POLICE
LINE DO NOT CROSS • P
And this TREE is MAME? REALLY?
Really.
But you un-wish it, right?
YES! I un-wish it! I TOTALLY un-wish it!
Your un-wish is my command.

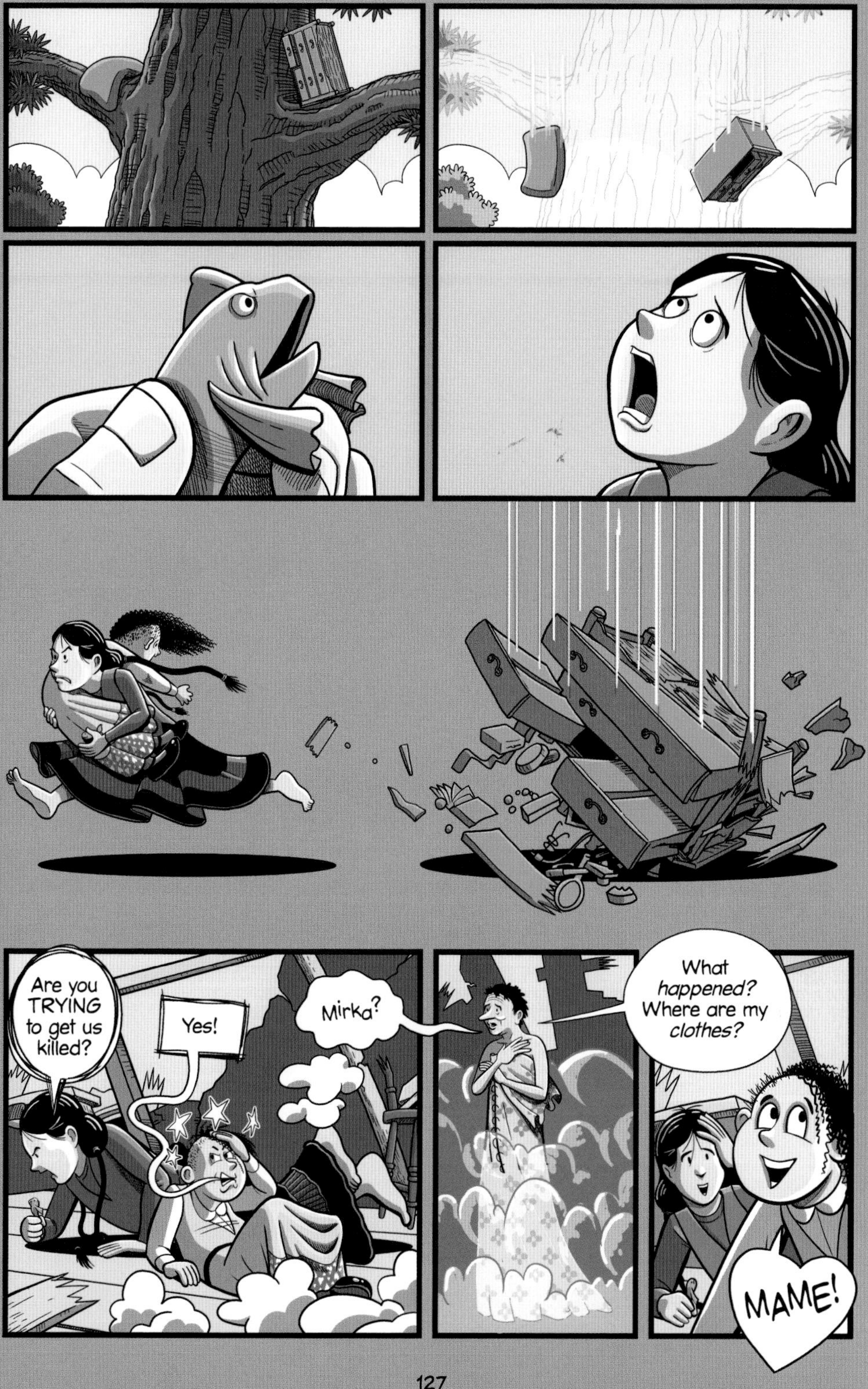

Are you TRYING to get us killed?
Yes!
Mirka?
What happened? Where are my clothes?
MAME!

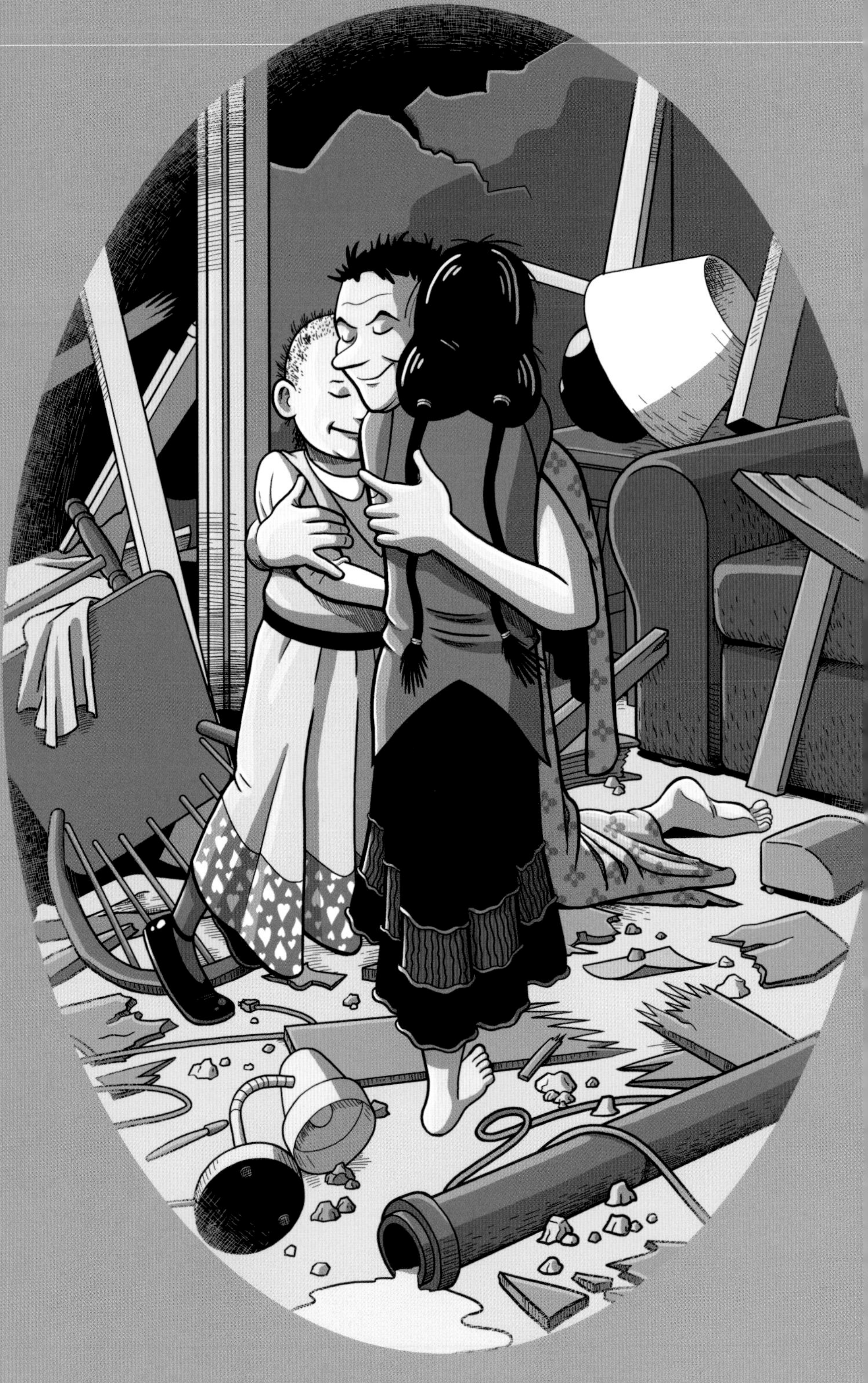

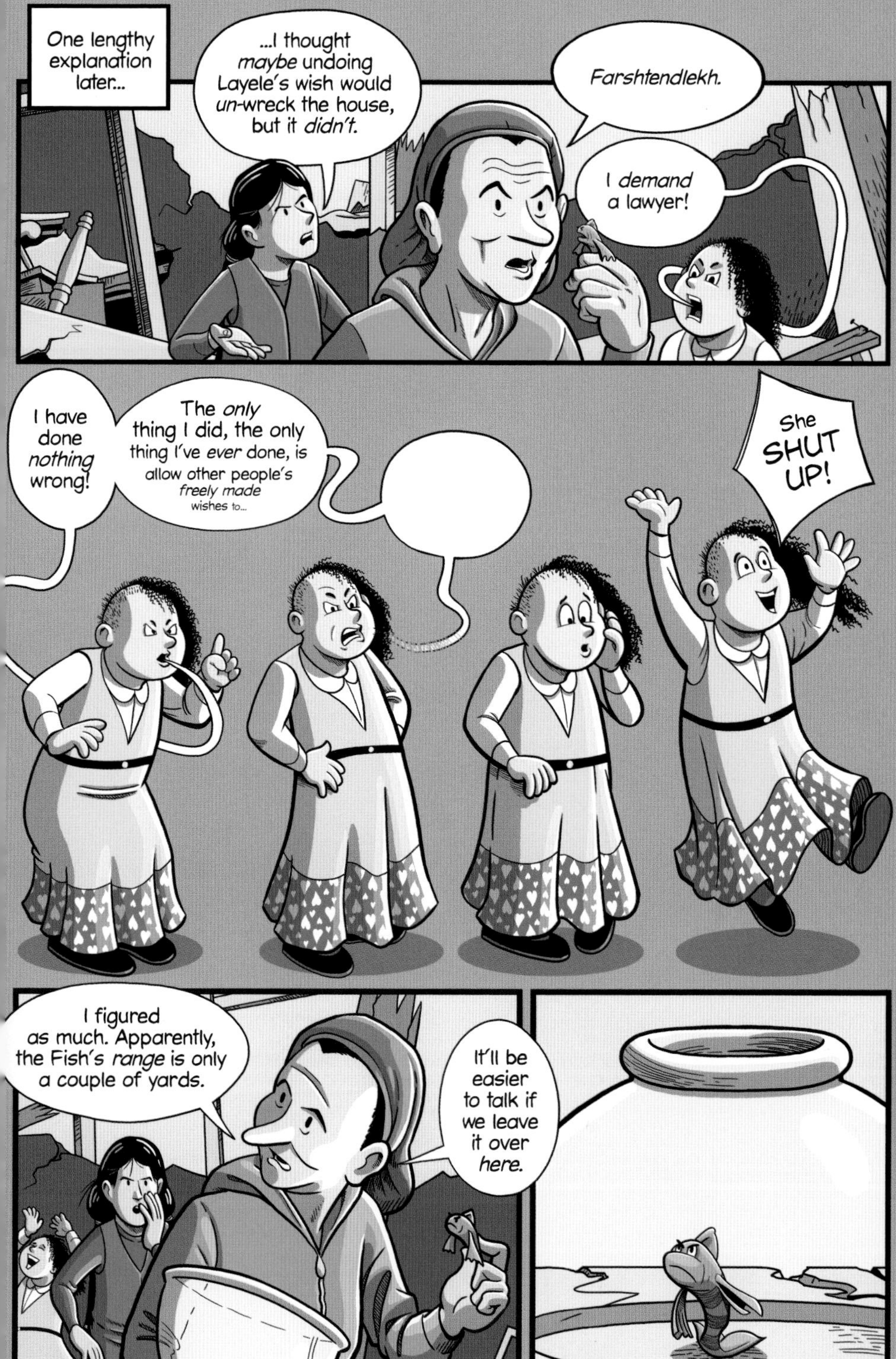
One lengthy explanation later...
...I thought *maybe* undoing Layele's wish would *un*-wreck the house, but it *didn't.*
Farshtendlekh.
I *demand* a lawyer!
I have done *nothing* wrong!
The *only* thing I did, the only thing I've *ever* done, is allow other people's *freely made* wishes to...
She SHUT UP!
I figured as much. Apparently, the Fish's *range* is only a couple of yards.
It'll be easier to talk if we leave it over *here.*

Farshtendlekh: Obviously

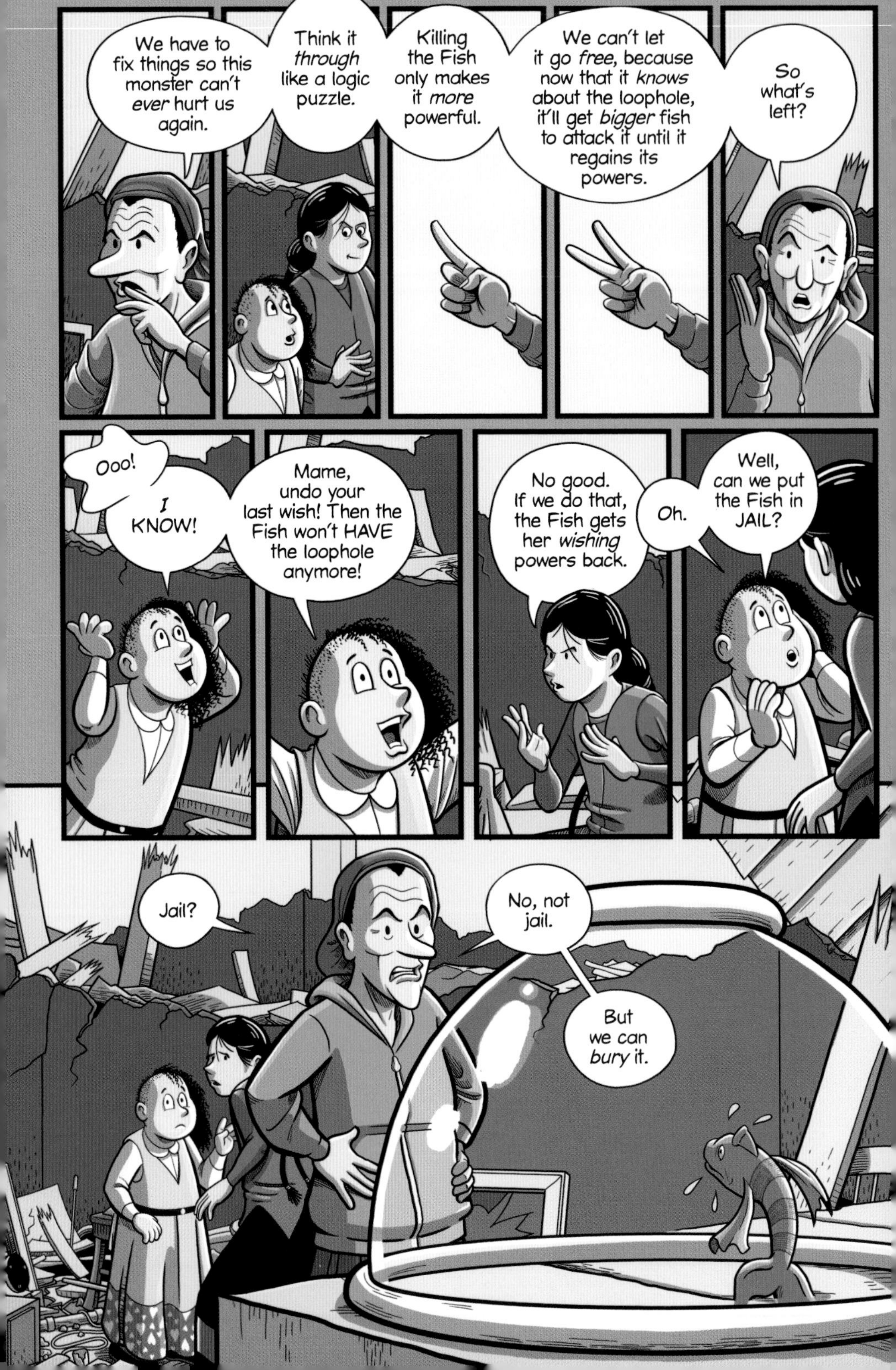

We have to fix things so this monster can't *ever* hurt us again.
Think it *through* like a logic puzzle.
Killing the Fish only makes it *more* powerful.
We can't let it go *free*, because now that it *knows* about the loophole, it'll get *bigger* fish to attack it until it regains its powers.
So what's left?
Ooo!
I KNOW!
Mame, undo your last wish! Then the Fish won't HAVE the loophole anymore!
No good. If we do that, the Fish gets her *wishing* powers back.
Oh.
Well, can we put the Fish in JAIL?
Jail?
No, not jail.
But we can *bury* it.

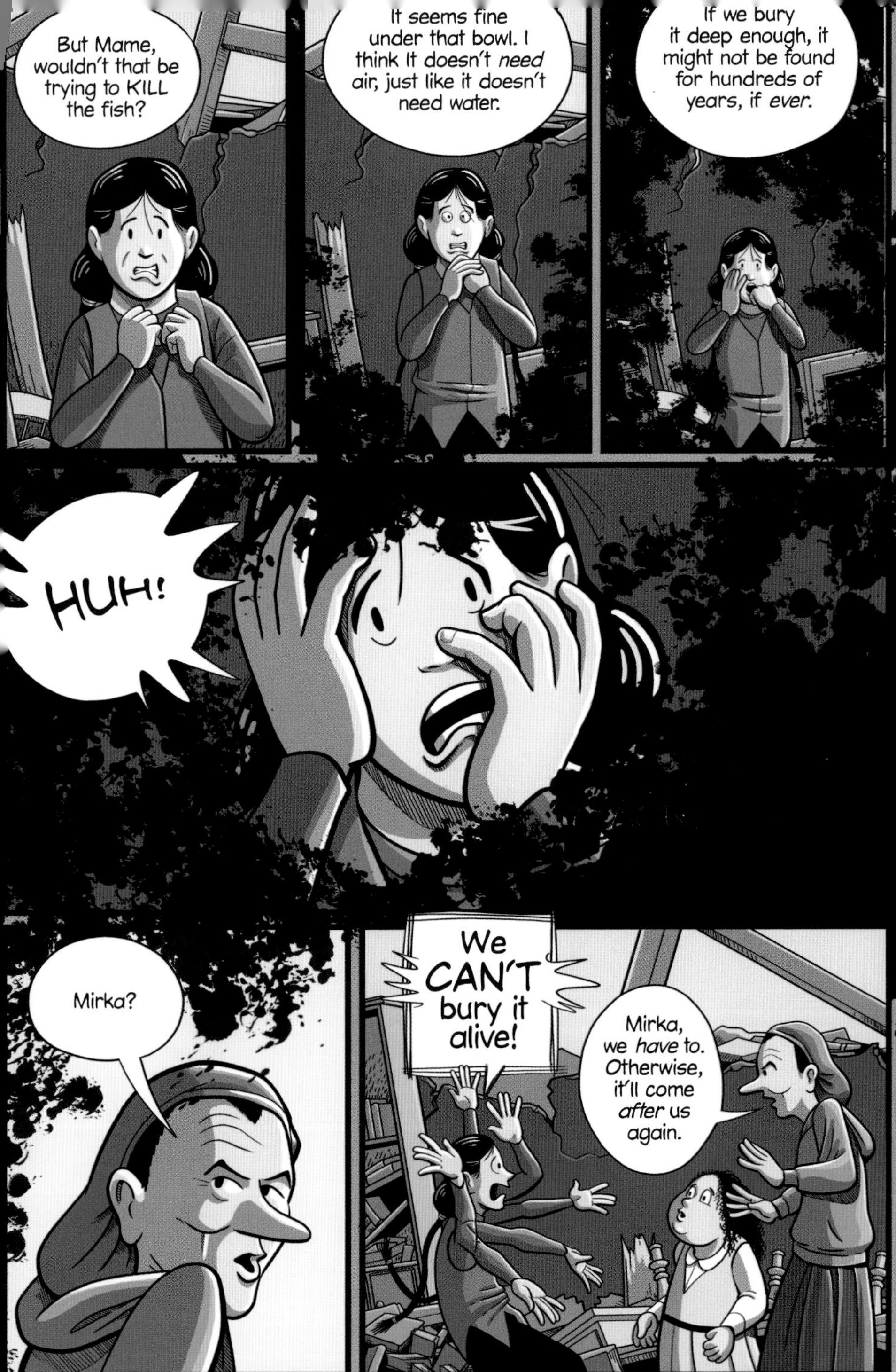
But Mame, wouldn't that be trying to KILL the fish?
It seems fine under that bowl. I think It doesn't *need* air, just like it doesn't need water.
If we bury it deep enough, it might not be found for hundreds of years, if *ever*.
HUH!
Mirka?
We CAN'T bury it alive!
Mirka, we *have* to. Otherwise, it'll come *after* us again.

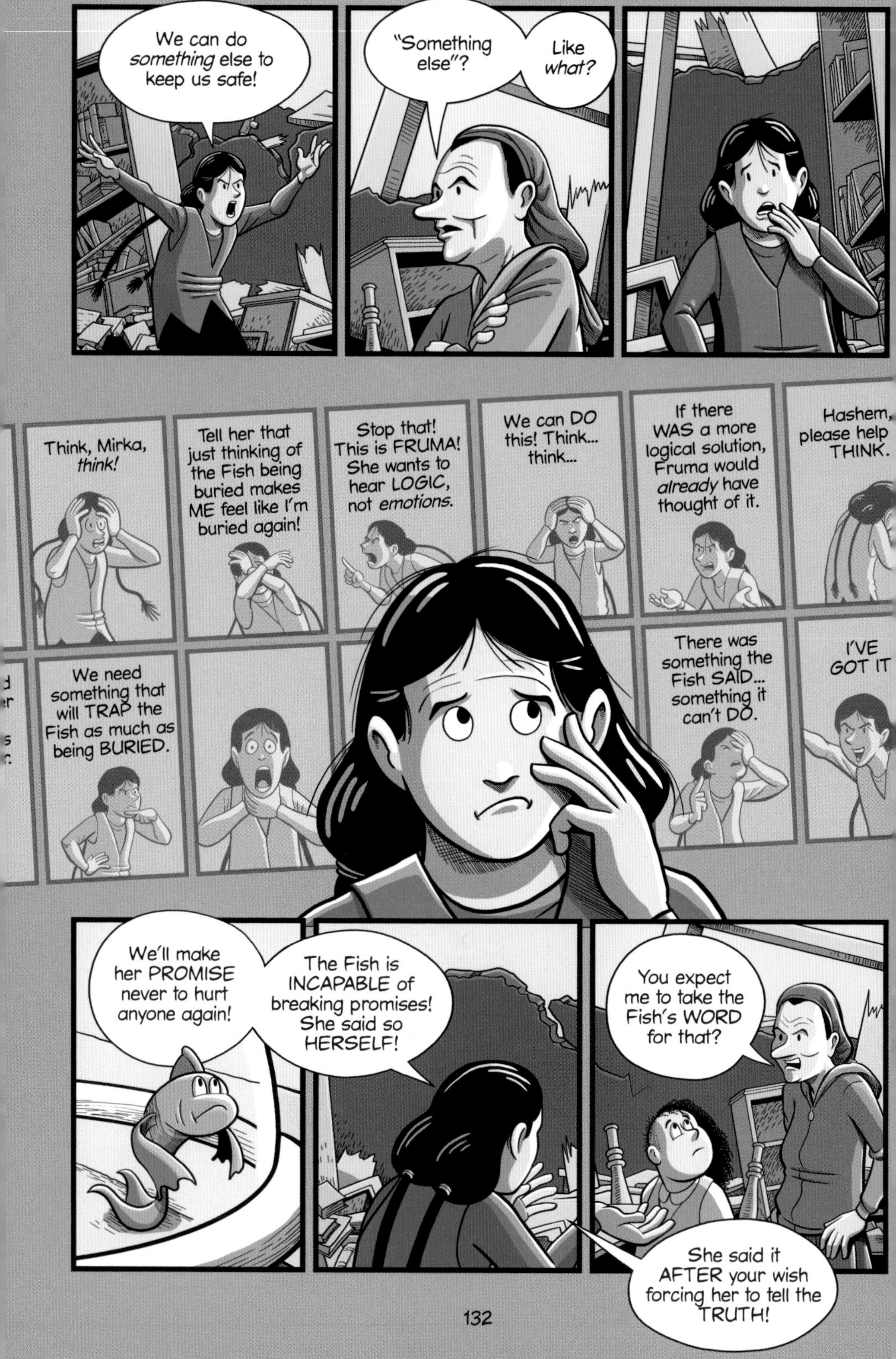
We can do *something* else to keep us safe!
"Something else"?
Like *what?*
Think, Mirka, *think!*
Tell her that just thinking of the Fish being buried makes ME feel like I'm buried again!
Stop that! This is FRUMA! She wants to hear LOGIC, not *emotions.*
We can DO this! Think... think...
If there WAS a more logical solution, Fruma would *already* have thought of it.
Hashem, please help THINK.
We need something that will TRAP the Fish as much as being BURIED.
There was something the Fish SAID... something it can't DO.
I'VE GOT IT
We'll make her PROMISE never to hurt anyone again!
The Fish is INCAPABLE of breaking promises! She said so HERSELF!
You expect me to take the Fish's WORD for that?
She said it AFTER your wish forcing her to tell the TRUTH!

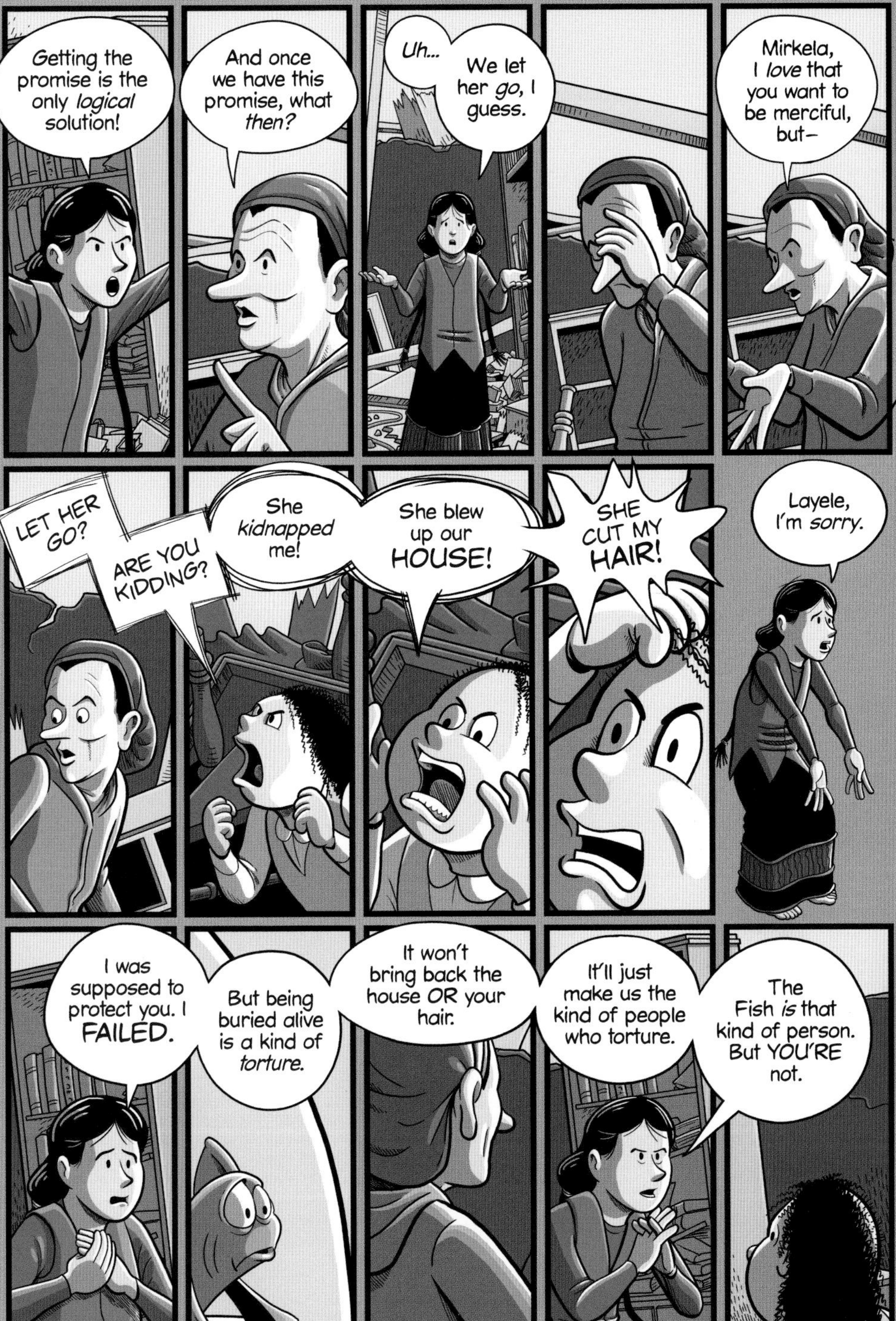
Getting the promise is the only *logical* solution!
And once we have this promise, what *then?*
Uh...
We let her *go*, I guess.
Mirkela, I *love* that you want to be merciful, but–
LET HER GO?
ARE YOU KIDDING?
She *kidnapped* me!
She blew up our HOUSE!
SHE CUT MY HAIR!
Layele, I'm *sorry*.
I was supposed to protect you. I FAILED.
But being buried alive is a kind of *torture*.
It won't bring back the house OR your hair.
It'll just make us the kind of people who torture.
The Fish *is* that kind of person. But YOU'RE not.

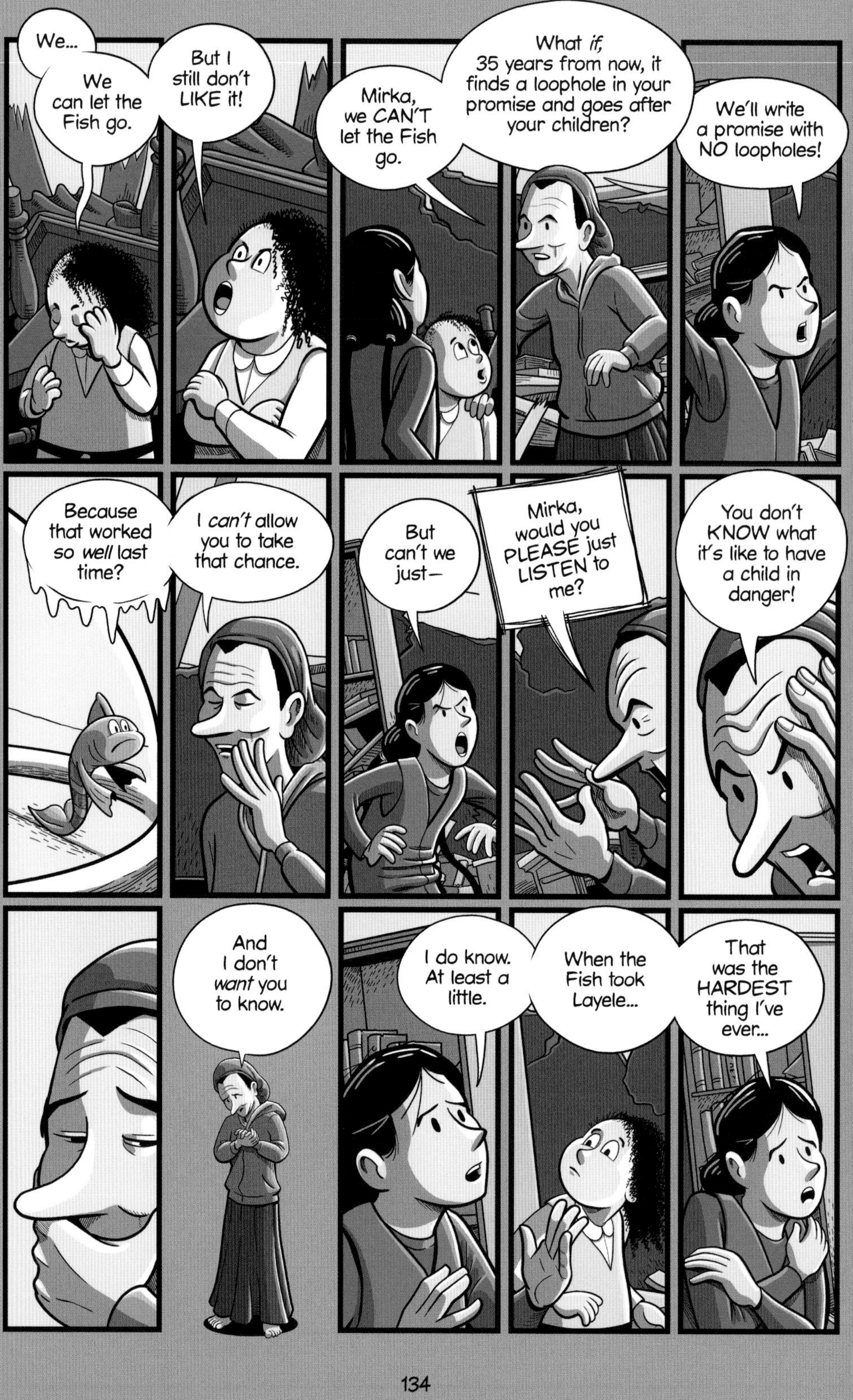
We...
We can let the Fish go.
But I still don't LIKE it!
Mirka, we CAN'T let the Fish go.
What *if*, 35 years from now, it finds a loophole in your promise and goes after your children?
We'll write a promise with NO loopholes!
Because that worked so *well* last time?
I *can't* allow you to take that chance.
But can't we just—
Mirka, would you PLEASE just LISTEN to me?
You don't KNOW what it's like to have a child in danger!
And I don't *want* you to know.
I do know. At least a little.
When the Fish took Layele...
That was the HARDEST thing I've ever...

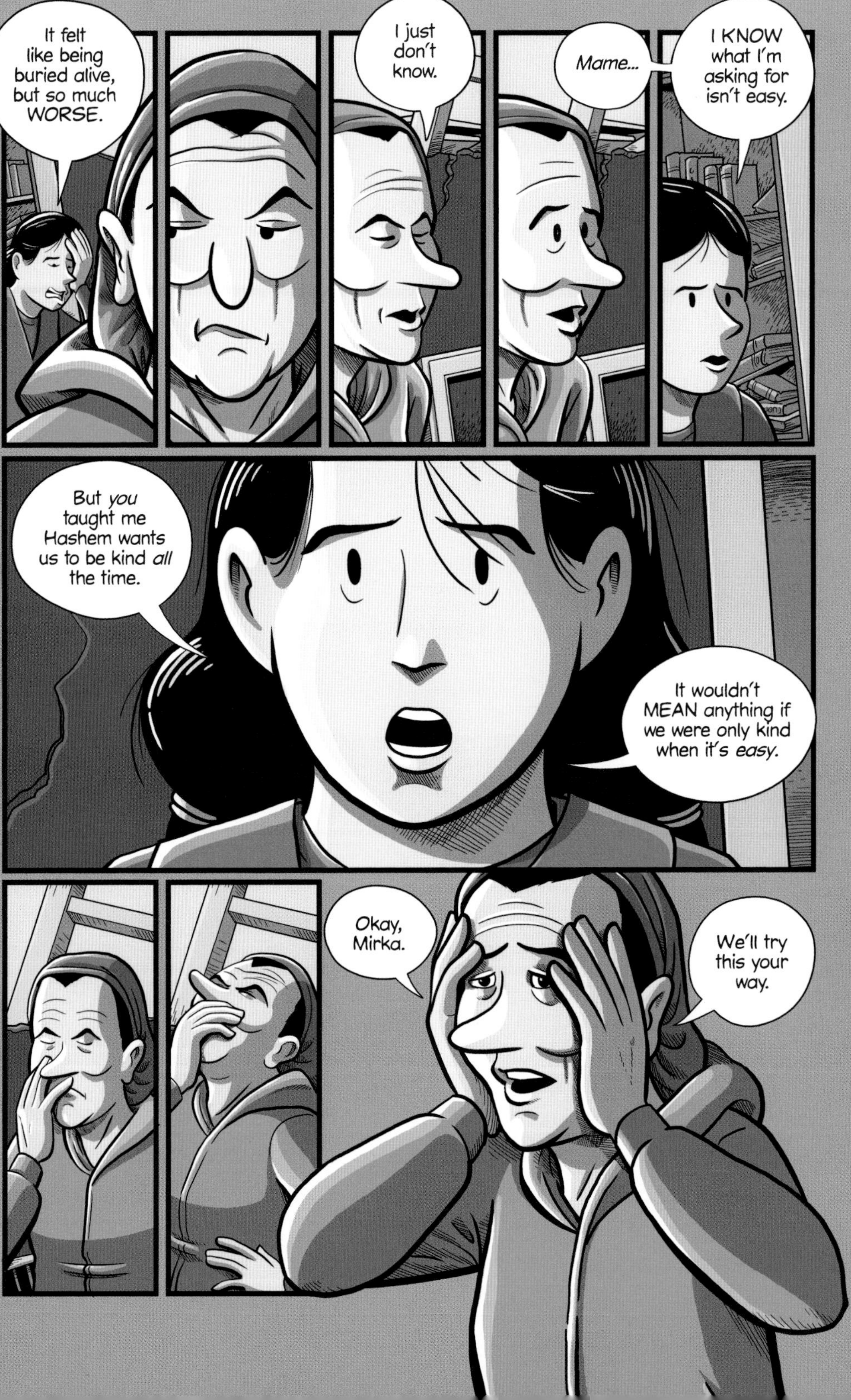

It felt like being buried alive, but so much WORSE.
I just don't know.
Mame...
I KNOW what I'm asking for isn't easy.
But *you* taught me Hashem wants us to be kind *all* the time.
It wouldn't MEAN anything if we were only kind when it's *easy*.
Okay, Mirka.
We'll try this your way.

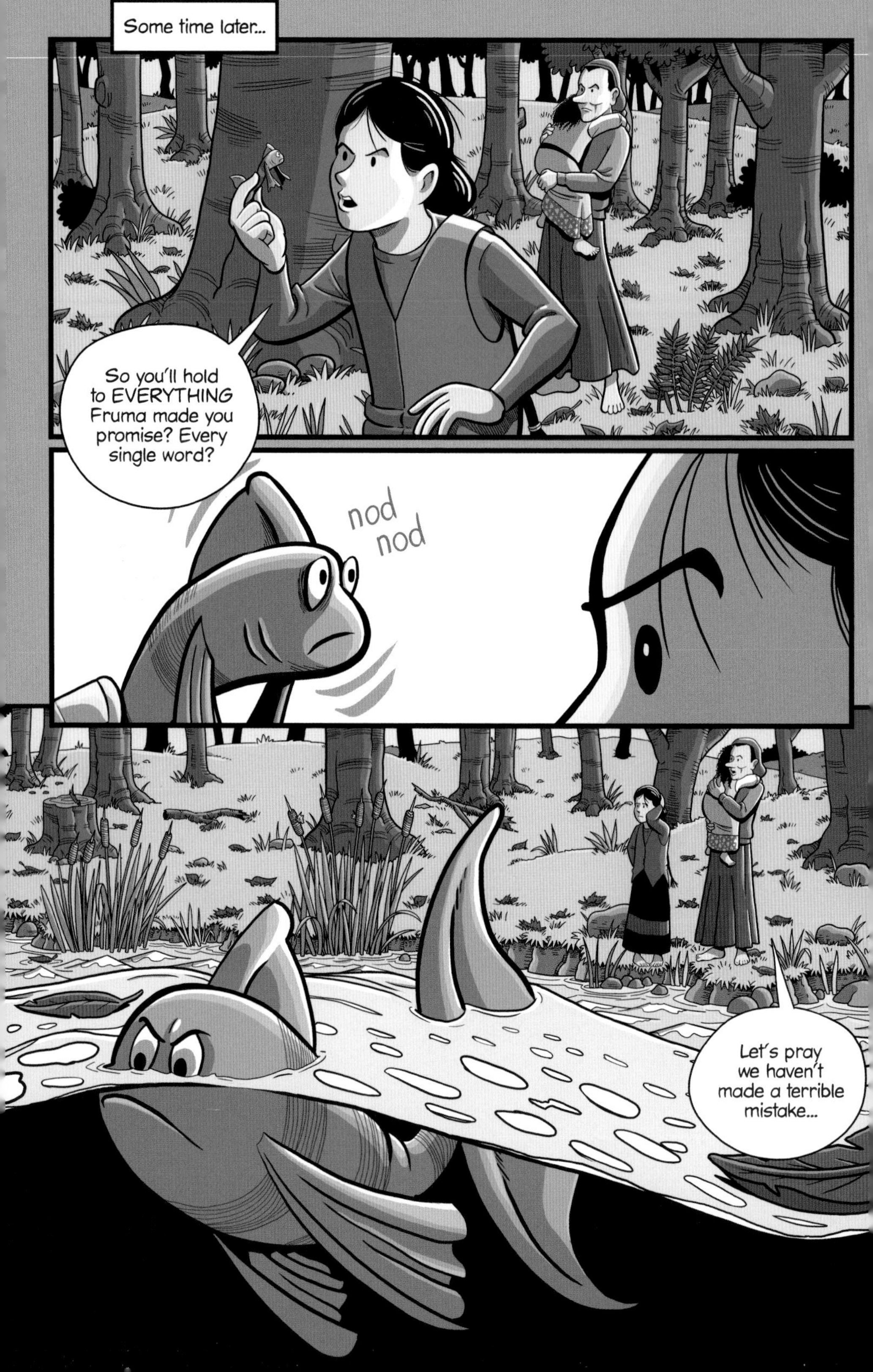
Some time later...
So you'll hold to EVERYTHING Fruma made you promise? Every single word?
nod nod
Let's pray we haven't made a terrible mistake...

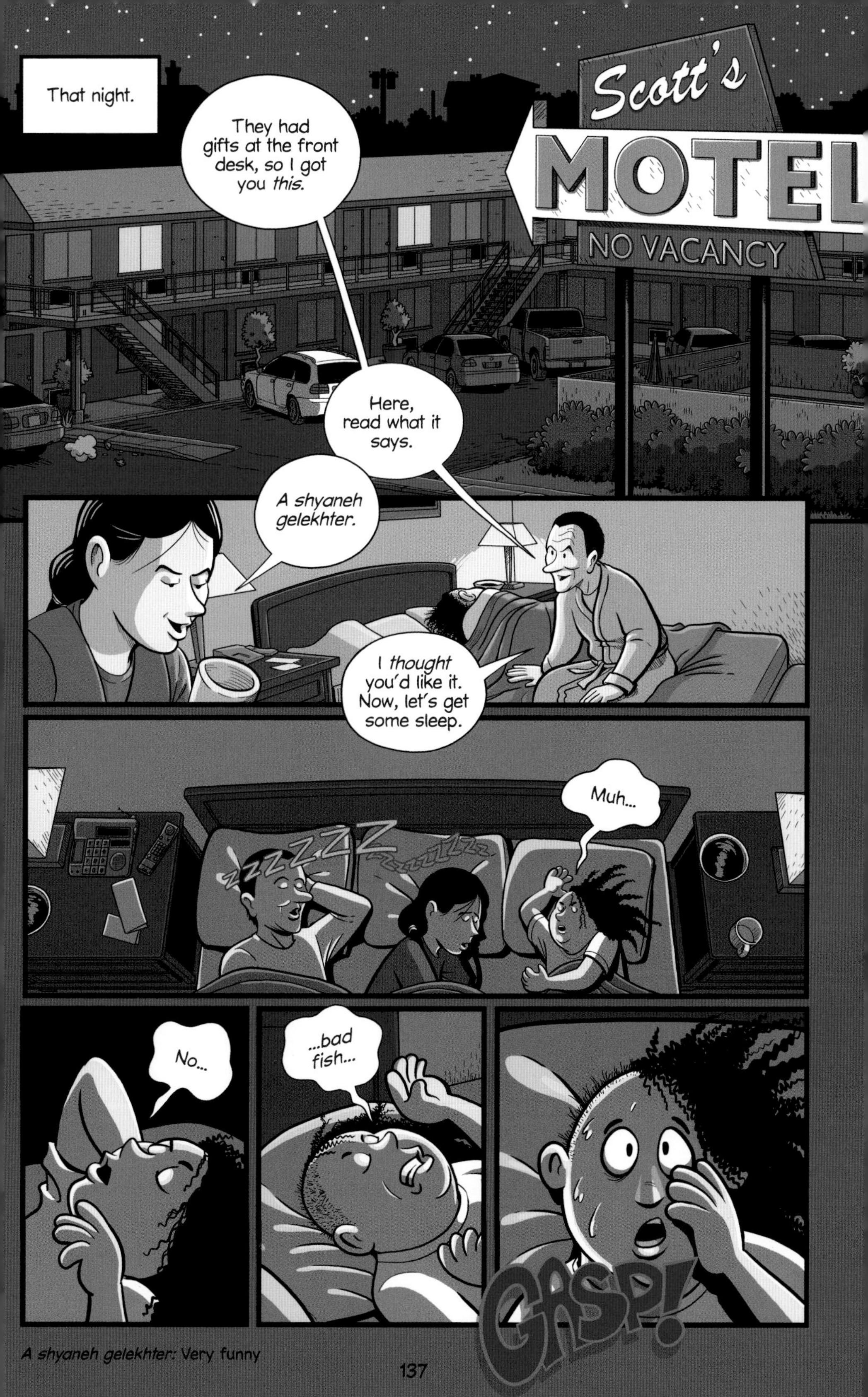
That night.
They had gifts at the front desk, so I got you *this.*
Here, read what it says.
Scott's
MOTEL
NO VACANCY
A shyaneh gelekhter.
I *thought* you'd like it. Now, let's get some sleep.
Muh...
No...
...bad fish...
GASP!

A shyaneh gelekhter: Very funny

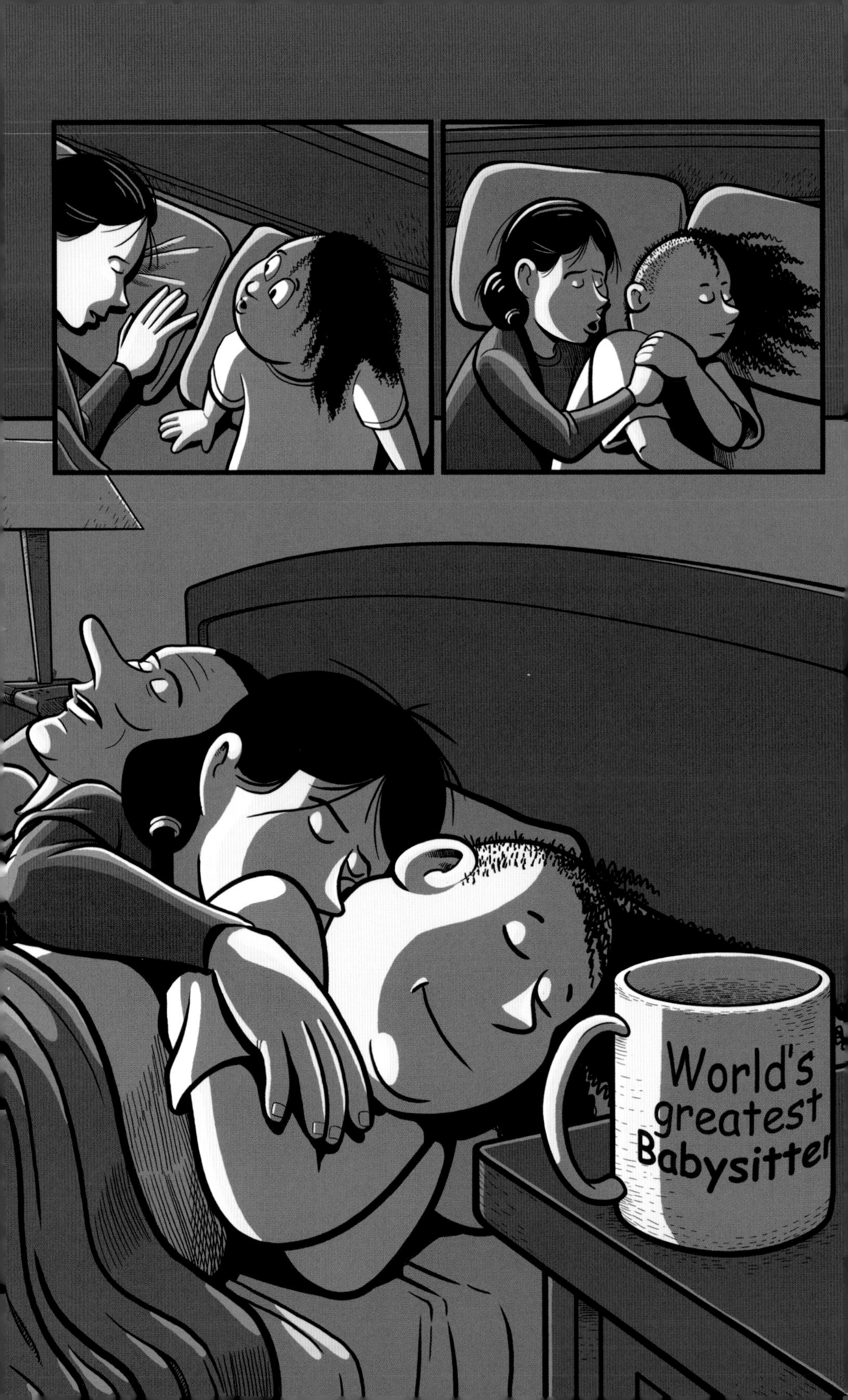
World's greatest Babysitter

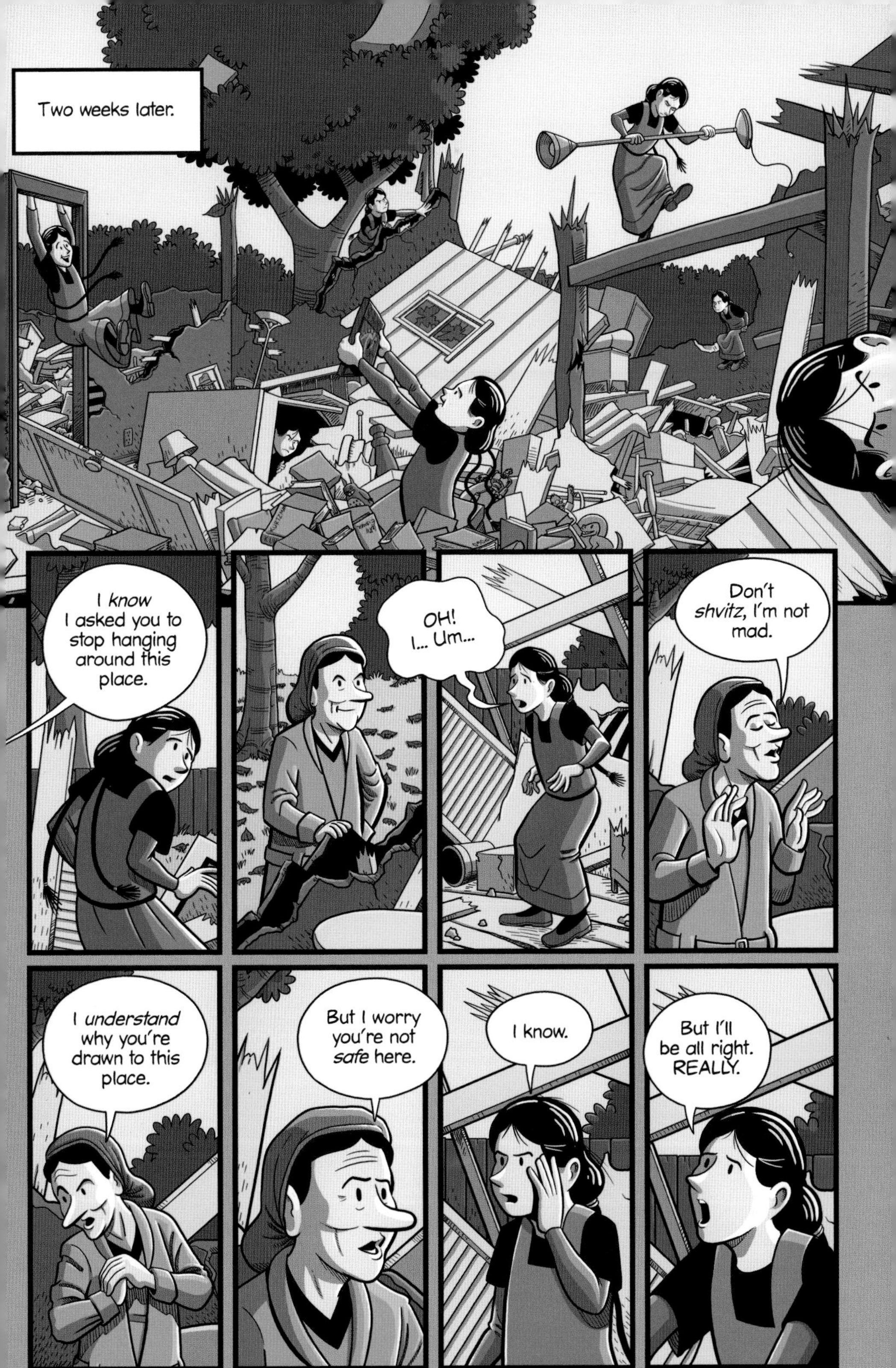
Two weeks later.
I *know* I asked you to stop hanging around this place.
OH! I... Um...
Don't *shvitz*, I'm not mad.
I *understand* why you're drawn to this place.
But I worry you're not *safe* here.
I know.
But I'll be all right. REALLY.

Shvitz: Panic (literally: sweat)

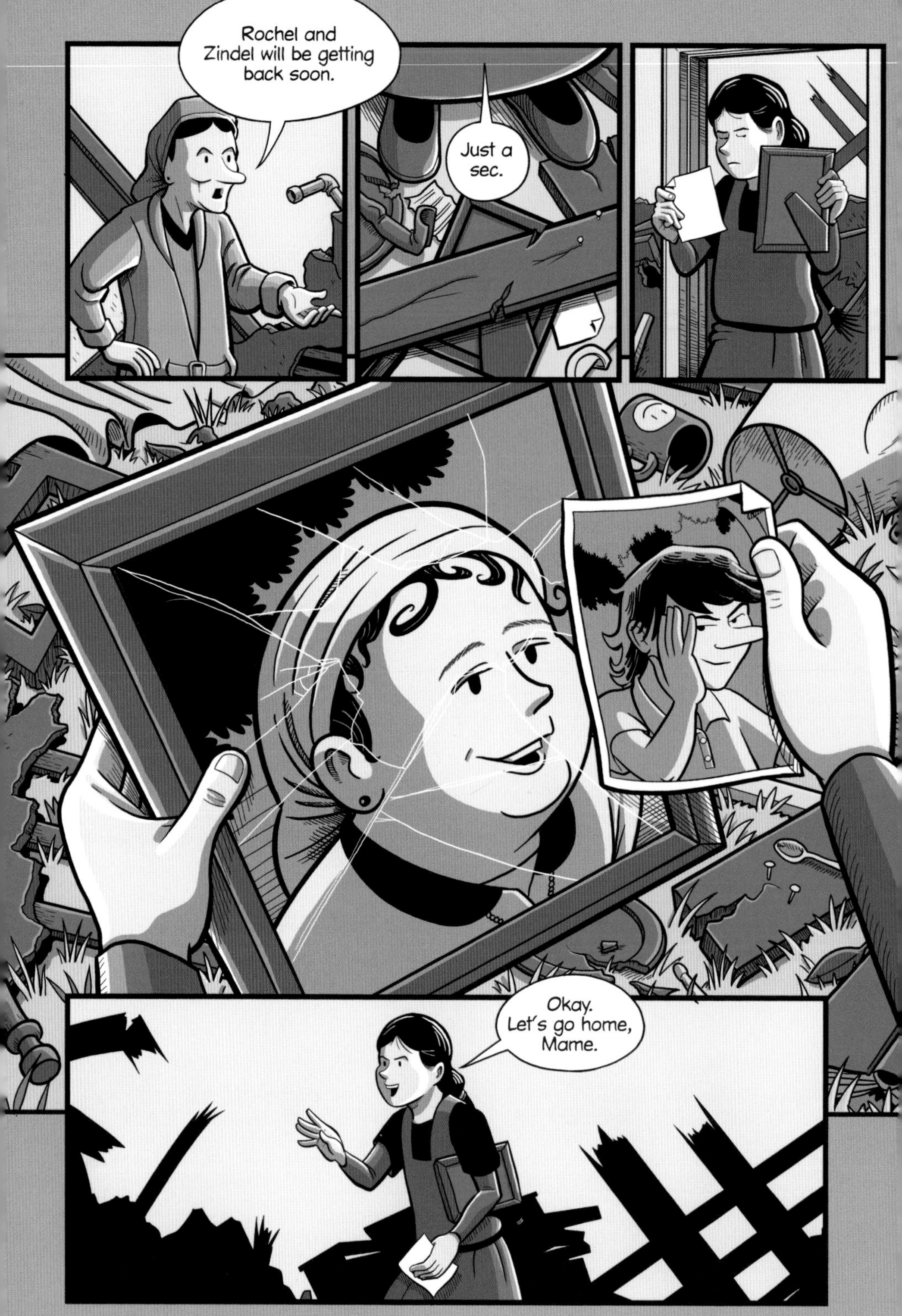
Rochel and Zindel will be getting back soon.
Just a sec.
Okay. Let's go home, Mame.

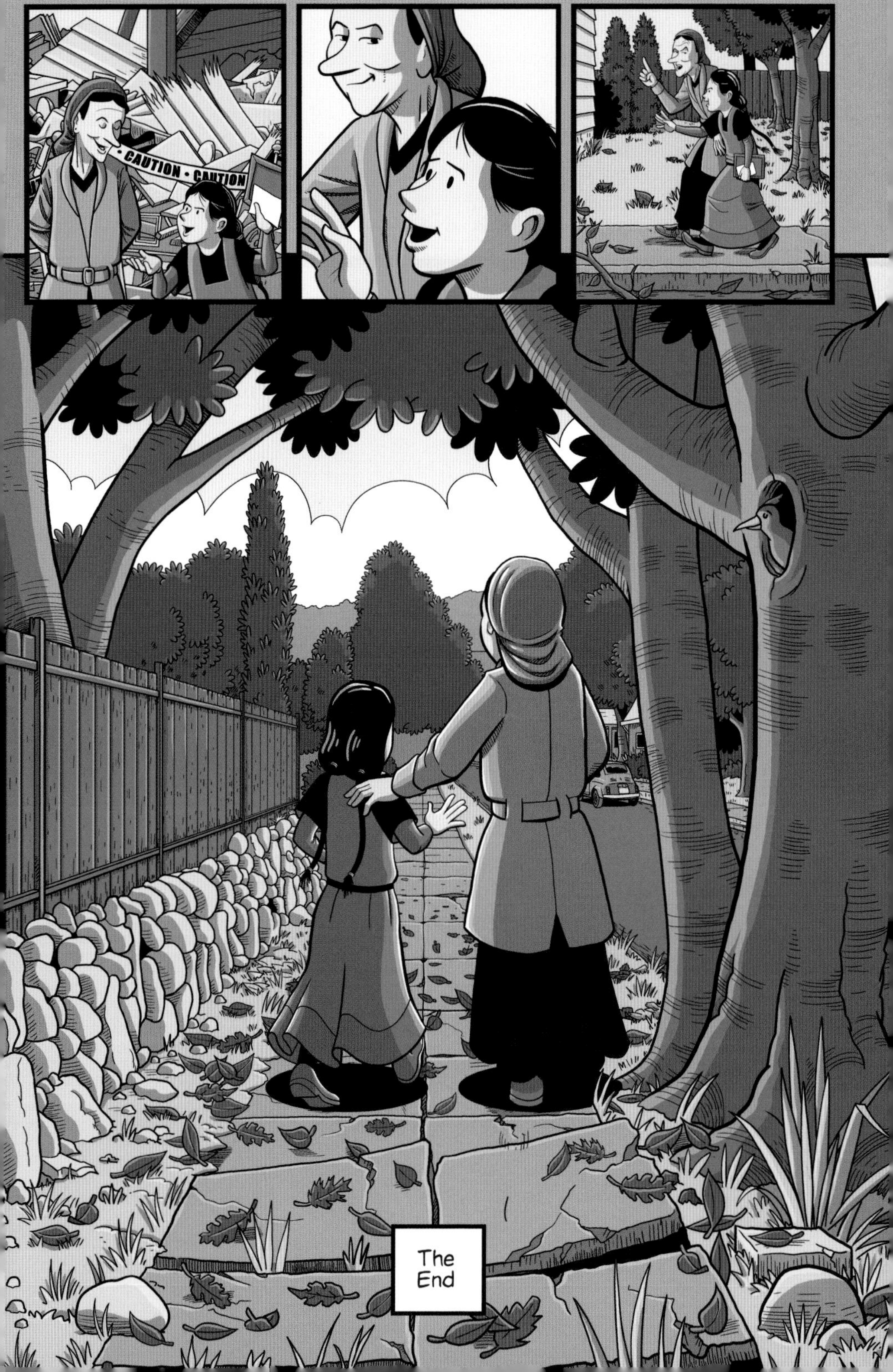
CAUTION
CAUTION
The End

To Toby Deutsch, the best *mame* any boy could ask for

ACKNOWLEDGMENTS

Thanks to my talented collaborators Adrian Wallace, Jake Richmond, and Melanie Ujimori; to my amazing and tireless agent, Judy Hansen; to the excellent Abrams crew, including Orlando Dos Reis, Charles Kochman, Carol Burrell, Sheila Keenan, Chad Beckerman, Jessie Gang, Jim Armstrong, and Kathy Lovisolo; to Rachel Swirsky, Becky Hawkins, Toby Deutsch, Sydney "I'm not gullible!" Schlotte, Maddox Schlotte, Jemma Andersen, Jenn Lee, Kip Manley, Naomi Rubin, Diane Riffe, Grace Annam, Erin Cashier, Tina Kim, and Rachel Edidin; to Yiddish mavens Fradle Freidenreich, Ed Goodgold, Beverly Koenigsberg, Shirley Stark, and Mark Hus; to cartooning mentors Scott McCloud and Dave Sim; to Noah Greenfield and Menachem Luchins; and to so many others who helped me.

ABOUT THE AUTHOR

Barry Deutsch lives in Portland, Oregon, in a bright blue house with bubble-gum pink trim. He has been obsessed with comics pretty much his whole life. This is his third Hereville book.

Library of Congress Control Number: 2015945771

ISBN: 978-1-4197-0800-8

Book and cover design by Barry Deutsch and Chad W. Beckerman

Printed and bound in China

10 9 8 7 6 5 4 3 2 1

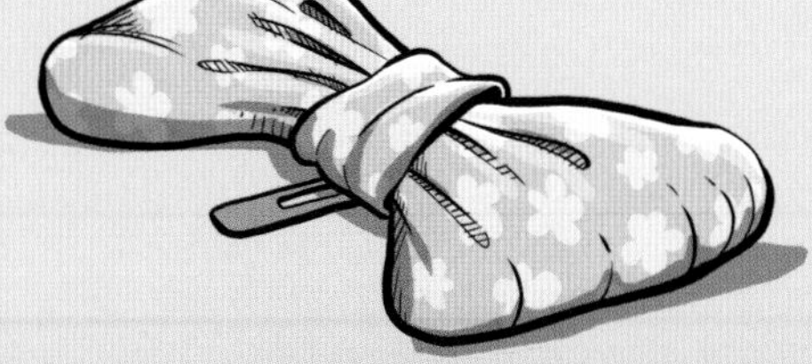

ABRAMS

THE ART OF BOOKS SINCE 1949

115 West 18th Street

New York, NY 10011

www.abramsbooks.com

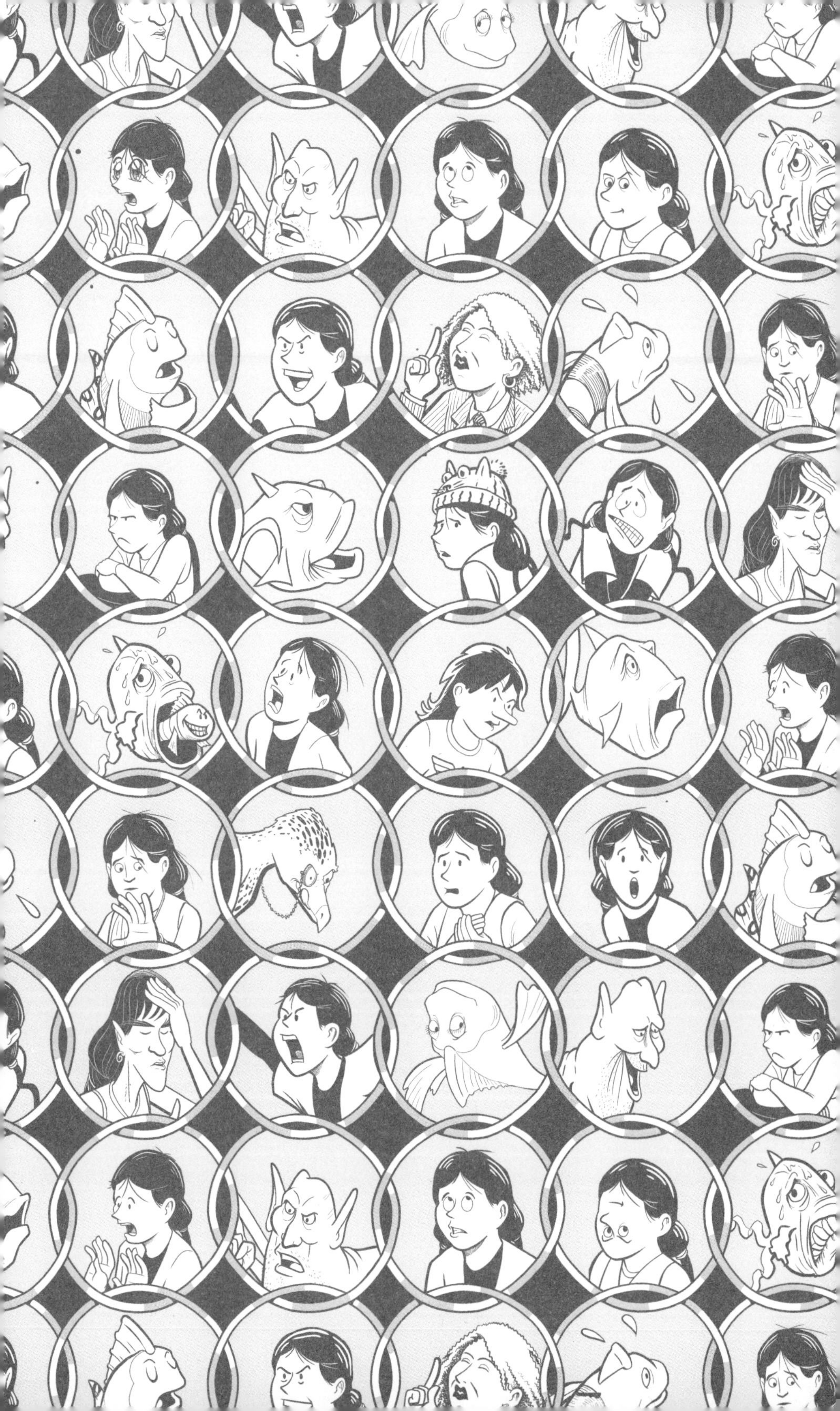

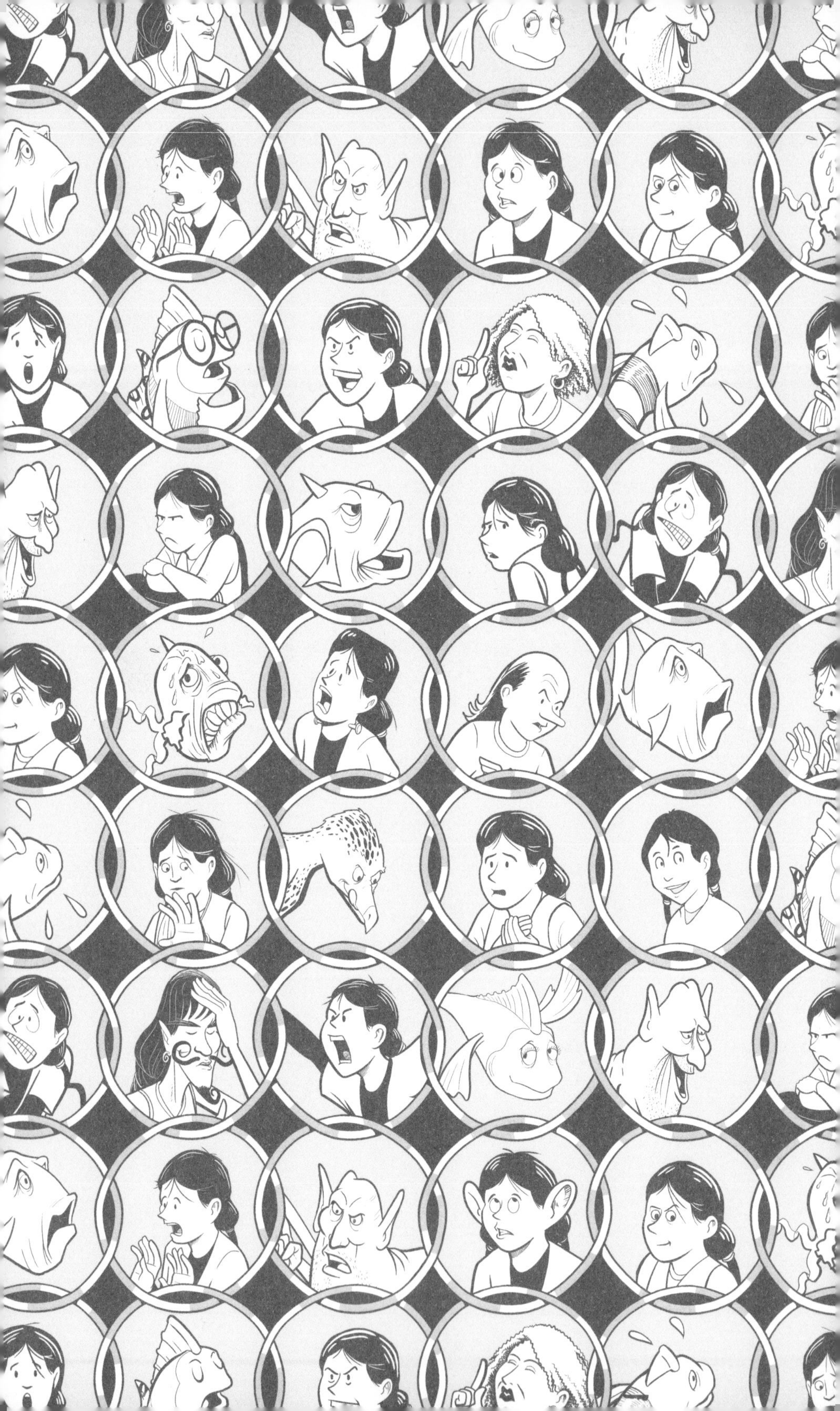